David LaPorte

ADRIENNE SHARP entered the world of ballet at age seven and trained at the prestigious Harkness Ballet in New York. She received her M.A. with honors from the Writing Seminars at The Johns Hopkins University and was awarded a Henry Hoyns Fellowship at the University of Virginia. She has been a fiction fellow at MacDowell, the Virginia Center for the Creative Arts, and the Squaw Valley Writer's Conference. She is the author of *White Swan, Black Swan,* a Barnes & Noble Discover Selection and a national bestseller, and *The Sleeping Beauty,* one of *Booklist*'s ten best first novels of 2005. *The True Memoirs of Little K* was a finalist for the California Book Award and has been translated into six languages.

Praise for *The True Memoirs of Little K*

"It's Paris in 1971, and ninety-nine-year-old Mala—ever the opportunist!—decides to set the record straight about her life in Romanov Russia in *The True Memoirs of Little K*. She has been—she would have us know—not just a *prima ballerina* of the Imperial Ballet but also a mistress to Tsar Nicholas II and mother of his illegitimate son. Sharp has taken equal parts truth and conjecture, and put spinning at the center of her story a charming, willful, and, at times, unreliable narrator. Mala's memoir fascinates."

—*The Cleveland Plain Dealer*

"The story is rich with historical detail, describing the decadent excesses of the Russian nobility, the intrigue of the theater, and the paralysis of Russia's rulers in their waning days of power. Sharp sweeps us into another place and time, blending fact and fiction into an engrossing tale of love, loss, and history." —*The Wichita Eagle*

"Sharp has brilliantly captured the last years in the doomed world of Imperial Russia. . . . Read these pages and shiver, but not from the cold." —*The Advocate* (Baton Rouge)

"These fictional memoirs, based on historical fact, describe the lavish lives of the Russian imperial family and the theatrical personalities of St. Petersburg ballerinas who served at their pleasure in the late nineteenth and early twentieth centuries. . . . Adrienne Sharp understands the devotion to perfection that drives successful dancers because she was a ballerina herself. *The True Memoirs of Little K* is an example of her attention to detail, shown by her extensive research and grasp of the history of this period."

—*Historical Novel Review*

THE TRUE MEMOIRS OF LITTLE K

The
TRUE MEMOIRS
of
LITTLE K

ADRIENNE SHARP

Picador

Farrar, Straus and Giroux

New York

www.picadorusa.com
www.twitter.com/picadorusa • www.facebook.com/picadorusa

Picador® is a U.S. registered trademark and is used by Farrar, Straus and Giroux under license from Pan Books Limited.

For book club information, please visit www.facebook.com/picadorbookclub or e-mail marketing@picadorusa.com.

Designed by Abby Kagan

The Library of Congress has cataloged the Farrar, Straus and Giroux edition as follows:

Sharp, Adrienne.
    The true memoirs of Little K / Adrienne Sharp.— 1st ed.
        p. cm.
    ISBN 978-0-374-20730-4
    1. Kshesinskaia, Matil'da Feliksovna, 1872–1971—Fiction. 2. Ballerinas—Fiction. 3. Nicholas II, Emperor of Russia, 1868–1918—Fiction. 4. Russia—History—Nicholas II, 1894–1917—Fiction. I. Title.
    PS3569.H3432T78 2010
    813'.54—dc22

                                                                    2010010289

Picador ISBN 978-0-312-61071-5

First published in the United States by Farrar, Straus and Giroux

First Picador Edition: November 2011

10 9 8 7 6 5 4 3 2 1

THE TRUE MEMOIRS OF LITTLE K

Paris, 1971

MY NAME IS MATHILDE KSCHESSINSKA, and I was the greatest Russian ballerina on the imperial stages. But the world I was born to, the world I was bred for, is gone, and all the players in it are also gone—dead, murdered, exiled, walking ghosts. I am one of those ghosts. Today in the Soviet Union, it is forbidden to utter my name. The authorities have wiped it from their histories of the theater. I am ninety-nine years old, an old lady with a hairnet and a pinched mouth and yet they still fear me. I stood barely five feet at the height of my fame—my shoe size a three—but now I neither stand nor walk. I sit with my eyes closed in my Paris home of fifty years and live in the past, the mementos of my old Petersburg life all around—sepia photographs of the imperial family and of my son, my father's icon of Our Lady of Czestokowa, his ring with the arms of Count Krassinsky, a medal from the tunic of my husband's old uniform from the Horse Guards. Like those things, I, too, am a relic. But traces of that old world remain, you know, buried somewhere beneath this world. The Winter Palace. The Maryinsky Theater. Tsarskoye Selo. Peterhof. I see that world more clearly than I see the avenues and trees outside my window here in the 16th Arrondissement. What is there to interest me here? The hippie boys in their psychedelic pants, the hippie girls in their short skirts and long, uncombed hair? The world I knew was grand, the court more elaborate than the French court under Louis XIV. I was the lover of two grand dukes, the mistress of the tsar. The last tsar.

He called me Little K.

it started like this

ICAN STILL SEE the imperial Romanov family, not that of Nicholas and Alexandra, but the imperial family of my youth—Tsar Alexander III and his wife and his children, of whom Niki was one. *The imperial family, the imperial family is coming.* I see them coming down the hall from the little school theater, with its wooden chairs set in rows before the primitive stage where we students had just performed—I in the coquettish pas de deux from *La Fille mal gardée*—toward the big rehearsal room where the celebratory dinner was set. This was the day of my graduation performance, March 23, 1890. I was seventeen. The Romanov tsars were patrons of a great string of imperial theaters—in Petersburg alone we had the Maryinsky, the Alexandrinsky, the Mikhailovsky, the Conservatoire, the English Theater—and patrons, too, of the artists who filled their stages and the students who filled the theater schools. Why, look what happened to the little girl who one year ran after the emperor when he made his annual visit to the school for the graduation performance. Breaking away from her chaperones and catching up with him, she kissed his hand, and Alexander, touched, asked her what she desired. Seizing the moment, like any good opportunist—and I have always admired an opportunist, being one myself—she whispered, *To be a boarding student*. And he said, grandly, *Done*. Just like that she was given a bed and with it a stature greater than the simple day student, over whom she could now lord herself. Yes, the family always attended the annual graduation at the school, and down its halls they made a parade far more thrilling than any royal processional we enacted on the stage. Down the broad corridor strode the emperor, taller than anyone, a trunk like a barrel, his forehead a stone wall, and behind him the empress, tiny like me. *Where is Kschessinska?* he called. He knew my name because I was the youngest daughter of the great Felix Kschessinsky, who had been dancing for the Romanovs for almost forty years. That was how the tsar knew my name and as for why the tsar liked me, called for me: perhaps because I was the theatrical expression of his consort, small, bright-eyed, dark hair set in waves. Yes, that must have been why. He saw how we were alike. I ruled my world with the same great vivacity she used to rule hers, and wasn't my world but a miniature of her own—its rituals, its hierarchies, its costumes an echo of the elaborate Romanov court? I lived my life in one world, but I planted my foot—my slipper—in the other.

That day, that day of my graduation performance where I took the first prize, a heavy volume of the complete works of Lermontov—which I never read but planned to use as a flower press and then never opened even for that!—the emperor moved the girl who was to sit at his left at the school's modest supper table and put me in her chair, placed Nicholas at *my* left, and then said, *Don't flirt*. By which, of course, the emperor meant the opposite. If the emperor was a giant, the tsarevich was a faun—small, slightly built inside his uniform, his cheeks pretty and soft. I had seen him before that day only from a distance, but now both he and I were almost adults—he would finish with his tutors and lessons that spring and later that year he would hide the childish softness of his face with his new beard, but on this day his cheeks and chin were exposed and it made him seem gentle; this gave me a courage that had he looked any more formidable I might not have had. I understood my talent had brought me into a new orbit, one with a path higher up into the heavens, and I was not afraid to fly there. At seventeen I knew better how to flirt than Nicholas did at twenty-two, and I was prepared to do so as soon as he spoke to me first. I knew at least that much: to wait. Until then, I pinched at the little blue forget-me-nots sewn to my dress to keep my fingers from pinching at him. And what did the tsarevich finally say to me? He gazed at the plain white drinking glasses set at each place rather than look at my face, which was, I am sure, radiant from the attention of his father and the proximity of the heir. I was never a beauty, my two front teeth tilt inward, the dog teeth protrude, the Russian tabloids drew me that way in caricature, but I was eager and I had those eyes, eyes like a fairy. Louis XV kept his mistresses in the Parc des Cerfs. The gossips would later call me the fairy of the Parc des Cerfs. So what did the tsarevich say to the fairy while he looked down at the table? Don't laugh. This: *I'm sure you don't use drinking glasses like these at home.*

That was the best he could manage. A few months later he would join the Hussars and begin to drink and carouse with his fellow Guards, who prodded him out of his timidity. But this Niki, slow and shy, made my work so much harder! Drinking glasses? What was I to say to that? Accustomed to the crystal of the Minister Service or the Petrograd Service, I'm sure Niki found those plain glasses clumsy, though I would never have noticed it. I pretended I had. Smiling, I flicked at one with two fingers to laugh at its dull ting. The milieu of the Romanovs was quite extraordinary, you know. I spent my life trying to imitate it. To join it.

It was no accident, our initial introduction. It occurred by the emperor's direct design, as did everything in Russia. After all, the country was the fiefdom of the tsar and it existed only for his pleasure. We girls at the Imperial Theater Schools were no exception. From our ranks, the emperors and the grand dukes, the counts and the officers of the guards, chose their mistresses, kept an eye out for a shapely leg or a pretty face. Why, one of them described the ballet as an *exhibit of beautiful women, a flower bed in which everyone can pick the flowers of pleasure*. The officers on horseback used to follow the coaches stuffed with girls as we traveled from the school to the theater—a tradition that dated back decades to even before the Maryinsky was built, when the coaches took the girls to the old Bolshoi Theater on Theater Square, where my father danced before it was razed—calling out to us and asking our names, which our chaperones forbade us to give, though we wanted to. I had to put my hand over my mouth to keep my name from spilling out: *Mathilde-Maria*. To keep us pure and to protect us from the syphilis that plagued the capital, we were sequestered from all outside influence—and equally sequestered from the schoolboys. Girls were penned together on the first floor of the school, boys on the second. Separate dormitories, schoolrooms, rehearsal rooms, dining rooms. We knew the boys existed, of course, for during ballroom class we practiced with them the minuet and quadrilles, where we were forced to touch, but we were not permitted to look into each other's eyes while doing so. The governesses watched us closely and they would swoop in to scold at any sign of forward behavior. Our day clothes were laughably modest, the dresses full of buckles and overlaid with aprons, and beneath our skirts we wore long, dark stockings; our practice clothes were a knee-length version of a street dress; our fur-lined coats were so dark and sober we called them penguins. And we looked like penguins in them, waddling around and around the courtyard—the only freedom we were allowed. We couldn't play wildly—no bicycles or balls, no ice sliding or ice-skating, no toy swords for the boys. We were property of the Imperial Ballet and if we were injured we were of no use to it and the money spent on us gone to waste. At lunch and supper the governesses counted us off two by two as we lined up for the dining hall. At night the other students slept in a single vast room of fifty or more beds, each bed dressed in white like the coffin of a child, and at the head of each bed a small table with an icon and the school number of each girl.

Why all the numbers, all the counting? To ensure that what had happened to a girl of some years ago did not happen again. Her elopement with an officer of the Horse Guards had made a fantastic scandal. Each afternoon she found some excuse to stand in the window of the dormitory and watch him ride by, a far too glamorous spectacle to be borne, in his white uniform and silver helmet, and driving two bay horses. He had to have been a spectacle, for Theater Street was normally empty of traffic except for the vast old-fashioned carriages that conveyed us students about. That he paraded unnoticed across the Anichkov Bridge and along the back side of the Alexandrinsky Theater must be myth, and in that myth, of course, his beloved had to be beautiful, very beautiful—girls in these kinds of stories are always beautiful, like princesses. So one afternoon she borrowed a maid's shawl—yes, the princess disguised as a peasant—and slipped out a side door into her future, which I hope was bright. And since her wedding day no girl older than fifteen was allowed home for a holiday other than three days at Christmas and Easter Sunday itself.

I myself was not a boarding student. My father was an Honored Artist of the Imperial Theaters, invited to St. Petersburg by Nicholas I, who loved dancers massed on the stage almost as much as he loved bayonets massed on the parade ground. And my father used his influence to spare me that spartan school life, so at odds with the ebullience of the actual theater we would soon serve. He didn't want my spirit broken. And perhaps that was his mistake.

Nevertheless, whether we lived at home or at school, our virginity was carefully guarded until our graduation day, when it was then offered up. Sewn into costumes that exposed our necks, our arms, our bosoms, our legs, we decorated the stage for the pleasure of the court, all those aristocratic balletomanes who handed down to their sons their subscriptions along with their titles, who sat in the boxes and first stalls of the Imperial Theaters for the best views and aimed their lorgnettes or opera glasses at us. In the smoking rooms, at the intervals, they debated our merits. It was a reciprocal attraction. We needed protectors to advance our careers and to supplement our miserable salaries with dinners, gifts, wreaths, and flowers. And as our costumes imitated the dress and jewels of the court, so we developed a desire to possess the silks and velvets we wore for a few hours each day, the gold that embroidered those fabrics, the gems to which our colored glass aspired. There were many girls at the school who came from nothing—why, Anna Pavlova was the daughter of a laundress—and whose liaisons could help the fortunes of their families. This was a long-standing tradition. Count Nikolai Petrovich Sheremetiev, in the eighteenth century—back when each nobleman had at his country estate his own theater and his own serf opera company, ballet company, orchestra—made a mistress of one of his opera singers and then secretly married her. In my time the grand dukes Konstantin Nikolaevich and Nicholas Nikolaevich, uncles of Tsar Alexander III, each kept a mistress from the ballet, and of Nicholas Nikolaevich's illegitimate children with the ballerina Chislova, the boy served in the Life Guards Horse Grenadiers and the girl married a prince. Sometimes these protectors married the girls they had made their mistresses and these girls became matriarchs of some of the greatest aristocratic families of Russia. Kemmerer, Madaeva, Muravieva, Kantsyreva, Prihunova, Kosheva, Vasilieva, Verginia, Sokolova, all were ballerinas of the 1860s and earlier who married noblemen. This possibility, rather than a reverence for the art, motivated many mothers to take a pretty child or a graceful one to the auditions on Theater Street. But some of us, of course, remained only mistresses.

The imperial wives saw to our suffering, you can be sure of that, even if a man's mistress came from the court itself, from a noble family. No matter. When Niki's grandfather Tsar Alexander II was murdered, his second wife—long his mistress, and no Romanov woman forgot those years—was barred from his funeral! Unfortunately, he died before he could make her his empress and legitimize the positions of his children by her. And so at his sudden death his first family moved immediately against her. The family would have taken her title of princess from her if they could. And what of this was her fault? She was seventeen to the emperor's forty-seven when she met him strolling in the Summer Garden, with its four long avenues leading to the Neva, its linden trees and its maples making green walls through which filtered the wet scent of that water, its wrought-iron fences barring as it should dogs, *muzhiki*, in their bright-colored shirts and high boots, the working class, and Jews. Who asked the young Ekaterina to wait for him in a secluded ground-floor room of the Winter Palace? Who gave her children? Who eventually moved her into that palace? She was a Dolgoruky, the daughter of a prince, from one of the oldest aristocratic families in Russia, and still the women of the court labeled her a schemer, a fornicator, a social climber. Imagine what they would say of me.

She was seventeen, a girl walking in a park east of the Champs de Mars.

And so was I seventeen. And that next week after graduation, in my best clothes, my hair curled in the fashion of the time, I walked not in the Summer Garden, but along Nevsky Prospekt, anxious to follow up my first meeting with Niki with another, during the great afternoon promenade that began each day after lunch and ended before twilight, at which time the workmen would drag their ladders from street to street, lighting each gas lamp by hand, before the evening's salons, parties, dinners, and balls.

Perhaps a word here about Petersburg, which those of us fortunate enough to live there called simply *Peter*. The city is a handful of islands divided by canals and rivers, all facing the Gulf of Finland. More than a dozen bridges join Peter's disparate parts— Admiralty Island with its palaces and theaters, Hare Island with the Peter and Paul Fortress, Vasilevsky with the German Quarter and the stock exchange, Petersburg Island with its wooden houses and later its art nouveau mansions, the Vyborg side with its military barracks and later its factories. We were once, in 1611, simply a Swedish fortress—*Nyenshants*, which means *Neva Redoubt*—but it was Peter the Great in 1703 who decided to build on this spot a capital city. *Here a new city shall be wrought. / Here we at Nature's own behest / Shall break a window to the West.* That's Pushkin, from "The Bronze Horseman." That, unlike the Lermontov, I read. Actually, Peter is a city neither Eastern nor Western, but both. It is European, like Paris, in its avenues, squares, parks, in its buildings of granite and marble, but unique in its long, low palaces reflected in the water, the rivers and canals that give the air its luminosity. When I dream of Peter I dream of light. Yes, the city is Western in design, but Eastern in its colors of brick red, mustard yellow, lime green, and cornflower blue, and Eastern, too, in the animals we kept like peasants in our courtyards by the great stacks of chopped wood—I myself, to have fresh milk, kept a cow at my mansion on Petersburg Island in 1907! And in the rooms, the private rooms, behind the granite classical façades, behind the pale, gilded salons, you will find the décor runs to patterned carpets, rich wall fabrics, the ubiquitous black or glazed tile Russian stove stoked from September to May, the polished silver or brass samovar full of scalding tea. We had no time to fully shed what was Eastern about us, for at Peter's command the city was erected as swiftly as a stage set, within fifty years. Russians say Peter made his city in the sky and then lowered it to the ground, complete. But it was not Peter who made this city. Serfs and conscripts dug the foundations for it with their bare hands, carried off the dirt in their shirt fronts, hauled and stacked the marble, granite, slate, and sandstone. Two hundred thousand laborers died of exhaustion, of cold, and of disease transporting and erecting that stone, and we say the city is built on their bones, and on their bones is where the *beau monde* of Petersburg paraded each afternoon.

Yes, Petersburg started as a fortress and even in 1890 Petersburg was a military town; sixty thousand men were garrisoned there in vast barracks on Konnogvardeisky Boulevard behind the Horse Guards Ménage or at the western edge of the Champs de Mars or by the Winter Palace or the Alexander Nevsky Monastery or the Obvodny Canal or in the Vyborg District, and the city was colored by the greenish-gray uniforms of the Grenadiers, the white and silver of the Horse Guards, the crimson jackets of the Hussars, and the blue and gold of the Cossacks. These men and their officers were not in Peter just to train but also to play. The high social season began in January, sparked by the twelve balls given by the tsar at the Winter Palace. Court servants in green jackets and black feathered caps and soft leather gloves delivered thousands of cards stamped with gold double-headed eagles inviting the deliverees to the palace. Its great halls on those nights would be lit by ten thousand beeswax candles and garnished with pruned fruit trees in enormous pots and vases thick with pink roses, Parma violets, and white orchids sent north by train in heated cars from the warm Crimea, along with bowls full of fruit embossed with the tsar's silhouette. Hundreds of troikas and carriages would clot the palace square, pulling close to the braziers, flames rising like red fountain spray to the black sky, their drivers carrying hot water bottles, sable blankets, and bottles of vodka—for even the blankets and braziers were not enough to keep these men warm. These balls went on until three o'clock in the morning, until the final polonaise. Too much vodka, though, while you waited for your master, and you felt overheated—if you tossed off your robe you might sleep your way to a frozen death. Although the square was shielded from the Gulf of Finland by the immensity of the palace itself, there are no words to explain the cold of a Petersburg winter. The lights from the palace lit up a white and black world—brittle ice and flakes and drifts of snow, the steaming black breath from the horses and the waiting men.

The season ended at Lent, after which society went to the country, to the islands outside Petersburg or to the Crimea at the Black Sea or to estates around Moscow, until the end of summer military maneuvers called them to the village of Krasnoye Selo near Peter, which boasted a great parade ground, around which the wooden villas of the officers lay like fringe. Ah, the lovely rhythm of those days. After maneuvers the court traveled to Europe, but by late August the ballet, the opera, the French theater had begun once again to adorn the stages, and their audiences eventually returned and began once again to adorn the blue velvet parterres and the loges to applaud the art we actors, dancers, musicians perfected just for them. During my time there were nineteen courts in Petersburg—the tsar's, his mother's, and seventeen grand ducal courts—several thousand people when one counted all the family members and courtiers; and these aristocrats along with the ambassadors and the Diplomatic Corps and the Guards and the occasional provincial nobleman came to the theaters every night during the season. You must remember we had no television, no radio, no cinema; Russian winter days are short, and there are many dark hours to fill. The Imperial Theaters produced plays, operas, operettas, concerts, and ballets, and of these performances at the Maryinsky, fifty were the ballet, and of those, forty performances were by subscription only. It fell to the director of the Imperial Theaters, Ivan Alexandrovich Vzevolozhsky, an aristocrat himself who could trace his lineage to Rurik and the princes of Smolensk, to supervise the production of

all these amusements, and to Marius Petipa, the French dancer who
had come to Petersburg in 1847 and clawed his way up to succeed
St. Léon as ballet master of the Imperial Ballet, to create all the *pas*
for them. He had help from the second ballet master, Lev Ivanov—
who became a family friend and who loved my father's meals, unfolding his linen napkin and saying, *Let's have a bite*, but who never
received the credit he deserved for his work, being a Russian in a
Francophile court. M. Vzevolozhsky favored the Petersburg theaters over the Moscow ones, and why not? The court, after all, was
here. At the Maryinsky one saw the same faces night after night.
We were like family facing each other across the footlights, they
very vocal relations, for the balletomanes would call out to us freely,
Go, Mala, or *More roles to Tata*, to urge us to dance harder or to urge
the directorate to reward exceptional talent. And, of course, there
would be boos and hisses, as well. It was the court's interest in the
ballet that led eventually to the great Tchaikovsky's composing for
it and to the flowering of the art. Once I became famous, I delayed
my return to the stage until later and later in the season, until the
more prestigious months of December and January, as if I, too, were
an aristocrat who had just returned from Europe to Peter. But that
is ahead. At this moment I am still seventeen.

Alexander III on the day of my graduation had instructed me,
Be the glory and the adornment of our ballet, and so I determined to
be just that; and as I had chased first prize at my school, so I determined to chase the first prize outside of it: the tsarevich. I took so
long with my toilette that April afternoon of my promenade I almost missed my chance to tag him. Now everyone has long, straight
hair parted in the middle, a generation of girls who wear their hair
like children in the nursery, but in 1890, we wore our hair tightly
curled, wet it with sugar water and wrapped it around curling papers, spent hours pinning it to dry. I had a rivulet of bangs at the top
of my forehead, tendrils fell before my ears, and that day I wore a
ruffled blouse with a doubled length of brocade secured at the neck

by a brooch, dabbed my violet scent behind my ears—for in 1890 each eau de cologne was made of just a single flower's scent—and in this costume of a young lady, my school clothes packed away now, I walked the fashionable section of Nevsky Prospekt, where in the shops one could buy soft French gloves or Chinese tea or English soaps, past the site where Eliseyevsky's would open in 1901, a shop so fancy it was hung with chandeliers and where one could buy the fruit and nuts of any region, to the Fontanka Canal, to the mustard-and-white façade of the Anichkov Palace where Niki's family lived while in the capital, his father having eschewed the Winter Palace except for official receptions. The imperial family lived among us then—it was only later that Niki and his family secluded themselves so completely from Petersburg society that people forgot what they looked like. Right away I spied the tsarevich sitting on the balcony with his fifteen-year-old sister, Xenia, he smoking, of course, the two of them leaning forward in their chairs to look through the railings at the passersby. I slowed my pace, the better to be seen. Niki blew smoke from his mouth and nodded to me. I nodded back. He nodded at me again but he did not rise and approach the rails. What could I do but walk on?

So. That was our second encounter and it was not much. I understood from it that it would not be as easy for me as it had been for Princess Ekaterina Dolgorukaya, whose tsar lover did not cower behind balcony railings but instead boldly arranged to meet her again in the Summer Garden on those paths beneath the linden, and just as boldly ravished her one afternoon in the Babigon Pavilion at Peterhof on a beautiful July day, the Gulf of Finland glinting in the distance, heat and perfume everywhere, flower petals crushed between her fingers.

No. Those next few weeks I would ride around and around the city with the family's Russian coachman I begged from my father. Not every family could afford its own coachman, especially a Russian coachman in his centuries-old costume who drove with his arms held out stiffly in front of him as if in balletic *port de bras* and who, as we plowed our way through the streets, shouted throatily at every other carriage, cart, and person in our way. Though I wanted to show him off, as well as myself, I might as well have stayed at home. For though I drove along the Morskaya, strolled Nevsky Prospekt, applauded the races at the Horse Ménage, even in a ridiculous act of desperation paced once again back and forth on Karavannaya Street across from the Anichkov Palace, the tsarevich took no notice of me at all. The stage for my seduction was not meant to be Petersburg, though I did not know this, but most unexpectedly the summer encampment at Krasnoye Selo in August.

The Imperial Guards of Petersburg and dozens of regiments from the provinces converged at Krasnoye Selo for summer maneuvers away from the Petersburg heat and swirling dust, 130,000 men in their pale canvas tents erected by the great parade ground along the Dudergov and Ligovka rivers. How the Romanovs loved their uniforms and their bugles and their horses! Niki's great-grandfather Nicholas I would weep at the sight of a great group of uniformed soldiers. There were white tunics and scarlet, the long blue coats and gold belts of the Cossacks, the Golden Grenadiers in their gray coats and tall gilded helmets—each regiment with its own epaulets, ribbons, braids, crosses, medals, ornaments, hats. Some regiments wore *papakhi* of bleached lamb, other Cossack regiments wore dark wool; still other officers sported visored caps festooned with feathers and medallions. Until almost the end of his life, Nicholas fiddled with the uniforms of his regiments, adding a row of buttons here, another golden braid.

He had talent as an artist, you know, had been taught to handle pencils and watercolors by Kyril Lemokh, the curator of art in the Russian Museum of Alexander III. He drew landscapes. I saw a few. One sketch held no figures, only a tree, a field, a red dirt road glowing like brick in the sun; in another a small wooden boat had just been pushed off from the shore, and one could see a lone figure hunched on it, two men on the very edge of the land who must have shoved the boat off for their friend, the tall, tall grove of birch trees in the background dwarfing them all. They were pictures drawn by a boy who loved the natural world and who found in it a place where a tsar was not a giant but simply part of a larger whole. But Niki gave up painting, other than making sketches in his record book of the gifts he was given. And later in life, I suppose, uniforms became the paper he drew upon.

The big show on the vast plain at Krasnoye Selo shimmered in the late July heat, the waves of heat soothed into stillness only when they reached the woods and hills that marked the boundaries of the big grassy space, which served as stage for the precision marching, the smart turns and lunges with saber and bayonet. The elite of Petersburg society turned out for the Great Review, seated in stalls near a thatch of trees, the women wearing summer whites, their hats and parasols caught by the breeze, undulating like the leaves and catkins of the beech trees above them. The ministers of the court stood in their tails and top hats beneath tents on the Emperor's Mound, and the tsar, the empress, and the grand dukes and duchesses inspected the troops from their horses and carriages, then joined the ministers to survey the rows and rows of men who filled the plain, marching in unison, flags held high. The next two wars Russia fought would be disastrous failures for her, leaving men like these and millions of others lying dead on the battlefields across Europe and Russia. But no one would have guessed this then.

No, that summer in 1892, at Krasnoye Selo these actors stood out on that great plain enacting battles they never lost.

This, however, was not theater enough. There must be evening entertainment, as well.

And so a wooden theater in the Russian style was built at Krasnoye Selo, a theater as big as the Mikhailovsky in Peter, a bright place of balconies hung with striped silk drapes and tasseled valances, and we artists performed there twice a week in July and the first part of August, when the grand dukes and the emperor and his family came to the camp, leaving behind their marble palaces to stay in their graceful wooden villas, with canvas awnings and wide verandas. In the evenings, all the theater artists stood at attention in the theater windows that overlooked the private imperial entrance to salute the imperial entourage as they disembarked from their landaus and troikas. The men wore their military regalia even to the theater. The grand dukes all sat in the first row; in the second and third ones sat their officers, with the ladies after and junior officers beyond, and in boxes opposite one another sat the tsar's family and the families of the ministers of the court and the military. I used to spot my turns by all the medals and decorations shining on the men's breasts.

The grand dukes and the emperor and the tsarevich always stopped by after lunch to chat with the dancers or to watch rehearsals, and they mounted the stage between the evening's entertainments— a comedy first and a ballet divertissement second—to greet all the performers. Great beauty, which I did not possess, could shape one's fate. And so I worked even harder to shape mine, with my pretty hands and my little feet and my lively conversation. Like my father, I have always been gay, with the gift to make those around me also so. And this was how Nicholas was finally drawn to me—by my charm. He would seek me out on that stage and stand in the sun to chat with me, showing his white teeth at my jokes, while I tried to hide my crooked ones. Sometimes I touched a button on his tunic or rose *en pointe* or made flying birds of my hands in my rapture at being so close to him. I had noted how Niki seemed most at ease around those who were merry, like us theater artists or like his rowdy cousins, the Mikhailovichi, or his fellow officers at camp, with whom Niki drank himself beyond drunkenness until they all played "the wolves," which involved crawling naked in the grass, howling and biting one another, before drinking on all fours from vats of champagne and vodka their obliging servants hauled out for the young men's pleasure. One afternoon, in my hurry to make sure I didn't miss the chance for conversation before rehearsal, I ran onto the little stage right into the uniformed belly of the emperor, who took one look at my flushed face and said, *You must have been flirting*. But he was wrong. I was just eager to begin! My brief moments with the tsarevich at camp were more important to me than the evening's show, and they were still all I had of him.

Yet it was not only with Nicholas that I chatted, for when else would so many Romanov men be assembled in a single place to which I had access? I attempted to charm every man with a title—who knew what use he might one day be for me?—including Grand Duke Vladimir, one of Niki's many uncles, who served as minister of the Imperial Theaters and was a great lover of the arts. An old man, but a valuable one—no?—given his position. He would come sit in my dressing room and visit with me while I painted my lips red. He didn't talk but rather boomed wherever he went, and his voice from his box could be heard all over the theater as he commented on the dancers. *What? What is this? A sparrow?* he cried when a young, thin girl appeared, poor thing, to perform a few spindly steps. Or he bellowed, *Let us all go home*, when the first-act curtain fell on a ballet he didn't like. Vladimir believed he should be a tsar rather than a grand duke and he acted like a tsar, despite the birth order that put his brother Alexander on the throne. Vladimir's wife, Miechen, the second-ranking woman in the empire, carried on like a tsaritsa herself. It was her annual Christmas bazaar in the Hall of Nobles which heralded Peter's holiday season. *The Empress Vladimir*, Niki's mother bitterly called her. The day the tsar's train derailed in 1888, almost crushing the imperial family as they ate chocolate pudding in the dining car, was for Vladimir a day close to triumph. *We shall never have such a chance again*, Miechen whispered indiscreetly to her friends at court. At Krasnoye Selo, Vladimir gave me his photograph to keep in my dressing room. Yes, the imperial family signed photographs of themselves for their intimates the way cinema stars do for their fans today—and on mine Vladimir inscribed the words *Bonjour, dushka*, which meant *little darling*, and he sighed that he was too old for me.

He *was* too old for me, but Niki was not, and just when it appeared my impassioned twice-weekly flirting with Niki the Hussar before the chartered train hauled me the thirty versts back to Peter had utterly failed to have the desired effect, and when only one week remained of maneuvers, Niki suddenly asked me to wait for him in the alley behind the theater after a performance that August night. He wanted to double back from his villa after supper to take me for a ride in his troika. Need I spell out my answer? What had inspired this sudden and uncharacteristic boldness on his part? I had seen him watching me with special interest from the imperial box, which at this theater was designed to look like a Russian peasant's hut. It must have been my costume that evening of tulle, the bodice embroidered with two great flowers that lay, one each, over my breasts. Or perhaps my little dance—for while the other girls had performed that night as a flock of birds or a school of fish, I had been given the adagio, the love duet, my hands laid tenderly on the forearms and shoulders of my cavalier. I remember Niki's invitation gave me trouble tying the sash of my white summer frock as I readied myself in my dressing room that night, and my hair sprang away from my face like the wild wig of Dr. Coppelius. The covered walkway to the theater was deserted by the time I came out, most of the dancers having already boarded the train back home to the capital, and the theater itself had gone dark. A tiny pulse flicked at the base of my throat. What if he didn't come for me? I would have to trudge to the villa where my older sister, Julia, also a dancer, visited with her beau and cry to her like a baby that I had missed the train. I went with some trepidation to the alley, where I stood alone, trying to smooth out everything about me, including my emotions, which were in a jumble. I waited. Before me the sandy yellow drive unwrapped itself, became dark and grainy, emptied into nothing. In the park and garden beyond the theater the summer insects made waves of sound, which crested and fell. Many are the stars in a Russian night, and here, fifteen miles from the capital, the sky made a plain well-furrowed with stars above the infertile, difficult earth below. Eventually I heard the bells of a troika and at the sound I was smart enough to feel a small moment of premonitory dread—on what journey was I now embarking and with what consequences? But I could not go back, *would not* go back. The troika appeared, the lanterns swinging from it shaking the stars from the sky and sticking them all around the tsarevich, who glowed like a saint on an iconostasis. He put out a hand with a grin and pulled me up onto the seat beside him for our wild ride, driving that troika across the parade grounds and through the small village, where all the streets and thoroughfares were empty, as if by decree. These streets, this village, these cities, Russia itself, one-sixth of the landmass of earth, belonged to him—or soon would—and when I was with him, it belonged to me, too. What was he showing off to me that night when he drove me across the plain, *abducted* me, as I later read in his journal—the countryside or himself?

It's not easy to drive a troika, you know. Of the three horses only the middle one wears the reins, and it takes all the driver's strength and skill to steer well. We Russians love speed, and Nicholas was flaunting his skill in the obstacle course of the village, on the dark mass of the parade ground. *He* wanted to impress *me*. He smiled at me without taking his flashing eyes from his horses, from the dusty yellow highway, sluiced down all through the day by barrels of water hauled from the Ligovka River on one-horse carts, wetted now by the evening dew. I was the one now too shy to look at *him*, though I peeked at him, sideways. The beauty in the family belonged to Niki—no pug nose and bulging eyes like his sister Xenia, no sunken cow face like his sister Olga. No photograph does justice to the balance and nobility of his face. And those eyes—no one who saw those pale blue eyes could forget them. But his eyes were more than tools of seduction. He used them to probe the soul. If I had the eyes of a fairy, he had the eyes of a god.

The country believed, you know, that its tsars were divine.

I ended up at the villa of my sister's beau, Ali, after all, in the early hours of the morning. He shared the villa with his friend Schlitter, a fellow officer, and what an entrance I made there, on the arm of the tsarevich—not as the baby sister blubbering at having missed the train, but as Venus triumphant! The five of us had supper and laughed for hours, Schlitter pulling a long face and saying, *No candle for God and no poker for the devil*, as he was the only man without a woman, a sally that pleased me enormously as it meant the tsarevich made up a pair with me.

For a moment, anyway.

I heard in the early months of his winter marriage to Alix, Niki took her, too, on nighttime rides, on a sleigh skimming the streets of Petersburg and the ice of the Neva.

And what kind of wife would I have made him? Could I have stood his future—imprisonment and a martyr's death?

I can assure you this: if I had been his wife, that would not have been his future.

our family's talents were our diamonds,
our rubies, our pearls

M Y MOTHER was twice a wife, and before that, for a few years, a dancer. She was a member of the *corps de ballet*, one of the girls who make up the row deep upstage, a Near the Water girl, or so we called them, those girls of the lowest rank who stood always in the back, their shoulder blades brushing against some piece of scenery inevitably painted with a large lake. My mother, Julia, left the theater to marry and have a family, and when her first husband, Ledé, died, she married my father, Felix. She was beautiful enough to marry as many times as she wished, with her round face and soft eyes. In the picture of her I keep by my bed she has her hair styled in ringlets, the front swept back, a braid like a crown anchoring it. She loved both of her husbands and with them had thirteen children, four of them by my father. I was their youngest.

My father was most famous for his mazurka. Poles dance the mazurka two ways, you know, one like the gentry, with elegant movements, the other like the peasantry, with feet stomping the floor, not softly sliding, and with much throwing of hats. Yes, Niki's great-grandfather Nicholas I saw my father dance the mazurka and had to have him for his own. On the Russian stage, my father performed not only the mazurka for him but also all the major character roles in our ballets for the next sixty years, his career three times the length of most dancers'. In the Imperial Ballet we cultivated two types of dancers—classical and character. Now, of course, no company can afford to do this. The troupes all have a small number of classical dancers, well under a hundred, and when they mount the big ballets, the stage seems sparsely covered. But then, with the tsar's purse, ah, well, we had a great many dancers, both classical dancers and character dancers, both types celebrated by the public and by the emperor. At times well over two hundred of us crowded the stage, and if we needed more bodies still, the tsar loaned us one of his regiments. My father was not only a great dancer but a great actor and a great comic. With his friend the dancer Timofei Stukolkin, when playing the robbers in *The Two Thieves*, the two of them not only ran about the stage but also clambered even into the orchestra pit, while the audience cried with laughter.

When I was a little girl, my father took me to watch him dance at the old Bolshoi Theater in Petersburg. Already I loved the theater and begged to be allowed to go. If my father would not take me, I cried. If he did take me, he complained that afterward I could not sleep all night. I pestered my mother to have a ballet costume sewn up for me so I could dance and pose before the mirrors of our ballroom, where my father gave his lessons in the mazurka. And so, on occasion, he relented and brought me to the theater. I remember the first time, a matinée. Like today, matinées then were full of children with their governesses and old ladies with their lorgnettes. I had the privilege of sitting in one of the artists' balcony boxes backstage, a special perch from which I could see not only the action of the performance but also that of the interval, when the curtain went down and behind it the stagehands lowered the new scenery and raised the old and the floor was swept and watered and the dressers stitched the torn strap of a costume while the wearer of that costume fidgeted impatiently. The performance that afternoon, I remember, was *Le Petit Cheval bossu*, in which my father played the Khan in his carpeted tent. All our ballets were based on French and German fairy tales until my father and his friends, who met Saturday afternoons at Stukolkin's, suggested to the old ballet master St. Léon that a ballet be based on a Russian fairy tale. St. Léon shrugged and confessed he knew none. At this, Stukolkin ran and pulled a storybook from the shelves of his children's nursery and right then pushed the samovar and the glasses of tea aside and read aloud the tale of *The Little Humpbacked Horse* by Ershov, while someone else translated each line into French so St. Léon could understand it. And so the tale of the Tsar Maiden and Ivanushka the Fool became a ballet—and St. Léon, inspired, took lessons in Russian and learned to speak it fluently—more than one can say for his successor as *maître de ballet*, the obsequious Frenchman Marius Petipa. And that is how I came to be that afternoon at the theater, watching my father play the old Khan of the Kirghiz Kaisaks who yearns for the young Tsar Maiden, only to find once he abducts her that she will not be possessed. At the end he is tricked by his passion for her into jumping into a barrel of boiling water, and she marries Ivanushka the Fool. In a few more years I would play my first child's role in that ballet as part of the undersea bacchanal. At the end of Act II the little horse and a peasant boy dive to the sea floor to find the missing ring of the Tsar Maiden, and that is where I, too, was found, in a tableau with all the inhabitants of the sea. But at this time I am telling you about I was only three and I was so silent in my rapture as I watched night become day on that stage and wind give way to thunder as the stagehands worked the machinery that my father forgot I sat waiting for him in the artists' box and went without me to his dressing room to wipe off his makeup and then traveled all the way home to Liteiny Prospekt. Only when my mother asked, *Where is Mala?* did my father cry, *Oh, my God, I've left her there!* and run back to the theater. He found me where I had hidden myself under my seat to wait for the evening's performance. Every artist has the story of his first enchantment with his art and that is mine.

After my father died, I found the leather journal where he wrote in his distinct hand the complete list of his partners. The last name at the bottom of the page was my own, underlined. At the sight of that black-inked mark I wept, for it told me he was still proud of me despite the disgrace of my personal circumstances. Yes, I was aware that while I considered my life a great triumph, to my parents it was a disgrace. My parents' friends were all, like them, Polish Catholics, and none of the daughters of their acquaintances became the mistress of anyone—before the revolution. After the revolution, of course, girls from the best families walked the Petersburg streets, selling themselves for pieces of soap. But we are not there yet. That is later. No, my private life was not what my father wanted for me. We were a proud family of artists—my grandfather was a tenor at the Warsaw Opera, his voice so beautiful the king of Poland called him *my nightingale*, and my father had hoped we would be a theatrical dynasty like the Petipas or the Gerdts, all of whom, fathers and children, worked at the Maryinsky and married fellow dancers. My brother Josef had already married a *coryphée*, Sima Astafieva, and he and my sister, Julia, and I had all graduated from the Imperial Theater Schools. We had all performed the children's roles in the company's ballets, as marionettes, cupids, nymphs, and pages. When we were cupids we wore headwear embroidered with gold thread, when we were nymphs we wore garlands of roses, when we were sylphs we were made to fly, a ring at the back of our costumes hooked onto a line by the machinist, smiles on our faces to conceal our terror as we were cranked into the air and tried to pitch our arms into the required poses. We watched the afternoon rehearsals at the great Maryinsky Theater from a box until it was our turn to rehearse on the stage, a little timid in the face of the theater so empty and so hushed, the great chandeliers and the velvet seats covered with brown canvas against the dust. Before the performance we were dressed, and then the lady chaperones used cotton wool to make circles of rouge on our cheeks. And then we were pushed onto the stage, where we tried hard not to stare out at the house, at the gold and white and blue of the four tiers, the parterres, the loges, the high-up gallery, tried not to breathe in the smell of chocolates and leather and tobacco, but attempted instead to focus on our little world on the stage. When we graduated, we all danced with the Imperial Ballet, my brother as a character dancer, my sister as a classical one. Julia was six years ahead of me; we were called Kschessinska I and Kschessinska II, until, of course, I surpassed her and was then simply M. Kschessinska. Our family's talents were our diamonds, our rubies, our pearls, and my father's talent was so abundant, the heap of it toppled off the stage and into our home.

In his spare time, he made a model of the St. Petersburg Bolshoi Theater, that building now demolished, though my father's model still survives, I hear, in the Bakhrushin Theatrical Museum in Moscow. It stands in a display case by the one that holds the little shoes I wore in my first performance in the undersea bacchanal of *Le Petit Cheval bossu*, though I have not seen either for eighty years. The little model my father built had real oil footlights and a velvet curtain and miniature canvas scenery that went up and down when you turned the handle, which my sister, Julia, never let me do, slapping my hands away if I reached for the crank. She thought she was the mistress of everything in the house. My father built, too, a big glass aquarium that stood by the windows in the parlor. Stone ornaments, like garden ornaments in miniature, decorated the vast bottom of the tank and fish swam like women moving in colorful dresses through the pillars of the watery estate. It was my father who designed the rooms of our large apartment at No. 38, Liteiny Prospekt in Petersburg and of our dacha on our country estate, Krasnitzky. There he tore down the walls of the dining room to enlarge it and built a bathhouse on the river. We had a farm there, an orchard, a vegetable garden, and beyond that, a forest thick with mushrooms. And I remember how each time we arrived at the country from the city, my father and my mother knelt down and kissed the land of our estate. We were not rich, but the money my father earned as principal character dancer and from his private ballroom lessons in the waltz and the mazurka, lessons given to the children of the nobility, even the children of the imperial family, gave us a comfortable life.

Christmas and Easter he turned into pageants and feasts. Christmas Eve day we fasted until the first star appeared in the evening sky, after which we gorged ourselves on the thirteen fish dishes my father himself had prepared—we, of course, had a cook, but this was a special day and my father a real culinary artist, with a secret recipe for fish soup made with cream, a Polish dish. He labored in the kitchen while we children played games—*rucheyok*, like London Bridge, and *chekharla*, leapfrog. Candles and glass pears shone in our tree, which was showered all over with silver tinsel that tangled with the gold paper stars and angels. On New Year's we drank hot Swedish punch and ate apple pies. For Easter my father baked a dozen *kulichi*, one for each apostle. Tall as a man's top hat, each cake was iced in a different manner and adorned with fruits or candies, and I would walk the length of the banquet table to admire their distinct beauty: a *fleur-de-lis* of sliced strawberries on this one, the crest of an ocean wave made of white icing on that, tiny toothpick flags a fence at the border of another. In France, the old Russian immigrants bake their *kulichi* in coffee cans to make them rise tall.

All the world was a theater to my father, and for my birthday in August no production was more grand. We were inevitably at our dacha in that month and the feast he prepared was followed by fireworks of his own invention. At the dessert table I sat in the place of honor; one year, my father hung a wreath of flowers on a string run though a hook in the ceiling and when my dessert was served, he lowered the petaled crown by pulley until it settled gently onto my head, while my big brother and sister and half-brothers clapped. Russian girls love to weave themselves crowns of flowers, and so my father wove one for me. Even the peasants in the nearby villages who did our haymaking and took care of our cows brought birthday gifts, baskets of eggs nestled in napkins, each linen embroidered with a small red cross, and they bowed low from the waist as they presented their treats. Some of the peasants had been serfs just ten years earlier, before they had been emancipated by Niki's grandfather Alexander II, and they kept still their serf manners, bowing low like that to their masters.

During those long days of haymaking and rye threshing and mushroom and berry picking, the lives of peasant and master were stitched tightly together in a single seam. Peasant children became the playmates of the noble ones, if only for the summer, and who does not remember playing *gorodki* with wooden blocks or bat and ball, *babki*, with any scrap of metal to be found, or *bory*, the game of tag, our bare feet brown with dirt. I remember the littlest ones bathed naked in what remained of our old bathhouse. The peasants joined us for lunch or for tea on Sunday, but when we returned to Petersburg, of course, they remained by the river Orlinka at their harvests to work the fields while I learned my art. I put on so much weight one summer from all the big meals that when I returned to school my teacher scolded I had become *regrettably fat*. But what is there to do in the country but play and eat? But wait, I've lost myself. That happens often to me now. It was the peasant women who as wet nurses and nannies raised the noble children, taught them folklore and fairy stories, played with them cards and lotto, put them to bed at night, accompanied them from country to city back to country again, wept when they went off to the lycée or joined the Guards, and then were cared for by the families as aging relations. Why, Sergei Diaghilev brought his nanny with him when he moved to Petersburg as a grown man!

We, of course, were of more modest means and had no nannies. My mother and father raised us, were devoted to us. Would it be wrong to say that of the four children he had with my mother, I was my father's favorite? After all, my parents are gone, their faces blackened in their graves; my brother Josef died in 1942, my brother Stanislaus died over a century ago, in 1864, at age four, eight years before my birth. This fascinated me, a brother I never knew, and I would gaze for long periods at the photograph my mother kept in a silver frame on her dressing table as if by that I could come to know him; he looked just like her, the rest of us like my father, with the long face, the straight nose, the close-set eyes. My sister, Julia, lived to be one hundred two, you know. She died the evening after Russian Christmas Eve two years ago, January 7, between seven and eight o'clock, right here in this room. After our husbands died, we lived together again, as we had as girls. My father lived to the age of eighty-three. Longevity runs in our family, though not in the Romanovs', but longevity is not immortality; it merely ensures you suffer the loss of everyone you love so that when death finally comes you are more than ready.

I am not writing this down. I am thinking it. I had two strokes this past year. To answer my correspondence, I dictate, and then I sign my initials MRK in a hand so shaky it looks as if some very old lady had written those three consonants. My handwriting used to be minuscule, but now it is loose and large, like a small child's. Yes, it is impossible to write, but I do not want to ask for help until I know for certain what I wish to share. Because, you see, there are so few of us left who remember how it all was. After the revolution three million of us fled to Berlin, Paris, New York, where we clung together, speaking Russian, reading Bunin, Tolstoy, Akhmatova, not the traitor writers, the ones who loved the Bolsheviks, but the ones who reminded us of what life was like before. We spent our days eating Russian breakfasts of tea, cream, ham, cheese, and hard-boiled eggs, attending midnight mass at Easter, sitting together in theaters where actors and singers and musicians from the tsar's great theaters now performed, traveling to the Riviera in the season, trying to live *as before*. That was our phrase, *as before*. Everything we did we tried to do as we did before. We were waiting for the Russia we knew to be returned to us. But death picked us off one by one as we waited, and our children who came of age in these foreign cities do not know the Petersburg and the Moscow that, as the poet Ivanov put it, *disappeared into the night*. Yes, if I don't tell, certain things will never be known, and when my memory is completely lost, even I will not know them. All will be rumor, which is nothing but the tail end of a vanishing truth.

The tsarevich and me and our fortunes together after that troika ride, yes, those details I can remember, but not so the names of the little girls I taught at my ballet school just seven years ago.

to the taste of the court

WHEN WE RETURNED FROM KRASNOYE SELO, the tsarevich called on me for the very first time, at my parents' house. My sister and I had a little sitting room adjacent to our bedroom, with a second door that opened directly into the central hall, which gave us some privacy for entertaining. As we were now eighteen and twenty-four, we could receive our own visitors, though we could not feed them, it still being our parents' house and the cook subject only to their orders! We both, like our father, enjoyed a party, and as my sister was six years older than I, my parents allowed her to serve as both hostess and chaperone while they retired out of earshot for the night. Some of the young officers of the Guards who saw us at the theater became our admirers and would visit us the evenings we were not performing. We were grown-ups now and did not have to shout our names from a carriage as we left the dormitories. The men could now ogle us at the theater and call on us at home. And so, you see, my sister had set the precedent for me with Ali—Baron Alexander Zeddeler, an officer in the Pre-obrazhensky Regiment whose family had been in service to the crown for a hundred years—who courted her and later became her official protector. She had not chosen a fellow dancer to love, and I, who copied her in all matters, would copy her in this. I would do better than copy her. In this, as in all things, I determined to trump her: I was prettier, my promotions came quicker, and so if she had a baron to court her, I would have a tsarevich. There is no greater pleasure than winning a competition with one's sister and no greater sorrow than to see her suffer because of it. In my journal that year I wrote of Nicholas, *He will be mine!* Yes, I used an exclamation point.

One evening in March the maid opened the sitting-room door to announce the officer Eugene Volkoff, but it was Nicholas Romanov who stepped through the threshold in his long gray overcoat, and the maid knew no difference. She had never seen the face of the tsarevich. But even those who had could mistake others for him. Niki's friends Volkoff and Volodia Svetschin looked so much like him, they were often taken for the tsarevich. Svetschin wore his hair and even his beard like Niki's and loved the moments of mistaken identity when Petersburgers stood straight and gave the eyes right as he passed—one was not supposed to look directly into the sovereign's eyes, you know—thinking Svetschin the heir. Yes, sometimes Niki was able to travel about unrecognized. If the tsar were to appear before you without introduction, would you know he was the tsar? At the head of a Bolshoi Vykhọd from the Winter Palace, surrounded by carriages and Cossacks and uniformed grand dukes, yes. But without such a production, perhaps not. Niki's own guards did not, on occasion, recognize him. On his march in the Crimea years later to test out the army private's new uniform, he was stopped by a sentry at the gate of his own estate. *You can't go through here*, he was told. And so the tsar of All the Russias turned without complaint and retreated.

Hard perhaps, now, to believe that the face of the tsar or the heir might be unknown to his subjects. The camera was not used to the extent that it is today. I have few pictures of myself before the age of thirty, and though the imperial family all had camera boxes and pasted pictures of each other in their scrapbooks at night, those photographs were private. The tsar almost never appeared in public. The official portraits issued in lieu of his presence were often painted photographs or colored lithographs, but those were idealized images. So my maid did not know this was the tsarevich, who did not want himself known as his intentions were not—and would never be—honorable. But at that time I did not care about this, and this "M. Volkoff" and I spent the evening in the type of light chatter I had learned so well by age fourteen. My first flirtation had been with an English boy, McPherson, I can no longer recall his full name, who had visited our dacha one summer and whose engagement my determined pursuit of him compromised. I must have entertained the tsarevich very well. For the next day, on ivory palace stationery with its gold crown floating above his blue-green monogram, Niki wrote me, *Since our meeting I have been in the clouds*. I had snared him as I had snared McPherson. Niki was always more expressive in letters than in person, though one could not know this from his journals, as terse and dull as a detective's report.

Once he had actually come to my house—which he told me he had feared would make him uncomfortable, as I lived with my parents—he came back again and again. My parents did not interrupt us in our sitting room. Could one tell the tsarevich that the hour grew late? That the frivolity grew too loud? For though Niki came sometimes alone, he came also at times with his fellow officers, Count André Chouvalov or the real Eugene Volkoff or Baron Zeddeler, or sometimes with his young cousins, the children of his grandfather's brother Mikhail Nikolaevich, the handsome Mikhailovichi—for that is how we refer to each branch of the Romanov family, as a group through the patronymic—the grand dukes George, Sandro, and Sergei. These last three and Niki constituted the Potato Club, their private joke. Out riding one day, some of them turned their horses into a potato field and the others, losing sight of them, called out to a peasant farmer, *Where did they go?*—to which the man replied, *They turned into potatoes!* And so to commemorate their brotherhood each man wore around his neck a golden charm in the shape of a potato.

The most handsome of the brothers was Sandro, with his quicksilver tongue and his solid gold ambition that had him pursuing Niki's sister Xenia, his second cousin. The dullest was George, who was quiet and who collected coins, of all things, and who grew quite bald at a young age; and there was another one at home, Nicholas, who preferred the bodies of men and who became renowned as a historian and whom later Lenin had murdered, saying, *The revolution does not need historians*. Of them I liked Sergei the best. He had a fine enough face, blond hair, his light eyes set far apart, and though he could be moody, a temperament I recognized well from the theater, he could also be the most fun—the first with a prank, the first to propose a caper. His favorite expression in those days was *tant pis*, so much the worse, but there was no sorrow to be had at my house. Together, I and the Potato Club laughed, talked, played baccarat, clapped to the Georgian songs from the Caucasus which the Mikhailovichi sang for us and which they knew so well from the twenty years their father served in Tiflis as governor-general. This province of Russia was so close to Turkey and Persia that the boys had only to look out a window of the white Italianate governor-general's palace onto Golovinsky Prospekt to see mules and camels, men with black fezzes and sheathed sabers coming to market or to consult with Sergei's father, and women in tall velvet headdresses adorned with scarves, their hair dyed a brilliant red and their necks hung with as many as two dozen necklaces of silver and gold. They came from straw huts laid with carpets or whitewashed *zindans* of mud to the palace where Sergei's father laid supper every night for forty. His father also had a two-hundred-thousand-acre estate in the countryside, in Borjomi, that a man could ride over all day and still not travel from one boundary to the next. The great white Kazbek mountain stood like the Buddha at the end of the big steppe and by its scale let men know their place.

As if the Romanovs ever knew their place until the revolution showed it to them.

The rest of the family looked slightly askance at the Mikhailovichi, as if their time in the Caucasus might have made them too much like the untamed Georgians they oversaw. Niki's father tried hard to Russify that part of the country, denying its residents their language, forcing even young students to speak only Russian at school or be punished, as the young Stalin was, by standing all morning in the corner, holding up a heavy plank of wood, but the Georgian language survived—and the Mikhailovichi learned it. I remember one song they sang, so haunting with its oriental sound, about a queen whose mellifluous voice drew lovers to her like a mythological siren's, though she sat not on ocean rocks but in her cushioned bedroom, in a castle by the Terek River. And when she had sated herself with the beauty of these men, she murdered them and threw their bodies down into the swift-running water.

Of the three brothers Sergei had the richest voice, and when he took the lead on that song he looked directly at me as if I were the coldhearted siren! Niki had told me Sergei loved his sister Xenia, but had stood aside for Sandro, who pursued her so aggressively and whom she seemed to prefer. I should say Sergei was the least handsome of his very handsome brothers and Sandro the most, probably why the butterfly Xenia had chosen Sandro. Sergei was teased sometimes by women who, like schoolboy bullies, would ask, *Why are you so ugly?*—which he was not—to which he would reply to cover his hurt, *In that lies my charm*. Had Sergei now fallen in love with another girl who could not belong to him?

For it was Niki who was pursuing me, and this was clear; this was the reason he and they were in my house and sometimes the reason they came to the theater: Niki wanted to see me in my little roles—as a tiny shepherdess who rode on a cart about the stage in the opera *La Dame de pique* or as Little Red Riding Hood running from the Wolf in *Sleeping Beauty*. One night, with a basket in his hand

and a kerchief on his head, the tsarevich entertained us by dancing my role of Little Red Riding Hood and then the role of the Wolf, pawing at the carpet with the toe of his boots, turning his head and looking at us from the side of his eye. He knew all the roles, little and big, from the opera and the ballet—he had a direct telephone line to the theater installed in his villa at Krasnoye Selo so he could hear the operas performed on the Maryinsky stage even when he was at camp. Niki mimed the wolf grabbing up the little girl and folding her over his shoulder, using one arm to still her imaginary petticoats, her imaginary kicking legs. Sometimes he called me *Miss Riding Hood*, looking down his nose at me with a long, serious face. *What, Miss*, he would say, *have you been up to in those woods?*

When we grew thirsty from laughter, I crept from the sitting room and, using glasses pilfered from my parents' pantry, I served champagne. These evenings sometimes lasted until five in the morning— we Russians love a party that lasts hours and then we sleep until noon—though one night our evening was cut short when the prefect of police came to tell us the emperor was enraged at having discovered his son's absence. A policeman followed Niki everywhere, to Niki's eternal irritation, and reported on him to his father. Apparently, Niki had metamorphosed from the effeminate child the emperor called *girlie* into a bit too much of the libertine for Alexander III, a libertine who nonetheless wrote in his journal, *What is wrong with me?* when he slept until noon and beyond each day. And at my own metamorphosis from child to flirt, my father was not enraged so much as worried. What risk would I take, what impetuous action would I regret?

But as yet there was no *real* intimacy between Niki and me, except for one brief moment in the entrance hall when, as he put on his woolen greatcoat one night, as a joke he drew me inside the flaps of the coat as if to button me within it close to him. He smelled of cologne—bergamot, rosemary, and leather—and I of my violet perfume, and the temperature inside the coat made those scents blossom. I bit at a thread on his shirt. Niki stopped my teeth with a kiss. I would have swallowed all the buttons of his greatcoat one by one if I thought that would keep me this close to him even a minute longer. Our real courtship had begun! But to my great frustration, Niki continued to feel his way toward me through letters rather than touch— *Forgive me, divine creature, for having disturbed your rest*. Pushkin's lines, I knew, because Pushkin I read, every Russian read Pushkin, his verse so accessible even a poorly educated girl like me could enjoy it. The words were not Niki's, but I treasured them anyway, though I was certainly too much a fool to understand that when Niki wrote to me one night after the opera *Taras Bulba*, in which the hero's passion for his beloved made him give up his father and his country, *Think of what André did for love of a young Polish girl*, that Nicholas himself would never be allowed to turn his back on his throne or on Russia for love of the young Polish dancer Kschessinska II. These were tantalizing words, but still, they were just words. For me, so used to the animating force of dance, the touch of two bodies, words, no matter what sentiments they expressed, seemed as flat as the paper they lay on. How to make them stand up?

That I had not yet figured out, but the tsarevich's attentions to me, such as they were, had not gone unnoticed by the theater administration, which saw fit to display me in larger and larger roles. In 1890 I was a *coryphée* dancing the part of the Fairy Candide in *Sleeping Beauty*, but with the flowering of my talent and the tsarevich's interest in me, I was quickly promoted to second soloist, and then to prima ballerina. By 1893, one year after the tsarevich's first visit to me, I would no longer dance the role of a fairy in *Sleeping Beauty*, but make my debut as Aurora herself, the first Russian ballerina ever to dance the role. Yes, the director of theaters Vzevolozhsky and the ballet master Petipa were eager to please the court, for the pleasure of the Romanovs was all that mattered. Why, when Grand Duke Nicholas Nikolaevich did not like the way a *galop* was performed in rehearsal, what we dancers called the *galop infernal*, which always closes the season at Krasnoye Selo, he came up onto the stage himself to demonstrate it to the company, and the dancers performed the *galop* as the grand duke wished. All was done to the taste of the court, and I had suddenly become its taste.

Let us be frank. I did not jump well, I was not ethereal. My feet were flat. My legs were too short—to disguise this last defect I had special tutus made with short waists and long skirts—but my audience did not notice my deficits. They saw only that I was bold, that I was fast, that I was brilliant. I was what was called a *terre-à-terre* dancer—I attacked the floor with my sharp, hard pointes. *Diamantine*, I was described. I gave off light. And I was dancing for a court that loved nothing more than diamonds, glitter, gold. In addition to my formidable technique, I had the ineffable something that makes a dancer a star. When I stepped onto the stage, one could look nowhere but at me until I left it. Scenery, stage business, the divertissements of soloists or *corps de ballet*—none of it could distract from the impact of my presence. And I could act, if that is the word for what happens when one opens the door to a role and steps completely within it, the canvas backdrop, the painted face of one's partner, more real than the walls of the auditorium and the men and women seated there. No one who has seen me as the tragic, bewitched Swan Queen Odette or the jilted Gypsy girl Esmeralda could ever forget it. When, as Esmeralda, I looked to heaven in the last act, my pain and my jealousy at Phoebus's betrayal changing to resignation, there was no one in the theater immune to my pathos. And while pining, I was glamorous. I pinned to my hair a wig styled by the most fashionable hairdresser of the time, Delacroix, I fastened jewels, at first just glass but later the real precious stones given me by my admirers, at my wrists and my neck, and I cinched beneath my costume one of the whalebone corsets I had made especially for me in a Petersburg shop. One could not bend much so laced, but a straight stiff back was the vogue then on the stage and off. They laughed at me later, Mikhail Fokine and the newer choreographers, when they pioneered a newer, free-flowing dance style at the turn of the century. In his *Petrouchka*, the stiff-bodied ballerina doll with the whipping legs was a caricature of me invented by Fokine, with his beak of a nose, and his little friend, with her nose in the air, Bronislava Nijinska—a Polish girl like me with a brother, Vaslav, who would become much more famous than she ever would, despite her airs. When she later joined Diaghilev's Ballets Russes along with her brother, she persuaded the older dancers not to wear their jewels on the stage, that it did not suit the character or costume to be so adorned. But that was the way we danced then in the 1890s—in corsets, in nineteenth-century three-act ballets, for emperors and kaisers and kings.

The court had already tired of venerating French, Italian, and German music, opera, literature, languages—where were our own? At the start of the nineteenth century, a parlor game in which the speakers could converse only in Russian became all the rage, and if one spoke, by mistake, a French word, his fellows would cry, *Forfeiture*—in French! because there was no word for this in Russian. It took Pushkin in the 1830s to give us our own language. But the Russian ballet of 1890 was still dominated by Europeans: imported Italian dancers and imported French ballet masters—Didelot, Perrot, St. Léon, and Petipa—woe to poor Lev Ivanov, who had the misfortune to be a Russian and therefore to be overlooked and underpaid as second ballet master to a Frenchman! I ask you, who looks to Italy or France for ballet now? It was Russia, under the Romanovs, that perfected the art, and I was its first Russian ballerina, not one of those Italian girls brought in to do the honors in the ballerina roles, while the Svetlanas and the Ekaterinas and the Olgas posed behind them. I was the first to learn the tricks of Zucchi and Grimaldi and Brianza and Legnani, the *fouetté*, the *double tour*, the *entrechats sept royal*. After my debut in January 1893 as Aurora in *Sleeping Beauty*—I am skipping ahead here again for a moment—Tchaikovsky himself came to my dressing room to tell me he wanted to create a ballet for me. It was like God calling on one. At my doorway, he bowed to me, his face very pink, his beard and hair almost entirely white, his dark-rimmed eyes glittering, his right hand playing with the pince nez he wore always on a black cord, and in his usual mishmash of French and Russian, he praised my dancing of Aurora. He was only fifty-two. We had just last year, on the fiftieth performance of *The Sleeping Beauty*, presented him on the stage a crown of gold laurel leaves. That's how we honored our artists in tsarist Russia—with ceremony and treasure. I remember because I myself had been elected to present him the crown and I was late to the backstage ceremony, having been flirting with a trio of grand dukes—and the company, which knew this, seethed at the delay but could do nothing about it! Yes, Tchaikovsky thought he had years ahead of him of making ballets with the great Petipa, many more spectacles and *féeries* to mount. Tchaikovsky, Vzevolozhsky, and Petipa—and, yes, Ivanov—together created the three masterworks of the ballet repertory—*The Sleeping Beauty*, *The Nutcracker*, and *Swan Lake*—now danced by companies all over the world, pieces of that music played on out-of-tune pianos in ballet schools on every continent as young girls practice their *battements* and *tendus*. (And Tchaikovsky was so kind to students! After the first performance of his *Nutcracker* in 1882, he sent two big baskets of sweets to all of us at the school who had performed children's roles in the ballet.) Petipa would send Tchaikovsky his notes—they each worked alone—then, in rehearsals on the little school theater stage, would have Tchaikovsky shorten or lengthen his music to suit his dances, though Petipa was deferential about it, for what serious composer could stand to work like this, on command take a scissor to his phrases? Tchaikovsky's reputation suffered at first because he wrote for the ballet. We usually had hacks like Pugni, Drigo, or Minkus—men on the theater payroll as composers or conductors—create the music for our steps. Who listens to *them* now? No one. But everyone can hum a bar or two of Tchaikovsky. For *Sleeping Beauty*, Petipa sent Tchaikovsky notes, *With a new wave of the fairy's magic wand Aurora appears and rushes onstage. 6/8 for 24. A voluptuous adagio. Coquettish allegro— 3/4 for 48. Variation for Aurora.* From these plain details Tchaikovsky dreamed the richly embroidered music. Do you know what Alexander III said to Tchaikovsky about his music after the dress rehearsal of his magisterial *Sleeping Beauty*, performed before an invited royal audience? *Very nice.* Perhaps he thought Tchaikovsky was satirizing him in the person of the bumbling King Florestan, who could not properly supervise his courtiers and thereby doomed his court to one hundred years' sleep. Tchaikovsky moped for days, always believing each of his triumphs to be a failure. Why, after the debut of his opera *Queen of Spades*, he walked the streets in despair until he heard three young officers singing the lines to one of the arias.

What music would Tchaikovsky have created for me? What story—for he created the story for his ballets, too; the libretto for *Swan Lake* was his own pastiche of fairy tales and bits of Wagnerian operas—would he have dreamed up to suit my talents? Perhaps *Undine*, the ballet he had thought about composing since 1886. Perhaps I was the final inspiration he needed? But I will never know, for Tchaikovsky died in the cholera epidemic later that year. Despite the large placards mounted everywhere in the city cautioning against drinking unboiled water, Tchaikovsky asked for a glass of it in a restaurant and drank it down like a man who wanted to die, a story that astonished me then, because I was young and knew nothing yet of the shame coiled about the body of love. When I went to the apartment of his brother Modeste, where Tchaikovsky was laid out in a black suit on a low bier draped in white satin, I could not understand how a man of his age, which seemed to me then so great, could still be driven by passion. I knew Tchaikovsky loved men, but I did not know until later that he was in love with his nephew and that his love was—even worse than forbidden—not returned. Was that hopelessness also my own? Before I kissed Tchaikovsky's pale forehead, all *his* thoughts of love blanched away, someone standing at the head of the coffin wiped the composer's nose and mouth with a cloth dipped in carbolic, and we were told to spit into a handkerchief of our own after giving to him our last kiss. Was it his disease or his torment we feared contracting? The emperor gave permission for the funeral service to be held in Kazan Cathedral, for which one needed a ticket, as if it were a performance, but for this goodbye, no one needed to reserve a seat. This farewell was for intimates, his fellow artists.

No, Tchaikovsky never made a ballet for me, but there were many extant roles ready for habitation. One I especially coveted was Esmeralda, the title part in the ballet based on Victor Hugo's *Notre-Dame de Paris*, that of the Gypsy dancer who loses her great love, Phoebus, to another woman. Though I coveted it, I would not dance it until 1899: I had not yet learned to go to the tsarevich, to the court, to get what I wanted at the theater. At twenty, I was still the obedient girl who listened to the *régisseur*, the *maître de ballet*, the *directeur*. Yes, I was mad to dance Esmeralda, but Petipa would not let me. *Écoute, ma belle*, he began when I asked him. He had been in Russia fifty years and still spoke only French—not a problem with the court, which also spoke French, but a problem for us at the theater, where other than ballet terms, which were always in French, Russian was what we knew best. No wonder Petipa was so good at mime. In his broken Russian he said to me, *You love?* And when I assured him that yes, I loved, he stroked his waxed moustache. *Do you suffer?* To which I responded, *Of course not*. That was the wrong answer. Only an artist who understood the suffering that accompanied love, he told me, could dance the part. He should know. He had been married twice, both times to ballerinas.

One day I would suffer, and one day Esmeralda would become my greatest role.

she was his doll come to life

B UT I WAS NOT SUFFERING in 1892. The tsarevich visited me at
home, sent roses and orchids to my box at the Sunday horse
races at the Michel Riding School, offered up little gifts of
jewelry, a gold brooch, a set of emerald earrings, which at
first I declined, but when I saw how my refusals saddened him and
because, after all, I really wanted those trinkets, I happily changed
course. Greed made in me its triumph over manners, and not for
the last time. Yes, the tsarevich's shyness and my innocence made
good partners in this long courtship. My desire for Niki was still not
fully the desire of a woman for a man, but more of a child for the
biggest prize that she could wave at others with glee. My parents
were somewhat mollified when they saw how Niki's courtship ben-
efited my career, and my brother and sister titillated themselves with
the possibilities such an alliance promised for them. While I accepted
the tsarevich's attention *off* the stage, it seemed I wore it *on* the stage
as well, and my being a favorite of the heir heightened both my appeal and the appeal of my whole family. The balletomane subscrib-
ers fought to get tickets for the nights we four Kschessinkys were
cast together in the same ballet. One night in *Sleeping Beauty* my
father played King Florestan XIV, I Aurora, my sister an attendant
fairy in the retinue of the Fairy of the Lilac, my brother Josef was

Prince Fortuné, a small part as Cinderella's *porteur* in the Act III divertissement.

Then one night at the theater, between Acts II and III of *Coppélia*, my long girlhood ended. I and my father's friend Stukolkin, who was playing Dr. Coppelius, a role my father himself often played, had just exited the stage—I as Swanhilda dressed up like the doll Coppélia, which the lonely doctor had made for himself as a daughter—just as Geppetto in the fairy tale *Pinocchio* made for himself a puppet to be his boy. Swanhilda had tricked the doctor into thinking she was his doll come to life, and Stukolkin had mimed his shock and then his fury at being tricked, and I thought his panting as he ran after me as the curtain lowered to be for comic effect. His rubber pate glued to his head, two big white tufts of hair shaking above each ear, spectacles teetering on his nose, he began to grip at the flats backstage right and with the other hand grope at his left arm. Beneath his orange makeup his skin made a shiny white sheath. And then, with a dense sigh, he collapsed, the piece of painted canvas he had been clutching swaying free as his hand opened, and when he fell, victim of a heart attack, he shook all the props on the stage and the hay-thatched cottage itself. In those several moments as I knelt by him in my doll costume I saw his eyes behind those fake spectacles grow dull. The thick face paint stood on his skin like a porcelain mask and with his dull pupils *he* looked like a doll. The columnists would eulogize him the next week: *He died like a soldier at his post, serving the art he loved passionately to his last minute*. Was this what I wanted—a life lived only on the stage? And a love affair that seemed to dwell there also, just for show? For Swanhilda had dressed up as Coppélia not only to fool the poor befuddled doctor but also to win back the attention of her beau, Franz, who had become mesmerized by the pretty new doll the doctor had posed, as if reading a book, on the balcony of his house. For the tsarevich, I understood I, too, was a pretty doll posed on *my* balcony, the Maryinsky stage, or the smaller stage of my parents' house, where I must appear to be a thing worse than a doll—a child! If I wanted the tsarevich to see me as a real woman, I would need to break away from my parents' embrace. I would need my own house—and quickly! For, after all, one does not live forever.

Of his own accord, Niki might never have suggested this. It was in his nature to drift, a small sailboat in warm, currentless water. Our little love affair would eventually have ended in the tall reeds of a marsh when he became enamored of someone else, perhaps an opera singer or a *kamer-freilini*, a lady-in-waiting at court. But it was not in my nature to drift. So after an evening of impassioned kissing, at my signal, of course, Niki agreed with me that, yes, he supposed it was time I had my own house. And so I learned—Niki the sailboat needed a push.

The tsar, Alexander, was not happy about this development. Niki's dalliance with me had suddenly become too serious for him. A flirtation with a clean Polish girl, the young dancer, Kschessinska II, yes. An interlude, yes. But take her as a mistress, set her up in a house, no. The emperor was notoriously straitlaced. The joke in the capital was that Alexander III was the only husband faithful to his wife. He did not want the heir apparent to set up a household in Petersburg with me, give me children, as his two uncles had done with their dancer-mistresses, as his own father had done with Princess Ekaterina. My father felt the same, of course.

I remember standing outside the door of my father's study for some moments, gathering my courage to tell him of my intention to set up household with the tsarevich, my intention and my father's hopes for me about to collide. I was not a girl from the lower classes. My parents traveled in the best Polish Catholic circles. My godfather was M. Strakatch, who owned the largest linen shop in Petersburg. My parents expected me to make a good marriage. My mother, I thought, being a woman, would understand what I had to do for love, but I was wrong about this; she would turn away from me for years, refusing even to see my new house. When I went to Liteiny Prospekt to visit my family, she stayed in her room and sent out no message—but I could not foresee any of this. No, outside that study door I worried only that I would break my father's heart. So I hesitated. I wanted in those moments to crawl into the study and lay myself beneath my father's big table as I had as a child, when just the warmth of my father's feet and the sound of his breath as he wrote or drew designs on paper for some of his inventions would provide an unfathomable comfort. I wanted to be a child again, to sit on the hands of a clock as they moved backward. I stood there so long my sister, Julia, whom I had left waiting in our bedroom, came to check on me. When she saw me standing there stolidly and silent, a mushroom under the beeches waiting to be picked, she raised her own hand to rap on the door. She believed the tsarevich's liaison with me guaranteed good fortune for our family. So she pushed past me into the room and told my father what I was afraid to tell him. *Mathilde is going to be kept by the tsarevich.* We three stood in silence as the clock ticked, the pendulum swung, the cuckoo bird slid out of the clock on its tongue of wood and gave twelve cries. An omen. The cry of the cuckoo tells you how many years you have yet to live. But this was a wooden bird, housed in a clock. My father's face rimpled above his great waxed moustache, the elegant erect posture eroded. Finally, my father said, *You understand the tsarevich can never marry you and your idyll will be short?* I nodded. I understood but I did not understand. Who at nineteen could? Hidden up my sleeve was the bracelet of sapphire and diamonds the tsarevich had given me in anticipation of our new estate and the gold clasp pinched impatiently at my skin.

Do the parents of all mistresses suffer as mine did? Did the father of the ballerina Anna Kuznetsova cry when Grand Duke Konstantin Nikolaevich built for her what was to become my house?

My parents would never visit No. 18, English Prospekt, out of principle. I had two floors, and behind the house two walled gardens, one a pleasure garden flush with flowers, the other a working one, with a row of vegetables, a stable, a barn, and just beyond that second stone wall lay the palace of one of the tsar's many uncles. Look how close I slept now to the Romanovs! Niki's great-uncle Konstantin had hoped to marry his mistress, but the tsar refused him permission to divorce his wife. Of course, Konstantin could have done so anyway, but he would have been stripped of his title, his income, his property, his country, and then what would he have? A new wife living with him in exile. Small compensation. So instead, he suffered in comfort his mistress's uncertain position and those of his five children. Eventually, though, before his death, he managed to have her and her children ennobled by the tsar's *ukase*. In Russia one's place can at any moment change. A tsar's decree was one way. For women it was done through marriage. For men by climbing the ladder of Peter the Great's Table of Ranks. One entered state service at the fourteenth rank, and with each year one accumulated more *chin*, or rank, until one reached the fifth rank and earned the right to be called *Your Honor*. After that, the top four ranks were filled with men appointed there by the tsar, and those men were given hereditary titles. Such a man was not a member of the imperial suite, he was not a prince or a baron, but he was a nobleman and had earned the right to be addressed as *Your High Excellency* or *Your Excellency*, and his name would be added to the list from which invitations to the twelve balls at the Winter Palace were drawn. Anna and her children had been given those rights. Why could they not eventually be mine?

Yes, No. 18, English Prospekt was an address with a rich history, a history particularly resonant for me, though from its hard lessons, I, of course, learned nothing. Because the old grand duke, a navy commander with a pretty face, expected, always, to be assassinated like his brother Tsar Alexander II—mutilated on the street by bomb-throwing revolutionaries, the People's Will terrorists—for the ground floor he'd had specially crafted steel shutters, as thick as the steel hulls of the ships he ruled. The rooms on the ground floor were otherwise outfitted fashionably in the European style, with heavy mirrors, French consoles, and delicate sofas. The bedroom I took for my own was the only room I bothered to change. Like a girl who fusses over one of her dolls and neglects all the rest, I changed not one iota of any other room in the house. For me, the bedroom was the only room of any importance—my fate would be determined there. Would I be worth the rubles Nicholas was prepared to spend on me?

For he paid my rent and paid also the salaries of my three servants—three, while the Winter Palace has six thousand when the imperial family is in residence—and this was the gossip of the capital. I remember one evening coming home from the Maryinsky, I passed my brother Josef on his bicycle, wearing his gray felt overshoes and a fur-trimmed greatcoat, and he called to me that I should hurry, that someone on the street had told him the tsarevich was already headed to my house! The whole city knew my business. In the theater that year on Nicholas's name day the audience laughed when the baritone in *Iolanta* sang, *Who can compare with my Matilda?* If the court only knew that at Niki's visits to my house of ill repute he sat not by me on the small sofa, but by himself in the Louis XIV armchair opposite, as if we were formal acquaintances and he had laid his card on the salver in the entry. The setting of our new house inhibited rather than advanced our flirtation. I realized too late: here is a man who likes to *dream* of love, who likes *the idea* of a woman, but not the woman herself, who prefers a white-skinned ballerina who dances on the other side of the footlights, a mistress who is a virgin and lives in her father's house.

I had made, perhaps, a mistake. I had miscalculated. But there I sat in the house he paid for. And there he sat, in his evening clothes, his frock coat with the gold braiding, his broad white shirtfront with the starched collar that cut a sharp vee. His body drawn away from me, he smoked his thin cigarettes in his holder with his left hand and with his right he stroked his moustache as he told me he would be tormented his whole life if he took my virginity, that if I hadn't been a virgin he would not have hesitated to make love to me. Even in my naïveté, I knew this to be an excuse, though for what I was not sure. What purpose had I and this house if not consummation? Why had he rented it for me—out of courtesy because I had asked him to?

I began to wish I had never moved away from my parents' house. I missed the bedroom I shared with my sister and our late-night family dinners when we had all returned from the theater, where, talking over one another, we would vie to tell my mother whose wig had slipped and who had forgotten what step and where a stagehand had begun to crank up the whirlwind and send branches and leaves flying before his cue. My father would employ his considerable talent as a mimic to demonstrate exactly how Pavel Gerdt, a little old now at almost fifty to play the Prince in *Swan Lake*, had come down flat-footed and huffing from a single, effortful leap. Why, he was so old that when Petipa had choreographed the pas de deux for him and his Swan Queen, the adagio had to be made a pas de trois, with the prince's friend Benno to do most of the dancing of it while Gerdt did the lifting as the ballerina's *porteur*. We would laugh, just the family, intimate and happy with one another, and my father would eventually bring out a bottle of cognac, but now I was alone, sitting awkwardly with this cipher in a frock coat, and they were still together, ignorant of my foundering. But I could not go back and face the humiliation my retreat would bring, my retreat as public as my advance, the gossip that even with privacy and opportunity I had been unable to lure the tsarevich to my bed. And, worse, I took it as proof that his feelings for me did not match mine for him, and I thought by force of will I could make his grow. And so I began to badger him, always an attractive behavior in a woman. *When*, I asked him, *when, will you sleep with me?* He told me, *Soon, soon.* And I would say, *How can you say you love me?*

Ah, and here's the thing. I fear he did not. He was already in love with someone else and had been for years.

His beloved? Princess Alix of Hesse-Darmstadt. Niki had met her when he was sixteen and she twelve. Twelve! Alix was all I was not—a granddaughter of Queen Victoria, a princess who was the daughter of a princess, though the house of Hesse-Darmstadt into which she had been born was not grand. She had first come to Petersburg in 1884, while I was still a student at the Theater Schools, to attend the wedding of her sister Ella to another of Niki's many uncles—in fact, there were so many Romanov brothers and uncles and sons that Niki's father was forced to reconfigure and reduce the *appanages* and titles, making some sons grand dukes and others merely princes so that the treasury would not run out of money. At her sister's wedding, Alix in a white muslin dress stood beside her sister the bride in a magnificent brocaded court gown. Alix's blonde, blonde hair was almost as pale as her skin, and Niki's soul bound itself to her pristine purity. And, I think, as well, to her sorrow, the black that saturated her at age six, when her mother and her little sister died of diphtheria in the same week, and she was left alone in a nursery with a set of new dolls staring at her with their black-pupiled eyes. Her old dolls had been thrown out for fear of contagion, their bodies and dresses and shoes burned to ash, her mother and sister abruptly buried, the house a tornado that left her untouched in the corner. Her nickname, Sunny, never suited her again, and this reserve tugged at Nicholas, answered a reserve in him, born of his grandfather's violent death and the domineering personality of his father.

Later that week they would use her tiny diamond ring to etch their names side by side onto a window at Alexander Palace at Peterhof, and when he asked his mother for a token to give her, his mother handed him a twelve-carat diamond brooch. This is Russia—for the imperial family, that was a token. He presented the brooch to Alix—a child giving a gift to a child. At a children's party the next day, she gave the brooch back to him. She was English and German and very proper, and she felt she had not behaved correctly in accepting it. He did not see Alix again until 1889, when she came at seventeen once more to visit her sister in Petersburg. Alix would not age well, but at seventeen she was a beauty—the cinched waist, bracelets at her right wrist, her face more European, almost English, save for that long German nose with its extra daub of flesh at the end that in later years would make a hook. I understood why Niki desired her so in 1889, though the court itself was not so taken with her. At public appearances she stood breathless and unsmiling, her face covered with blotches. *Devoid of charm, cold eyes, holds herself as if she'd swallowed a yardstick*, the court said of her. His parents liked her no better. That year Niki pasted her picture into his diary and silently determined to marry her.

How do I know this? Because he would read to me on occasion from his diaries, from the entries about me and from the ones about her, to flatter me, at first—to caution me, later. He kept a diary for thirty-six years, his first one begun at fourteen when the empress gave him a book of souvenirs. The edges of that first book's pages were gilt, the binding made of inlaid wood. Only that was good enough for the heir, though later he wrote in plain lined journals, the pages numbered by hand in the upper right corner in advance

and pasted up with pictures and mementos. In this first book he recorded the murder of his grandfather on the street alongside the
Ekaterininsky Canal. After this, his father became tsar, moved the
family to Gatchina outside Petersburg, surrounded the palace park
with sentries. Alexander III had crushed the revolutionaries, or so
he thought. The young terrorists from the People's Will who had
assassinated Alexander II—after seven unsuccessful attempts!—
had been hanged, signs that read TSAR KILLER pinned to their chests,
and their bodies had dangled from their nooses for hours so all
could see, and after their hanging, Alexander III rescinded almost
every one of his father's liberal *ukazy*, the Great Reforms that freed
the serfs, loosened censorship, reformed schools, allowed local self-
government, the ones he thought had led, so inadmissibly, to his
father's assassination. The revolutionaries who wanted to rid the
country of Alexander II were afraid his reforms and his proposed
constitution would satisfy the people so much that there would be
no revolution, no abolition of the throne. Alexander III meant to
ensure there would be neither reform nor revolution. He was a tsar
of the old school, the father who ruled by the whip. He thought he
was preventing a revolution, though he actually induced one, but
he never lived to see this or the murder of his brother, his cousins,
his sons, his nephews, his grandchildren. No, the revolutionaries
never disappeared, no matter how Alexander III squeezed them.
Why, he even hanged Lenin's older brother in 1887 for plotting to
kill him as he made one of those processionals from the Winter
Palace to the cathedral with a phalanx of royalty, the smaller parade
called the Maly Vykhod, and the larger the Bolshoi Vykhod, with
which the Romanovs reminded the court and Petersburg at large of
their power. Yes, to be a tsar was to be the preordained victim of a
regicide—killed eventually by revolutionaries, by your guards, by
your own family. Perhaps Niki had a premonition of this. On the
inside front cover of his very first journal, in his angular hand, Niki
wrote out the lyrics to an old folk song, one where the ancient

gnarled hag uses a comb on the hair of a young dead man who sprawls in her lap. Youth and Death. Yes, in his first notebook he recorded the murder of his grandfather, and his last notebook, the fifty-first, from 1918, was only half filled, the numbers floating in the corners of the empty pages.

Later, in Paris, after the revolution, when his journals were published, I read all the entries, glossing for the private matters of his heart. I know. Of all the great events recorded in those books, the coronation, two wars, the completion of the Trans-Siberian Railway, Bloody Sunday, I was seeking only mention of me. Some of those earlier entries, I had, of course, already seen. It was a Russian custom for the bridegroom to share his diaries with his bride on the eve of their wedding, to reveal to her his life previous and whatever attachments and liaisons it contained. Tolstoy did this with his wife, Sonya, and Niki did this with Alix, who began to write in the pages, who wrote on their wedding night, *At last united, bound for life*. And so, there was some significance, yes, to the fact that Niki shared his journals with me? He did not give them to me, I did not take a pen and write in them for all of posterity to see, but he read to me from them. At my first appearance, in 1890, he read me just a few notes: *Gossiped at her window with little Kschessinska* or *I like Kschessinska II very much*, but later in 1892 he read, *It is over three years I have loved Alix H. and I constantly cherish the thought that God might let me marry her one day . . . But ever since camp in 1890 I have loved Little K passionately.*

She was the someday. I was the here and now and perhaps beyond. But it was not until 1893, when Alix refused Niki's first proposal of marriage, that I truly triumphed. In his journal of that year, Niki recorded the tale of his failed endeavor and included in his entry a few lines from Alix's letter in which she proclaimed it *a sin to change the belief in which I have been brought up and which I love*. To marry the heir to the Russian throne she must convert to the Russian Orthodox Church and this she would not do—though I would have done so in the snap of a finger. Where do I sign? To whom do I bow? What statue do I kiss? But Alix was a Lutheran, the entire religion a reaction against the Roman Catholic Church with its spectacle, its idols, its fancy vestments, and its insistence on the necessity of a priest's intercession to reach God. Alix could speak to God on her own in her own plain church, *danke schön*, in which she had just two years ago been confirmed, that sacrament as important to her as the one of marriage. How could she now, suddenly, renounce this? But she could not be Lutheran *and* be the future empress of Russia— the emperor stood as head of the Orthodox Church and any heir to the throne must be born of an Orthodox mother. The calendar of the Russian court year was ruled by Orthodox observances. It was impossible for the empress to be Lutheran. So Niki's parents, who didn't much like Alix anyway and who had been withholding their permission for the match, were pleased by Alix's refusal to convert, although their pleasure could not approach mine, and they began suggesting instead this alliance and that, perhaps to Princess Hélène of France or to Princess Margaret of Prussia. But all this was to be considered eventually, and eventually is a long day's ride from immediately. For now, at least, the long-haired phantom of Alix that had stood sentry over Nicholas at my bedroom window receded, whisked into the distance, and, in despair at her disappearance, Nicholas bedded the little Polish princess instead of the German one. That happened January 25, 1893. I could tell you the hour.

I cannot, of course, describe to you what it was like to make love to the tsarevich because such things are private. But his naked body impressed even the Bolsheviks who dragged it from the cold water of the mine shaft twelve miles from Ekaterinburg the day after his murder. Before they chopped him up and burned him, they marveled at how fit he was, his cheeks so red from the icy water that he looked alive. That January night with me he *was* alive, his body whole and warm beneath my fingers and my mouth, his limbs all stitched to their proper places, after which he recorded in his diary, *Flew to my MK . . . am still under her spell—the pen is shaking in my hand*. He was not a Pushkin, not a Lermontov, I grant you, but he was the tsarevich, and so he did not have to be.

I'm afraid for a while at the theater I became intolerable. I received my *own* diamond brooch from him, and to mark the delight of our consummation, a necklace of large diamonds—each diamond as big as a walnut—which I wore showily onstage with the brooch, whether I played a peasant girl or a princess. It was not unusual for a dancer to do this, to wear on the stage the jewels her protector had given her, but no one else had ever been given a necklace like that. The Romanovs knew their jewels, mined from the rich earth of the Urals in Siberia since the seventeenth century, and the tsars had first pick of the best of them. Alix, age twelve, may have returned her diamond brooch to Niki, but I kept *my* brooch *and* my necklace, which all came to know as the tsar's necklace and which I valued most and for years refused to sell. With that around my neck, I was untouchable at the theater. When I did not get what I wanted, they at the theater called my fits of pique *Her Imperial Indignation*.

Our idyll. Let me tell you about our idyll. Niki often left his parents at Anichkov Palace in the evenings and made my house on English Prospekt his second home. I can still recall my excitement at returning from the theater to see his coat already in the front hall and the way my body flushed as I moved from the violet-scented warmth— for the violet was my flower—of my carriage to, for a brief moment, the frigid Petersburg air and from there into my house, my own house, where my lover waited, when all the other girls my age lived still with their parents. What a triumph! And in my house, on the marble-topped table of the front hall, lay the dark greatcoat of the heir to the Russian throne. Some nights we ate a late supper alone; other nights we had suppers together after the theater with friends from the ballet or opera companies or with his cousins, the Mikhailo-vichi, or with his fellow officers. I served *zakuski*—mushrooms in cream sauce, little sausages, eggs, and onions—sturgeon, and then *kuropatka*, partridge, and we toasted our health with the eight gold-painted vodka glasses encrusted with semiprecious stones the tsar-evich had brought me as a housewarming present. No more plain drinking glasses for me! The meals were followed by games of cha-rades, where Niki would hold his cigarette between his teeth and pretend to conduct an orchestra that spread above us across the ceil-ing, while we had to guess at the symphony, the plaster lifting away to accommodate the musicians and instruments. I can still see the set of his jaw, the way he threw down the cigarette to grab me up and kiss me, while his cousins pounded the table in approval. Or there were games of baccarat, the beginning, I suppose, of my nasty infatu-ation with cards and gambling. Later in life I would become a habi-tué of the gaming tables at Monte Carlo. They called me Madame 17, for I always bet that number. Can you guess why? After all this Nicholas and I would climb into the bed, which I had made so comfortable—not at all like his camp bed at Anichkov Palace. Yes, the emperor, so as not to cosset his children, had them sleep on camp beds and wash in the morning with cold water. Niki's cousins all did this, as well, some odd imperial tradition of deprivation for those children who would grow up to have so much, as if a hard bed and a cold bath could bring with them humility and strength of character. Nor was my bed like a bed in the Winter Palace, sheathed with a comforter that bore the monogram of Catherine the Great, the coverlet so stiff and slippery it slid to the floor if one shifted posi-tion. No, I had a coverlet of sable, which we lay under or upon, and Niki stayed with me some nights all the way until the morning. I slept with my arms around him or his around me and sometimes in the hour before he left, we would study one another in the winter light, where naked we were a different color than we had been the night before by oil lamp, this paler version of ourselves no less pleasing. He called me *Mala, Maletchka, Panni*—short for *Pannochka*, the endearment for a young Polish girl—or *my M.K.* I called him *my Niki* and this interlude in the months before he became tsar and assumed the responsibilities that governing demanded were the last days of his youth. Why, he played like a boy up until a month before his father's death that next autumn, when he and his cousin Georgie pitched a great chestnut-throwing battle out at Gatchina and a few days later fought another match with pinecones. Chestnuts, pinecones, theatricals, cards, a few imperial duties, and me—that was how Nicholas II, before he became Nicholas II, spent the year 1893. That year the tsarevich visited me almost every week, and some weeks twice, and between visits we wrote one another our love letters. His to me I lost in the revolution, but mine to him are preserved—they sit today in the State Archive of the Russian Federation in Moscow. He had saved my letters as I had saved his, and they, along with every other bit of his property, were confiscated after his arrest and death. My letters are now testament: the last tsar once lived and loved—loved me!

The ballets I danced that season teased me with possibilities.

That winter I danced Paquita, a new role for me in the ballet of the same name, wearing a fetching costume with one big white flower on my breast and another in my hair. The ballet was set during Napoleon's occupation of Spain. Paquita saves the life of a French officer, Lucien, but the two, though in love, cannot marry: she's a Gypsy, of no birth at all. Only when she shows Lucien a medallion she's owned since infancy does she learn she is really of noble family after all, abducted as a baby by the Gypsies she thought were her kin. And so the lovers can now wed, for in this ballet, as in all of Petipa's ballets, the series of scenes and acts culminated in a celebration, usually a wedding, at which a variety of classical and character dances could be performed. All talents must be accommodated, you remember. Paquita's story is a bit like my own, you know. Imperial blood runs in my veins from my Polish ancestors on my father's side. My great-grandfather was the son of Count Krassinsky. He was orphaned at age twelve and entrusted into the care of his French tutor. Apparently the count did not trust his brother to be guardian and with good reason—in 1748, this brother sent assassins for the boy, and the tutor had to flee with him to Neuilly. This uncle usurped his birthright and his property and all that was left to my father was a ring with the arms of Count Krassinsky: a silver horseshoe, a gold cross, a crow with a gold ring clasped in its beak, the crown of a count, all set against a background of azure. I had a ring, Paquita had a medallion. Perhaps this would make me imperial enough for Niki. I determined to ask my father for that ring, to show it to Niki, and to tell him the story behind it. Once he knew that I, too, was from a ruling house, or almost a ruling house, he might speak of it to his father, and who could predict the effect of that on the tsar? But there was no hurry then, and so I wastefully dreamed my way through that winter and spring, summer and fall, until early 1894, when Niki's father suddenly took ill.

my life, at twenty-one years, is over

THAT WINTER OF 1894 Niki came to see me less and less, as his father's intractable illness drew him back to his mother and father, to his brothers and sisters. A cough the doctors could not cure, weakness, and pain in the kidneys, which rendered the tsar unable to stand, brought with it concerns about the succession and made urgent what had been put aside—the matter of an appropriate bride for Niki. How many times have I thought—has every Russian thought—that if only the tsar had not sickened and died at age forty-nine, how different the future might have been. If we had even one more year together, I thought then, like a simpleton, perhaps Niki would have gone to the tsar with my name instead of Alix's. The doctors had diagnosed Alexander III with nephritis, brought on by the injuries sustained in that train wreck six years before that had almost enthroned his brother Vladimir and made Vladimir's wife croon, *So close, so close*. Alexander III had, like Atlas, held up the world, or in this case, the heavy ceiling of the dining car to keep it from crushing his children, and was now paying the price of a mortal trying to do the job of a Titan.

It seemed even the days shortened themselves in mourning. I remember how, at a certain hour, the shadows seemed to race across the streets and canals toward my house and then engulf it. All the soft white spokes of the blossoms and the green leaves had long fallen from the beech trees, and they lay sodden and rotting beneath the snow. The heavy white branches of the trees crept so close to my bedroom window the ends of them scratched against the glass as if a woman were perched out there, clawing to get in. One night, waiting for the tsarevich, I sat at the table in the long narrow dining room and stared at the oak paneling that ran from floor to ceiling. The nicks and swirls and grain of it seemed to assemble themselves into the features of my father's face, and once I had seen it as such I could not unsee it, could not dismantle his likeness from the striations of the wood. I stood and still I saw him. I moved left and right and his eyes followed me, and then, as I stood in the dining-room doorway, it seemed the full figure of my father emerged from the paneled wall, and grained just like the wood, but diaphanous, stood there, gazing at me sadly. But when I jumped up to touch him, running my hands over the paneling, I couldn't find his shape—all was smooth.

That was the night Niki told me that he was going to Coburg in his father's place for the wedding of Alix's brother Ernest, the grand duke of Hesse-Darmstadt, and there he was going to propose once again to Alix. His right hand pulled at his collar; his left closed over his cap and gloves. His position obliged him to take a consort from a ruling house and Romanovs had been raiding the German principalities for their wives for a century: Leuchtenberg, Wurtemburg, Saxe-Attenberg, Oldenburg, Mecklenburg, Hesse-Darmstadt. He would, he said, take care of me, but I must understand that we ourselves could never marry. Alix was a princess, she was the sister of his uncle's wife, she knew Russia a little through her sister, and here I interjected, *She doesn't even know the Russian word for yes!* His parents had agreed to the match. So Niki's father had gone soft with suffering, soft enough to consent to Niki's desire to marry this stiff-necked, minor German princess who clung to her Protestant religion as if it were a lover. I had lost my ally and it seemed I might now lose Niki, who seemed determined this time that Alix accept his proposal. *She'll refuse you*, I told him, and he shook his head and smiled. I put my hands on my hips, but I could not summon the energy for an exhibition of *Her Imperial Indignation*. I could see that what Niki wanted at sixteen, at twenty-one, at twenty-six, he still wanted, and that something was not me. I was not solemn and reserved, I was not educated, I spoke only Russian, a child's version of Polish, and a smattering of French ballet terms, and none of those was the language of the court. I had read few books, my religion mattered little to me, I was trivial, I adored cards and parties, and worst of all, I appeared half-naked on the stage. Everything I was was wrong, everything I lacked he desired. What had been for me a passion had been for him a diversion, or worse, a dress rehearsal. My body had only further primed his desire for Alix's, with the red-gold hair, the pale skin, the long, manicured fingers, Alix's body with its own distinctive scent waiting to be discovered, with its own distinctive cry waiting to be provoked. I did not want to be reasonable, I did not wish to behave, as he put it, like two *adults*.

No one likes her here, I told Niki, and *You will be her only friend.* And when those announcements did not seem to move him, I began to rummage about for the ring of Count Krassinsky I had begged from my father and stuffed away like a fool. Perhaps it was not too late to tell Niki the story behind it. Niki watched me for a while, perplexed and concerned, as I pulled open drawer after drawer and thrust my arms into them, begging him, *Wait, wait.* And he did wait, until I had given up looking and stood, a little lost, a doll flung down in mid-play by her distracted mistress. Then he finally lowered his omnipresent cigarette and told me, *You will always be among the happiest memories of my youth*, and I told him, *Go then. Go to your despicable Alix.* And those were the last words I said to him before his engagement.

————

It was March and snowing in Russia when Niki left for Coburg. My life, at twenty-one years, was over. I lay like a frozen corpse in my bed that week, watching the white blur the wind made outside my dark bedroom window, the ring of Count Krassinsky, which I had found, too late, a tiny bit of ice in my fist. In Germany that year, though, March brought with it an early spring, lilac blossoms, pendulous and heavy, making soft purple bows as Niki strolled through the palace park with his consort, Alix, on his arm.

Later that March, Niki dispatched his cousin Sergei, one of those Mikhailovichi cousins, to my house to tell me that Alix had at last accepted his proposal. Niki had written all the family from Germany of his jubilation that his prayers had been answered, of how Alix had wept for three days, saying, *I cannot, I cannot*, before finally agreeing, *Yes, I will marry you*. If I had been there, I would have slapped her. What could possibly be her hesitation?—not that I was sorry she hesitated. But, apparently, according to Sergei, it was only when Alix apprehended that her brother's new bride would replace her as the first lady of Hesse-Darmstadt and that Alix would now become the spinster sister-in-law that she changed her mind. How better to upstage the bride, Victoria Melita—and oh, I must tell you this, she was not long the bride, for she later divorced Alix's brother to marry one of Vladimir and Miechen's sons (is that not unbelievable?)—what better way to upstage the bride than to become the future empress of All the Russias? Niki and Alix's engagement, Sergei told me, immediately became the talk of Coburg. Even Niki's mother wrote to *dear Alix* to ask if she preferred diamonds, sapphires, or emeralds. Why, Alix liked diamonds, sapphires, emeralds, *and* pearls, apparently: to honor their engagement, Nicholas gave Alix a matching ring and necklace of pink pearl, an emerald the size of an egg dangling from a bracelet, a sapphire-and-diamond brooch, and a *sautoire* created by Fabergé of so many ropes of pearls Alix could drape them from her bodice to her hem. Niki could not have paid for this—any of this. That last piece alone cost 250,000 rubles. The money had to have come from his father. The first of many imperial rubles spent on Alix of Hesse.

I walked the floors of my Petersburg house, the house I hated now, and as I walked I could hear the pistol-shot sounds of the ice of the Neva cracking and breaking up, and soon enough the cold water would begin to move again, blocks of ice hurtling along with the current from Lagoda and the current bringing with it Alix of Hesse-Darmstadt. Sergei followed me awkwardly in his overpolished boots, his voice a trail of vapors, the syllables breaking apart as soon as he uttered a word. *Poof*. Poor Sergei, following a madwoman through her rented home, trying to reason with her. I did not want to be reasoned with. I believe I actually pulled at my hair. I ran through the austere reception rooms, their octagonal tables crimped with gilt, their feather-stuffed settees, their dark-wood rococo-revival chairs with backs like laced antlers, all the artifacts of that old grand duke's ambition and the artifacts of mine, and then circled back into the private rooms, the Russian rooms, with their mustard and lime walls, their bloodred oriental rugs, and the framed photographs of my parents, who had warned me not to leave them. Sergei followed me all the while, his high, broad forehead all twisted up and his gentle eyes full of pity—no jokes to tell me now! No, instead he tried to tell me how Niki planned to settle on me 100,000 rubles and the house on English Prospekt. I knew the tsarevich did not have unlimited funds. The 100,000 rubles represented his entire *appanage* of a year, the only money whose use he did not have to account for. The house itself, at 400,000 rubles, would have to be bought for me, as I found out later, by the Potato Club—for Niki's cousins each earned a grand ducal *appanage* of 200,000 rubles a year, as well as income from their own and their father's enormous estates. Yes, Niki was quite the stepchild, in comparison, as tsarevich. So in an act of brotherhood to help the tsarevich wash himself clean of me, the Potato Club made a great fountain of its money. Apparently, the tsar Alexander III, who had seated me with Niki on my graduation day and who now hung ropes of pearls on Alix, would not put up a single kopek to pay off Niki's little Polish whore.

As I sat stonily on a chaise, Sergei drew a sheaf of papers from a leather satchel and made as if to explain them to me. All I needed to do, Sergei said, was to sign a few documents transferring the title and agreeing to the settlement, how lucky was that? How lucky? This lucky. I spat on the papers like a peasant woman from Borjomi and he folded them up at once and apologized. This could wait a few days, he said. A few days? How quickly they wished to settle accounts! Did they really expect me to capitulate so immediately? Perhaps they hoped to knock me over with their generosity. After all, it was no small sum, even though that day I spat on it. I have to confess, even as I spat, I felt a small thrill of pride at the amount. My salary at the theater was a thousand rubles a year. So Niki thought me worth a hundred years, five hundred years if one counted the house. But if I signed the settlement, I knew I would never see Nicholas alone ever again, and that I could not bear. And so I did not sign. But it wasn't until Sergei had bowed once again and left that I found the great big tears of self-pity I could not locate earlier.

It was through Sergei that I extorted a last meeting with Nicholas. As Niki was now engaged, it would not be proper for us to meet at the house where we had conducted our affair, and yet Niki wanted the meeting to be secret. I can see now, of course, that he did not want to meet me at all, but courtesy was a cardinal virtue for him, so he agreed to my request and Sergei arranged a rendezvous for us near an old barn out on the Volkhonsky High Road, halfway between Petersburg and Peterhof, that grand country retreat Catherine the Great had built in imitation of Versailles. By then it was May, the time the Neva had been declared open for navigation and the imperial family traditionally left the city for the country. The High Road allowed glimpses of the sea between the trees and occasionally those trees thinned out to reveal fields where cows wandered grazing. The High Road terminated at the Grand Palace, its gilded cupola topped by a crowned triple-headed eagle so that from every angle the bird had two heads. But I would not travel so far.

I rode out in my carriage with the same Russian coachman who had driven me two years earlier on my afternoon promenades along Nevsky Prospekt and Morskaya Ulitsa, driven me in circles around Petersburg in my desperation to surprise the tsarevich in his carriage. I studied the back of the elaborate costume worn for the last hundred years by all the old Russian drivers—the green blouse closed by silver buttons under the left arm, the belt embroidered with gold thread from which hung a hunting dagger, the low hat with a long flap that shielded the back of the neck from the sun. What did this man think of me, this little girl who had flung herself like a fleck of mud at the tsarevich and was now about to be scraped off by his fingernail? That I was lucky to have flown so high? Or that it was time I learned my place? Society would be so divided— some would pity me, others would grow slippery with pleasure. But no longer would anyone envy Mathilde-Maria Felixovna Kschessinska unless I could effect a great feat. I touched at the orchids I had pinned in my hair and reviewed what I would say. I had a plan, concocted over these long two months during which Alix began her study of the Russian language and prepared for her conversion to the Orthodox Church and during which I alternated between hysteria and despair. My behavior terrified my family—and then, when I hatched this idea, I became suddenly calm—which worried them still more. They begged me to return home to Liteiny Prospekt and to resume my old life with them, with my sister, but I knew if I did that, within a few months, whatever comfort home provided would pale and then I would be plagued by longing, for Niki, for the world of the Romanovs whose slice of this life was so much tastier in every way than the life of anyone else on earth. I wanted to keep eating from their golden plates. And so I intended to persuade Niki to keep me as his mistress after his marriage—after all, his grandfather had had both wife Marie Alexandrovna and mistress Ekaterina Dolgorukaya. Why should Niki not do the same? I could think of no reason why not, and once I suggested this to him, I was certain he would slap his forehead and say, *Mala, I should have thought of that myself!*

I arrived first at the barn just off the High Road and so I was able to watch the figure of Nicholas as he slowly approached—at first like a dot, then a smudge, a shape, a centaur, a sovereign astride a horse. He looked as heavy, as immutable, as the statue of his father on horseback that he would one day unveil in Vosstaniya Square and about which this ditty would spring up, making everyone laugh—

Zdes stoit komod
Na komode begemot
Na begemote sidit idiot

Here stands a chest of drawers,
On the chest a hippopotamus,
And on the hippopotamus sits an idiot.

But Niki was not an idiot. His face was cautious and grim, for he had come here against his better judgment to hear the trouble I was prepared to make him. He was on his guard against me, but he needn't have worried, because once he dismounted, I could not find my voice. I could do nothing, I could not even move. He saw this and the careful, polite look left his face and one of compassion replaced it, and he offered me his arm. We walked in silence a short way around the barn, the wood warm and splintering against my palm, just out of the sight of my coachman. My shoes, not made for walking in the grass, got their heels stuck here and there, but the tsarevich in his knee-high military boots walked easily over the matted grass that hid the buds of incipient wildflowers, and he helped me along, gently. If only this grass went on forever, if only we could never stop walking. I gripped his arm, the material of his summer dress uniform so formidably starched, so crisp, I could have bitten into it. Let the grass turn to dirt, let the length of this barn never run out. But it did. And that's when Niki said, *That's a pretty flower in your hair, Mala*. He smiled at me. *You look beautiful today*. I looked beautiful today! I would not have to say anything to him, after all. He was thinking what I thought and all I had to do was say, *Yes, I agree*. He unlocked my fingers from his sleeve and kissed my palm before raising my other hand and kissing its palm also. That's how we Russians sign our letters to our friends and family, *I kiss your hands*, a sentence full of love and fealty. The sun became so radiant about me I felt it would scorch my silhouette into the barn wall. I shut my eyes. Next I would feel his lips on my lips. Instead, Niki released my hands. I opened my eyes to see why. From a pocket of his white uniform, he drew out the papers Sergei had shown me in March, in April, in May. And Nicholas said, *Mala, I need you to sign these*. He held out next a pen, a blue-and-gold enameled fountain pen, these pens being a fairly recent invention, and he unscrewed the cap of it. While he held one paper and then another against the rough barn wall, I signed my name once, twice. *Mathilde-Maria Kschessinska*. I remember thinking even then how strange it was that a few ink marks on paper proposed to dissolve a human bond. One hundred thousand rubles and the house on English Prospekt were mine and Niki rode back to Peterhof.

You would think I would have the sense then to give up. But I did not. I had lost all sense. Grief had stolen it from me.

I must tell you I was not the first of the tsarevich's mistresses from the Imperial Ballet. There was one before me—Maria Labunskaya: long blonde hair, in certain lights too pale to be called blonde, long legs, the face of a Russian aristocrat, not of a peasant. Those broad eastern faces with the strong bones, thick lips, and almond eyes were not so prized by the court. The more delicate northern European features were preferred. The first Slavs, you know, mixed with the Normans when they came down from Scandinavia to Russia, and Ingwarr eventually became Igor and Waldemar became Vladimir, and the legendary Norse prince Hroerekr became the first Russian ruler, Rurik, in the historical chronicles of the ninth century. Traces of that northern heritage still appear on occasion on our faces. So Maria Labunskaya. When the tsar's advisor Konstantin Pobedonostsev suggested to the sovereign that they find someone suitable for Nicholas to enjoy before the rigors of marriage, the chief of police, a good friend of the tsar's, pointed his fat finger at Maria in the *corps de ballet* and told the tsar she would be perfect. I've told you the men came to the ballet for a mistress. They drove their carriages right up the private drive of the Maryinsky Theater reserved for the imperial family, right up to the low windows of our dressing rooms so we could lean out and chat with them before performances. Maria Labunskaya was a few years ahead of me at the school and engaged to an officer in the Guards, but her new duties as mistress so appalled her prospective mother-in-law that her marriage plans were jettisoned. In what position was Maria to say no to the sovereign? She was paid eighteen thousand rubles a year from the tsar's purse to make herself available whenever summoned to the palace. But Nicholas with his baby face and his beginnings of a moustache preferred sketching his country scenes to an awkward assignation with a pair of legs paid for by his father. Two years later she was still on the imperial payroll and Nicholas had yet to summon her—he had, in fact, begun to flirt with me.

But I worried: Why would the tsarevich ever call on *me* when the beautiful Maria Labunskaya still raised her white arms on the Maryinsky stage?

I've told you I was not beautiful?

So at the theater I began to spread rumors in her name— Labunskaya had said the tsarevich was a syphilitic, the emperor a fraud, the empress a whore for having first been engaged to the emperor's brother—and within a few months Labunskaya was exiled from Russia, dismissed from the Imperial Ballet.

And so I thought perhaps the same incantations I had used to chase Maria from the tsarevich in 1892 would repel Alix from him now. What else can one do in a beauty contest in which one's beauty is second but lessen the beauty of the rival?

I wasn't close enough to Alix to whisper my slurs about Niki into the air and let them buzz and stumble on their black wings to her ear. So I wrote the spells down in my own tiny hand—I know, I was twenty-one years old—sealed the papers with wax, and sent them to her in Coburg. Niki was not the only one with documents! I had said things so terrible Alix could no longer possibly love him, and when she opened my letter, the pages would spit out their slanders and she would recoil from Nicholas as Petersburgers had once recoiled from the deformities in Peter the Great's scientific museum: a man with two fingers, a hermaphrodite, a two-headed fetus. I wrote her that her fiancé had taken the virginity of a young girl and then discarded her, that he could not be trusted, that the whole capital was saying the tsarevich was a rake, a libertine, a fornicator, that it would be bad luck for her to marry a man with such a black soul and their marriage would be cursed from start to finish. *Stay away*, I finished, *Stay out of Russia!* But Alix was then still very practical, not yet a superstitious Russian, not yet one of us with our icons and our candles and the acrostics we make of our names, look-ing for omens, though she would make up for lost time and double so. There would be no empress more medieval than she, eventually. But in 1894, when she saw my girlish handwriting on paper, she showed my letter to Nicholas, who had gone back to visit her, and he immediately recognized the handwriting as my own. Hadn't I written to him enough plaintive letters on that same paper, in that same hand? *I am terribly bored if I do not see you. The time drags end-lessly. Who did you look at so long in the stalls?*

It was Sergei who told me how angry Niki was at my letter and I cringed to imagine him reading it. In my imagination—in a sce-nario not terribly well thought through—Alix alone would look at the pages, swoon in disgust, and then, revived, would begin to pen a letter of her own to Niki, expressing her revulsion. *Your life*, she would write, *is regrettably debauched. I am enclosing the diamonds, emeralds, and pearls to be given to another girl more deserving. Surely you must know of one.* Something like that. But that was not what happened. Instead, she showed him the letter, the other possible out-come, of course, and Niki, who could not find it in his soul to lie, was forced to tell Alix about his ballerina mistress from the *demi-monde*, to open up the pages of his journal a little earlier than his wedding night to show her all the entries about Little K as he had once shown me all the entries about Alix. Whereupon she wrote in the margins by his entries, *I love you more since you told me that little story*.

That was what I was reduced to. A little story.

But I did not taste this humiliation yet. So certain was I that this trick would work that foolishly, ridiculously, the little story began to strut about the theater and to boast, *We shall see who will win, Alix or me*, and the other dancers snickered even as they slinked away from such seditious talk. Yes, I made indiscreet proclamations. *We shall see who will win*, I cried, and the dancers looked away, embarrassed for me. My father finally sent my brother to English Prospekt to scold me, to remind me I was a Kschessinsky, not the daughter of a laundress or a scullery maid. Where was my dignity? I had no dignity. If I could not behave myself, he told my brother to tell me, they would forcibly bring me home. But they were theater people, dancers, they had not moved in the circles I had, so how could they understand what I had lost? Yes, I had become the poor girl in every ballet, the hysterical peasant girl thrown over for a princess, the hysterical temple *bayadère* thrown over for a princess, the hysterical Gypsy girl thrown over for a princess. Worse, I had become a matter of state. Finally, Polovstov, a member of the State Council, was told by the director of the Imperial Theaters, Vzevolozhsky, who abandoned his usual exquisite eighteenth-century manners to report on me, about my disturbing outbursts at rehearsals and in the hallways. And Polovstov went in turn to Grand Duke Vladimir, minister of the Imperial Theaters and therefore minister of me, who ordered me to the Dvortsovaya Embankment, to his painstaking imitation of a Florentine palazzo with its 365 rooms, one for each day of the year. Its long façade faced the Neva and the sunlit water made the gold-brown bricks of it glow like God's face. A gondola floated at the pier. A gilded carriage waited at the street. No one lived closer to the Winter Palace than the grand duke. I stood at the entrance portico for a few moments enjoying its small protection and it's a good thing I did, for the sober façade did not prepare me for the shock of the interior. The entrance hall rose several stories high around me, with walls of scarlet and gold, each arch, each cornice, each recess so heavily gilded and ornamented I felt I had stepped into a church. My mouth opened. Two giant bears, stuffed and mounted, flanked the grand curved staircase, dwarfing me further, one bear offering a tray of salt, the other a tray of bread—an old Russian custom of welcome, but I did not feel welcome. I was in trouble. The grand duke's servants wore scarlet coats and the square caps of the

Renaissance courts and carried both swords and maces, which made me feel I was being delivered to Vladimir by armed guard. It was a palace that evoked both East and West but it spoke with one voice of the Vladimirichi's power and ambition. I had the ambition but not the power. I meekly followed a liveried servant to the library, the two-storied room a cherrywood box, domed like an aviary, with books everywhere above and below instead of cages of spring larks and winter finches, and at the great table in the center of the room, presiding over all this wood and paper, was the grand duke, *Emperor Vladimir*, with his muttonchop whiskers, his booming voice.

His palace is now the House of the Scientists of Leningrad. His bones lie in Russia, his wife's and children's scattered about France.

But on that day he was master of the house, master of me, and he had me sit down at the big table in a leather chair opposite him in which my feet barely skimmed the floor. If I'd put my thumb in my mouth I could not have looked younger. Vladimir looked at me sternly, the white whiskers of his sideburns plumped up with alarm. By this time Vladimir's beard was also white, though his moustache still had color, and his face had thinned the way the faces of old men do as life begins to seep from them. As a young man the grand duke had had a fleshy body, a face full and voluptuous, but as he aged his face became quite elegant—hollow cheeks, the dark muttonchops gray, then white—it became an intelligent face, no longer the face of a drunken lecher. He looked like an ascetic, but he was not one: he still loved food and theater and power and women, and thank God I was a pretty young woman. Pretty enough.

My actions were upsetting to the tsarevich, he told me, threatening the security of his new fiancée, did I understand that? Nicholas and Alexandra were one day to be the father and mother of a nation, Russia's Batiushka and Matiushka. I could not go about shrieking this way and slandering Niki in letters to Alix. I put my hands over my face. Yes, he said, he knew about the letters. Furthermore, I must know that Niki had to marry. Had matters not been settled properly with me? I nodded. So why was I still making such a fuss? The state secretary wanted me sent from the capital, with a monthly allowance to be stopped if I ever returned, he told me. Was that what I wanted for myself? I shook my head. And then I felt it—the great patriarchal fist squeezing the breath out of me like the boned corsets I danced in. I could be another Maria Labunskaya, dismissed from the Imperial Ballet and sent all the way to Paris, the city where the tsars had, for decades, sent the wayward members of their families. I did not want to be so far from home. I did not want to dance as Maria had at the Parisian Gaîté-Lyrique Theater. I was one of the tsar's imperial dancers, not a common entertainer.

So I put on my smile. I used two shaking fingers to wipe at my tears. I agreed to stop making a fuss. And the grand duke called me his *dushka*—thank God I had once been his *dushka*—and he kissed the top of my head. *Good girl*.

And there was something else. The grand duke promised if I behaved I would be named *prima ballerina assoluta* of the Imperial Ballet. So my hysterics had some benefit, after all. And to the envy of all about me, the laughingstock was promoted. Just like that.

soul and spirit, body and heart

YES, PATRONAGE HAD ITS ADVANTAGES and the lack of it disadvantages. My hundred thousand rubles from Niki and the Potato Club would not allow me to live like a Romanov. The money was intended only, I understood, to tide me over until fortune brought me a new protector. At the theater, without one, I would eventually be subject to the whims of the administration or perhaps eclipsed by my rival Olga Preobrajenska, who despite her modesty and lack of cunning was being promoted right behind me, kicking at me with her muscular legs and shoving her plain face right next to mine. And both of us would soon enough be trampled by the younger girls, the ones graduating from the school every year and marching out onto the Maryinsky stage. No, I needed a protector with ties to the court to help me keep my footing at the center of that crowded stage. But Vladimir was, as a brother to the tsar, perhaps a bit too old for me—not that I didn't think about it! But I was not yet in straitened-enough circumstances to take an old white-bearded grandfather to my bed. Sergei Mikhailovich, however, already making regular visits to my house on Niki's instructions, might do. When a master tired of his serf mistress, he gave her a dowry and married her off to one of his hunting serfs, one of the elite serfs on the estate. And that is, in essence, what Niki did to me, giving me, well, not quite a dowry, but a purse, and sending it along with his proxy, the serf Sergei Mikhailovich, who was, as general of the artillery, a hunter of men! Clearly, Niki wanted Sergei, whom he trusted above all others, to look after me, and perhaps, too, Niki had intuited as I had that Sergei's feelings for me ran quietly alongside his own. So Sergei was not a poor choice. His father was the brother of one tsar and the uncle of another, and as such Mikhail Nikolaevich received one of the treasury's largest *appanages*; he owned land and estates all over Russia to which his sons were heirs. In time Sergei would be one of the wealthiest men in the empire, and he was certainly wealthy enough now. And because Sergei was so very close to the tsarevich, on his visits to me he could report on Niki's summer idyll with Alix in England, on her lessons with Father Yanishev, on Niki and Alix's service as godparents to the first son of his English cousin George of the chestnuts and pinecones and his wife, May, and of how the baby was not dunked in the baptismal as was the custom here but merely sprinkled with a few drops of holy water. How European Niki was becoming! Yes, Sergei knew all about Niki and Alix's vacation in Osbourne on the Isle of Wight, where Niki rolled up his trouser legs and trekked down the palace lawn to the sandy beach to count the white sails of the boats he spotted out on the sea. In Sergei's company, you see, I was never very far from Niki. And I liked Sergei. He taught me how to smoke one of those little yellow cigarettes smoked by the court between dinner courses and how to ride a bicycle, and he promised when I had to travel to Krasnoye Selo in July he would let me use his personal train car. What better way to convince Niki I thought no more of him than he did of me than to quickly take Sergei to my bed? And there was always the chance Niki might become jealous.

I plotted all this while Niki was on the *Polar Star* in the Baltic Sea, sailing back home to Russia now for his sister Xenia's wedding to Sergei's brother Sandro, a union that did not make the royal family very happy, Sandro being one of those Caucasian Romanovs. Yes,

I plotted while Niki was on the water, away from Alix but dreaming of her, I'm sure, probably reading over her notes in his journal about me—*When we are young, we can't always hold our own against temptation*—as if I were the serpent himself and Niki the innocent! And I worried that Niki, upon his return, might rebuke me in some way for my letter, perhaps by a letter of his own: *Dear Mala*, it would read, *Vengeful demon, dark where Alix is light, turbulent where she is smooth, soiled where she is pure*. Soiled by him! And so, being soiled, there was no reason I should not accept the attentions and the protection from Niki offered by Sergei. But what if Niki was so angered by my letter that he yanked Sergei away from me? Where would that leave me then?

And so on July 25 Xenia married Sergei's brother and Sergei said goodbye to his dreams of her and on July 28 I performed at the gala in honor of the bride and groom at the old Peterhof Palace theater, which had been renovated for the occasion, the galleries lined with tropical plants and both the theater and the long drive to it from the Great Palace fitted with electric lights. The tsarevich sat with his family in the imperial box made to look like an enormous red velvet tent, supported by columns and beams of gold and topped with a crown, and he did not approach to congratulate me after *Le Réveil de flore*, as was the custom. I knew then not only Sergei's dreams were in the past, but mine as well. And so, while Xenia's maids packed away her wedding gown and while Niki was inspired to write Alix, *You have got me entirely and forever, soul and spirit, body and heart, everything is yours, yours*, Sergei stood behind me in my Petersburg house and took the pins and ribbons from my hair as if I were a little girl being put to bed, and then he began to comb out my hair with his fingers and to roll the long, curled strands of it between his palms. He said nothing, and neither did I. It was late in the evening, eleven o'clock, and the sun had just set so that the air in the house was soft and furred and we felt our way to one of the bedrooms, not the one I had shared with Niki. It took some time to remove all our garments—we wore clothing then, we were dressed, not like today with two or three articles. I myself wore an underskirt to match my overskirt, a frilled blouse, a hooped petticoat and a soft cotton one, a plump cloth pad that had just recently replaced the bustle and that when untied revealed an S-bend corset and its corset cover, a chemise embroidered with tiny roses, frilled drawers that tied at the front with two satin sashes and reached to my knees, and beneath that, high stockings. Yes, I wore all this in July. It was enough to give one pause, a chance to reconsider, but we did not reconsider. Sergei put his hand down my drawers and did something gentle with his finger until I was so full of cries out and whats and wherefores that finally Sergei had to stop to laugh at me and ask, *What has Niki been doing with you all this time?* (I have to say here that Sergei and his brother Sandro were known as the two great rakes of Petersburg, and now I understood why.) And when I said to him, *Nothing like this*, I think for him at that moment the ghost of Niki flew out the window, where it was saturated with the scent of grass and drowned by dew, for it was clear Sergei had trumped Niki in matters of the bedroom, if not yet in matters of my heart. *Tant pis.* So much the worse for Sergei, who began to love me though I did not love him, who would, all his life, seek that love, a woman's love. Though I did not know this yet, by his bed in Mikhailovsky Palace he kept a framed photo of himself as a toddler standing in his mother's lap, her winter dress thick with heavy trim, her head bent to his so her chin just touched his hair. Though she holds him close for those minutes before the camera, she did not pet him much—she was too busy for her children. She was quite strict and had a sharp tongue to boot, and Sergei had therefore resigned himself to the perpetual deprivation of affection. Now, with me, he thought he had found happiness and it made him expansive.

Soon after our first night together, he opened up his fat purse and bought me a dacha at Strelna on the gulf, at No. 2, Berezoviya Alleya, where the nobility summered, where my property ran right up to the edge of Konstantin Palace, separated from its stables by only a slender canal. My house with its wooden turret lay by a grove of birch trees; a private road led to my own beach. Ornamental iron gates with hedges on either side guarded the entrance to my park. A stone pig, a stone frog, and a stone rabbit made as if to drink from a fountain on the back lawn. My park stretched to the gulf, with trees that hit the sky at the edge of it and shook like black feathers in the night wind. Eventually, I would have an orangerie, an ice house, a greenhouse, a barn, and a pier for my own boat. Better than a diamond necklace, no?, for at Strelna I could string Romanovs about me each summer. Why, Grand Duke Konstantin Konstantinovich, Niki's cousin, later put me into one of his poems, so thoroughly did I make certain to ingratiate myself with them, bicycling up and down the roads to their various palaces, learning with what they thought was their help to do fine figure eights on my cycle, holding receptions and parties, which the grand dukes, without their wives, began to attend, for, like my father, I knew how to entertain well and could do so on Sergei's money. Yes, K.R. memorialized one of those afternoon parties:

> A stream trickles down from the hill,
> Swaying a tulip's petals with its water,
> And there Bayaderka in the flowers
> Dances passionately to the sound of timbrels.

That *bayaderka* was I, at Strelna, at my dacha down the hill from his palace! So easily could I have been forgotten. But Sergei, upended by love, let the rubles from his pockets fall all over me and made me shiny.

In a show of my gratitude, I designed a gold medallion for Sergei with a portrait of me in the center and engraved in a circle about my face the inscription *August 21st—Mala—September 25th*, in memory of our first happy days at the dacha he'd bought me. To the medallion I added a ten-kopek coin from the year of Sergei's birth, 1869. He was only three years older than I, but in his hands he held so much power. And in my hands I held his heart. He would wear that little charm the rest of his life.

Should I have felt guilty? Why? Love, even unrequited love, is still a gift. Who knew this better than I?

Do you remember the queen in her castle by the Terek River from the Georgian song Sergei and his brothers used to sing, the one who ravished her lovers and then pushed them out her bedroom window? If they survived the fall, the rocks beneath that swift-moving river cut their bodies as they tumbled in the current. Those rocks, for Sergei, were no doubt the purgatory of our conversations, which were so often about Niki, or Niki and Alix, conversations that were idle lovers' talk between us at first but then became, to Sergei's discomfort, obligatory before bedding me. But if he was the suitor, I was the river queen, for to me, as well as to her, was appended a dreadful reputation. I was now yet one more debased mistress of a Romanov, and mothers warned their daughters not to talk to me. That fall when I saw a little group of students from the ballet school toddling in their penguins in the frigid air, I had my driver stop for them, and I called to them, *Girls, girls, come in here with me.* But they would not ride in my carriage, not even the few hundred yards up Theater Street. They shook their heads, said, *Spasibo,* but would not climb up into the perfumed warmth, would not nestle with me beneath my sable lap robes. *She's wicked!* I heard one of them say to another as I gave up and shut my carriage door. *Wicked.*

a tsar should die in russia

THEN THE ILLNESS THAT HAD WEAKENED the great tsar at the start of 1894, that had sickened him further in the summer, in the cold of autumn, cut him down. He died in Livadia, in the Crimea, at the bottom of the country, near the Black Sea, which was not black but a brilliant blue, wild roses and honeysuckle everywhere on the slopes that led down to it. So many varieties of flowers grew in the Crimea they were sent by train all winter to Petersburg to decorate the great ballrooms of the Winter Palace, the Vladimir Palace, the Mikhailovsky Palace, the Sheremetiev Palace. But the old wooden palace in Livadia where the great tsar died, with its wood balconies and galleries like those of the palaces of the old Crimean khans, was not grand but dark and damp. I saw it only when it was abandoned. A white cross drawn on the floor of Emperor Alexander's sitting room, where he had sat suffering in the big chair and breathed his last, remained there still, flecked and faint, but visible. An hour after his death the new tsar, Nicholas II, took the oath of allegiance on the palace lawn while the old tsar received his last salvo from the warships out in Yalta Harbor. Alexander's doctors had wanted him to go abroad, to the dry air of Egypt, but the tsar had agreed only to go south, to the Crimea, because he knew he was dying and because a tsar should die in Russia.

A tsar should die in Russia, the place where he passed marked, like the floor at Livadia. The chair in which the tsar died and the props that surrounded it were treated like relics, pieces of the divine. It was the same for all the tsars. The bedroom in the Winter Palace where Niki's grandfather died stood as it had in his last hour—a cigarette butt propped in an ashtray, handkerchiefs resting on the tables and chairs within easy reach, the stained linen unchanged beneath the coverlet. At Gatchina, behind a sealed door, was hidden the bloody bed from the Mikhailovsky Palace in which the body of Paul I, murdered by his guards and officers, had been laid. Niki told me once that he and his sister Olga used to see Paul's ghost flickering past the windows of the Mikhailovsky, searching for his bed. And what would he do when he found it, I wondered. Lie down in it? Would he finally be able to rest? But he never found it, and so it remained, sealed off, a relic no one wanted to venerate, an evil no one wanted even to see. The House of Special Purpose in Ekaterinburg where Niki was murdered stands empty, I hear, untouched; the bullet-pocked basement walls have not been replastered.

When I dream now of Nicholas, I see him as I imagined he looked on the day of his death, aged, great creases running the sides of his face and disappearing into his beard, blue eyes cosseted by pouches of flesh. His khaki tunic is bullet-ridden, ruined by dozens of holes, the edges of them charred and ragged, but his face, his limbs are intact. In my dream, Niki stands before me with those sad eyes and raises a hand to me. *What? What do you want?* I ask him. What could I possibly give him now that I hadn't offered him when he was alive? But he doesn't speak, just offers his hand. What else can he offer but that hand, the hand of a dead man?

———

Did I tell you that in London, at Buckingham Palace, when Niki's sister Xenia arrived there at the end of her flight from revolutionary Russia, her servants fell to their knees at the sight of King George? They beheld what they thought was the resurrected figure of their tsar. He looked just like Niki, you know.

But I was speaking of his father's death.

Because Alexander III died so far from Petersburg, his body journeyed by train one last time across the Russia he had ruled—three thousand miles north from the station at Sevastopol in the Crimea to the Nikolaevsky Station in Petersburg, up through the Ukraine to Moscow and from there northwest to Petersburg, through the countryside where the barons and squires lived in manor houses that would be, in twenty years, ravaged to their foundations, stripped by the peasantry of every good, including the door frames and window-sills so that the walls stood gaping, guarding nothing. But in 1894, the old order stood intact and the peasants lined the tracks to see their tsar's body borne back to the capital.

In Moscow the body lay in the Kremlin overnight as if to rest before making the long journey to Peter. Black carpet covered the station platform where a catafalque housed the coffin, its columns bound up in black cloth, the horses that bore it also draped in black. Even the court carriages had been covered in black—no red and gold for this occasion. It took four hours for them to ferry the family, living and dead, across Petersburg, along Nevsky Prospekt lined with a hundred thousand guards, the guards and the mourners on the street silent, the only sounds those of the carriage wheels, of the church bells ringing in counterpoint in that special way of Russian bells, the guns of the Fortress firing each time the clock clicked past a minute, the horses' shoes ringing against the slushy streets, the wheels making a deep rumble as they traversed the cobblestone Palace Square.

All tsars are given a week of masses before burial. When Niki's grandfather died, the embalmers could not fully put back together the bits and pieces he had become by the force of the grenade thrown at his feet—both legs had been destroyed, his abdomen split open, his wedding ring broken into splinters of gold and drilled into the flesh of his right hand. So they camouflaged what they could. In his death photograph—those of the tsars were published in the papers or reproduced as lithographs, hand-tinted and sold as *mementi mori*—he wears his uniform with epaulets, but his face looks sunken, the mouth open, the bushy whiskers dry as straw, his mangled hand covered by the intact left. At his funeral, his body was covered up to the chest with an ermine and gold cloak, his face covered with a veil until the time when the coffin lid, covered with flowers and the tsar's sword and helmet, was placed on top. As for Nicholas's father, when the time came, he was mutilated not by death but by his embalmers, who somehow miscalculated their chemicals and imposed upon the emperor the disgrace of rotting before his subjects' eyes. It was almost a month from the day he died that Alexander was finally interred. By the time his body reached the fortress, his face had blackened, his head had shrunk, and no flower could mask the smell. The family by custom kissed that face on entering and leaving the church each of those seven days mass was said, *Come ye all that love me and kiss me with the final kiss*, until even his wife cried, *Enough, enough*. Imagine such a thing to happen to so great a man—and to the father Niki worshipped and feared.

At the thought of it I gripped my father's hand as we walked with my mother, my sister, and my brother through those quiet, slushy streets to St. Catherine's, our own parish, on Nevsky Prospekt, where we Catholics worshipped and where the last king of Poland was buried in 1798, here in the country that took his country from him and made it its duchy. Attendance at the funeral service at the Peter and Paul Fortress on Hare Island was for the imperial family, the court, and its diplomats, and yet the crowd that had traveled over the bridge to stand respectfully in the streets about the mustard-colored cathedral was so great I heard the Prince Dolgoruky could barely clear a path for their majesties to enter. The city, which was normally so lively, now seemed to be populated by the dead, shuffling and inert, following the boxed corpse of their king.

He was the only tsar I had known. My parents kept his portrait in the house, and portraits of him hung in the ballet school and in the theater. In my first year at the school I used to cross myself when I passed by the big picture in a frame so heavy it could kill a child if the portrait fell from the wall. In my mind, I mixed up the tsar with God, and his eyes looking down at me from the canvas seemed to know me all the way through. I remember St. Catherine's that day as crowded with many black coats and black dresses, black hats and black veils. My mother wept that afternoon, as did I, but as you might suspect, I did not boo-hoo for Alexander III but for myself, for Niki now so burdened with all the duties of the empire would have very little thought of me. When Sergei brought back the funeral program for me to see—the silver imperial eagle stamped on the front of the dignified plain black portfolio—I blinked twice at reading Niki referred to as the emperor. The emperor. At twenty-six! So quickly my Niki of last year was no longer my Niki. And, of course, Alix would soon be empress. Not me! For she was there, too, even if, as fiancée of the new emperor, she had no official place, no official funeral duties to perform, as did Niki. For after the eight major generals of Alexander's suite lift the funeral cloth, the program informed us, *His Majesty the Emperor will approach the coffin to fold the imperial cloak on the mortal remains*. His Majesty the Emperor. Niki's portrait would soon replace the one of his father in the school, in the theater, on the ruble, and that paper face would be all I would see of him. All I was hearing of him from Sergei I could put to no use, and because of the protocols of mourning, Niki would not even return to the theater this winter! And so I wept wildly, alongside the rest of my fellow Poles, my father casting sidelong glances of surprise at me and the vehemence of my grief, while across the Neva, at the Fortress of Peter and Paul, the court prepared to inter the body of Alexander III in the small cathedral where all the Romanov tsars since Peter the Great were entombed.

Alexander III would be the last tsar buried there.

Alix had knelt by the tsar's coffin, had kissed the tsar's face with a final kiss, had been witness even to the tsar's final hours—this last we learned from Sandro, already with Xenia and the family in the Crimea that fall for the deathwatch, and it was he who delivered to Sergei and me all the details of the agony of the sickroom, of Niki's panic at the thought of the throne, of his pleas to his father to be allowed to abdicate, just as Alexander I's brothers, the grand dukes Konstantin and Nicholas, each tried to abdicate before Nicholas I finally accepted the crown and became the Iron Tsar. Niki's father refused to even consider Niki's abdication—his son might be *an imbecile* but the tsarevich's brother Mikhail was an even greater fool and Niki would have his mother to guide him. And so Niki bowed his head, but Alix, he insisted, he must have Alix. And so he was allowed to send for her at Darmstadt. He went to the railway station at Simferopol himself to retrieve her, and by the end of their four-hour ride from the station to Livadia Palace, their carriage overflowed with the lemons and oranges, the roses and lilac and oleander offered as tribute by the Tartar peasants along their route—the seat of their carriage was like a marriage bed, strewn with symbols of fertility. While she may have brought courage for Niki with her from Germany, she also brought death with her: after her arrival the emperor lived only ten days more. Alexander's funeral cortege would be the first time that Petersburg saw Alix. In the procession she rode alone in her own carriage behind the rest of the family, her place still uncertain, and the women in the street crossed themselves as her carriage passed as if to ward off bad luck. *She has come to us from behind a coffin.*

If Alexander had not died so young, Niki would never have married Alix so quickly—and who knew what change of heart those months of delay might have brought? It wasn't fair! But Nicholas, in his first decree as tsar, named his fiancée Alix *The Truly Believing Grand Duchess Alexandra Fedorovna.* And in his second he declared that his marriage to The Truly Believing Grand Duchess would take place one week after the burial of his father. As the peasants say, *It is very high up to the tsar*, and Niki now flew so far away from me I suppose only his grand duchess could reach that great height.

The details of the wedding I could not help but pull from Sergei, who as one of Niki's four best men had, so to speak, a view from the imperial box, the best seats in the house. But he did not want to tell the tale to me and thereby contribute to my agony. I had to kiss him for each word.

What did she wear?

A silver gown and a gold cape.

And on her head?

A diamond *kokoshnik.*

Her jewels?

Pearls. The 475-carat diamond Imperial Rivière.

Her bouquet?

White roses and myrtle.

The train of her cape?

Lined with ermine. Carried by four pages.

She rode to the palace in?

A gold coach.

Nicholas stood?

In the palace chapel, wearing his Hussar uniform and boots.

They carried?

Each a candle.

And the vows?

Niki stumbled over them, needed prompting.

And then?

The priests blessed the couple, who kissed the golden cross.

And it was done?

Just before one.

And when they left the palace in their coach?

The crowd on Nevsky Prospekt cheered.

What theater, no?

I did take pleasure in *this*: At the reception, Alix found herself in one of the rooms of the long *enfilade* quite alone, abandoned in the confusion by her young pages from the military school, the Corps des Pages, who had been charged with the duty of carrying the new tsaritsa's train, and then misplaced both the train and the empress. There in her heavy court dress, with its underskirts and overskirt, its thick sleeves and long train, with the weighty *kokoshnik* and the 475-carat diamond necklace and the diamond earrings so laden with gems they had to be strung up with wires so as not to tear the flesh of her earlobes, Alix realized she could not move at all. And so she remained there, rooted to the spot, in that empty, high-ceilinged hall. I wonder what she thought, stranded there in the palace of a country so foreign to her she would never come to understand it. If I were there I would have hissed in her ear, *Go home!*, and given her a push west. But eventually, her brother, Ernest, realized she was missing and went to look for her. Her brother, mind you, not Niki.

That night I cried as only a young girl fed daily on theatricals could cry. And Sergei, whose family had begun to call him my *lap dog*, could find no trick to distract me. Though he tried.

I myself would not be a bride until I was forty-nine years old. There was no *kokoshnik* for me, no silver gown, no golden cape, no cheers on Nevsky Prospekt. Petersburg was a ghost town by the time I married, in 1921. No gold carriages rode the streets. No imperial crests rode the façades of the Winter Palace. They'd been hacked off and laid in the palace square like stone angels dropped from the heavens. Three-quarters of the houses stood empty. Dead horses lay in the streets. Trash floated in the canals. By the time I married, I stood at the beginning of my old age. My lips had begun to line. The skin of my arms had turned crepey and soft. My hair had to be tinted black. As a bride, I was Petersburg.

I've told you I live now in Paris, dressed this month for Christmas, with the lights like fork tines riding up the sides of the trees on the Champs-Élysées, the big pine tree knotted with lightbulbs and bells at Notre Dame, the wood stalls of the Christmas market hung with boughs and lights that recall for me so well the Shrovetide markets on the Champ de Mars where the peasants sold their Christmas crafts and toys. I have lived here in France for fifty years, but that time lies like a thin veneer over my real carpentry. By day I speak French when I must, but not *en famille*, and at night I dream in Russian. I settled in Paris rather than Berlin, where so many writers and artists and musicians fled after the revolution, drawn by the cheap mark and the large apartments like the ones we once had in Petersburg (in Peter now stuffed with worker and peasant families, one family to each room), all those southwestern suburban Berlin apartments left vacant by the suddenly destitute middle class whose finances had been completely destroyed by the Great War. But the Romanovs, what was left of them, moved in large part to France, to their villas on the Riviera, and therefore so did I, and from there, as all our finances declined further, to Paris, where the light and the squares and the boulevards of the old city are so like Petersburg's. Paris in the winter smells of chestnuts roasting over charcoal; Petersburg's streets in winter were spotted with bonfires, not to cook on but simply to warm the air. In Paris, White Army officers worked as taxi drivers and chauffeurs, businessmen as factory workers, counts and barons as waiters. And dancers of the Imperial Ballet opened ballet schools. I taught ballet on the avenue Vion-Whitcomb for thirty-five years at my own studio, the Studio of Princess Krassinsky. I closed the school in 1964. I was ninety-two years old. I gave a few lessons to the great Margot Fonteyn, you know, and to Pamela May—both from the Vic-Wells. I taught Mia Slavenska and Tatiana Riabouchinska—the latter from a great Russian banking family—who both became stars of the Ballet Russe de Monte Carlo, that company made up of what was left of Les Ballets Russes after Diaghilev's early death. I taught *Swan Lake* to Alicia Markova—the English girl Alice Marks, who dressed herself up with a nice Russian name because, thanks to the tsars, Russia was synonymous with ballet, and what dancer worth her salt was not Russian? And I, once the greatest imperial ballerina of them all, now live on the charity of old friends and my former students. Yes, I, Kschessinska, am a charity case.

In my drawer there with the pity francs I have a receipt for eleven boxes of silver and gold, deposited in 1917 in the vaults of the Petersburg Bank of Azor and Don. Eleven now-empty boxes. In 1920, Lenin liquidated the banks, took everything in them that didn't belong to him to prop up his tottering regime. Do you know what else I have tucked in my drawer? Old money, paper money, rubles, printed with the imperial eagle or the tsar's face, Niki's face. People hoarded those bills during the revolution, spent their Provisional

Government rubles instead, or later, their Bolshevik rubles with their hammers, sickles, or the face of Lenin, as if by hiding the tsar's money they could protect the tsar, the regime, and themselves.

The Orthodox priests here in Paris won't give their blessing to my desire to contact my dead through a medium, and I have so many dead. The church never liked the séances that were all the rage in Petersburg during Niki's reign, with the trembling tables and the spirits knocking on the walls and making the clocks chime out of time. The dowager empress used to open her bible at random, the words that lay on that page read as prophecy. How is that so different from a séance? No, the nobility were not that different from the peasants, with their *domovoy*, the impish household spirits who took the blame for any kitchen mishap. The peasants left pancakes for them on their windowsills at Carnival. We sat in dark drawing rooms in our silks and furs and called out the names of our dead. The priests are jealous of their travel ways to heaven and beyond, so even now they tell me that such an effort would disturb their souls, which I doubt, anyway, are at all peaceful. What do the priests imagine, that the soul stretches like a white cirrus cloud above the body in the stone crypt? Or that it sits on an armchair in heaven, dressed in phantom flesh and phantom clothes, motionless, and that the tendril of my yearning could be perceived as an itch or a pinprick?

la bayadère

In 1896 the court came out of its year's mourning for Alexander III and the imperial family returned to the theater and so did I. During that truncated season of 1894–1895 at the Maryinsky, my family had endeavored to distract me. My brother had taken me with him to Monte Carlo to dance an engagement there for those members of the imperial family who vacationed on the Riviera to escape the rigors of mourning demanded of the court back home. After that, my father brought me to Warsaw, to the Grand Theater, where we danced together the czardas and the mazurka, my father's specialty, even at his age of seventy-four! I was gone so much from Petersburg that rumors began that I had died of a broken heart, the very broken heart my family tried so hard to stitch back together. They hoped that with Niki now married and the routine of the theatrical seasons restored, I would recoup the exuberant high spirits of the Maletchka they once knew. But the routine of the theater was not exactly the same. Niki no longer visited the school or applauded the annual graduation performances of the students. Grand Duke Vladimir took over that responsibility. Alix, apparently, did not want Niki in such close proximity to the harem or me ever again. And though Niki still attended the theater, soon enough he never attended on nights when I performed. This seemed to be the new order, as permanent as a tsar's decree, as permanent as the sentinel ordered by Catherine the Great to stand in the Summer Garden after she spotted a lone flower, ahead of its fellows, rising up through the snow. A soldier was stationed in the garden that day to brush away any flake that fell on the petals of that flower, and because Catherine never revoked her order, every day, for years after, a guard was remanded to that spot. Rain, snow, heat, there he stood. So did I imagine Alix's order stood equally absolute.

Yes, so, 1896. I went back to the theater after Russian Christmas, which never falls on the same day as Western Christmas but two weeks later, nor does our Easter match the day the West celebrates the Resurrection of Our Lord. We went by the Julian calendar, you know, until the revolution, at which time in 1918 January 31 suddenly the next day became February 14, in line with the Gregorian calendar used in Western Europe. But the church never made the switch. So who is right? In 1896, after Russian Christmas, I danced a new role, that of Nikiya, a *bayadère*, a temple dancer, in the ballet *La Bayadère*, another of Petipa's fairy tales, this one fitted with bangles and saris, banana trees and the Himalayas with their mourning veils of silver snow. A Hindu temple dancer falls in love with a warrior prince, a *kshatriya*, who, alas, is already promised to the daughter of a rajah. Both the rajah and his daughter conspire to rid themselves of the *bayadère* and she is delivered a basket of flowers, an asp hidden deep within the stems and petals, an asp which springs out and plunges its fangs into her breast. After her death, her Shade haunts first the prince's opium dream and later his wedding, unnerving the bride and groom. Before the ceremony can be completed, thunder, lightning, and earthquake destroy the great hall of the rajah's palace and bury within its ruins all the participants. A perfect vengeance. Odd, don't you think, for me to be cast in the role of the dancing strumpet who spoils the young couple's wedding bliss? Perhaps Vzevolozhsky, having failed to get rid of me by tattling to Polovstov and to Grand Duke Vladimir, thought he'd try again, by sticking me in a role designed to remind Niki and Alix of my past with Niki and of my present as the girl whose ghost haunts their bedroom as Alix's ghost once haunted mine.

If true, Vzevolozhsky's plot almost succeeded. All innocence, I performed the ballet on a Sunday, January 28. I remember the date because it was the last Sunday I was to dance almost that entire year. It was not hard to see the imperial family that night, situated as their box was to the right of the stage and not very far above it. One had to ask their permission to perform an encore, which the highest-ranking member of the family granted with a nod of the head, so we had to be able to see them. Their faces were as clear to me as the faces of the dancers who played my beloved prince Solor, the rajah, and his daughter, Gamzatti. I could see Niki in his red dress tunic, and his sash, braids, and medals, all gold; his mother, hair piled high and loaded with the jewels convention dictated should have been given to Alix, the reigning empress, but which Sergei told me Marie Fedorovna could not bear to give up, having given up so much else the past year; and Alix herself. It was the first time I ever saw her, and I felt—I felt cold, as if I had drunk a pitcher of ice water in the wings and it had filled up my limbs instead of my belly. She looked, with her red-gold hair, exactly like the German and English princesses in the fairy-tale book my sister used to read to me when I was four. My sister read while I studied the colored engravings of the princess in the tower, the princess asleep in the woods, the princess trying on a slipper, the princess disgorging pearls and flowers from her open mouth. Alix wore a gown of silver cloth that rendered her skin a luminous white, and the pearl-and-diamond tiara planted in her curled hair she must have wrestled from her mother-in-law in a palace catfight. And I stood before them in a ridiculous pair of pantaloons, copied exactly from an engraving in the *Illustrated London News* that documented the Prince of Wales's journey to India in 1876, my arms stacked with bracelets, my skin tinted brown like an old cup of tea, and around my neck, in deliber-

ate provocation, the tsar's necklace. I admit it: I was not all innocence. I might not have recognized the echo of our lives in the ballet,
but I certainly recognized an opportunity to vex Alix and the new
tsar. And I did vex them. Niki's face I had not seen since that gala
for his sister's wedding, and yet he did not look happy to see me. He
regarded me from his box with an expression both stern and wary.
Sergei had told me Niki was displeased with me—I just hadn't understood how much. It had been a mistake, perhaps bigger than I
realized, to stage crying fits at rehearsals, to have written those letters to Alix, to have worn the necklace tonight. And with that real-
ization, the ice water sloshing around in my limbs turned solid, and
I had to drag and hoist my arms and legs through all the movements of the first act. I supposed I would be given no signal from
the emperor to dance an encore.

Thank God much of Act I is mime—my horror at the Great
Brahmin's declaration of love for me, my filling of a vase with water
to offer it to the other temple dancers and the *fakirs*, the men who
jump through fire and wave daggers and knives in their religious
ecstasy, my conversation with Solor in which we declare our love—
for I don't think I could have danced. But somehow I moved my
arms. Our theatrical miming was so elaborate the court balletomanes
took lessons in it to understand what we gesticulated about up on
that stage. Yes, it was during one of those extended mime interludes
that I peered over the shoulders of my beloved Solor and witnessed
a small commotion in the imperial box. Big splotches now reddened
Alix's face and she breathed as heavily as if she had been the one
dancing here on the stage, not I. She leaned toward Niki, made a
gesture of distress, at which signal he stood immediately and pulled
her chair back into the shadows of the box—into her own Kingdom of the Shades. Let her remain there. What did I care, if only
Niki reappeared. But he did not. Vzevolozhsky's ploy had succeeded, though not the way he had intended. He had rid the theater
of the emperor and empress, not of me! After that the sovereigns

and I shared the Maryinsky. It was arranged always to have me dance midweek, on unfashionable Wednesdays, the nights the imperial family did not come to the Maryinsky, while Pierina Legnani, that Italian pigeon, short, stout, plain-faced, performed her bag of tricks each Sunday for the tsar. I had been made *prima ballerina assoluta* of the Imperial Theaters, but I would never dance before the sovereigns. I might as well be dead.

When I danced Act II of *La Bayadère* now, on my Wednesdays, after the great procession of *Badrinata* I put down my little guitar and picked up a basket of waxed flowers; within the wicker recesses lay not the prop master's rubber snake, but a live one, drugged, and that is what I thrust to my breast to simulate its bite. I have always been fearless on the stage—no one comes to the theater to see a performer restrain herself—and on the stage I never restrained myself: nor off the stage much either, if truth be told. The other dancers reared back when, snake licking its way up my arms, I circled the stage to show them my injury and my inevitable fate. Some nights, under the hot lights that bedazzled me and the colorful dervish of pantaloons and saris and veiled headdresses, I wished that snake would wake and in its confusion bite into me—and then, like the famous Gypsy singer Varya Panina, who one night, spying her former lover in the audience, sang to him a song of ruined love and drank a glass of poison, I, too, might die right there on the stage. Better to become a legend than to be known as a scorned lover dancing to a vacant imperial box on Wednesday nights.

At the end of the year, I learned with delight I had been given a Sunday to dance—only to hear that Vzevolozhsky had persuaded the tsar to see a French play that night at the Mikhailovsky instead. When I heard this, my delight turned to a bitterness so fierce, I raged through my house, absolutely raged through it like the propellers of the imperial yacht, the *Standart*. I would not be so thwarted. I would not be entombed at the theater like a piece of old scenery or a decrepit prop. I sat down at my little writing desk and wrote a

letter to Niki in hysterical script big as a placard, and at the end of
it I signed my name with its grand flowery *M*. I wrote in Russian
and when Sergei arrived that evening, as was his habit every night
duty did not require him to be elsewhere, I planned to beg him
to translate the letter into French, which I would then copy over
neatly in my beautiful, tiny penmanship. I had no real education,
you know—the academics at the Imperial Theater Schools were
laughable—even Vaslav Nijinsky, a true imbecile in the school-
room though a genius on the stage, managed to graduate. But it was
important to me to write the final copy in French, the language of
the court, as this was a formal letter from a wronged subject to her
tsar, not a love note from some *petite danseuse*. I had written that if I
had lost the privilege of dancing for the emperor I no longer wished
to dance and if I did not dance then I had nothing, not him and not
my art; that I accepted the punishment of not seeing him privately,
but I could not be doubly punished by not seeing him even at the
theater. Was I or was I not his *prima ballerina assoluta*? And as such,
were my talents not the ones he should be applauding, rather than
those of some imported *il secondo*?

Sergei that night read over my letter—I had rushed to him at
the front hall and stuffed it into his hands like a child with a broken
toy for her father to fix—and when he finished, he said, *So, Mala,
you are delivering an ultimatum to your tsar? Are you sure you want to
do this?* I nodded, though truth be told I had not thought much
beyond Niki reading my Gypsy song of lamentation. What if his
irritation with me now was so great he said, *Fine, leave the theaters?*
But my desire to have him understand the injustice done to me was
greater than my interest in the outcome. And so, reluctantly, Sergei
translated my letter for me after which I covered him with kisses,
and the next morning he put it in his pocket to take to the tsar, for
he served that day as Niki's aide-de-camp, a privilege the grand
dukes rotated among themselves. Who else could have delivered to
Niki such a letter and from whom else would Niki have accepted it?

Once it was in his hands, I knew he would read it, not only because I had written it, but also because even this early in his reign he had shown he took pleasure in dealing with little matters—the budget of a provincial school, the petitions of peasants who wished to officially change their names from the crude monikers the village had assigned them, such as Ugly or Stinky—even the notorious Rasputin's name came from a nickname, *Rasputinyi*, meaning *dissolute*— petitions that required the tsar's attention. Well, this was my petition.

On that Sunday I prepared as I usually did the day of a performance—I stayed in bed all day, ate a few spoonfuls of caviar at noon, refused to drink a drop of liquid, even water, arrived at the theater two hours early to warm up. This habit of arriving early to the theater had been with me since I was a little girl. Because of my father's position, when the theater needed a tiny child to pull the Tsar Maiden's magic ring from the fish's mouth in the last bit of *Le Petit Cheval bossu*, I was chosen—and though I did not set foot on the stage until almost the end of the ballet, I insisted my father take me with him to the theater one hour before curtain. On the stage this night behind the lowered curtain, the other dancers grumbled as usual about having to dance with me when my presence guaranteed the emperor's absence. If the tsar and his suite were not in the theater, even the audience was affected, for the court came to the theater as much to see the tsar as to see us. And we artists longed to be seen by him, as well. I cannot explain this—his power conferred on us heightened senses, as does love.

I had not received a reply to my letter and Sergei had not watched Niki read it, and so I myself could only pray that what mattered so much to me still had the power to move him a little. I walked, as if casually, through the forest of trees, the bananas, amras, madhavis, their branches intertwined, and along the side of the pagoda, for I was dancing, once again, as luck would have it, *La Bayadère*. It had an elaborate set, for the court loved to see a lavishly outfitted stage and loved, too, the machinery of it—flying figures, apparitions, whirlwinds, trap doors, fountains and floods, creeping webs and thickets, the crumpling of great castles, floating barques transformed into sparkling palaces—Vzevolozhsky earmarked most of the year's budget for the opera but made sure there would be spectacle enough for the ballet. I made my way through the stage to the peephole in the blue velvet curtain.

The imperial box was deserted. Vzevolozhsky I could not see at all. It was his job to greet the emperor at the private drive, and with his peculiar gait—his back was bent, curved perhaps from so many years of bowing to the sovereigns?—to escort him through the private hallway and salon to his box. Perhaps Niki had gone after all to the Mikhailovsky to see the French play. Vzevolozhsky would be there to meet him. I put my finger to the peephole as if by crooking it I could draw Niki toward me. *Come here. Come here.*

In the pit the musicians tuned their instruments, and broken bits of various melodies from the score floated up from below—now the *turti* and the *vina*, the bagpipes and the small guitar of the *bayadère*'s dance, now that of the violin used in Act II in the Kingdom of the Shades. With the imperial box still dark, the curtain drawn at the back of it, I felt myself shrink and my bracelets slipped past my wrists. As I bent to retrieve them, I heard all around me, competing with the orchestra, a great cacophony of voices as the news spread from the house to the wings to the stage: *The tsar is here. The emperor is here.* It was like the French farce the emperor would not, after all, see tonight—the theater administrators colliding with one another in their rush to phone the Mikhailovsky Theater and have Vzevolozhsky, in his formal blue coat with the star of Vladimir pinned to the left lapel, rerouted to the Maryinsky to greet Niki, in their efforts to reach the private drive to greet their sovereign themselves in case the director could not hasten back quickly enough. What had Niki told Alix to explain this change of plans? Did she know what I had written him? My smile as I turned from the peephole was triumphant. *I knew he would come*, I told the court of the rajah Dugmanta now assembled in their places for Act I. *I was looking out the curtain for him*. And I put away my poor, drowsy reptile and took in its stead the rubber one from the prop master's cabinet. I was dancing on Sundays again.

It was a great night, for I knew I still held some power, however small, over his majesty the emperor. What would I do with it?

S O WHEN THE DOWAGER EMPRESS STRUCK my name from the special list of imperial artists scheduled to perform at the coronation gala later that spring of 1896, saying, *It would be an insult for her to dance before the young empress*, and when Niki stood there silently while she did so, I acted. Surely Niki would want me in Moscow to witness the moment when he placed the majestic nine-pound state crown of Catherine the Great on his own head. Why had he not said so when his mother uncapped her pen and drew a line through my name? Because to contradict anyone was considered by the tsar to be impolite. His ministers never understood this about him, were perpetually astonished when the seemingly agreeable tsar did not do what he had been advised to do, when the tsar smiled at them one hour and asked for their resignations the next. Why, this happened to Prince Volkonsky, who succeeded Vzevolozhsky as director of the theaters, and who, after a contretemps with me, offered Niki his resignation. Niki asked him to reconsider, but when Volkonsky arrived home he found sitting on his desk a letter from the tsar accepting his resignation! But I will tell you more of this later. Niki always knew his own mind, though his ministers did not know it. I did.

This time I did not go to Sergei for help, but to Grand Duke Vladimir, who as head of the Imperial Academy of Fine Arts was the ultimate arbiter of all things theatrical and who as blustering uncle of Niki held his young nephew in his palm. It was Vladimir and his brothers who decreed that Niki could not marry Alix quietly in the Crimea as he had wished but must wait and have a formal state ceremony at the Winter Palace in the capital. It was Vladimir who choreographed the funeral of Alexander III. And it was he who planned this coronation. And so I knew already that Vladimir loved to exercise his power and with his older brother the tsar dead and his young nephew the new tsar so raw, this was Vladimir's best opportunity to play the tsar himself for a while. Why, Niki had already had to reprimand him for using the imperial box at the Maryinsky without Niki's express permission. I could have gone to Sergei about this matter, but this was not the matter of a Sunday-night performance but a matter of state, and I was afraid the dowager empress would not listen to her great-nephew. No, Emperor Vladimir was the better choice, and anyway it is always better to have two allies than one, and I was certain Vladimir would help me countermand the dowager empress's order because he hated her and because Alix had insulted his wife. When Alix first arrived in Petersburg, Miechen tried to take her under her wing. After all, they were both brides brought to Russia from small German principalities, both women quiet and bookish and unprepared for the spectacle of the Russian court. When Miechen looked at Alix, she saw her long-ago self, modest of dowry and social graces, though Alix was a fairy-tale beauty with her red-gold hair and Miechen looked like a bulldog. But like Miechen before her, Alix had no one to guide her through the intricacies of the elaborate Russian court. The dowager empress was busy helping her son choose ministers and hold on to the crown. So the wily Miechen saw an opportunity to slip her hand into the pocket of the new empress. But Alix slapped it out. The puritanical Alix found Miechen far too sophisticated, far too comfortable with the luxury-loving, sexually amoral Russian aristocracy, and so Alix made the first of many enemies in Peter.

No, I was the first. And I was also Vladimir's obedient *dushka* who had shut her mouth like she was told and who was *still* being punished. And so on my behalf Vladimir spoke to Niki, who agreed that, yes, my name should be put back. He did want me there! I knew it! Unfortunately, Petipa had already created a ballet called *La Perle* in honor of the occasion.

The pearl was the empress's favorite gem. She had the first pick of any pearls obtained from the icy waters of Siberia by Fabergé, Bolin, and Hahn, Russia's greatest jewelers. And so, it was specifically to flatter Alix that Petipa designed this ballet to be performed at a gala at the Bolshoi Theater, one of many entertainments planned for the new tsar and tsaritsa. That was Petipa's job as imperial choreographer—to stage occasional pieces for coronations, state visits, royal weddings, and if he could at the same time flatter the court, why, so much the better. His detractors used to say the old man always had one eye on the stage and the other on the imperial box. But who did not? Most men had both eyes on the tsar, so at least Petipa saved one of his for me. Already Petipa had devised divertissements for pink, white, and black pearls, and suddenly he was forced to create new steps for a new rare pearl, a yellow pearl, and new music had to be composed for me *immédiatement* by M. Drigo. A yellow tutu had to be hastily confected for me by Mme. Ofitserova. These preparations for me, no more than the preparations made for the others, but done so long after their own, drew special attention. Drew ire, one might say. Such a fuss over Kschessinska, the tsar's exconcubine. Why is it so important to the tsar that she be included?—for, of course, everyone knew the theater would not go to this trouble were it not a direct order from the tsar. And so the rumors began then that despite the attentions paid to me by Sergei Mikhailovich, Nicholas came still to my bed, rumors I did nothing to dampen. There were even rumors that I had given the tsar a son and that this son was hidden, disguised in our midst, no, secreted away in Paris, but there *was* a son, maybe two, and *this* was the mystery of the tsar's loyalty to me. How else to explain Kschessinska still sitting in the pocket of the tsar? If only that were so, but as it was, the only explanation I could find was that the tsar still loved me. I was rich with happiness during those weeks when everyone hated me. Was not a pearl formed when a grain of sand irritated an oyster?

And so I prepared to dance *La Perle* at the coronation gala of Nicholas II at the Bolshoi Theater, which had been renovated at great expense for the occasion—fifty thousand rubles to hang new red velvet drapes at the boxes and to reupholster the chairs, sixty thousand rubles to regild all that shone like gold and to freshen the ceiling's mural, fifty thousand rubles to refit the crystal chandeliers and to replace the sumptuous red carpeting. More rubles than Niki had settled on me! More by half. Of course, he had access to many more rubles now. I didn't know this yet, but the ballet would find itself crushed between the first and last acts of *A Life for the Tsar*, a minor divertissement, and as such, it would not command the undivided attention of the audience or of Niki. While his Yellow Pearl danced for him, he would greet dignitaries in his box, Alix beside him in a silver brocade dress. As it turned out, they were not vexed or irritated. Why, they never looked down at the stage at all, no matter how furiously I spun. Not once while I danced the steps Petipa made for me to the music Drigo had made for me in the costume Ofitserova had made for me did either of them take note of Little K. Tiny K. Grain of sand.

Nicholas wrote in his journal that night that *The Pearl was a beautiful new ballet*. Reading that line even seventy-five years later—for I read his journals over and over—still infuriates me. For, really, how would he know?

The coronation of a tsar always takes place in Moscow, no matter where circumstances dictate his initial oath of allegiance is pledged. Moscow is the site of our Slavic origins as tribute payers to the

Mongols before we wrested our destiny from them—and before Peter the Great wrested the court from the heart of the country and spun it around to face the west, and Moscow is where the new tsars must formally pledge themselves to the Russian people. So Niki went to Moscow to be crowned on May 9, 1896, after the official twelve months of mourning for his father were well over. The planning for the coronation had begun in March of the previous year. Scale models were built so the three-hundred-year-old Cathedral of the Assumption and the processional routes to it could be studied by Niki's uncles Vladimir, Pavel, Sergei, and Alexei, who served on the Coronation Commission, so that every step taken by every person involved in the three weeks' events could be measured. Every hotel, palace, and lodge was rented—the imperial artists were housed at the Dresden Hotel—and any doorway, window, and rooftop with a view of the processional route was rented for the day for a fortune! Almost a million rubles were spent to refurbish the city streets the processional would traverse. The only element not under the jurisdiction of the Coronation Commission was the weather, and so, of course, it did not behave. The week before the ceremony, it rained each day, the storm cold, windy, grim; only on the day of Niki's entrance into Moscow did the sun make its entrance. Good omen.

So, on May 9, the tsar and the court rode the four miles from Petrovsky Palace to the Kremlin. Members of the Imperial Horse Guards, the Dragoon Guards, the Hussar and Lancer Guards, the Grenadier Guards, and the Life Guards Ulan Regiments stood in lines two men thick, the mounted Cossacks behind them and the Moscow police behind *them*, at the sides of the road all the way from the Tver Gate to the Nikolsky, all of them charged with protecting the life of the tsar—during his father's coronation the police uncovered various assassination plots, one that even had bombs concealed in the caps of the terrorists, and so the tradition of throwing one's cap in the air as the sovereign passed by was banned. But Niki's father's coronation had followed his own father's murder and those times of unrest were long behind us now. Alexander III had died in an armchair, not in the street. The avenues had been hung with bunting to welcome Niki, and ribbons of blue, white, and red, the colors of our flag, dried slowly in the sun on their poles in the square. The buildings all along his route had been whitewashed just for him and clippings from pine trees had been strung, for good luck, over the doorways that faced the road, their scent stingingly, acridly fresh in the nostrils of those of us who waited, one million of us, flags in our hands, to see the new tsar and to be transported by the vision.

Yes, I was there, leaning out the window of my hotel, above the herds of peasant women who wore their kerchiefs knotted under their chins, the fabrics yellow or brightly printed or striped, above the smarter of the women who opened parasols against the sun, above the city girls, more fashionable, who wore hats with ribbons made to stand in fat bows or sprigs of flowers—I saw one woman in a pointed hat that made her look like a Pierrot—all of them as excited as if they were at a circus, and who doesn't like a circus?

We could hear the parade long before it reached us—the twenty-one-gun salute that rang out at the commencement of the processional, the obligatory sounding of the church bells, hundreds of bells ringing Russian style, the ropes pulling the clappers to the bells, not swinging the bells against the clappers, and then the hurrahs of the crowd ahead of us, the thudding of boots and horses, the trumpets and drums of the court orchestra who strode with the costumed men. The Imperial Guard came by us first, in their golden helmets, then the Cossacks with their sabers, the Moscow nobility, the orchestra behind them, the Imperial Hunt, the master of the horse and the master of the hounds, various platoons of Asiatics in the costumes of their subjugated provinces, because after all, we are a vast people, we reach far east and far west, far north and far south—the court footmen in their white powdered wigs, the black Abyssinian Guards in their tasseled caps and embroidered tunics, the Petersburg court in full military regalia traveling in carriages or phaetons, then Niki on his gray charger, Norman, onto whose hooves had been nailed silver shoes that, like my little shoes, now stand in a museum as historical objects. Behind Niki rolled the grand dukes in their gilded carriages, Sergei among them, and then the red and gold carriage of Catherine the Great, a replica of her crown mounted to the top of it, pulled by eight horses, that ferried the dowager empress, weeping because only thirteen years ago it had been her husband's coronation and her own. Behind her carriage, another one: the gold carriage of the Truly Believing Alexandra Fedorovna, her face stony and unsmiling, because the crowds grew silent and suspicious as she passed. *Put up your hand and wave, you fool*, I thought. *Smile.* Did she think she was the only one ever to perform before a hostile audience?—why, with all the intrigues at the theater and all the claques of the balletomanes who cheered their favorite dancers and booed the rest, I had learned long ago to smile into the faces of my enemies, to woo them into my camp. If only that had been me in that carriage. I would have stuck my arms out the windows and waggled my fingers. But Alix had not learned my lessons, and by the end of the procession at Cathedral Square, when she and Niki bowed to their people three times on the Red Staircase, Sergei told me she was openly weeping, the idiot. Behind her came the carriages of the other grand duchesses, who knew how to behave better, and then all the various foreign princes on horseback. *A gang of princes*, as Niki described them in his journal, princes from Germany, England, France, Greece, Italy, Denmark, Romania, Bulgaria, Japan, all there to witness what would be the coronation of the last tsar of Russia.

The processions were filmed, you know, for the first time in Russian history, by the two brothers Lumière of the Lumière Cinématographe, who cranked by hand their movie cameras. But the black-and-white film and photographs of the time cannot capture this event. Any grand moment is diminished by a photograph—all is small and brown and silent. But it was anything but silent or brown as the horses and carriages and regiments trooped past us in a shimmering undulation of red, purple, green, silver, and gold, so much gold that this must have been what it was like to gawk at the court of Louis XIV at Versailles. I wonder sometimes what happened to all of those steps, all of those programs, all of those costumes, all of those scripts spoken by the priests and the sovereigns. Are they packed away somewhere, diagrammed, preserved? No matter. They have not been needed again. That day the women below me raised their arms and cheered as Niki passed and men all along the route fell to their knees and called out, *We would die for our tsar!* They thought he belonged to them and their desire to die for him proved that. But I watched silently as he rode past my hotel window, a stranger to me, my face a pale cousin to his. He had no idea I floated above him. He gripped the reins in his left hand, right hand raised in a permanent salute to all and no one in particular. To symbolize his humility, as he entered the Kremlin and the formal beginning of his reign he wore his plain army tunic. He could play at being humble only because no one else and nothing else around him did, lest anyone mistake the new tsar's humility for weakness. But he rode in the middle of a spectacle so vast, so gaudy, so proud, that I'm afraid a glint of it must have reached up to heaven and pierced the eye of God.

Yes, I was in Moscow for the coronation of the last Tsar, the last Emperor and Autocrat of All the Russias, Tsar of Moscow, Kiev, Vladimir, Novgorod, Kazan, Astrakhan, of Poland, Siberia, of Tauric Chersonese, of Georgia, Lord of Pskov, Grand Duke of Smolensk, of Lithuania, Volhynia, Podolia and Finland, Prince of Estonia, Livonia, Courland and Semigalia, Samogotia, Bialystok, Karelia, Tver, Yougouria, Perm, Viatka, Bulgaria, Lord and Grand Duke

of Lower Novgorod, of Tchernigov, Riazan, Polotsk, Rostov, Yaro-
slav, Belozero, Oudoria, Obdoria, Condia, Vitebsk, Mstislav, and all
the region of the North, Lord and Sovereign of the countries of
Iveria, Cartalinia, Kabardinia, and the provinces of Armenia, Sovereign of the Circassian Princes and the Mountain Princes, Lord of
Turkestan, Heir of Norway, Duke of Schleswig-Holstein, of Stor-
man, of the Ditmars and of Oldenbourg.

It would have been easier to list what he *was not* emperor of.

Of course, I was not among the two thousand guests invited to the
Cathedral of the Assumption for the actual coronation itself, nor
was I on the guest list for any of the breakfasts or luncheons or
dinners or military reviews or balls. No, I watched the processions
with the common crowd and with them pressed toward the Grand
Kremlin Palace to see the spectacle of lights that evening. Great
projectors sent beams of flashing white into the sky and across the
balcony that overlooked the left bank of the Moskva River where
Niki and Alix stepped out, so illuminated, to greet the crowd. The
mayor of the city presented a bouquet of flowers on a silver salver to
the new empress and when she took the tray from him a hidden
switch sent its message to the Moscow power station which in turn
sent its current back again to light up all at once the little bulbs of
red, green, blue, and purple that had been strung along the steeple
of St. John the Great and all the cupolas and roofs and ledges of the
churches and all the trees in the courtyards and all the tall buildings
within the Kremlin. I whooped with the rest of them, but really, it
was an old trick. At Easter, the priests at St. Isaac's laid a long oiled
string across the tops of the dormant votive candles that lined the
cornices and encircled the dome of the cathedral, all far above the
congregation. At midnight, the string was lit at one end and a flame
coursed about the church, lighting the wick of every candle in turn,
the lighting of them an echo of the miracle of the Resurrection.

Why was it arranged for Alix to perform a similar miracle? Why, to make her seem divine to a people who wished to believe she was so, to make it seem that it was her will that made the city sparkle, that from her palm alone blew the magic dust that turned Moscow into a fairyland. And what did she think, this German princess, when she looked out on the lit-up ancient capital from which the first Rus princes ruled this part of the world? Did she believe herself then truly Russian? Because she never would be.

I could imagine how she felt, though, in that moment, being made such a fuss over. After all, such theater was *my* milieu and I had been the object of such fuss and the purveyor of such stagecraft myself. It is easy to forget when you stand there glittering that you are not the wizard who conjured up these spells, though you are made to look that way to your audience, which gasps, thunderstruck by you. Yes, like Alix, I, too, had enjoyed such moments. Just two months after the coronation I stood at Peterhof in a little grotto on Olga Island, named so for Nicholas I's favorite daughter. A stage had been built out on the lake and the guests were rowed in small boats to their seats in stands constructed on the island. When the ballet began, I stepped from my little grotto onto a mirror, which floated on the lake, supported by pontoons, and the stagehands worked the pulleys that drew me to the stage proper. It was like the *reika*, a small platform on a long track constructed first for *The Nutcracker*, on which the Sugar Plum Fairy stands in arabesque, her hand in her prince's, while the stagehands winch the wire to draw the *reika* across the stage, the fairy gliding upon it as if by magic. To the assembled, it looked as if I walked on the water and their *oohs* and *aahs* skipped toward me. I walked on water. Alix lit a city with her fingers. But her action impressed far many more than did mine.

The coronation weeks, though filled with miracles, were not without their casualties. Eighteen people died in the mayhem that ensued when heralds in their gold tunics and black-and-red-feathered hats distributed souvenir parchments announcing the date of the coronation—the carriage in which they rode was robbed by a sea of bodies and stripped of its imperial emblems, which became also, I suppose, souvenirs. That, though, was nothing compared to the two thousand peasants crushed to death on Khodynka Field outside of Moscow, where four days after the coronation, according to tradition, the peasantry were to be fed and barrels of beer were to be sprung, filling red, blue, and white enameled cups stamped with the tsar's initials, the Cyrillic H II, with the image of the crown above it and the date 1896 below. Unbelievably, the tents and tables had been pitched on a field pocked with ditches and trenches where the Moscow garrison trained. How imbecilic was that? Tents and tables rocking on pitted ground. Even at Alexander III's coronation a handful of peasants were trampled to death there, but this year five hundred thousand peasants were on that meadow, and when something—a rumor, a cry, a woman fainting—ignited a panic, the crowd began to push. Some were suffocated standing up, others fell into the ditches where they were trampled, mud pressed onto their cheeks and into their open eyes and mouths. The crushed bodies, arms like the arms of paper dolls flapping across their flattened trunks, lay like a tarp over the field, as if protecting the ditches and potholes that had killed them all. The chaos was filmed by the horrified Lumière brothers, there to record the banquet, but the police confiscated their film. They had time to think of that while they and the Cossacks laid the corpses on sheets and, when they had no more sheets, on the bare ground. And then they gave even that up and waited for the peasants' carts filled with straw to arrive so they could clear the field before the ball given by the French ambassador that night at the Sheremetiev Palace in the city. The carriages of the partygoers would have to pass this field on their way to Moscow.

The dowager empress told Niki to cancel the evening's ball, but Niki's uncles insisted he and Alix attend while the corpses lay in piles in makeshift morgues—or lay where they had been stuffed, the ones that could not be carted away in time, beneath the field's imperial viewing stand. Niki's mother had a keen political nose—we had that in common, I would have gotten along with her well—but the uncles said their French hosts had trucked in tapestries and chandeliers and fountains and gold plates for the event and France was Russia's most important ally and sentimentality was useless. At this point in his reign, with only seventeen months as tsar, Niki was still the obedient nephew who heeded the uncles who had been serving the empire for longer than he had been alive. His father might have considered them incompetent fools, but Niki felt there was no one less competent or more foolish than he. He was terrified of making a mistake. Every bureaucratic or ministerial appointment suggested to him by his father's—and therefore his own—minister of the interior, Sergei Witte, was met with the same response—*I shall ask my mother*—which had M. Witte laughing up his sleeve at Niki. Still, to make up his own mind and make it up badly was the greater humiliation. He was so young, so young, we have to forgive him. Even at the ball itself, when Sergei Mikhailovich and his brothers took Niki aside and urged him to walk out with them, telling him it was not too late to cancel all the balls and performances and reviews and to hold instead a religious service, Niki, spying the steely faces of his uncles Vladimir, Paul, Alexei, and Sergei Alexandrovich, could not bring himself to do what his own conscience dictated. The hot-tempered Potato Club walked out, minus one, creating a stir Niki was afraid to be part of, the uncles hissing after the young men, *Traitors*. Sergei abandoned him to those uncles, whose conservative policies Niki would follow, to his detriment, for the next two decades. Better Sergei should have linked arms with Niki and reasoned with him in the soft way Sergei reasoned with me when I was wrongheaded. But, no, Sergei left him, and Niki stayed to dance for three hours that night in the foyer of the Sheremetiev Palace sweetened by one hundred thousand fresh roses from the

South of France. Niki held a luncheon the next day at the Petrovsky Palace. He attended a state dinner that night at the Hall of the Order of St. Alexander Nevsky. He danced again at the governor-general's ball. And then he led the military review of sixty thousand men from the cavalry, artillery, and infantry. The review was held on Khodynka Field.

Nicholas had longed to model himself after his favorite tsar, Alexei I, *Alexei the Peaceful*. But by the time he returned to Petersburg, the people were already calling him *Nicholas the Bloody*.

Have you seen the coronation Easter egg Fabergé made that year for the wife of Nicholas the Bloody? Its golden shell, wrapped in gold netting, opens up, and a miniature of a gold and red imperial coach slides gently from its nest of gold velvet. Fabergé made fifty-six Easter eggs for the tsars before he fled Russia in 1918. Alexander III ordered one each year for his empress beginning in 1884, and after his death, Niki ordered two a year, one for his mother and one for Alix, each egg reflective of a momentous occasion of the reign—a coronation, the canonizing of a saint, the completion of the Trans-Siberian railroad, the Romanov tercentenary—and if there was no great event to commemorate, then an egg full of whimsy and de-light. The Easter egg of 1916 during the war looked like death— the gray steel shell, a grenade more than an egg, was elevated by four bullet casings, the sheen of the egg embellished with the double-headed eagle in gold, the tsar's miter-shaped crown fixed at the top where the grenade's pin sat. Inside, a miniature portrait on a minia-ture easel depicted the tsar and the tsarevich at the front consulting with the commanders of the army, a bleak leafless tree in the back-ground, the sky gray and cloudy. The Easter eggs Fabergé made for the year 1917 were undeliverable: by then Niki had abdicated and was imprisoned with his family at Tsarskoye Selo. But Fabergé still sent him the bill.

I know I dream of a Russia that has disappeared, a Russia that *exists not / On the map, nor yet in space*, as wrote Marina Tsvetaeva in exile here, a prominent poet in Moscow, but who, like me, lost both her country and her audience after the revolution. I saw her last at the funeral for Prince Volkonsky in 1938 at the Orthodox Church on the rue François Gérard, standing off to the side, speaking to no one, no one speaking to her. She had rallied behind the Provisional Government that deposed the tsar and no monarchist in Paris would ever forget it. After that, she returned with her family to Moscow. There were those of us who did this—who found our loss of purpose and place here so great that it overpowered our fear and distrust of a Russia under Lenin or Stalin. Yes, she returned, as did others—the composer Prokofiev, the writer Gorky—Stalin loved those artists, gave them apartments and dachas and prizes: the Stalin Prize! But Tsvetaeva found herself a pariah there, her poetry too sympathetic to the old regime and to the Provisional Government that had briefly replaced it. It was as if she had been tainted, as well, by her time in the West. Without Stalin's protective embrace, people were afraid to be seen with her, to speak to her there. Her husband, who had fought for the Whites, was arrested and shot shortly after their return on suspicion of spying for the West. Her daughter, Alya, was sent to serve seven years in a labor camp for the same reason. Eventually, Tsvetaeva hanged herself. She had found the answer to her own question, the one she asked in "Poems to a Son": *Can one return to a / House which has been razed?*

No, one cannot return, except in dream or memory.

So let's return, by memory.

B Y 1897 NIKI AND ALIX HAD TWO CHILDREN, Olga and Tatiana. You would think, after witnessing such a spectacle of consummation, I would have given up loving Niki, but though the country had twice celebrated the birth of daughters, with hundred-and-one-gun salutes, the country was only as happy as the birth of a daughter could make it, and therein lay my hope. What if Alix could give Niki only daughters? The country had reacted with disappointment, as Niki must have, especially the second time, when the guns stopped firing just past one hundred instead of going on to a glorious three hundred that announced a son and heir had been born. Niki needed an heir, but in lieu of one, the family used its daughters' beauty as bait to secure the love of the people, distributing photographs, postcards, and calendars with images of Niki's daughters dressed in their petticoats, in bonnets trimmed with fur, and jackets buttoned up to fur collars, and as they grew older, photographs of them dressed in pearls and lace, their long hair partly tied up with ribbons, partly hanging down their backs and shoulders. The beautiful faces of these children who had been born in the purple inspired worship: the Cossacks who guarded them saved as holy icons each flower or stone the girls offered them as little gifts. But pretty as those children were, they were not boys. And though

Elizabeth Petrovna had been empress, as had two Catherines, and though Victoria sat on England's throne, none of Niki's daughters could be heir. For the past one hundred years in Russia only men had inherited the scepter and the orb. Paul I had decreed this, his laws born out of hatred for his mother, Catherine the Great, the German princess who married Tsar Peter III and then had him murdered, seized the throne for herself, and sidelined her son by sending him to a provincial palace from which he was not liberated until her death in 1796 on the way to the toilet. Then she left him a letter that told him the tsar had not even been his father, that he was the son of her lover, an officer—a letter of dubious veracity, for Catherine *had* shared her husband's bed for a while before denying it to him, this letter designed as a final stratagem to undermine her son even after her death. And it did rattle him: Was he not even a Romanov? For in a country with a king, birth is everything. Paul resealed his mother's letter and kept it with instructions that it was to be read only by each new emperor over the next hundred years. So Niki knew he needed a son. Alix's sisters had all had boys. Niki's sister Xenia would have six of them. And yet Alix could bear the tsar only daughters.

When I walked in the Summer Garden and saw the wet nurses strolling there in their gold-embroidered *sarafans*—blue silk or cotton beneath the gold thread if they were nursing a boy—their breasts hung with necklaces of amber beads that kept sickness away, I thought: *If only I had given Nicholas a son.* And when I saw a little boy play with a hoop and ball or ride the swings in the summer and in the winter take a sled down the great ice hill built at Admiralty Place, I thought: *I should not have worn the beeswax cup my sister taught me how to wear to keep my father and mother from dying of shame lest I have a baby.* And during the week before Lent, I would have stuffed this son with blini soaked in butter. And just before

Easter, I would have baked him little cakes shaped like the larks who bring with them warm weather, planting in the dough raisins for eyes. I would have bought him red-painted eggs and chocolate eggs and wooden toys, a miniature wooden palace with a matching coach of wood, tin, and glass waiting out front. At Christmas he would have had gingerbread cookies and a bear marionette who danced when his string was pulled and a live bird in a cage. Sergei Mikhailovich was a good courier of Niki's secrets and of mine, but a son would have been better than a courier—a snare. If I had had a son, Niki would feel compelled to see him, and therefore, me. The first Christmas after Niki became engaged to Alix I went between Christmas and New Year's to have my fortune told, as was the custom: young girls always want to know who their husbands will be. I wanted to know something else. Not, *What is his name?* But, *When will I see him again?* And yet all the tricks of the fortune-tellers told me nothing. The candle melted into a bowl of water but formed no discernible shape. The piece of burning paper held up to the wall made not the shadow of a figure, but a blur. The mirrors reflected into one another only empty walls. The passerby in the street was a mute and could not tell me if he was a Sergei, an Alexander, or a Nicholas.

But the portents did not say Niki would *not* come back to me. They just could not say exactly when. The only way I could keep him thinking of me was by making a commotion at the theater. And so, I made a commotion. Many of them.

magnificent mathilde

I HAD OCCASION TO, as Prince Volkonsky was appointed the new director of the Imperial Theaters. M. Vzevolozhsky had left the post to become director of the Hermitage Museum, to take up residence in a cramped office there with a view of the Neva through his small windows, charged with the care of the statues, *objets*, paintings created by the great European masters and collected over the centuries by the Romanovs—which left us at the Maryinsky to the abrasive Volkonsky, who immediately suggested I share my role in *La Fille mal gardée* with one of those imported Italians. I refused. The role was mine and a Maryinsky ballerina did not share her roles with anyone. When Volkonsky insisted that Henrietta Grimaldi dance the role, I complained to Sergei, who first spoke to Volkonsky and then, when he did not get satisfaction, sent him a blistering letter, saying, *By wronging Mathilde Felixovna, you insult me!* and promptly called the tsar who was visiting his mother's family in Denmark. Niki had the minister of the court, the all-powerful Baron Freedericks, send a cipher telegram to Volkonsky with his order not to give my role to Grimaldi. What other dancer but me could complain of her treatment to the tsar, for as you remember, it is very high up to the tsar! No other dancer, and that is the truth.

And Volkonsky was from an old Russian family, the grandson of the Decembrist Prince Sergei Volkonsky, one of the guards who confronted the Iron Tsar, Nicholas I, in the Senate Square in 1825 in an effort to unseat him and was sent to Siberia for thirty years for his trouble. The Volkonskys had served the throne for generations, and yet the tsar sided with me, not with him. You would think that the great Volkonsky would have learned his lesson about who was the greater, but he was new to theater and had accepted the position only to please his father, and soon enough we locked horns again. When I balked at wearing a hooped petticoat beneath my skirt for *La Camargo*, explaining that such a billowing petticoat beneath the Louis XV–style costume would dwarf little me, Volkonsky insisted I wear it. Well, I did not! He even sent the theater manager to my dressing room before the performance to once again demand that I wear the hooped petticoat. I refused! By this time, every dancer in the company and half the audience out front had heard of our battle, *l'affaire of the hoops*! I appeared on the stage in the requisite costume—and who would even know that I had left the petticoat behind had there not been such a fuss? But when Volkonsky fined me a trifling amount of rubles for an unauthorized costume change, a deliberate provocation, posting the notice on the hallway board as if I were some Near the Water girl, I wrote to the tsar myself, and not in French this time, and the tsar canceled the fine, ordering the director to post *that* notice on the board. At which point Prince Volkonsky resigned his post, and I became known as *Magnificent Mathilde*.

And I was magnificent—both powerfully connected and powerfully talented. At twenty-seven, I had mastered all the specialties of those Italian ballerinas who had performed in Peter for the last hundred years, even Legnani's astonishing series of thirty-two fouettés, one leg whipping the body round like a top over and over and over. And so I asked the tsar to clear the theater of Zambelli, Legnani, Grimaldi, and their like. We didn't need them anymore.

The theater had me. And I wanted to be the one onstage when the tsar came to the Maryinsky on his Sunday nights.

Yes, I kept the tsar very busy with matters of the ballet.

And he was also kept very busy, apparently, with matters of the bedroom, for in 1899 the tsar had yet another daughter, his third, Marie. *Tant pis*. So much the worse. So much the worse for Alix.

In 1900 I was asked to dance at the tsar's private theater, the Hermitage Theater in the museum attached to the Winter Palace, for the first time. Was the juxtaposition of the birth of Marie and my invitation to the Hermitage a coincidence? I didn't think so. How many daughters could a tsar endure? This intimate theater had been built by Catherine the Great, who had her gilt and upholstered armchair dragged right up to the rim of the orchestra pit to better enjoy the spectacles her artists had concocted just for her. Tsar Nicholas II and *his* family sat before the stage in the gilt armchairs now and the court of 1900 sat behind them in the wide semicircular pews to watch the private entertainments created for their pleasure alone. The ballets performed there were always trifles devised for the occasion and danced only by the finest artists in the company, its soloists and ballerinas, never by the *corps de ballet*. Yet I had never been invited to the Hermitage before. But now, I supposed, with all those Italians sent home, my name stood at the top of the list and Alix could not draw a line through it without looking petty. Or perhaps Niki expressly requested my presence, in which case, she could not say no.

The stage of the Hermitage Theater was a small one, the wings crowded with wooden wheels to raise the scenery and with bellows to blow wind or smoke, but from it I knew I would be able to see the royal family at close range. And then, after the performance, we artists would be invited to sup with the imperial family and their guests in one of the Hermitage picture galleries. It was like being stabbed with a steak knife to hear those dinners described by the dancers lucky enough to have been invited here before: the caviar on shaved ice, the hot stuffed mushroom caps, the smoked salmon and sturgeon, the salted cucumbers, sausages, blini, the lobster bisque, the steaming borscht, the liver pâté of the Lota fish, the filet mignon, suckling pig, roasted partridge and quail with croutons, lamb in cream sauce, venison and veal, the pyramids of pineapples, watermelons, grapes, strawberries and cherries, the Italian fruit cake flavored with violets, frosted bowls of chocolate, vanilla and fruit-flavored ice creams and sorbets, pastries and tortes, the decanters of whiskey, cognac, sherry, champagne, and cassis, the silver jugs of lemonade and milk flavored with almonds and the vodka flavored with lemon peel or cranberries. At the end of the meal, the tsar would dispense a small gift, a gold medallion, the imperial eagle stamped on the back, to each of the artists.

Yes, those close enough to the tsar to hold out their hands found them filled with gold and it had been that way for four hundred years, though by the end of the year all the expenses of his court depleted the treasury and the tsar was out of money. But these customs of the old Russia in which the tsar stood absolute and all wealth flowed through him were customs Niki loved. He loved the story of Catherine the Great's standing order for a sentry perpetually at post in the meadow. He loved that by right he had first pick of the pelts, vodka, timber, and metals hacked from the mines of Siberia. In 1900, he even debated changing court dress to the long caftans of the fourteenth century and changing the spelling of words to that of Old Muscovy. He wanted to turn back the clock even as the world was hurtling forward. In medieval Russia, custom once kept the tsar and his empress shielded from the people, even from their own *boyare*. They observed court ceremonies from their *terem*, through secret windows, the mysterious, unseen source of power, and as

Niki did not like to be stared at and Alix did not like to appear at court, perhaps a *terem* would have suited them both. But they came to the little theater at the Hermitage and let us all look.

That night the divertissement Petipa devised was *Les Quatre Saisons*, for which he had choreographed four dances—Rose of Summer, Winter's Frost, Bacchante, and Harvest Time, and I represented this last as an Ear of Corn. The choreography I cannot remember, but no matter, it was not a masterpiece. Vegetables do not inspire great works of art. At the Maryinsky the court was held at a distance, but Niki sat before me now on a chair next to Alix, just beyond the orchestra pit and the proscenium of the stage, which projected forward in a half circle. If I leapt from it, I could almost land in his lap, but my legs trembled so much when the stagehands cranked up the curtain I wasn't sure I could walk. I knew Sergei was out there and I sought his face for comfort. He nodded at me, gave me the little one-sided smile, the secret smile we gave each other. Like two-faced Janus, I returned it. I stood as decoration for much of the first few divertissements, a husk of corn in my hand as a prop, and good fortune, for I could not remember whatever it was I was supposed to do whenever my eyes met Niki's luminous blue ones. It seemed to me he gazed at me with affection.

At this close range, Alix looked, at twenty-seven, at least a decade older and she would that year consult her physicians two hundred times for her heart, her nerves, her sciatica; when these men failed to satisfy her, she would begin her long and ultimately disastrous journey of consorting with healers and holy men. All this was before her and yet one could see something of it in her face: in the exhausted expression, the grim eyes, the long nose beginning now to droop, the frizzled hair that rose like a turban from her too high forehead, the hair brushed and then pinned around the plump cloth pads that gave her coiffure its elaborate shape. Around me danced women equally unattractive—the young Anna Pavlova with her beaked nose, my plain-faced rival Olga Preobrajenska, and Petipa's daughter, the stout Marie, who looked like a Viking warrior and who owed having a position at all to her father. No, there was no competition on the stage or off for Niki's attention and I began to note how often and how discreetly his eyes—just his eyes—flickered to where I stood to take in my form before returning to the general action on the stage. He wanted to look at me in my shimmering gold tunic and bloomers, cut much shorter than my usual skirts, at me in my gracefully curled wig. Well, who would not take pleasure in such a sight? And suddenly I began to relish this evening. The nervous sweat that had enveloped me and soaked my hair beneath my wig began to dry and I became impatient for my turn to take center stage and dance, for the moments when Nicholas would not have to drag his eyes from me.

I remember it was Nikolai Legat, my dear Kolinka, who partnered me in my adagio and oh, he was lovely to look at then, with dark, curly hair, eyes as large as two slices of orange, and a lower lip a woman would enjoy biting. It was Kolinka Legat who uncovered for me the secret of Legnani's endless series of *fouettés* by scrutinizing her during rehearsals for Act III of *Swan Lake*, and it was he who coached me until I too could snap my head round while focusing on a spot center front, the trick by which one could whip the series of thirty-two turns without pitching over. (I presented him with a monogrammed gold cigarette case for his trouble.) I was an Ear of Corn, but I decided to behave that night not like a cheerful vegetable in a raspy husk, but like a flesh-and-blood woman bewitched by her lover. Our formulated and regimented choreography—put one's head together here with one's partner's, then turn and place this hand there and that one here—so often produced a mechanical effect in adagio, a cursory approximation of love. But tonight, and not for the last time, I decided to channel my feelings for Niki, using the unwitting Kolinka as medium. I didn't think he, being already a friend, would mind. Perhaps I overplayed my part a bit, looking too amorously into his eyes and then turning to the eyes of the tsar so close to me. At one point, I held out my hand to the tsar before furling my arm back and touching my palm to Kolinka's. This went on for some time, until finally Kolinka whispered from behind while supporting me in arabesque, *Mala, what are you up to?* I almost laughed.

And did my efforts have the desired effect? I believe so. The tsar had no eyes for Winter's Frost, Rose of Summer, Bacchante, for the empress herself, sitting there looking at him with an increasingly dour face. I forgot to look for Sergei's. The empress might not be pleased by what she saw on the stage, but the Ear of Corn certainly pleased the tsar.

Sergei told me later that in the Hermitage gallery Niki had leaned toward him beneath a Rembrandt after the main courses and salad but before dessert while lighting up his little yellow cigarette to say, *Mala looked very beautiful tonight.* Which Niki expected Sergei, pleased by the tsar's approbation, to dutifully repeat to me. And Sergei was pleased, but he was also wary.

What would happen next?

A meeting of sorts.

It was only a few months later that the chief of police called to tell me the emperor would be passing by my dacha on the road from Peterhof to Strelna at one o'clock and that I must be sure to be standing in the garden where the tsar could see me.

It was the first of such calls, which time would teach me to receive with greater dignity than I did that day. When I put down the receiver I screamed. Then I ran about, for I had little time, sprinting around the garden from this bench to that flower bed, trying to decide which perch would offer the best sight lines from the road. I believe I even considered sitting on the top of my fountain, but I ended up choosing the obvious stone bench, upon which first I sat and then I stood, on tiptoe, so eager was I to be certain Nicholas could see me over the clipped hedge that divided my garden from the road. In the heat the air seemed to me to be swirling and liquid, thick with the sea lapping at the bottom of my garden, which was suddenly and ferociously in bloom, as happens in Russia—after the long winter, the sudden spring, so sudden it shocks one. I felt a bit like one of the dwarves or Africans kept by the old Russian counts for amusement—or worse, like one of the unfortunate serfs forced to paint herself white and pose in the garden like a statue as her master rode past.

At the sound of Niki's approach I stood on tiptoe and arranged my hair, which I had pinned only half up, leaving the bulk of it down my back like a young girl who has not yet been presented—it was my garden, I reasoned, where one could expect to be left alone, and so if my hair was in charming dishabille, it seemed circumstances might allow it. Girls dance without wigs now on the stages of Paris, London, and New York—but for me that is hard to imagine, one's hair is as private as the hair on one's body beneath a tutu; to expose one's head to an audience is like undressing before it. No. I always wore a wig. But not for this impromptu program.

The sovereign's carriage at last appeared over the edge of the hill and its appearance surprised me—I had been expecting Nicholas to approach on his horse. And then I saw: the empress sat in the carriage beside him. The empress? Why? Did she feel Niki needed a chaperone on his ride by my dacha? As they neared, I curtseyed and they bowed, but I saw her eyes were on him as he inclined his head toward me, one hand raised against the sun. A bit of a smile, forced, flat. Nothing from her but that bent head. They passed. And I understood it all. She had bristled at his ogling of me at the Hermitage, and they had fought and he had denied it and she had insisted on this ride by my dacha for the purpose of watching his face, to see if her suspicions were correct, that Niki was tiring of her, of her illnesses and of her predilection for producing girls, and that his thoughts were curling back to me. And Sergei—Sergei must have known this and yet he must have been concealing it from me in order to keep me for himself. Selfish. I said a quick selfish prayer myself to the back of Niki's carriage, the wheels raising yellow dust mixed with pollen, praying that the one minute in which Niki's carriage rode past my garden would be long enough to remind him of the color and texture of my hair and the alabaster sheen of my skin, which I once pressed beneath his brown body, browned from his naked summertime dips in the Black Sea, and, more important, that his face would reveal his memories of this and that he would fail his test, fail it miserably.

I'm sure he *meant* to come to me, soon, and alone, but that spring of 1900 while he lingered in the Crimea, where he should have been safe from the cholera and typhus of Petersburg, Niki was stricken with the latter. Niki called Peter *the bog*, and he left it behind each spring for the fragrance and the blossoms of the Crimean tropics, the lilies, the lilacs, the violets, the orchids, the wisteria and roses and magnolia, left behind Peter's flooded streets and gardens and stairways. For in the late spring the Neva rose as the ice melted and water flooded the city. Rats swam through the rivers made of the streets, long tails a whiplash in the eddies, their basement houses drowning pools. Disease had become a problem now that the city had become clogged with factories and the factories clotted with the peasants who left their villages at the end of the summer harvest to look for work and ended up staying here year-round, shackled to all the new industries: the metalworks, the engineering works, the electrical plants. You'd see whole families, women in their homemade blouses and kerchiefs, men with their bowl haircuts and filthy beards, and this was a new phenomenon in Peter, not the peasants, for we always had peasants there, working as our maids and chauffeurs and stable hands and bath attendants and laundresses and prostitutes, but these peasant *families* working at the factories now crowding up to English Prospekt and spotting the Vyborg side of the city, filling the adjacent Little Neva with their waste. The workers slept together in flophouses or cellars or stairways or shared apartments, sixteen to a room, or they slept on plank beds in the factory barracks or on makeshift mattresses of dirty clothes piled by the side of their machines, and they filled the backyards of the tenements with excrement, and that was why we had so much typhus and cholera all of a sudden in our city.

I've told you Tchaikovsky died of cholera from the drinking water? Well, even the tsar's daughter Tatiana would grow sick one year from the water. I had to pinch my nose when I stepped out of my house at No. 18 and I no longer wanted to stroll by what were now the putrid canals and river. Unfortunately, in the early 1900s disease lurked everywhere in beautiful Peter, and it surprised even the tsar, while his ministers refused to build the suburban housing that could help alleviate the crowding and the disease, saying, *But we're an agrarian society*, when clearly what we were was something else entirely. Russia's land, not much of which was fertile, was so overworked the peasants couldn't farm it. In 1892, the peasants in Simbirsk starved in a famine so terrible that when a charity sent children's clothes to the province, the clothes were returned. There were no children left to wear them. You can see why over the next decade peasants flooded the cities.

And from this devastating famine the sentiments of the Decembrists of 1825, long suppressed, were reawakened. Those nobleman officers who had fought Napoleon alongside the peasant infantry saw that the foot soldiers they commanded were men, who deserved to be treated by the regime as men, not as serf beasts. And now, this

new generation at the end of the century, a generation of intellectuals and students and revolutionaries, saw the same and said so. They
demonstrated against the regime and joined the Union of Libera-
tion, the Marxist Social Democrats, the Social Revolutionaries, and
so just as his father had, Niki was forced to repress what threatened
the crown. He hunted down and conscripted, exiled, or imprisoned
the groups' leaders. Did I think of these things then? Ponder the
unjust treatment of the peasantry or the need for a constitution? I
wish I could say yes, but I had more pressing concerns.

For I heard that while in the Crimea nursing Niki, Alix discovered she was pregnant again, and she told the family she was certain
that she was carrying, this time, a son. This news from Sergei—that
Niki was gravely ill and that Alix was carrying a son and heir—had
me halfway between frustration and despair. Her pregnancy and
his illness were her great victories, her chance to revive his flag-
ging affection for her with his gratitude. What an opportunity! She
could have designed no better one and she must have known this
for she kept a steady vigil by Niki in the darkened bedroom. If only
the tsar had been this sick with me—I would have nursed him so
well I would have won him over completely! Sergei told me Alix
reported Niki was so weak he could not crawl from his bed to his
dresser. The light hurt the tsar's feverish eyes and one small ray sent
spasmodic pain through his neck, back, and legs. He was so weak
he could not hold a spoon or a pen or scratch out the few words of
a *ukase*. If only when he opened his aching eyes he could have seen
me before him with the spoonful of broth and the cool rag for his
forehead. But he saw Alix. The old palace at Livadia, always humid
and moldering, seemed to be decaying about them. The whole of
the Great Palace was dark, covered up by shrubbery and arcades and
loggias all run over by honeysuckle and wild roses and ivy, which
shut out the sunlight—and the mahogany paneling of the interiors
quickly absorbed whatever light pierced that fortress. Against even
that, Alix shut the drapes and so shut out the world. Alix's panic

had stolen from her the pains of her weak heart and her sciatica, the pain that usually kept her in bed or confined to a wicker wheelchair, and now she had energy, the frantic energy terror provides. While her children and Xenia's ran back and forth along the "imperial trail," the brambled path between Livadia and Xenia's palace of Ai Todor, a progress Alix normally assiduously monitored, she sat instead in her sweat-soaked muslin feeding the tsar spoonfuls of soup, relieved only by Mrs. Orchard, the one servant she fully trusted, this her own nanny whom she had brought from England when Olga was born to help her carve order from the free-flowing splendor of our long Asiatic Russian summer days and the long darkness of our winter ones. Mrs. Orchard had been there when the black cyclone of diphtheria had sucked up Alix's mother and sister and then let them fall back down lifeless, and surely with Mrs. Orchard by her God would not dare take her husband from her as well. Without him, she had no center to her world, only these children, these *tinies*, little leaves, the oldest of them five, and this baby inside her, a life of so few weeks it did not yet have a discernible shape and without Niki would have no discernible future. She knew what would happen: if Niki died she would be consigned to one of the palaces to quietly raise the children of the former tsar, while someone else moved into Tsarskoye Selo, Peterhof, Livadia, the Grand Kremlin Palace, her *appanage* and those of her children reduced and their places at court pushed upstage, against the water. Instead of being grand duchesses, her daughters would be merely princesses, and her son, instead of tsar, a prince. Here in Petersburg, Sergei told me, Count Witte and Baron Freedericks and the grand duke uncles and great-uncles were already conferring about the line of succession and the dowager empress was maneuvering to have Niki's brother Mikhail made heir to keep Vladimir or Nikolasha from crawling onto the throne. Niki's brother George, who had been the heir apparent, had died the year before, in the Caucasus, at Abas Tuman, where he had been living quietly, isolated from the family, hoping the climate would cure him of his tuberculosis. But no such luck. He had had a hemorrhage while riding his bicycle and he was found by the side of a road by the attendants charged with his care, dead in the shadow of the great Kazbek mountain. And now the tsar's handsome but foolish youngest brother Mikhail must quickly be declared heir, for how likely was it that Alix would produce a boy? Not likely. No, Mikhail was heir and he would remain so until Alix produced a boy. The family rose up against her in a dress rehearsal of their complete retreat from her a decade and a half later, when they would plot to force Niki's abdication and her own confinement in a convent. This time the family merely stirred and rustled and strutted, but from this, Alix understood that Niki's family were her enemies. But if the tsar recovered and she had a boy, they would have to walk on their knees to her.

And so Alix put her lips to the whorl of her patient's ear and whispered: *Make me regent for your son. Declare your brother only temporary heir, not tsarevich. Ignore your mother. I am sure I am carrying a boy.* I had to give her credit: she was not without plots and schemes and capers. And in his superheated dreams Niki, too, could see what she saw, the landscape of disempowerment, trees without leaves, stalks without flowers, smoke and ash. Even I, in St. Petersburg, could see it—for that future was also my own and it rolled toward me with the news of Niki's illness. I might never have a chance to complete my destiny with Niki and I had so many plots and schemes and capers myself. I had seen Alix as my nemesis for so long I forgot to worry about assassination or illness. Many people died of typhus. I might never see Niki alive again. I tried to bring up the picture of him as he rode past my dacha, but I kept seeing my own self in my white dress with my pretty long hair instead. I should have worn a ribbon. I lay on my bed at Strelna one whole day in my nightgown—an eternity!—waiting for news of the tsar's death, but that news never came, and, after all, how long can one stay in bed? I had to get up. And so, eventually, did the tsar.

By December, he was sitting up in his chair.

By January, he was back in Petersburg, to the relief of his mother and brother, and to the concealed disappointment of his grand duke uncles and older cousins.

By June, he was at Peterhof, where on the fifth of that month, to the curses of the entire imperial family, Alix gave birth to her fourth daughter, Anastasia.

And by the end of June, Niki rode the Volkhonsky High Road to my dacha at Strelna. His two Cossack bodyguards remained at the stables while we walked together back to the house, the wind trying to take from us our clothes, which we would take off soon enough, small leaves and twigs making targets of our faces and bodies, the whole afternoon suddenly aroar.

AH, IT IS ALMOST TOO PAINFUL to recall that triumphant afternoon as I lie here on *this* bed.

I will say that it seemed, after all, Niki had yielded to the ravenous nature of his grandfather who, not fully sated by his wife and mistress, commissioned from the artist Mikhail Alexandrovich Zichi pornographic engravings for further pleasure. This erotica—in one, Zichi had women impaled by winged phalluses as if the woman on her back receiving the phallus of the devil was not enough for him, that disembodied members must also be fornicating simultaneously beside him—was discovered locked in Alexander II's desk at the Winter Palace by the Bolsheviks when they ransacked the place in 1917. They later published the painting in books for all the world to see. What would the world ever come to know of *this* woman on her back, receiving the phallus of the tsar?

When we finished to his satisfied bellow, Niki sat up to locate his cigarettes, which were tucked, as always, in the pocket of his tunic or the pocket of his greatcoat, with him wherever he went; he put one in his holder, which was like any item he used or owned, no matter how small—a pen, an inkwell, a brush, a bottle—exquisite, made of silver or gold or inlaid with mother-of-pearl or encrusted with gems. He kept a collection of Fabergé cigarette cases in the dressing room of his bath. Did he possess any plain objects? I never saw one. The Bolsheviks couldn't find any either when they stuffed their pockets with palace trinkets—even the embossed cakes of imperial soap made them pretty prizes. I sucked at one curled end of my hair, a childhood habit, and stared at the tsar, who sucked at his embellished cigarette holder, leaning forward every now and then to offer me a smoke, which, thanks to Sergei, I knew how to do. I would like to say I thought of the *feelings* of Sergei Mikhailovich at this time, not just the tricks he taught me, but I did not. I was thinking about the discouraging fact of the gold band glistening on the ring finger of Niki's right hand and about the marvelous fact that he nonetheless lay naked in my bed. And he was now no longer a faun but a man; he wore a greater weight than he had six years earlier and grooves now scratched at the corners of his eyes, and those six years as emperor of the country and emperor of the bedroom had erased his hesitation, his reticence as a lover. I rested my chin on Niki's thighs and made an idle fig leaf for him of my hair, while he sat against the pillows, smoking and looking out my window at the tall yellow and purple heads of the tulips in my garden, the boldest of those tulips so proud, so big, they couldn't possibly know how the wind would peel them from their stalks before summer. Was *he* thinking of Sergei, whom he had just displaced? Of Alix, whom he had just betrayed? My mind was empty—pleasure and triumph had wiped it clean, but I could feel in a cupboard there a few words scrambling into formation, which then broke ranks when Niki said abruptly, *Let's walk*.

He wanted us to wear little—my chemise and petticoat, his shirt loose over his breeches. He wanted to enjoy in the fragrant afternoon the nothingness of private people who can walk half-clothed in the gardens of their empty houses. I think he wanted in that moment not to be tsar or even to be himself. But my house was not empty, though to him it must have seemed to be. I had only my houseman and my cook and my yardman, but any one of them could look out a window and see Nicholas II in his billowing shirt walking beside me past the violets, the orange tips, the dahlias. And with what surprise would my servants regard him! And what would they think when they did? That the fortunes of this house were soon to rise? The tsar's boot soles bent the grass. My bare feet skimmed the grass. At his coronation four years earlier Niki had been eclipsed by Alexandra's height, made greater by her heels and her crown, and eclipsed also by her breadth, made wider by the stiff skirts of her court dress. By her side *he*, rather than she, seemed the consort, meager of stature, his chin receding into the neck of his mantle. She made him look slight, but at my side he stood majestic, his stride the stride of an emperor. It's all in the proportions, as any scenic designer knows. A small castle on the backdrop is made to loom large in the distance. The second floor of a storefront is constructed at half the size of the first to give the illusion of greater height. A large spinning wheel dwarfs the girl. A dwarf by her side makes her a giant.

We walked all the way along my private road to the gulf, and his silence was so deep I thought wildly that when we got there perhaps he would expect us two fornicators to drown ourselves. The wind lifted his shirt and my chemise, but when we reached the water, he stopped walking and he made no motion to rope me to a big rock and roll me into the surf. No. He had in mind to talk. Whatever he wanted to say, he wanted to say here, outside, as if he did not want to be held accountable for these words, but to let the wind over the water take them from him as he spoke. *Alix has been seeing a spiritual advisor, a Monsieur Philippe, and he has assured her she will bear me a son.* He turned his face to me. *He said this last child would be a boy.* At the sight of yet another baby daughter in Alix's arms, Niki told me, he had had to excuse himself from Alix's bedside and walk the Peterhof palace park to master his disappointment. His sister Xenia's reaction? *My God, another girl!* It had been six in the morning, but the dew had already dried from the speckled planes of the flowers, and Niki's hope and faith had dried up along with it.

I had heard of M. Philippe Nazier-Vachot, the butcher's assistant from France. All of Petersburg had heard of him. He lectured, in his ungrammatical French, about the heavenly orbs and the earth, which was once, according to him, a globe of fire, and offered up prophecies, all the while asserting, *I am nothing in myself, I am the receptacle of God, I act in the name of the divine*. His women disciples called him *Master* and they revered his psychic powers, believed that if he proclaimed them invisible they were so. Why, they would not even greet one another in the streets, for each believed herself as invisible as M. Philippe had promised, and therefore could not be seen by the others. If M. Philippe promised Alix she would bear a son, she would flatten herself beneath the tsar every night to make it so. But Niki had lost his taste for making love to Alix, he said, these six years of illness, paranoia, and desperation stripping from him his patience and his desire. Even her increasing mysticism he met with dismay. *My mother barely speaks to her, my father, if he were alive, would have her put away*. Niki had begun to use his study as a refuge, his ceaseless paperwork as barrier, darkness as tool of last resort. When it was her time of the month to conceive, he told me, grimacing, he managed his part by conjuring up his memories of *my* body, which was, here and now, exactly as he recalled it, exactly as it had been when I was twenty. And here he kissed my arms. Well, of course, I had not had four children and I was a dancer—an occupation that preserves the body better than a dip in formalde-hyde. But I did not say any of that. Let him think what he wished about the marvelous condition of my beauty and the decrepitude of hers. Let him kiss the length of my arms. No, I reveled in his words. All this was what I had waited to hear, the thoughts too private for the tsar to reveal to Sergei, impossible to reveal given Sergei's rela-tions with me, relations Niki could halt with a word. If the tsar wished to reassume his place in my bed, Sergei, of course, would be nudged from it. Did I think, *Where is the lighthearted young officer I fell in love with ten years ago and who is this beleaguered man in his place?* No, I did not. I thought only about how I couldn't wait to run back to my family, and to my father in particular, to tell him, *The tsar still loves me! You were wrong. My idyll, after all, is not so short!*

All those long summer afternoons of 1901, when Alix and her four daughters lay down all unknowing at Peterhof for their naps, Nicholas would set aside the papers his ministers had brought him from Petersburg in the special leather pouch stamped with the imperial insignia, and he would mount his horse and ride the twelve versts to my dacha. He had asked me to empty my house that summer for his visits—Sergei was with his regiment at Krasnoye Selo, I hosted no parties, invited no one to stay, gave my servants each afternoon off—and so there was no one to see us when we walked into the woods in search of the mushrooms Sergei had had planted for me or when Niki himself filled my birch-bark basket with the black and brown caps, which I would stew with butter and cream. I did not have my father's culinary talents, but I could do this much for the tsar. We would sit on the veranda and eat with our fingers, like two children left to their own devices while the adults went out visiting. Before we went to bed, we licked each other's fingers clean. The fingers he once licked of butter are puckered now and dry, but not then, and not his either. That summer I did not wear my cup of beeswax nor did the emperor wear a sheath, and though he said nothing I knew what he wanted, a son, against the drip, drip, drip of all those girls. The sun rises before five in that month and makes a leisurely arc across the sky, and because the sun took so long a roll west, our afternoons together were endless; our lovemaking was slow and long and breathless in the heat. When it neared the dinner hour, only then did he rise from the bed, and I drew him a bath in the dacha's biggest tub, which still was not deep enough or long enough for him. In the bathrooms in each of his apartments in each of his palaces had been installed a sunken tub in which he could completely immerse himself. In my mansion on Kronversky Prospekt I would build him such a tub, but we are two years from there yet. We take our bathing seriously in my country—every estate had its own bathhouse and the blocks of every city were dotted with them—bathhouses complete with Persian carpets, wood paneling, potted palms, and male attendants bearing trays of brandy and cigars. The men, smoking and drinking, would dip in the pool. Then they sat in the sauna while the pages beat them with birch twigs or else they retired to a private room where a page would allow himself, for a fee, to be corrupted. For Niki, I served as such a page, and in my dacha he folded his limbs into my tub, where I poured in the oil he loved of bergamot, bitter orange, and rosemary, and sponged him first with that water and then with fresh as he lay there, cigarette between his teeth, head back against the porcelain rim. The window above the tub let in air pungent with grasses, pine, and birch, the scent seized and intensified by the steam rising from the water. In this sweet haze his fingers would play against my fingers and sometimes he would turn his face to me, and I would begin then to dread his leaving, the emptiness of the dacha once he had, and the specter of Sergei, which seemed to walk the rooms at the tsar's exit. I would sometimes run after it to say, *I'm sorry. You know he was my first love.* Sometimes my fingers would drum the rim of the tub in anticipatory dread, and the tsar would calm my fingers with his own. Finally, though, Niki would have to stand, water sluicing off his body as the waters in the fountain at Peterhof sluiced down the gilded body of Samson, the estate and the evening there a relentless slice of boredom to which the tsar must now return, to face dinner, embroidery, reading aloud, perhaps the showing of a film from which, at the empress's insistence, the indecorous moments had been removed. To all this the tsar was subject, as he was subject to the continuing predictions of M. Philippe, who assured him that for Anastasia to have been born when all signs of the sun and moon and stars pointed to the birth of a son must mean that she was marked for an extraordinary life. The next child would most certainly be a son, for Anastasia had paved the way. And through all this nonsense, the tsar kept his silence.

Poor Anastasia. I met her briefly in Paris, in 1928, with my husband, in the compartment of a train at the Gare du Nord, eight years after she had been fished out of that Berlin canal and given her name as Frau Tchaikovsky. Yes, Anastasia had had an extraordinary life, though I doubt M. Philippe could have foreseen its exact dimensions. None of the Romanovs but Niki's sister Olga would see her, and then denounced her as a fraud. Olga had known Anastasia best, having been the one member of the family still visiting Niki and the girls even as late as 1913, when the family summered, as usual, at Livadia, where she gave Anastasia painting lessons. But it was hard, you see, to know for certain if Frau Tchaikovsky was in fact Anastasia, as girls change so much in appearance between the ages of twelve and twenty-seven, even girls who had not seen their families murdered and who had then crawled across Russia to Berlin. And as Niki and Alix broke completely from the rest of the family after the tercentenary of 1913 over the issue of Rasputin, no one saw the girls after that. By 1916, Niki was no longer even exchanging Christmas presents with his brothers and sisters and cousins and their families. But I saw Anastasia, in 1917, just before Niki abdicated. She was then almost sixteen. And so, I knew it was she in the train compartment. Or, rather, I knew an opportunist when I saw one. And why should she not have her opportunity? What harm was there in it? I stepped from the compartment and said, *I have seen the tsar's daughter*. In 1967 I said it again to the French director Gilbert Prouteau for his documentary *Dossier Anastasia*. He came to film right here in my bedroom. He addressed me as *Princess*. I was considered an expert, an insider, an authority on the Romanov family. More of an authority than he knew. *Yes,* I told M. Prouteau, *she had the tsar's eyes. I could not mistake them. I knew those eyes very well.* Ah, that made M. Prouteau very happy.

So. So. Where am I?

At the end of that summer of 1901, just before the emperor was due to join Sergei and the court for maneuvers at Krasnoye Selo, I knew I was pregnant. If I was pregnant with a son, this would change the tsar, me, and the country. So to prepare the way for this announcement, I brought the tsar sturgeon, black bread, and caviar to his bed. I found his cigarettes. I drew his bath. I would tell him while he lay in the tub, when his mind was relaxed and his heart open to me. In my mind's eye I could already see his smile, his slow disbelief turning to comprehension, and the birth again of hope and faith: he would have a son. When I came to the bedroom to tell him his bath was ready, he was still lying on his back, smoking, his slow exhalations sending long shots of smoke up to the high ceiling, which then disappeared halfway there. At my entrance, the tsar sat up and stubbed out his cigarette on the small porcelain dish with the remains of the bread and cleared his throat. *Mala*, he said, *I have something to tell you.* And so, of course, I let the tsar speak first.

How many times have I replayed in my mind the different unfolding of events had I spoken first! For what he told me was that Alix was pregnant again and that M. Philippe, *la surprise grande*, had declared with dead certainty that this time she would have a son. I would have laughed had I not been choked by a spasm in my larynx that kept me from either breathing or speaking. Probably a good thing, for if I had spoken, I'm sure I would have said something to regret, as always. I felt the way I did a thousand times over when trumped, unexpectedly, at vint. Why, our afternoons together had been just another wild troika ride across a great plain, and that ride had brought us to this same place. I had been deceiving myself all summer. I had not had Niki to myself as I had thought. I had counted on his fidelity for at least the eight weeks that followed the birth of Anastasia in June, at least until Alix stopped the bleeding that follows childbirth. But no, the French butcher's son and the German baby-making machine had not waited even that long before their quest for an heir began in earnest once again. There were three of them in the bedroom at each coitus, Alix and Niki in the bed, M. Philippe in the corner, intoning some prayer. *I am nothing in myself. I act in the name of the divine.*

But for once I did not behave impetuously. I did not shriek at the emperor for relishing a diversion with me while still at the labor of sleeping with his wife. I did not pitch at him the hard sponge which I held in my hand. No, I closed my mouth around my secret. I, who had never kept a secret in my entire life, who ran to my father, to my sister, to this grand duke or that to prattle on about every perceived injury or splendiferous triumph—why, the hour after the tsar bedded me in 1893 I gave the telephone exchange my sister's number so I could crow to her—yes, the details of that night flew from my mouth, but this summer and its secrets lay under my tongue and had no feathers. I thought, *Better to wait, let Alix have another daughter, and then I will tell the tsar I had had his son.*

So, Niki dressed and left me that day for the Great Review at Krasnoye Selo knowing nothing, and I have no memory of what else he said to me or what I said to him, whether he took the bath I drew for him or not, whether I watched him dress or not, or whether we kissed goodbye. I knew only that he would return to Alix and remain by her side during her confinement, and I would not see him for a long time. As soon as he disappeared over the bridge, I began to worry. What if I did not have a son? Another daughter would be of little interest to Niki and that lack of interest would not be enough to counter the scandal I was certain to endure. Not that I was that much afraid of scandal. Still, this would be scandal on a far grander scale than *Will Mathilde wear a hooped petticoat?* In this scandal the tsar had returned to his mistress and given her a child.

Society women who carried illegitimate children as the result of an affair retreated from public life, went abroad for the birth if they could, and adopted out their children. A woman who was a mistress gave birth at home and raised her child at the fringes of society, employing her protector's connections to ennoble her child or find for him a place at court, in the Guards, or in the diplomatic corps. Even the child of a servant and an aristocrat could find some position—why, the governess of the tsar's own children was such a one as that. And girls who had no protection, such as the poor girls in the ballet who had been made pregnant by the young officers who abandoned them, well, those girls were dismissed and went home to their families, and each in her own way struggled with the disgrace. I did not fit exactly into any of those categories. I was a mistress, but my child did not belong to my protector. I was a dancer who had been made pregnant, but my impregnator was not a young officer but the tsar. If Alix and I both had sons, she would campaign to send me and my son into exile, probably to Paris to live side by side with Ekaterina Dolgorukaya and *her* son who had some claim to the throne. But what if I were not carrying the tsar's child? What if I carried the child of, say, Grand Duke Sergei Mikhailovich? If I had a daughter, Sergei would find her a husband from one of the great Russian families, for I would not subject her to the limited life of the theater, and if I had a boy, well, the possibilities were endless for a boy. My child could study at the Alexander Lyceum or at the Corps des Pages. He could join the Guards. He could have a career at court. And if Alix should have another daughter, well, that would be another story still. My son could be tsarevich. But for now it was better for my son to be the son of Sergei Mikhailovich.

You must see how I could not let conscience overwhelm expediency—not that I ever had—and on Sergei's return I said only that I had rested those summer weeks while he was gone at Krasnoye Selo, putting the troops through their exercises, absorbed by that world of men, weapons, and uniforms to which all Romanov males periodically retreated. If Alix had not given birth that summer, Niki would have been there with him, with all of them, instead of rolling around in bed with me, his Cossack bodyguards playing cards in my stable the only witnesses to what were supposed to be the tsar's long rides through the countryside. Yes, I took Sergei back into my bed with a haste and a false ardor that made him smile. Yes, I licked at him with my black tongue and I rubbed my ash, coal dust, and sooty pebbles all over him, and he only smiled and said, *How you've missed me, Mala*, before my body spit him into a sleep where he lay spent, so terrifically unaware of the malignancy of me.

By late October, my body had begun to change in ways only I could notice but soon enough Sergei would, as well. The theater season began, too, and though I could hide my pregnancy for now beneath my high-waisted tutu if I took care with the profile I presented on the stage—thanks be to God we did not perform in the leotards of today—eventually, I would have to withdraw from the season with some excuse of illness and with a more intricate fabrication for Sergei. I chose a gray afternoon as we rode in his carriage on Nevsky Prospekt during the usual promenade—in a few years more the carriages would be joined by motorcars, but for now we shared the wide boulevards with bicycles and *drozhkis* and horse-drawn taxis called *izvozchiki* and troikas and electric streetcars. I wore, like all women who rode in these contraptions, a veil that shielded my hair and face from wind and grit. Better to be veiled when one is two-faced. The rains of September had gone; the November snow had not yet arrived. It was neither here nor there, a good day for a lie. Strolling about us were officers in their winter uniforms with gray mantles, men in greatcoats and dark caps with cockades to signify their rank, students in their black cloaks, peasant men in belted tunics and sheepskin jackets, *muzhiki* in red shirts. Peasant women in kerchiefs carried their children, and governesses—foreign ones and Slavic girls—led their charges by the hand or in a small parade and the ones with infants pushed elaborate buggies. I touched at my hair, at my wrists, at the spot beneath my collarbone. As I opened my mouth, the tall slender windows of the city watched me from the four-story buildings that lined the streets. *Sergei, I'm carrying your child*, I said, and the hot words scorched the material of my veil. I held my breath. Would he believe me? He turned to me, his bearded face suffused with joy. Ah, yes. He believed me. Terrible. We had to hurry to my house on English Prospekt to drink to the child's health, Sergei pouring the vodka into the little jeweled glasses Niki had bought me as a housewarming present ten years before.

But don't pity Sergei too much. He could have offered to marry me yet he did not. A morganatic marriage to me would have jeopardized his income and his titles. But he would put his name down as father on the child's birth certificate, give my child his patronymic, which no Russian child can be without. It was like an identity paper, and with Sergei's patronymic, Sergeivich, my child's future would be assured.

Unfortunately, of course, I gave birth a month too soon, in June, at Strelna, during the white nights, in the heat and privacy of my dacha. In an act of deliberate impudence, I had covered the walls of my bedroom in a silk with the same floral pattern Alix had selected for her bedroom at Tsarskoye—green wreaths dotted with pink flowers, each one tied up with a pink ribbon, or so Roman Meltzer, designer to the crown, had described it to me—and the flower-and-leaf-covered walls seemed to breathe with me as I paced. Sergei, alarmed by what he thought was this emergency of a premature delivery, had called in his brother Nicholas's private doctor (for Nicholas, in addition to being a homosexual, was an inveterate hypochondriac), a doctor who demanded I lie flat on my back in bed, a command I promptly disobeyed. I could not obey him. Instead, like a peasant woman, I walked the room, my fingers sliding against the silk walls, the green leaves as prickly as if they were real leaves beneath my wet fingertips, the bright print of the flowers and bows deepening and seeming to bleed. This kind of pain was unknown to me, this pain tightening across my abdomen, this pulling at my tailbone. Peasant women in labor, I'd heard, tied themselves under their arms with rope and hung themselves from the rafters of a barn to enlist gravity as midwife. I understood the impulse. Some gave birth in the fields, stepping away from their plows to squat. But I had a doctor who treated the imperial family and who implored me to lie in a dignified manner flat on my back.

As I lay beneath the sheet that protected my modesty and blinded him, with his unwashed hands he periodically checked the progress of my labor. I would be sick with childbed fever for a month following the birth from his ministrations, my body weak and rubbery and my brain dark. My sister was the only one I could stand to have in my humid bedroom, the only one in my family not mortified by the disgrace of my confinement. While Sergei paced on the veranda, she distracted me, retelling from memory the old stories she used to read me when I was a child, the Russian fairy tales, about Grandfather Frost whose breath makes thin icicles and who shakes the snow to the earth by rustling the long hair of his beard, about the Snow

Maiden who rises from that snow and melts each spring, about Baba Yaga, the witch who inhabits a house that stands not on stone or dirt but on chicken feet, and so the house could be turned to face north, south, east, or west, depending on Baba Yaga's fancy. But any way I turned, north, south, east, or west, I found only pain.

Somewhere during this long day children played in the gardens of the villas around me and lovers took little green boats across the lakes between the islands and the boatmen sang for pay, and on a barge a concertina band played as it did on summer evenings, and on a veranda I could not see a gramophone was cranked and bits and pieces of its music turned to splinters and pierced the air. At night there was no sun but also no darkness, the sky streaked magenta, blue, and pearl; the yellow of the Russian virgin's bower with its spidery bell-shaped blossoms did not disappear and the birds did not hide themselves. I did. In my room the wet heat came off me and no number of cool towels could stanch it. Although there was only Julia in my room, I saw others—the shadows and outlines of bodies, the flicker of a face—just as I sometimes see today, now that the dead are arriving to sit with me. By the early hours of the night I understood I might die; my labor was going on too long. I was being punished for my duplicity, which I longed now to confess, and I began to pray, *Gospodi pomilou*, Lord have mercy on me. But my body was strong—I had my father's robust health and I would have his longevity, though I did not yet know this—and finally, between one and two in the morning, the earth opened between my legs and my son was born.

My sister caught my boy as I squatted silently, clinging to a bed post, while my doctor smoked cigars with Sergei in the next room until the baby's cries hurried him in, and she and I whispered to each other, *It's a boy, it's a boy.* And though she shared in my delight, she did not know the whole truth of it. *Look at his fingers, look at his feet, look at his face, his beautiful round face.* My son had the wide Russian face of most Romanov babies, and a widow's peak of hair that lapped at his forehead. My sister held him to me so I could kiss him there. By age six, he would retain only the broad forehead; the rest of his face would narrow, chiseled into a long triangle. I whispered *lyubezny*, my dear, and *milenki*, my little darling, to the son I had dreamed of having. If I were married, I would have lit then for him the candles I saved from my wedding, as a symbol of his parents' love to light his safe passage through the world. If I were married, I would wrap my child in the shirt his father had worn just the day before today, another old Russian custom to symbolize the father's protection offered to his newborn. But there were no candles or shirts for my son.

And when the doctor ran from the room to tell Sergei that the baby was a boy and, no, quite robust and certainly full term, Sergei, my sister said—for she had followed the doctor with the baby in her arms—blanched, for he could count backward as well as I to the summer he was gone. He put out his cigar and, without even looking at the baby she held, went to the stables, and to my sister's amazement, saddled his horse and rode away from the dacha, from Strelna, from me. I suppose I had thought nothing could take him from my side. *The doctor's a liar*, I railed to my sister, *he's trying to ruin me*, as I struggled up from the bed in time to watch from my window as Sergei rode his horse through the garden and, I worried, might ride it into the sea. It looked as if God would punish me, after all.

My mother came to visit me at Strelna for the first time the day after my son was born. She had never come to my dacha before or to English Prospekt, out of moral principle, but when my sister reported I was sick and all alone, having been abandoned by Grand Duke Sergei, my parents' worst fears were realized and my father dispatched my mother to nurse me and then bring me home. For now, Sergei still paid the expenses of my house and dacha, but who knew how long he would continue to do so and how could I afford either on a dancer's salary? My parents wanted to move me back to Liteiny

Prospekt with my illegitimate son, whom they said my sister and her new husband would adopt. For Julia had married her beau, Baron Ali Zeddeler, that very year and she had become a baroness, and I, for all my conniving, was nothing but my parents' disgrace. My mother sat by my bed, and in my sickroom I breathed in her soft skin and her lilac scent. Too ashamed to look at her, I slept or pretended to. I was too weak to talk or to eat. My mother had to feed me by tipping a spoonful of broth into my mouth as I lay there, just as Alix had done for Niki. Then my mother tucked my son into bed with me and crooked my arm around him, cinching us so close I could not help but inhale the intoxicatingly sweet smell of him. I was lucky, she told me. I had a healthy son. And whatever shame his birth caused me could not compare to the pain of a stillbirth or a dying child. I've told you she had thirteen children. What I didn't tell you was that she buried five of them, my brother Stanislaus when he was four years old, and four other children in their infancies, children from her first marriage. She had had to place each little child in a box in the ground and let the rain pour over him, let the sun bake the earth but leave him cold. That, she said, was unbearable, not this. And I suppose it had been, for looking at this round-faced infant, his mouth working as if to suck even in his sleep, I could not imagine him in a box or anywhere but in the crook of my arm. Niki's father, on the twenty-first anniversary of the death of his second son, Alexander, an infant who had not been even one when he died, wrote to his wife of his intolerable pain that their boy was not with them, that he was not there to enjoy his days with the other children, their other boys, that they would never have their angel with them in this life, that this was a wound that would never close. Alexander III. The bear with a trunk like a barrel, a forehead like a stone wall.

Sergei, too, had lost what he thought was his child and his grief was so great it drove him over the hedge in my garden and onto the High Road. Ali had told my sister that Sergei had wept to the tsar that I had betrayed him, that I had given birth to a son of another man and that he was now lost, and that the tsar had held him and said nothing. But Niki must have known then that I had given him what he had wanted. At times it seemed the tsar and then Sergei appeared at the foot of my bed on horseback, thundering over me, and then like Hades, one of them swept up my son, and, cloak flying, made off with him while I wailed and walked the empty ground they left behind. I left a damp mark wherever I lay in my bed, and when eventually I recovered, the bed was thrown out, the mattress burned, and every piece of furniture and each wall wiped down with disinfectant.

When I was well enough to lie on the couch, Grand Duke Vladimir began to walk to my dacha each afternoon to visit me, to stroke my hair, and when I could sit up, he read to me, and when I could hold cards, we played *mushka*, and when it came time for the baby to be christened and I had no name for him—I could not call him Sergei, and I could not, though I wanted to, call him Nicholas—the grand duke said, *Give him my name*. On that day, July 23, he presented my son with a cross hung on a platinum chain, the crucifix itself a dark green stone hacked from the Urals and polished in a Petersburg shop. And so I knew Vladimir would protect me and that I would be able, despite my disgrace, to return to the stage. His attentions to me, of course, did not go unnoticed, and the rumors began that my son was his, and Miechen tightened her lips whenever someone whispered my name. Would she tighten her lips still further if she knew Niki was my son's father, my son's paternity pushing her yet one square further from the throne?

During this time, also, my sister told me Sergei had begun an affair with a woman he had known a long while, Countess Barbara Vorontzov-Dashkov, who had married into an old and important family of Moscow *boyare*, long associated with the court, and at this news my heart shrank like a desiccated old nut in its shell and it rattled there in its place behind my rib cage. Niki's father had years ago bought the old Vorontzov estate in the Crimea, with its waterfall, its pine tree forests, its view of the Yalta harbor, and its French château, done Third Empire–style, and Sergei and Niki had played there and at the Winter Palace and Gatchina with Barbara's future husband, Vanya. They, along with the other Vorontzov-Dashkov children, the Sheremetiev children, the Dariatinsky children, had run on the palace lawns, ridden the miniature railways, taken tea at the Huntsman's Lodge. Niki and Vanya had each married, but Sergei had not. And now Vanya was dead and his wife was a widow and in her Sergei found another vulnerable woman to love. I did not know whether the countess visited Sergei at his palace or he called on her at her mansion on the English Embankment. I did not know if their love-making involved a bed or a garden bench, the sound of a clock chiming or the smell of crushed rose petals, but in 1905, the countess went to Switzerland, where she quietly gave birth to Sergei's son, whom she named Alexander. At his birth, he was adopted by the countess's friend Sophie von Dehn. Why did the countess not keep her son? Why did her liaison with Sergei not end in a marriage? Wait, and I will tell you.

Now August 1902.

I sat on my veranda, my tiny son, my faithful little man, in my arms, and I prayed one thing over and over, that Alix would have a daughter.

But prayers are rarely answered as you request. For Alix, alas and alack, had that summer no baby at all.

In early August, Alix began to bleed and though she bled and bled, there was no baby. It was, the doctors said, simply her *Mrs. Beasley*,

as she called her monthly, after nine months of what she had thought
was a pregnancy. When her waist had thickened and her breasts had
swelled, she had refused all those medical doctors access to her body.
She had admitted only M. Philippe, who had pressed his hand to her
womb and said, *You are with child*. And she had not wanted the doctors to contradict this, to in any way impede the progress of the necessary, the essential fantasy, and so only M. Philippe, who had been
decreed here in Russia by one of Niki's *ukazy* a doctor of medicine
and who had been made a state councilor, observed the progression
of this phantom pregnancy. I suppose even a tsar's decree cannot
make a doctor of a charlatan. Perhaps Alix had guessed where Niki
spent those long summer afternoons while she nursed Anastasia,
and so she had hastened too soon to try for another child. Her pregnancy had long ago been announced and all the country was awaiting
the birth of the tsar's fifth child. When a bulletin was published, finally, on August 20, explaining away the hysterical pregnancy of the
past year as a miscarriage, the wildest rumors began to circulate in the
capital: the empress had given birth to a monster with horns, to yet
another girl who was spirited out of the country, to a stillborn buried
on the grounds of Peterhof under cover of night. I ask you, was the
truth of it any less fantastic?

No, there was no child buried or sent away. That fate belonged to
M. Philippe, with the black hair and the black moustache. At last
Niki had had enough of the *znakhar*. Philippe's last words to them:
Another will come to take my place.

His prediction was not as outlandish as you might imagine. The
sorcerer, the holy fool, the idiot *muzhik*, the peasant through whom
God speaks, the madman who is not mad but prescient—these are
men for whom Russia has long had tolerance. Wearing rags and

chains, they wander from village to village on pilgrimages, fed by handouts, sleeping in the open or by a borrowed fire, begging a few kopeks from some peasant or prince who hopes to buy a bit of grace. On occasion, these fools and spiritualists were brought to a palace to pray or to rebuke or to heal. In the Petersburg of my time, the two princesses from Montenegro who married cousins of the tsar—they were known as *the black sisters*—brought with them to Russia along with their dowries their interest in the occult. It was they who brought Mitka the Fool, Philippe Vachot, and, finally, Rasputin to the palace. In Montenegro, they claimed, witches and sorcerers lived in the forests and they could speak with the dead and see the futures of the living. They and their friends at court held séances in closed rooms or hung on the ravings of spiritualists in trances. Alix, the German-English Alix, found all of this to be nonsense, until her desperation for an heir reached a high-enough pitch, until she turned one wall of her bedroom into an iconostasis before which she prayed, as if in church, for God to give her a son, and then the gates to Tsarskoye Selo swung open to these peasants, these *startzy*, to whom she surrendered utterly.

You could say, I suppose, that M. Philippe *had* wrought a miracle— for me! I sat down and wrote a note to Niki, which I gave to my sister without a word and which my sister gave to her husband, Ali, to deliver to the tsar. Ali was quite close to Niki, you know. On the eve of Niki's coronation Ali was one of five Guards officers invited to join the tsar at his uncle's estate at Ilinskoe. My sister's marriage could not have worked out better for me. I needed a new courier now that Sergei had vanished. And Ali personally handed to the tsar my note, which said simply: *Come see your son*.

So, when the birds began their annual migration from Petersburg to the more temperate climates of the Crimea and Persia and Turkey, for the weather, which had been warm, had suddenly turned cold and soon it would begin to rain, as it does for weeks and weeks until one longs for snow, which at least brings light to the city but does not, for some reason, feel as wet, and when Niki returned from the provinces of Rishkovo and Kursk, where he had toured monasteries and hospitals and governors' houses, the chief of police called me to say Niki would be coming to Strelna and the police would close this afternoon the highway between Peterhof and my dacha, so that Niki, before he went home, could make one last official visit, this one to me, at my dacha, where I had remained, later in the season than usual, out of sight.

I had been waiting for him since noon, uncertain exactly when he would arrive, and by now the light had already begun to fade. When I finally heard the cry of my stableboy's greeting and the slog of the tsar's approach to my house from the stables, I opened the door to greet him—and there was the shock of the sight of him—tall in his *papakha*, his face ruddy from the cold, his eyes a sparkling blue—and I thought, *Will my desire for this man ever leave me?* He kissed me on both cheeks, the scent of his bath oils still present on his chilled skin, present even at the end of the day, and when I put my hands to my cheeks against the cold he left there, he laughed. *My Little K, did I chill you?* And I wanted to kiss the tips of his fingers but instead I took from him myself his *papakha* and his greatcoat, which I handed over to my houseman to clean and brush, and off the man went trembling with the honor. Niki looked at me, one part of his mouth still smiling, and he said, *So, Mala, I've heard a rumor that you have given me a son.* I laughed with surprise—our meeting was going to be lighthearted, not at all like the weather or the weather I imagined inside the palace at Peterhof. And the tsar said, *Does he look like you or like me?*, teasing a bit, but I detected a stress note beneath that tone—remember, I have been listening for the notes beneath a melody all of my life—and so I said, teasing also, *The sovereign will himself decide*, and I brought him my son, almost four months, sleeping, swaddled in his blankets, and just the sight of him sent milk to my breasts, which were bound up with strips of cloth to prevent exactly this. My maid followed me, carrying the cradle, and when she set it by the tsar, I placed my son in his arms.

And around me it seemed the house, even the earth, wobbled. Niki bent his head over our child. My son did not look a Kschessinsky. He was made of different parts, Romanov parts. He had the tsar's ears, which narrowed almost to a point and bent outward at the top, the tsar's same straight, small nose, not the pug nose of some of Niki's daughters, handed down to them from their grandmother but skipping over my son, nor the long nose of their own mother. And as my son grew, when people passed him, they would say, *That must be the emperor's son*, that's how much he came to resemble the sovereign. This Niki now was discovering for himself. *Look*—and he held up the baby's palm against his own—*he has my fingers*, and then, as if the thought suddenly occurred to him, he opened the baby's diaper, and at this my laughter pealed out of me like a bell and rang around the room.

I have a son, Niki smiled. *I have a son.* And he looked about him as if to tell someone the news, but I was the only one there and so he told it to me.

Yes, I said. *You have a son.* Niki stood with him and my son kicked spasmodically and stretched and contracted his small arms, his little fists the fists of a tsarevich, and Niki spoke.

Maletchka, why did you tell poor Sergei Mikhailovich you were having his child?

Did you want two sons by two mothers? I asked. *Are you that greedy?*

And the tsar laughed.

I said, *What does Sergei know?*

He thinks it's the son of the prince of Siam—or of the Hussar Nikolai Skalon.

Two men I'd had flirtations with in 1899 and 1900.

But since he doesn't look Siamese, Niki said, *and as Skalon is long dead, the boy must be mine. What is his name?*

When I told him, Niki said immediately, *We shall call him Vova*, using the diminutive. We. So Vova would not be adopted by my sister and her husband. Niki put the baby in his cradle and then he knelt, abruptly, before me and kissed my hands, and at this, the heavens released their heavy rain, which rushed to meet the treetops, the grass, the roof, the windows, the doors, the cobblestones, the garden, the High Road, its cousin the gulf, and the rain also fell upon the crowns of the triple-headed golden eagle on the cupola of the Grand Palace at Peterhof.

By the first snowfall, Niki had bought for me three plots of land on Petersburg Island, across the Great Neva, across from the Winter Palace, at the corner of Kronversky Prospekt and Great Dvorianskaya Street. The purchase of the land was kept secret. It was not registered in my name so as not to draw attention to the 88,000 rubles paid for it, which everyone would know that I—abandoned by Sergei Mikhailovich—could not afford. This side of the city owned no metal works or electricity plants or printing presses, only a smattering of new mansions amid the old wooden houses that Peter the Great had once decreed were to be the only type of house to be constructed in this part of the city, as the granite from Finland, the marble and travertine from Italy and the Urals, the porphyry from Sweden, and the sandstone from Germany were to be used only for Admiralty Island, for the imperial section of Petersburg, demarcated by its canals, the Fontanka and the Moika, and by its avenues, and by the two palaces of the tsar, the Winter and the Summer, and by its stone. And so until 1830, little else was built on Petersburg Island but wooden shacks for the workers, a wooden fort, a wooden house where Peter himself had lived while his city was assembled. Even after that, the land remained barely developed. But when the Troitsky Bridge was finished the next year in 1903, it would connect the island to Peter proper and the building of mansions would begin in earnest, and mine would be one of the best of them, built by the court architect, Alexander von Gogan, and taking a silver medal from the city for its art nouveau design. From my new property, Vova and I would look across the Neva to the Fortress of Peter and Paul, the Summer Garden, the Champs de Mars, the Vladimirichi Palace, the New Mikhailovsky Palace, to the Winter Palace itself.

So that Niki could visit us discreetly, whenever he wished, he planned to have a tunnel dug beneath the Neva, stretching from the basement of the Winter Palace to the basement of my new palace. I hear that visitors to my mansion, now the State Museum of Political History, to this day ask to see the entrance to the secret tunnel that once linked the palace of the dancer Kschessinska to the palace of the tsar. Political history does not interest them. I interest them. The secret passage, the underground tunnel, was not without precedent, given our Russian winters. In Moscow, tunnels connected the Yusupov Palace and the palace of Niki's uncle, Sergei Alexandrovich, with the Kremlin. In 1795, a five-hundred-foot tunnel was dug between the basement of the Alexander Palace at Tsarskoye Selo and its kitchen, located on the other side of the garden. In 1814, the engineer Marc Brunel proposed to Alexander I that a tunnel be built under the Neva, and when the emperor decided to build a bridge instead, Brunel built a tunnel under the Thames. So the Neva would now have its tunnel, and Kschessinska would soon have her palace. Until then, I would have to satisfy myself with Niki's infrequent visits to my dacha, where I lingered, out of sight, as out of sight was the only place Niki could see me, and where, once or twice, I managed to persuade him to spend a genial hour in my bed. Yes, yes, I agreed. I must be patient. But patience, I will admit, was not my strong suit.

Almost all the great emperors had two wives, you know—Mikhail Romanov, Alexei Mikhailovich, Feodor Alexeyvich, Peter the Great. Not that Niki said anything *directly* about this to me, but I understood it to be a possibility, as he must also. Of course, the first wife must be disposed of. Peter the Great's first wife did not have the grace to die, and so after almost a decade of marriage he forced her to move into a convent and take the veil. Later, Peter married a peasant girl who worked in the regimental laundry. It was *her* son who became the next tsar. Did you know that at the end of his short life, Niki's grandfather was maneuvering to make Ekaterina the empress, to place in the line of succession their son, Georgy, instead of the son of his first wife, Alexander, Niki's father? Alexander II had never liked the cool reception the children of his first wife gave to his second one—or to his children with her. What would the country and his family bear? Could he pass over the thickset Alexander in favor of his delightful Georgy, son of the love of his life? Niki would have to maneuver equally delicately. Yes, first he would make me a palace. Then he would give me a title—Princess Krassinsky-Romanovsky. Then he would pack Alix and her herd of girls off to Paris—or return her, daughters hidden under her big skirts, to Hesse-Darmstadt, where they could all become Lutherans if they wished. Yes, if Alix did not want a second wife for Niki she would have to give him a son. *Tant pis.*

To prepare for my fabulous future, I decided to retire from the stage (as if anyone could forget I had once danced upon it) at the end of the season. In 1700, perhaps, the empress could be a laundress, but in 1900, she could not be a dancer.

My sister had already retired with my parents' blessing, although she had done this after twenty years at the theater and with the receipt of her pension. But when I went to Liteiny Prospekt to tell my father that I would retire, he was not happy with this latest enterprise of mine. I trapped him in the ballroom where he gave his dancing lessons—the little children were just filing out, ribbons crooked in their hair, to meet the governesses who stood in the ante-room holding their charges' fur-lined coats and fur-trimmed felt boots. The large ballroom stood luminous and humid and within it my father a tall willow in a frock coat. Those at the theater who gave ballroom lessons wore white ties and tails to do so, sometimes wear-ing them even to rehearsals if they had scheduled themselves too tightly, and these men were known as the *frock coat set*. My father looked thin, a little too thin, in his frock coat. He was getting old, I saw. Just four years before, he had celebrated sixty years on the tsar's stage. He had received so much tribute that it took four stagehands to hoist each chest of gold plates and silver cups from the orchestra pit to the table set out on the stage, where, at the interval, the curtain remained raised so the audience could appreciate the great esteem in which my father was held.

At that time I thought, *My father will dance forever*, but now I could see he would not. In a voice smaller and much less bombastic than my usual one, I told him of my plans, and before he spoke, he took a small towel from the chair by the mirror and carefully wiped at his face, wiping off his smile as well. I knew then what he said would not be good luck and good wishes. No. *Mala*, he said, *your sister, bless her, was a good-enough dancer. Let her play the mother. For you, Mala, you are a different story entirely. Remember, from your art comes your power*. Perhaps that was where he garnered *his* power, but I now had another source, one less ephemeral than art, and I would not give up my son to my sister, no matter how my parents pressed me. As a dancer one must eventually retire, but I could live into an old age greater than my father's and still die an empress. My father must have seen the obdurate look on my face, for he folded the towel over his shoulder and held out his arms to me. *Come, Maletchka*, he said, and for a few moments we took on the ballroom for a waltz; in the doorway a few students lingered to watch the tall man and the tiny lady make their slow, graceful circuit around the bare room, where they themselves, just a few minutes before, had struggled to execute the polonaise, the mazurka, the quadrille, this very waltz.

I KNOW YOU PROBABLY WOULD AGREE with my father that I was far too great a talent to leave the stage, but I must tell you the fashions of the stage were so rapidly changing, so it was not *only* for my son that I wished to leave it. The new director of the Imperial Theaters was Colonel Vladimir Teliakovsky, who had been director of the Moscow Theaters and an officer in the Household Cavalry. I had hoped he might, being an old-style aristocrat, have, as well, old-fashioned tastes, but unfortunately, when it came to art, Teliakovsky was a modern man, one who proceeded to open his purse to even more free artists—that is, artists not on the imperial payroll—than had his predecessor Volkonsky. And so it was *not* with a heavy heart that in early 1903 I returned to the theater to dance for one last triumphant time in a ballet mounted in honor of my retirement from the Imperial Theaters, for I could not retire quietly, just slip away after my confinement and the birth of my son. No, I had to first return, and then retire in style, raking my tribute off the tables on the stage.

Petipa had planned the ballet *The Magic Mirror* while Volkonsky was still director of the Maryinsky, and perhaps if it had been produced under his aegis the ballet would have been a success. But Teliakovsky now hired the modern artist Alexander Golovin, one of

those avant-garde painters known as *les décadents* to create the sets
and Teliakovsky allowed his own wife to design the costumes and
the modern composer Arsery Koreshchenko to write some of his
new symphonic music, and these parties carried with them in their
mouths and ears and eyes a taste for the new century, the twentieth
century of which we were all so newly, and some of us reluctantly, a
part. Yet *The Magic Mirror* itself was not a modern ballet, but a
nineteenth-century *féerie*, what Petipa did best, what *I* did best, a ballet of four acts, thirty scenes, and innumerable tableaux, its libretto
based on Pushkin's retelling of the German fairy tale *Snow White and
the Seven Dwarves*, save that in Pushkin's version the dwarves were
gnomes. The ballet was nineteenth century, its audience nineteenth
century, our circa-1860 blue and gold theater, named for Alexander
II's first wife, Maria, nineteenth century. Our attendants, standing
stiffly at the sides of the aisles and flanking each doorway costumed
in their powdered wigs, red livery, and high white stockings, hark-
ened us back a century earlier even than that. And the balletomanes this theater served did not like innovations in music or set
design or costume any more than they would like the other innovations of the new century, the political ones that threatened to strip
them of their wealth and status.

Petipa himself had complained the costumes made caricatures of
the dance artists: his immortals were wrongly costumed as nymphs,
his court ladies sported contemporary dress that made them all look
like café singers, the gnomes resembled hunchbacked trolls, the prince
in his gymnast's clothes was a dressed-up circus horse. During rehearsals Petipa fretted about the ballet that he should have done
instead, *Salammbo*, which he had wanted to mount before Volkonsky left, but Volkonsky had canceled it, and now Teliakovsky had
forced Petipa to use these decadent free artists whose determination
to modernize would destroy his creation. Poor Petipa. Teliakovsky
endeavored to soothe him. *No, no, M. Petipa, the ballet is perfection*.
Yet Petipa knew that his dryads and flowers and zephyrs and stars

and queens and kings and peasants and gnomes must be cushioned in a setting appropriately antiquated, and that, deprived of it, they became absurdities, as did the ballet master himself. Not to mention the ballerina.

I, of course, played Snow White, *the Princess by Her Father the King's Previous Marriage*. You see, families were full of previous marriages where the new wives wielded power over the children of the former wives and contrived to put their own children on the throne! The entire imperial family of 1903 Russia, old wives, new wives, recycled wives, and various permutations of children, were assembled in their boxes to witness my last performance on the Maryinsky stage. My father and brother, who were performing with me that night—for my father played *Her Father the King* and my brother Josef a Polish magnate in full court regalia—crowded at the curtain peephole with me. We did not know whom to look at first—Niki or his mother; Alix or her two oldest daughters, the grand duchesses Olga and Tatiana; Niki's sisters or their husbands—and the grand ducal boxes were full, as well, of Niki's uncles and cousins, his father's brothers and uncles and cousins, the Konstantinovichi, the Vladimirichi, the Alexandrovichi, the Nikolaevichi, the Mikhailovichi—why, even Sergei had come to the theater, though I saw he was there with a woman by his side, Countess Vorontzov-Dashkov, I presumed, an hourglass of jewels, silk, and compensation. Yes, it was a full conflagration of Romanovs gathered here to mark my exit! How astonished they would be—all but Sergei—if they knew of my plan to vault from this stage to their boxes, right to the imperial box! My father could drag me from my post as peephole spy only just before the curtain was raised.

The first act went well enough—a garden tableau in which men and women weave baskets and garlands and present them to the queen, the king, and the courtiers at their entrances—and for this scene, at least, Koreshchenko had composed a traditional and melodious waltz. When I entered, I bowed to the tsar, who nodded to me, and at his nod Alix frowned, and then to the audience at large, and at last to my father, the king, and to my subjects. I had my figure back, which all of Peter could see, and nothing, not even a scandal that would pitch any other dancer off the tsar's stage, could unmoor Kschessinska from the beautiful trappings of her theater. Act I, Scene I—all was well. But when the scene shifted to the palace park, the laughter began, provoked by the sight of a tall bush painted rather impressionistically on the canvas with wild daubs of green and yellow splotched here and there. The court was accustomed to seeing meticulous depictions of vegetation with decorously overlapping leaves and stems, and it was as if that one bush pricked at the dream of make-believe and the audience did not like one bit being awakened by something so little like a kiss. The snickers began and worsened when Petipa's daughter, not Marie, but Nadezhda, *tant pis*, began to mime. The Stepmother Queen is delighted with the magic mirror a merchant displays, a mirror with the power to reveal the image of the most beautiful woman in the kingdom. Petipa's daughters were character dancers rather than classical ones, but even in that category their talents were more limited than most. Despite their father's grace, they grew to be big clumsy bosomy girls, and so Nadezhda's miming was bad enough, but when the wicked queen gazed into the tall mirror and asked her famous question, *Who is the fairest of them all?*, just as the quicksilver of the mirror held my own image, the mirror abruptly shattered, shards of it making a brittle waterfall, pelting us as we struggled to continue our scene. A piece shaped like an arrowhead attached itself to the silk threading of my pointe shoe, and like a peasant farmer who stepped in manure, I had to shake it off. In their efforts to avoid the glass, the other dancers began to bump into one another and one courtier and then another fell flat on his derriere and the audience, at this point, began to laugh outright and then to talk, which we on the stage perceived only as a buzz that rivaled the discordant music from the orchestra pit.

During the interval we dancers retreated to our dressing rooms and to the wings to shriek and moan, and some, less concerned, to eat sandwiches!, while the audience outside made a ruckus in the small salons behind their boxes and in the hallways and foyers and smoking rooms. And as if all this were not happening, Colonel Teliakovsky came to my dressing room, as is customary, to present me with the tsar's gift upon my retirement. The imperial present, as it was known, was normally for a man a gold watch and for a woman a jewel set in gold, the setting stamped with the crown or the double-headed eagle, but I knew I would be getting a gift far better. As my father and brother bent over me, the feathered plumes of their hats skimming the bare flesh of my arms, Teliakovsky made a little ceremony of handing me the velvet jeweler's box, and with a little trepidation and much expectation, I unlatched the clasp. What would Niki have chosen for me? Inside the box lay a coiled serpent, its scales specked with diamonds as it strangled a cabochon sapphire, the polished convex shape of the gem a smooth blue apple. *The brooch*, Teliakovsky told me, *was designed by the empress herself for this great occasion. The serpent*, Teliakovsky continued into my silence, *is the symbol of wisdom*.

Really.

The serpent was a deceiver, a trickster, the offerer-up of apples.

The gem is very valuable, said Teliakovsky the salesman, *at least fifteen carats. A great tribute.*

Tribute? This was no tribute, this was an insult, a provocation, and my retirement performance had become an inadvert comedy full of broad slapstick and shenanigans with the audience dissolved in laughter. While my father *ooh*ed and *aah*ed and handled the brooch as carefully as if it were a real snake, my brother peered around him at my dark face. I snapped closed the jeweler's box and announced that I was going to dress and leave the theater, but my brother and father erupted, my brother in protest, my father in bafflement, *leave the theater?*, while Teliakovsky stood there with his mouth as open as the box had once been. I was Kschessinska, not some *coryphée*, Josef said, while my father nodded vigorously, and I was still for this last night the figurehead of the Imperial Ballet. I could not abandon it just because a few pieces of canvas did not please the antiquities out front. I've told you my brother was a modern man. But it was not just the scenery that bothered me. *What about this brooch?* I said. And Josef said, *Pin the brooch to your costume and show the empress you do not care*, and then he pinned it deftly to my bodice himself. *There!* So did I go home? No, I did not. I remained at the theater. I would dance Acts II, III, and IV. My brother had appealed to my pride. I could not walk out on my own farewell performance and I would not let Alix think her serpent had stung me.

By the time the curtain rose on the third act and the balleto-manes saw the grotto of the gnomes, which looked like a thick forest of tree stumps, cut flat across, some hanging from the ceiling like stalactites and others sprouting from the stage floor, all decorum had fled the house and the audience began to whistle, to catcall, to hiss. When the gnomes led me to their rough hut to dress me in a costume of leaves, they did so to a chorus of laughter from the boxes and parterres. I had been booed before on the stage by claques loyal to Preobrajenska or more recently those loyal to Pavlova, but this differed in the totality of the disruption. Although we were not re-sponsible for any element of the physical production, this act of pro-test did not punish Teliakovsky, Golovin, or Koreshchenko so much as the dancers. I and the other dance artists bore the humiliation of it, while Teliakovsky and his brethren cringed in the wings. M. Pe-tipa stood back there, too, slightly away from them, such an old man, eighty-four years, his waxed moustache a silvery white, his face trembling and his hands made into impotent fists. And so it continued throughout each scene, each act—and as I counted them earlier, they are many. There was no escape, no retreat for me as Grand Duke Vladimir brayed from his box, *Let us all go home!* I could see Colonel Vintulov quite clearly as he shouted, *Get rid of Teliakovsky—he will ruin the theater!*, his bald head slick with indignant sweat. And in the midst of all this the emperor and his entire family sat politely in the imperial box, watching the *pas d'action* on the stage, though their presence there did not suppress the hubbub in the slightest. Yes, I picked my way through my delicate variations with the zephyrs and the stars, my romantic pas de deux with the prince against the backdrop of the moon. I bit into the poisoned apple and laid myself in my glass coffin. I mimed my awakening and my betrothal in a castle hall painted in bold diamond patterns and ornamentation that looked like giant pineapples and cabbages, but I did all this in a state of mortification so extreme I have no memory of any of it. In the imperial box, the women spoke to one another occasionally behind their fans. Alix smiled now and then and lifted a hand to conceal a laugh. Niki, though, watched the ballet steadily, and at its curtain, amid a frogs' chorus of croaks and boos, I looked up at him. He pulled a droll face, *Who cares?*, and gave me a conspiratorial wink.

Right after the curtain came down, with the dancers crowded about me, Teliakovsky presented me with the theater's gift: a crown of gold laurel leaves, each leaf engraved with the name of a ballet in which I had over the years appeared, and wouldn't you know, the top front leaf read, *Le Miroir magique*. Gold or not, I snapped it off.

Teliakovsky blamed Petipa for the whole debacle and forced him to retire along with me after that night. Petipa consoled himself with the writing of his memoirs. I remained in Petersburg and consoled myself with the triumph coming to me soon on a stage far more vast and far more public than the Maryinsky's. I told my family all about it the next day to prepare them for what awaited me and, by association, them. *The tsar has come back to me*, I said, and they stared at me as if I had gone mad. They all thought the loss of Sergei and the disaster at the theater had robbed me of my reason. *He comes to visit me at my dacha.* My mother shook her head as if I were some sad creature. Even Julia looked askance at me and said nothing in my defense. *My son is the tsar's son*, I told them, *not Sergei's, and one day he might be tsar.* My father said, *Mala, enough*, as my brother scoffed, *Your son as the Tsar of All the Russias? Does your ambition know no bounds?* My judgment must have been toppled by all those grand dukes who supped at my tables and entertained themselves in my bed, he said. By no stretch of the imagination would Vova be anything more than the illegitimate son of a dancer, as marginalized by society as any other illegitimate son. Did I think that by all my tricks I could ease the circumstances of his birth? I snapped my fingers at him. My father instructed my sister to talk some sense into me. I stared at her indignantly. She had *seen* the letters I sent with Ali to the tsar. She had *driven* in my carriage past the three plots of land the tsar had purchased for me on Petersburg Island. Did she, too, think all this was fantasy on my part? Had she only been humoring little Mala? I suppose she thought that Ali had crumpled up in his fists my letters to the tsar and that my plots of land belonged to Baron Brandt, next door. I hated her looking down her long Kschessinsky nose at me. Well, she would soon see. Everyone would soon see. And everyone included Alix, who I knew would be doing her best to rid herself of me.

I didn't have long to wait.

For as soon as the Neva began its spring thaw and the ground was broken for the foundations of my grand new house on Petersburg Island, Alix began once again promoting the canonization of the monk Serafim of Sarov. Just the year prior, she had wanted the canonization done before the birth of what she thought would be her son, but the procurator of the Holy Synod, the head of the Russian Orthodox Church, had resisted. If the monk was *now* made a saint, she believed, he would intercede with God on her behalf and God would this time give her a son instead of a phantom. Serafim of Sarov, the monk from the Sarov Monastery who died in 1833 and who had lived as a hermit in a hut outside its walls, was said to have performed miracle after miracle in Siberia, and he had made prophecies, as well. He had predicted Niki's reign, named him and Alix as tsar and tsaritsa fifty years before they were born, had even predicted the tsar and all his family would one day come to Sarov. Alix believed if Seraf had known of her when she existed only in the mind of God, then he might also know her son, the child she was meant to have, whose spirit still waited to be called. In anticipation of this, Seraf would be made the patron saint of Nicholas and Alexandra.

By now she had lost all patience with the church. She did not care if Seraf did not meet the standards for sainthood. She did not care if his body was decomposed, when the corpse of a saint should be sweet and uncorrupted. When Bishop Anthony of Tambov, himself of the province where Seraf had lived, protested the glorification, Alix insisted the bishop be posted deeper into Siberia, like a silenced revolutionary. She told the procurator, *Everything is within the emperor's power—even the making of saints*. Finally, Niki had to step in: the canonization must be done if only to calm the tsaritsa. I knew Niki was only trying to pacify her, to make his eventual break from her easier if she believed they had tried everything and she had failed him utterly. So the church declared that hair, teeth, and bones were enough evidence of sainthood, in which case, of course, every corpse lying in a tomb would qualify; and despite the hundreds of letters of protest, the Holy Synod presided over a canonization it did not want. Let Alix canonize every wandering monk in all of Russia, I thought. Not one of them could guarantee her a son.

In July, while the beams and supports of my palace were being raised, the entire imperial family rode the train to the Arzamas station in the middle of absolutely nowhere and from there they climbed into open carriages to journey to Seraf's old monastery. Peasants, thousands of them, lined the unpaved roads, and Niki stopped the convoy to let the people greet him, kiss his hands, touch the sleeves of his tunic, call to him, *Batiushka, Father-Tsar*. Before his return to St. Petersburg, over a hundred thousand peasants would gather to see Niki in all his divinity, and he had been carried through the crowd on the shoulders of his aides so the people could see him without trampling each other. *Little brothers*, Niki called to them as he tried to make his way through the crowd before his adjutants finally lifted him to their shoulders. Each day there were miracles and cures in the cathedral, at Seraf's cabin in the wild, by the stream where seventy years before Seraf had scrubbed the dirt from under his fingernails. Children were cured of epilepsy, men with withered legs could walk, etc., etc., and Niki and Alix visited that miraculous stream themselves on their third night in Sarov. Naked, they submerged themselves in the dark, chilled water, guarded at a distance by a few discreet officers of the cavalry. Meanwhile, my house and I had become the subject of intense gossip in the capital. Drawings of its projected design appeared in the journal *Architect*. I had sent them to the editor myself!

Was I worried by all the miracles and prayers and bathings in streams? Not in the least. Not even in October when I learned Alix was pregnant again.

My house was built in the art nouveau style all the rage then—the pale brick shone like yellow gold in the sun, ironwork wreaths and boughs draped themselves above the many windows, the glass walls of the winter garden reached two stories, these windows closed by bronze latches I ordered extravagantly from Paris. My White Hall could host a concert. Yellow silk kissed the walls of my small drawing room, fumed oak the large. I had a dining room, a billiard room— for the tsar loved his billiards—a study, a dozen bedrooms upstairs, a kitchen and wine cellar below, a wing for the servants, a carriage house, stables, and a barn with a cow so my little tsarevich could drink fresh milk. The balcony of his room overlooked Kronoversky Prospekt. I hired a *dvornik*—a housekeeper—two footmen, a pantry man, a chef, two cooks, a scullery maid, a boiler man, a chauffeur, two maids for me, and a valet for Vova. My house was completed in the summer of 1904. I sold No. 18, English Prospekt to Prince Alexander Romanovsky, Duke of Leuchtenberg and one of Niki's many relations, and only when I crossed the Troitsky Bridge to Petersburg Island did my family then believe what I had been telling them. I even became the subject of a new ditty that circulated throughout the capital:

> *Like a bird you flew over the stage*
> *And without sparing your legs*
> *Danced your way to a palace.*

Yes, let Niki stand by Alix's side for her confinement, for I had danced my way to a palace.

And I would be in it, perhaps in a posture of repose on one of the chaises in my White Hall, when Niki came there, rather than to my dacha on one of his surreptitious visits, to tell me Alix had given him another girl, named Ekaterina or Elizabeth or Elena, or that yet again there was no baby at all! I would try not to whoop in triumph, *I, Mathilde-Maria, have won!*

———

Yet I had no sooner unpacked my clothes in my wardrobe room—
each outfit numbered by a little plaque above it—when the great
guns of Peter and Paul began to fire the traditional salvos that signaled a child had been born to the tsar. It was July 30. I ran to my
son's balcony and turned my ear toward Hare and Admiralty islands. No one in Peter listened more fervidly for their number than
I. Ninety-nine. One hundred. One hundred and one. One hundred
and two. And the guns did not stop. I thought at first I had mis-
counted, or perhaps I had been tricked by echoes peculiar to the location of my new house, but the salvos continued, so many of them
and for so long that I knew I had not been a fool at arithmetic but a
much bigger sort. By the 150th, I was weeping. By 210 I had composed myself. By 300 the telephone began ringing—have I mentioned
I had the prestigiously low telephone number of 441?—but I did
not take any of the calls from the artists at the theater or from my
ridiculous family who wanted to say, *Do you think it is true?*, and
who had no idea the disaster this event meant for me. By afternoon
confirmation that the tsar had fathered a son appeared in every newspaper: *By the manifesto of 28 June 1899 We named as Our successor
Our beloved brother the Grand Duke Mikhail Alexandrovich, until such
time as a son was born to Us. From now on, in accordance with the
fundamental laws of the Empire, the imperial title of Heir Tsarevich,
and all rights pertaining to it, belong to Our Son Alexei.*

Alexei. They had named him after Alexei Mikhailovich, Alexei I,
Alexei the Peaceful, Peter the Great's father, the gentle tsar Niki
had long admired. It was an unusual name for a Romanov, for
a family so full of Konstantins and Nikolais and Vladimirs and
Mikhails and Sergeis and Alexanders, but Niki worshipped the last
Muscovite tsar, the last one before his European-loving son Peter
stamped out the old Russian customs, had all the men shave their
beards and the women put on corsets, and set the two down to dine
and dance together as they did in *la France*. Why, at his own coronation Niki had sat on Alexei's throne encrusted with 750 diamonds!

But there was a reason the family had only sporadically given that name to its sons. The name belonged not only to the father of Peter the Great, but also to Peter's son, the son Peter had clandestinely murdered when he began to suspect his son might be plotting against him. This murdered Alexei was the one the people remembered when they began to whisper about the bad-luck name for the poor boy born to that woman who had come to them from behind a coffin.

I folded the newspaper back over the tsar's *ukase*. I went up the small staircase of seventeen steps that led to my bedroom suite in this house that was so newly mine and might so soon be mine no longer. I went into the very grand blue-and-silver mosaic-tiled bathroom that housed the great sunken tub I had built for the tsar and in which no one had yet bathed, plugged the drain, and turned on the faucet. I climbed in fully clothed, my plan unfolding before me as I enacted it. The water slowly covered my body, saturated first the fabric of my dress, then even the elaborate layers of my underskirts, and finally the silk of my chemise, my corset cover, and the canvas of my corset, all of which acted as weights. As the water rose, my hair and then my arms began to float toward the surface and when my head was fully submerged, I looked out at the rippling bathroom, its silver-and-blue mosaics shot with little rivulets of light. They would find me here, preserved like an oddity from Peter the Great's Scientific Museum, and my plaque would read *Former Mistress of Tsar Nicholas II*. I should have worn a better dress, but too late for that now. I should have been holding a crucifix in my hands, but too late for that, too. I opened my mouth to breathe in the water but at the influx of bathwater rather than air, my body exploded in outrage and I shot up, coughing. It appeared I did not have what it took to die, to disappear, which would clearly be better for everybody, except, perhaps, my son, now eating bits of chopped apple in the kitchen with my cook. With me gone and the tsar occupied with his legitimate son, Vova would in short order be adopted by my sister and shunted off into the ballet school like everyone else in my family, where he would vanish into that warren of a theater and emerge sixty years later an old man with a gold watch. Was there no other career for a Kschessinsky? No. Apparently not. Only if I were alive could I ensure this would not happen. Only if I were alive could I make certain Vova had the life he deserved. So I stood up, my skirts weighing a hundred kilos, and wringing what water out of them I could, I hoisted my leg over the edge of the tub. Dragging my dress behind me, I sloshed my way in my sodden shoes to my bedroom to pack for Strelna, as if it were time for my usual summer holiday. There I would figure out what to do next.

Yet within not even a week of my arrival at Strelna, where I had not even planned to be, the chief of police called to inform me he was closing the bridge from Peterhof to Strelna and that the emperor was on his way to see me. The police tracked the whereabouts of all persons of importance at all times. Why, they could tell you exactly whom the various ambassadors and grand dukes called upon each afternoon and exactly when. And so, of course, they knew I had left Peter for Strelna, and therefore so did Niki. And I thought, Niki's come already to take the key to my palace from me, to pay me another hundred thousand rubles. He has already drawn up more official papers for me to sign. But he had no papers with him when he arrived. Before I could even greet him, before he had even come up the steps of the veranda where I had gone to stand when I heard his horse, he said, *Mala, the baby is sick*. And when I looked at him uncomprehendingly, he said, *Alexei is a bleeder*, and he sat down abruptly on the bottom step and I came and sat by him. He put his head in my lap and the bright sunlight streamed down from the sky and slowly, slowly my former despair was bleached to pity. I stroked at the tsar's hair the way I had just stroked the hair of my child to put him to sleep for an afternoon nap.

This bleeding disease had made its appearance in Alix's family before. Queen Victoria and her daughters and granddaughters carried this disease in their bodies, for women were the carriers and men the sufferers and because these women married cousins who were princes and kings, the disease had infiltrated the royal houses of England, Spain, Germany, and now, apparently, Russia. When Alix was just a year old, her brother Fritzie had died from a fall he suffered in the morning that killed him by day's end. When she was twelve, her uncle Leopold fell and died of a brain hemorrhage. Just six months before Alix's son was born, her sister Irene had lost her son. It had taken Alix's nephew Henry, four years old, several weeks to die after a bump on the head, weeks of his screams and weeks of the most terrible helplessness suffered by his parents. Alix had gone, pregnant, to the funeral. Bad omen. So Alix knew if a child was a bleeder each fall, each stumble, each bang, each bump could mean weeks of painful bleeding, swollen knots of corrosive blood beneath the skin that could immobilize a joint, damage organs, even kill. Niki said to me that he should have married the French princess Hélène or the Prussian princess Margaret as his parents had wished. No mention, of course, of me! He believed now that this was why Alix had wept so uncontrollably on the day of their engagement. Fate held this black card at the back of her hand, out of sight, but Alix had somehow seen it. He himself was born under the sign of Job. He was that card. He was destined for a terrible trial. He would not receive his reward on this earth, nor would Alix. When her contractions began, Niki said, she was sitting on a sofa in the drawing room in the Lower Palace at Peterhof, and the mirrored panels hanging behind her spontaneously shattered and covered her with glass, just as the quicksilver of the stage mirror had done in my last ballet. One did not have to be Russian to see the omen in that. And all the while he spoke, I stroked at his hair and made unintelligible murmuring sounds, *there, there*, and I was glad he could not see my face, which I am sure shone with a slowly waking bliss. His son was sick.

He would not live long. It was not my life God wanted to take but Alexei's. Despite all Alix's efforts to thwart me, fate had intervened. Heaven did not want Alix's son to be the next tsar. Heaven did not want Alix as empress. Niki had left her at Peterhof and had come here to me. The key to my new house would remain in my pocket.

Come, I said to Niki finally, and I took his hand and led him to the nursery, where Vova, now two, slept, his cheeks two red apples, his forehead a charm. *Is he breathing?* Niki asked. *It's too hot in here, Mala.* I laughed. *He's breathing*, I told him, and I lifted our boy from his little bed and put him in Niki's arms. Niki rocked him standing there in the warm room. *We cannot see each other for a while, Mala*, Niki said over my son's small back. *I cannot undermine Alexei's legitimacy. He may live for some time. There is no way to know for certain.* Meanwhile, I would have my palace. The minister of the court would continue to transfer a monthly stipend to my accounts. He and Alix would have no more children. *We have enough daughters*, Niki said ruefully, *and the risk is too great for another son.*

Yes, the risk was too great. The House of Spain had two hemophiliac sons. The little princes wore padded suits to play in the palace park where the trees had also been padded but still the boys suffered. Both of Alix's sister Irene's sons were hemophiliacs; before his death, she had kept the younger son Henry hidden in the palace in Prussia to conceal the evidence of his illness, lest the country know both the heir and his brother were bleeders and the House of Prussia was riddled with disease. So Alix had decided she would do the same with Alexei. The next year, the family would move to Tsarskoye Selo and hide themselves in Alexander Palace, hide Alexei and his illness so completely that almost no one knew of it. It would be 1912 before even the children's tutor, Pierre Gilliard, understood what illness the boy suffered from, why he was so pale, his face so pinched, and why he spent weeks at a time in bed. Alexei's doctor, Eugene Botkin, never spoke a word of Alexei's condition even to his own family. Niki's family themselves for more than a decade would not know what was wrong with the boy. Photographs of Alexei were fed to the press, but he would rarely appear at state occasions, with various excuses given for his absence. And so the rumor-mongering commenced yet again: the child was retarded, an epileptic, the victim of a revolutionary's bomb.

As for *my* son, Niki issued a secret *ukase* granting him the status of a hereditary nobleman. And that was all Vova would be until the inevitable, the unspeakable, occurred, for which I waited, wickedly, impatiently, even lamenting the wait! I remember thinking, *Oh, if the theatricals at the Maryinsky had taken this long to create, the tsar would have sat in his box for decades with nothing to see.*

FOR THE GLIMPSE OF NIKI I longed for, now I was obliged to attend public events, and so in January 1905 I went to the Dvortskaya Embankment to watch the ceremony of the Epiphany. This blessing of the waters began the cycle of Carnival, an explosion of gaiety that climaxed with Butter Week, just before Lent. Soon booths would be set up on that very spot and in the streets and on the Champs de Mars, and the next few months would be boisterous ones. The peasants kept themselves alive between harvests with their sales at those wooden stalls, slapped up in a hurry and hung with bunting and flags, and jugglers and Gypsies danced between the booths for the kopeks we would throw. I planned to take Vova to watch the puppet shows where harlequins were clobbered on the head by villainous blackguards with sabers and clubs, to hear the Gypsies sing their folk songs, to stuff ourselves with blinis, *themselves* stuffed with caviar and slippery with butter, to feed Vova gingerbread or hazelnuts or Ukrainian nuts or Greek nuts roasted right out in the open on charcoal braziers just like the vendors do here in Paris, using their brass shovels to scoop the nuts into paper bags. You've seen the ballet *Petrouchka*? Then you've seen a Shrovetide Fair and the puppets upon which this ballet is based, the little harle-

quin Petrouchka, the Blackamoor with his sword, the Columbine-
cum-Ballerina with her stiff pink skirt. At one of the stalls, I would
buy Vova a caged bird and a wooden toy. Today, on the way to the
embankment, I promised him that as soon as Carnival began I
would find him a wooden cart with wheels that really turned, the
sides painted with the vivid red, yellow, and blue of eastern Russia.

The blessing itself was an annual ritual in which the tsar and his
family walked out onto the frozen Neva on a long red carpet that
ran from the Winter Palace, down the steps of the quay and over
the ice to a makeshift chapel, assembled of gleaming crucifixes,
plaster pillars, a wooden altar and silver chalices, and the banners
and icons of St. John the Baptist. Guards regiments lined the strip
of carpet and made a circle around the chapel. A hole in the shape
of a crucifix was cut into the ice there and the cold water swam
sluggishly beneath it, while snow dust blew across us above. On this
day, we pretended the Neva was the Jordan, and for once, the imperial guests waited inside the palace while the plain Russian people
stood witness to a ceremony. It was our day, a rare one, to be with
the emperor. Some women carried pitchers to fill with the Neva
water once it had been blessed: a child or a husband was sick or
crippled at home. Some women carried an ailing baby to be dipped
quickly into the freezing water and then swaddled in a fur lap robe.
I had brought Vova, though his only ailment was his illegitimacy,
and a dunk in the water would not cure that, nor would a glimpse
of the emperor cure what ailed me. Still, Vova and I waited anyway.
No guard stirred a finger or uttered a word but stood like lead soldiers, their heads bare and their helmets at their feet as the wind
whipped across the ice and rattled the props of the chapel.

Then exactly after the morning service in the palace chapel, the
bands began to play the national anthem and the soldiers we could
not see shouted out the salute and then Nicholas, looking quite re-
gal, led the imperial family and their Cossack retinue down the stone

steps of the quay to the river; from the women's jeweled *kokoshniks* floated long white veils, and it looked as if their souls floated behind their bodies, so pure as to be colorless, part of the gray-white sky. Niki's head, by tradition, was as bare as his guards', for today he played Christ ready to be baptized by St. John, and he played the part well, for didn't he, like Christ, suffer the dark knowledge of what was to come? The local metropolitan and his bishops and ar-chimandrites and priests wore gold vestments so grand one would think they, and not the emperor, stood at the head of the church, but the truth was Nicholas held the appointments of these church-men in his palm. From where I stood holding Vova, who wore a tiny beaver hat, the exact words of the liturgy were not distinct; only the sounds of the priests' voices skimmed over the ice on the scent of cloves and roses. The wind puffed up its lips and blew its cold, wet, voluptuous breath across the ice, as well, and Vova buried his face into the sable collar of my *shuba*. He buried his face because he was cold. He was too young to know shame, but soon enough he would begin to ask, *Where is my father?* And what would I answer? *Your father is far away*—for after all, is it not very high up to the tsar?—although at that moment he was less than a verst from us.

At the climax of the ceremony, the metropolitan dipped three times a large silver cross hanging from its long chain into the hole cut in the ice and with it he blessed us all. The bells from Peter and Paul chimed and the guns and cannons made their thunder, and the women next to me began to scream—at the sound, I thought at first—until I realized some invisible weapon had begun to pock the ice all about us. Small pieces of ice flew up and bit at our faces and hands, and Vova began to whimper. The women near me began to run, children tucked under their arms, slipping a little despite their felt boots, dragging with them their empty pitchers. We found out later that a terrorist had managed to substitute live ammunition for the usual blank rounds, and as the guns continued, some of it flew all the way over to where we were standing. The imperial party was sprayed with shrapnel, too, and they scattered in shock. On the quay I saw a policeman fall, his blood a red thread unraveling from the crimson carpet, and we could hear the windows shattering in Nicholas Hall, where the guests waited in court dress for the return of the emperor. I patted Vova's shoulder to soothe him and strained over him to see. I could not flee until I knew Niki was safe. I saw Niki was now surrounded by his guards; other guards encircled the rest of the imperial family, and when the cannons quieted, Nicholas moved through his party, calming its members, having his group, a bit like a woman with her dress mussed, gather and smooth itself and make a dignified recessional. I had never seen him called upon to lead in any public situation that had not been tightly choreographed— and it appeared his ten years as tsar had prepared him for this departure from the expected better than he knew. This, too, was part of being emperor. The office involved, after all, not only receptions and processionals and ceremonies but actual governance and the protestations against it. Niki at his coronation had spoken against the *senseless dreams* of those who, like the generations before them all the way back to the war with Napoleon, hoped to bring reform to the monarchical government of Russia. Perhaps Niki would find his way with as much aplomb through the jumble of that. When the imperial family vanished into the Winter Palace, the ice quickly cleared, but I lingered on it, stooped to pocket a piece of the shrapnel that lay there, unnoticed, the edges of the metal warm and jagged to the touch even through the leather of my gloves.

Have I mentioned at all that Russia had been at war that year with Japan? It's no wonder if I haven't. It's a war best forgotten. While Niki was building my house on Petersburg Island, he was also busy completing the Trans-Siberian Railway, shortening its planned route by laying track right across Manchuria, Chinese land that had obstructed the track's direct route from Irkutsk to Vladivostok, Russia's furthermost eastern outpost. The Chinese had been bribed with rubles and with the promises of an alliance with Russia against China's enemies and respect for her sovereignty. But while his men were laying the track, Niki decided in violation of that agreement to annex Manchuria, to make it another of his Asiatic conquests, which the Chinese, despite their protestations, were too weak to prevent. Had Niki stopped there, all would have been well. But he did not stop there. He wanted to claim the forests of the Korean peninsula, as well, to become master of even more Russian lands. After all, was he not tsar? Unfortunately, the Japanese also wanted those Korean forests, and so, when Niki refused to sign an agreement with *the yellow monkeys* to contain his interests to Manchuria and to leave the Korean forests to them, the Japanese attacked. The yellow monkeys that we had laughed at—in the newspaper cartoons our Cossacks scooped the Japanese up by the dozens in their fur hats—not only bottled up the Russian fleet and sank our ships in the Straits of Tsushima, a disaster Vladimir's son Kyril, a commander in the navy, barely survived, but also mowed down our men making their old-fashioned bayonet charges in Manchuria. It took seven months for the Baltic Fleet to sail around the world to reach Port Arthur to assist our men, endless days for supplies to travel the six-thousand-mile route by rail from the big cities of western Russia to the Manchurian-Korean border. Niki at one point sent his men a shipment of icons to aid them in battle—beautiful oval portraits of the Savior in gold chains—and at that, unpacking those boxes, a general had laughed, *The Japanese are beating us with machine guns but never mind: we will beat them with icons*. I suppose the war was the match to the tinder, and the shrapnel I held in my hand an artifact of an attempted assassination. The coming year would bring a wave of assassinations: Niki's minister of the interior, Plevhe; his Russian governor-general of Finland, Bobrikov; his governor-general of Moscow, his very own uncle, Grand Duke Sergei Alexandrovich; and later, his prime minister, Stolypin. Yes, these men would all be killed, though not yet the tsar.

Now for the tinder.

Just three days later, on January 9, it exploded when Father Gapon, a priest who had been working with the poor peasants laboring in the factories, felt compelled to lead these suffering people to the Winter Palace to tell the tsar of their sorrows. Gapon wanted the tsar to hear of the poisonous fumes that filled the unventilated factories, of the typhus and cholera spawned from the industrial waste, of the peasant children working sixteen hours through the long Russian night, of the machinery that tore out an eye or severed a limb, after which the worker was paid a few rubles and fired, of the searches the workers endured at the factory gates, of the floggings they endured for violations, the pay docked for using the toilet, the piles of clothes used as bedding in the factory barracks or the cellars and stairways where the workers slept like serf beasts at the mercy of their factory boss squires. The irony of Gapon's desire was that he was paid by the tsar's police to sponsor unions expressly designed to *keep* the workers enduring these conditions, to keep them from joining the radical Socialist Democrats and *their* unions, which urged the workers to revolt rather than endure. At Gapon's meetings, decorum reigned: the workers drank tea, recited the Lord's Prayer, sang the national anthem. But I suppose Gapon's pity for them ultimately overwhelmed his mission to subdue them, and so he dreamed up the idea to stage a great theatrical *allée*, to provoke a solution to their great enslavement. Their tsar would help them. It had been only because the tsar's windows looked out onto the beauty of the river that he had missed their misery. Or perhaps the enfilades were too many rooms deep and word of the workers' misery did not penetrate. Or perhaps the tsar had been too busy with the papers on his desk and the mighty worries of the war with Japan, his mind on matters far away, and so he did not see the suffering right there within a half verst of his study walls. But once he knew of the intolerable conditions under which the peasants toiled at his factories, their Tsar-Batiushka would surely hold out his hands and smooth everything over with the right strokes of his pen. For, after all, the tsar always says yes; it is his little dog that barks no. So with this hope pounding in his breast, Gapon and the workers gathered by the hundred thousand at six points in the city and proceeded on foot along the streets designed like the spokes of a wheel by the European architects of the beloved eighteenth century—Lambert, Trezzini, LeBlond—spokes that led to the Admiralty and to the Winter Palace, the hub of it all.

But Niki had no intention of hearing the pleas of the striking ironworkers and the workers of the electrical plants, had no intention of receiving this crowd. And why should he? Walking in the wilds of Sarov with his Rus peasants, his humble little brothers, he would allow them to touch his hands or kiss his shadow or tell him their troubles, but why should he have to receive angry rabble at the doors of the palace, especially rabble corrupted by socialists and intellectuals who cared nothing for the peasants and used them as tools for their own ends, ends the peasants knew nothing about?

Vova called me to his balcony when he heard the first of what sounded to him like a big parade, and I joined him there to watch the procession cross the Troitsky Bridge toward the palace. I pointed out to Vova how the men and women and children carried icons and portraits of the tsar and flags and banners, including one that stated, disconcertingly, *Soldiers, Do Not Shoot at the People!*, which the children at the front of the column gripped in their small hands. *Do Not Shoot at the People*. Posters had been pasted up around Petersburg inveighing against the march, and cannons had been placed in the palace square and cavalry assembled in front of the palace and in the Alexandrovsky Gardens, and twelve thousand soldiers had been posted along the streets, on Nevsky Prospekt, on the Troitsky Bridge, at the Neva Gate. The line of people marched as solemnly as a church processional of Holy First Communicants, past the soldiers and the Cossacks stationed along the bridge, while my skin began to tingle with foreboding. The Cossacks liked to kill and to kill at close range. Why do you think the tsar used them for his personal bodyguards? Bystanders at the edges of the bridge and the curbs of the street just beyond pulled their hats peaceably from their heads or crossed themselves as the column plowed past—after all, a priest carried a large cross at the head of the parade. The workers' petition had been sent ahead to their tsar and was later printed in the papers: *Sire, we come to thee to seek justice and protection. We are impoverished; we are oppressed, overburdened with excessive toil, contemptuously treated. We have reached that frightful moment when death is better than the prolongation of our unbearable sufferings. Batiushka, hear our plea.*

As Vova and I stood there, Vova dancing from the cold, I heard shots, the sounds faint but a fat number of them, and Vova began to pantomime the firing of an imaginary gun. I thought, *Surely no one would be firing on those women and children*, these men holding portraits of the tsar, but I called to my maid anyway to bring Vova inside, and he went off wailing that he hated me, that he wanted to stay and see, he wanted *to see the people*. I learned later that as the marchers approached the Narva Gates, a squadron of cavalry charged through that green arch that bore the figures of medieval Russian knights in their helmets, boots, and armor. And when the marchers still continued to press their way forward—for how easily can a crowd turn itself back?—remember Khodynka Field—the infantry pointed its rifles at the marchers, fired off warning shots, and then aimed into the crowd, suddenly, without any further delay. And who ordered this shooting of the people? Grand Duke Vladimir, *Emperor Vladimir*, monitoring the situation in his tall polished boots, brother of Alexander III, commander in chief of the Preobrazhensky Guards and of the St. Petersburg military district, father-disciplinarian of wayward dancers. To such a monarchist no demonstration by the people was permissible, no dissent tolerated. Hadn't I learned that myself? Though the crowd began to scatter and stampede in confusion, the cavalry continued firing and like a shock wave from a bomb, the disorder spread outward from the gates toward the Troitsky Bridge. From Vova's balcony, I watched the excitable Cossacks drive their horses right into the crowd stalled there and bring their whips and sabers down upon the hats of the men and the kerchiefs of the women and the blades split the face of one man into two faces and he fell with his faces onto the street. At that I bolted into the house where my son was waiting to flail at me with his fists and cry as if he had missed the sight of a pack of Siberian wolves skulking past his door. I held him, a small angry puddle, in my arms while outside in the pandemonium, people tried to flee back the way they came, back down Nevsky Prospekt, pressing themselves into the Alexandrovsky Gardens as if to hide among the trees or lose their pursuers on the garden paths, and the Cossacks and the mounted Guards cut through the procession and then back again, shooting so wildly that children, who, like Vova, had found themselves some high perch by which to view the parade, some tree or garden statue or top of fence, were felled like small beasts. In the middle of this chaos, Father Gapon, that *yourodivi*, that idiot, stood in the palace square in disbelief, his big crucifix at his feet, hundreds of bodies bleeding into the snow that stretched white and wide into the distance all around him, and cried out, *There is no God. There is no tsar.*

Ah, but there was a Tsar. He was at Tsarskoye Selo, playing dominoes. And I thought, *Perhaps Niki will not do as well with all this as I had believed.*

––––––

This day came to be known as Bloody Sunday, and the bleeding from it lasted all that year of 1905, the blood being all the loudly expressed dissatisfactions of the entire country—not only the factory laborers who requested decent hours and housing, but also the citizens angered by the costly war with Japan, the peasants who had survived the famine of the last decade and now claimed a right to the land they tenanted, the *intelligenty* who demanded civil rights and who, along with a few liberal noblemen, called for a national parliament, a national *zemstvo* in which they all, not only the tsar, had a voice. It seemed the whole country began holding meetings and coming up with manifestos to send to the tsar and his ministers, and to the Winter Palace were sent sixty thousand petitions, like the *cahiers*, the letters of grievance, sent by the French people to King Louis XVI in 1789, and all these letters asked the tsar for reform. The petitions for a cabinet of ministers and a Land Assembly of representatives of all the tsar's subjects came from the tsar's own ministers; the petitions for the redistribution of land from the squires to the peasants came from, of course, the peasants; and the petition for a Union of Unions in which every worker would belong to an association concerned with political freedom—lawyers, professors, clerks, bookkeepers, teachers, Jews, women, railroad employees, peasants—came from the liberals, the *intelligenty*. And these petitions were followed by action. More than a hundred thousand ironworkers and electrical workers struck spontaneously later in January, and once again I watched men march over the Troitsky Bridge, ten abreast, and for a few days we had no light. The schools had to be closed in February. In September the printers struck and so for weeks there were no newspapers, rail workers struck and there were no trains and no telegraph. So many of the previous revolutionary troublemakers had already been sent or had fled abroad to avoid arrest that a new cadre of leaders had emerged— the writer Gorky and the nobleman Prince Lvov and others like him who had long sought to help the peasantry and advocated reform. They wrote articles and gave speeches, and soon the agitation in the cities spread to the countryside. In Russia's provinces, in Tomsk, Simteropol, Tver, and Odessa, the great agricultural swath, the peasants cut down their squires' forests, took their hay, destroyed whatever machinery they couldn't load onto their carts, and stole their squires' crystal and porcelain and paintings and statues. The peasants of one village hacked a piano to bits and divided among themselves its ivory keys. Other manor houses were burned, their libraries and tapestries and grand pianos and oriental carpets turned to ash—and the houses they didn't burn, they desecrated, squatting to leave piles of excrement on the carpets and floors, smearing the wallpaper with their filthy hands. *We were here in your house*. The squires fled to the cities to petition the court for help, while in the countryside the skies turned ocher from the fires and the peasants like plowhorses pulled their loaded wooden carts of stolen goods across the fields. In Moscow the students at the university burned portraits of the tsar and hung red flags from the roofs of the buildings. Even in Latvia, in Finland, in Georgia, in my own Poland, there were strikes and barricades and street fighting from the people who had never enjoyed, but had simply endured, Russia's dominion. Yes, Russia's old unrest of the 1820s had returned, suddenly, and with a vengeance.

During this terrible year, Niki took Alix, Alexei, and the girls and retreated into the routine of the imperial year—winter at Tsarskoye, spring at Livadia, summer at Peterhof, Poland in autumn for the hunt, back to Tsarskoye for the long Russian winter. But in retreating from his people, he also retreated from me. He had not been seen in the capital since the Feast of the Epiphany. Might he not forget I existed, and as long as Alix's son remained healthy, forget my son's existence, as well? For not all hemophiliacs died young. Prince Leopold of England had lived to thirty-one. It was possible my son and I might wait here for thirty years or more before Niki turned his head toward us again. By then Niki and Vova would be strangers! Niki and I would be strangers and I an old woman! Away from the theater, sequestered in this palace and by social position, Vova and I were invisible to the court and therefore to the tsar. And I had never been invisible. And so, in February 1905, I determined to return to the Maryinsky stage. As I had already completed my obligatory ten-year term as dancer and therefore had repaid the treasury my debt of free schooling, I could now negotiate a better contract for myself with the court minister, asking fees per performance in addition to an annual salary. And I knew the tsar would approve any fee I asked. As my father had said, from my art came my power, though this is not *exactly* what he meant.

In my short absence, though, I had gotten out of shape and put on weight, and so I began to fast and to practice, which I did privately, at home. One trick I had was to set four chairs about me and test my precision and my nerve by executing *grand battements* without tipping over a chair or breaking a leg—and when I thought I was ready, I met my sister at Liteiny Prospekt, in my father's ballroom, where I danced for her the variations from all the ballets in my repertoire and where she pronounced me fit, for of course, that was what I wanted to hear. But I returned to the theater in triumph only to find that life there had gone on without me—the curtain rose, the stagehands lowered and raised the scenery, old dancers retired and younger students graduated from the school to take their places, Pavlova, Karsavina, Fokine, and Nijinsky, who would all eventually make their names with Les Ballets Russes. You've heard of them because they danced in the West—but my name, perhaps, is a mystery, for I always preferred to dance in Russia, in Peter, for the tsar. But worst of all, my rivals had been assigned to what had been *my* roles alone in *my* ballets. At the Imperial Theaters, a ballerina did not share roles. Once a dancer had made her debut in a ballet retired by another, that ballet belonged to her until *she* retired. While I was gone measuring my head for my crown, my old rival Olga Preobrajenska had inherited my part of Lise in *La Fille mal gardée*, and upon my homecoming, I, of course, demanded back my old role. But Colonel Teliakovsky, a rather straitlaced boob who had never really liked me for my debauchery with the Romanovs, and who once walked in on me as I sat chatting with Sergei Mikhailovich in my dressing room, wearing only a robe, and who raised his upper lip as if he had seen a pile of offal, and who in 1924, like the rest of the exiles, would write his memoirs and in those pages would slander me unforgivably not only as a woman, but also as a dancer, calling me *vulgar* and *trite* and describing my beautifully formed legs as *fat*—yes, we had all lost our country, our tsar, our theater, and yet we continued our ridiculous rivalries about which no one cared but ourselves—this Colonel Teliakovsky refused to let me reclaim my role. I suppose he thought with the loss of the tsar and Grand Duke Sergei, I had become powerless, a puffball of tulle easily blown about by his hoary breath. He might have to let me back into the theater but he thought he did not have to schedule me to dance. I could have gone to the tsar but I did not wish him to see me as a supplicant but as his equal, his consort! So I took matters into my own duplicitous hands. Literally. Before the first scene of *Fille* one night, I, descending from my artists' box and chatting gaily with the dancers backstage, surreptitiously unlatched the door of the chicken cage. You know the ballet *Fille*? Set in a provincial French village of the 1750s, it opens in the barnyard of Madame Simone and her daughter Lise. The use of live animals on the stage is gone now, but in the early 1900s in Russia we often used the furred, feathered, and hooved. Painted backdrops were not enough enchantment for the tsar and his court. We employed horses for *Sleeping Beauty*, a goat in *Esmeralda*, chickens in *Fille*—horses decked out in embroidered blankets and plumed bridles, a goat led about by a braided rope with a bell on its collar, chickens pecking at seeds in their cages in a French barnyard. For animals more difficult to obtain—like monkeys—we used children in costume from the school. Why, the great choreographer George Balanchine, then little Georgy Balanchivadze, swung from tree to tree in a monkey suit in *La Fille du Pharaon* while I took aim at him with my pretty bow.

I was safely ensconced in my box for Act I when one of the chickens thumped against his wire door and open it flew, followed a moment after by an eruption of squawks, feathers, and claws, while the stagehands and some of the dancers dressed as village boys chased the birds in circles and then, snatching them up by the neck or feet, or tucking them under their elbows, attempted to shove the reluctant chickens back into their cages. How the audience laughed! Olga stood flat-footed to watch the chaos, the length of blue ribbon with which she had been ready to rope her beau Colin to her hanging slack in her hands. My little trick had so unnerved her that the next divertissement in which she and Colin make pretty patterns with that ribbon and wind one another up in it was made all a ruin of knots, one from which my old partner Nikolai Legat could not shake himself, and all that while the laughter from the audience continued. Don't click your teeth. A loose chicken, a snipped thread that held closed a bodice, a small price to pay to ensure the audience saw whom they really wanted to see. By such tricks and capers, I retrieved my old roles one by one, and I waited for Niki to appear in the imperial box to see me perform them, to remember how bright, how lively, how pleasing I was. How loyal.

But as the season progressed and Niki did not make an appearance at the theater, the revolution did. Inside the theaters, believe it or not, the revolution was also felt in its way. The actors and dancers and musicians began to agitate, just like the feverish workers in the streets, though their demands were different. Students at the music conservatory asked for monthly opera productions and a library, and they wanted M. Auer to stop hitting his students over the head with his bow. Rimsky-Korsakov, my old landlord until the tsar bought his house right out from under him, was dismissed as director of the conservatory for supporting the students, and as if that wasn't enough, the tsar also barred his music from the Imperial Theaters. From my brother I heard that dancers held furtive meetings in the apartments of their disapproving parents, and these were, of course, the younger dancers, the newest graduates from the school with the least seniority. What these children wanted—to rule the theater by committee—was an absurdity. Petitions circulated all through the schoolrooms and the dressing rooms, calling for freedom of speech, freedom of conscience, freedom of the printed word. As if they could write! Why, one day a little student from the school, white bow in her hair, proffered a paper for *my* signature at a rehearsal for *Sleeping Beauty*, of all ballets, created by Petipa and Tchaikovsky as a paean to the monarchy! The children had prepared a petition demanding lessons in applying theatrical makeup, better instruction in academics—and the older of them wanted to wear their own cuffs and collars with the school uniforms. Ridiculous. Of course, I sent the child off with a pinch. The dancers themselves, rather than the director or the ballet maître, wanted to decide what ballets would be done and who would dance them, what salaries would be paid and how many days they would dance. Of course, I had been for many years deciding those things for myself, but the difference was I had *earned* that right—I was a decade on the stage and I was La Kschessinska. One could count in months how long these children had been dancing for the tsar. They weren't electricians like the workers at the Petersburg electrical plant and therefore could not, as those workers had, plunge the city into darkness. And they were not laborers at the Moscow waterworks and therefore could not keep water from filling the pipes. But they could try to make the theaters go dark. At the Alexandrinsky Theater the actors threatened to abandon their lines and instead lecture their aristocratic audience about the need for governmental reform before striding offstage. But the revolutionary actors could not get enough of the other actors to agree to this. At the Maryinsky, committee members barged into the dressing rooms before curtain and began haranguing the *corps de ballet*, busy gluing on their wigs, to refuse to dance the matinee, to answer the obstinacy of the theater administration with an obstinacy of their own—but these new committees did not have the loyalty of the entire company and the dancers yawned and the matinee performance of *La Dame de pique* went on as usual. Even my brother Josef, radicalized by all the strikes and marches and all those pamphlets and petitions, took part in these actions, at great embarrassment to my father and me. And when I heard that the imperial family planned to remain at Tsarskoye Selo for the entire social season, I decided I myself had had enough of this strange and desolate season and of the theater to which I had returned with such great hopes. I took Vova and, with my parents, retreated to our family estate, Krasnitzky, for the summer. My brother, of course, stayed in the capital.

But I found Krasnitzky changed, too. When I took a stroll on the roads I knew so well from childhood or along the familiar sandy path by the swift-running river Orlinka, if I should happen to pass a peasant from the estate he gave me only a curt nod, and I felt even that was offered reluctantly. And after all the kindness my father had shown to them! Our neighbor found a wall of his barn smashed one morning; another one had his farming tools stolen. Other neighbors complained the peasants were measuring the land and pretending to divide it up between them, and they did not stop their chatter even when their squire walked by. And so, reluctantly, I curtailed my walks and stayed closer to our dacha. My boy was old enough now to toddle alongside me to the fringe of birch trees, to yank up the mushrooms I pointed out and drop them, some of them squashed and others in bits, into my own bark basket carved long ago with my initials, MMK. In the evening's soft light I rocked him on my lap or my mother took him onto hers, while we gazed at the trees that rose twice as high as our roof. My father gave Vova a pet pig, which Vova would take on a walk as if it were a dog, a rope leash to pull it and a stick to prod it, and he would call to me to watch him strike the animal until I had to take the stick away from my miniature Ivan the Terrible. Because Vova was so particular at table, my mother spoiled him by cutting his food into shapes—an acorn, a butterfly, a rabbit, and coaxed him to eat as only she could, with honeyed words and a few twirls of the spoon, and after dinner, she and I taught him *durachki*, which means *little idiots*, the card game learned first by all Russian children. At night Vova slept in my bed, covers thrown back, face flushed; underneath that red fever the sun had tinted his white skin brown. I lay awake beside him sometimes for hours, while the wind shifted the limbs of the trees, the top page of a sheaf of paper, the hem of a tablecloth, the tea in a glass. I felt as if I were a girl again and Vova were my much younger brother, but this was not the life I had envisioned for him, slow summers with Petersburg's Catholic circles. Just ten versts away, at Tsarskoye Selo and at the palaces lining the avenues leading to it, the imperial family and the court had also retreated from the unrest in the capital, but those ten versts might have been ten thousand versts, so far had my life drifted from theirs. At Tsarskoye Selo, I'm sure the trees also grew lush and green and stirred with the wind as they bent over the canals Empress Elizabeth had once intended, before the project had been abandoned, to lead all the way to Peter, so the tsars could be rowed the nine versts to the capital like pharaohs on a barge. In the Alexander Palace there, I imagined Niki spent his days as we did, playing cards with *his* children, perhaps bezique and aunt, reading aloud from the novels of Tolstoy, Gogol, and Turgenev, pasting photographs into his picture albums. But I did not hear from him and had not for almost a year now, though money was regularly transferred into my account each month by Baron Freedericks. By midsummer I had grown restless and dispirited, and then my spirits were destroyed further by calamity.

During a dress rehearsal for *Sleeping Beauty* this past season, a trap door on the stage had abruptly snapped open and my father, who had had the bad luck to be standing on it, dropped through. He arrested the plunge with his elbows at the very last moment, but the shock of the fall, like a curse in a fairy tale, had cracked his robust health; the unrest in the capital and in the theater only ruptured it further. The doctors had put him to bed, as if whatever was wrong might mend itself there, but for eighty-three years my father's life had been predicated on motion, and he refused to lie flat with the covers drawn up. Yet, once out of bed, he told me, he felt the parts of him seemed to be assembled in some manner that was not quite right, that he moved like a mechanical man, metal bones covered over by paper. Though none of us could see this, assuring him the summer at Krasnitzky would cure him, who knows his own body better than a dancer? My father died suddenly in July, a month after our arrival. He had lain down with a headache and when my mother sent me to check on him, I couldn't rouse him. I said to myself, *He is just sleeping*, and I crawled next to him on the bed and curled my arm around him, laid my face by his face from which I had inherited so many features, and then I looked out the window at the blazing blue sky. I thought, *If he does not get up, I will not get up*.

It was 1905, twelve years after the cuckoo in his study had called out twelve times as I struggled to tell him of my plans to become the mistress of the tsarevich.

My father had come to Petersburg in 1853, and he had danced for four emperors—Nicholas I, Alexander II, Alexander III, and Nicholas II. My father was in Peter even before the Maryinsky! He had watched the circus burn down in 1859 and the Maryinsky

Theater rise in its place. He had given me his adopted city and his theater and this life, and I could not imagine any of it without him. At Ivanov's funeral a few years earlier, in 1901, my father had sighed, *Very few of us oldsters remain*, and now they were one fewer. Perhaps I could close my eyes and when I opened them my father would open his. I closed mine to try my magic but then I was afraid to open them. My mother eventually came looking for us both and had to slap my hands and call to the maid to help pull me from the bed.

Within a day, my brother and his wife, Sima, and my sister and her husband, Ali, converged at Krasnitzky, and at the supper table that night, after we had drunk too many glasses of vodka and cognac, and had laughed over my father's habits, the face he made while seated in his dressing room gluing on his horsehair beard, drawing his lips wide in a ghoul's grimace, or the time my brother came stomping through the kitchen and sank two of my father's *kulichi*, which he then had to build up with a tower of icing so sweet no one could eat the cake at all, or the way my father had sat all three of us down—me, Julia, and Josef—to lecture us as if we were third-year students about the sedition at the theater, reminding us that we were Kschessinskys, servants of the tsar, and we served at his pleasure, and how we had sat in our chairs, cowed, not even Josef daring to look up. And as we were laughing at ourselves, my brother pushed aside his plate and said perhaps my father should have called in all the workers on the estate that day, as well, sat all of them down in chairs beside us, for from what he heard today, the peasants could have used this lecture. And then Josef sang for us a tune he'd heard that afternoon while walking along the river:

Nochyu ya progulivalsya po okrugeh
Ih mne ne vstretilsya nih odin bogach
Pust tolko popadetsya mne khot odin
Ih ya razmozzhu yemy cherep.

At night I strut around,
And rich men don't get in my way.
Just let some rich guy try
And I'll screw his head on upside down.

I listened to it, wondering, *Who was the rich man they sang of—
my father?* Was it *his* head they wished upside down? And then, after a moment, I pushed Josef's plate back at him, all the pleasantness
between us dimming, and cried, *See what you have wrought? You killed
him, trying to turn his theater upside down.* And he said, *I? Because I
refuse to take orders from Teliakovsky like a slave? I cannot lie beneath
the emperor and his cousin as you have, Mathilde-Maria, and from that
position give my orders.* And I said, *Ha! Some Bolshevik! I see you
picked a princess to marry*—because his wife was Serafima Astafieva,
the daughter of a prince who served as a general in the Imperial
Army, so Josef did not always turn up his nose at the court but
kissed the fingers of some members of it—and then my mother's
tears and my sister's shushing sent my brother from the table so we
could scream at each other no further.

But because of the troubles Josef so supported we could not
travel to Warsaw to bury my father by his own father as he'd wished.
I had always thought of my father as a real Petersburger, but perhaps my father, a Pole from one of the empire's duchies, had never
felt truly comfortable in Russia's hard embrace, which had left Poland, as my brother put it, *poor, broken, and depressed.* Why, Poles
hated the Russians so much that if one used Russian to order a meal
in Warsaw, the waiters refused to hear it. But we could not take my
father home. The Russian countryside was on fire. The trains were
not moving. And so we could not move his mother's body, either,
which had lain in a Petersburg cemetery all these years and which
my father wanted buried with him and his father in Warsaw. We
had no choice but to take my father's body back to Petersburg and
place his coffin in the crypt of St. Stanislaus until the maelstrom of

that summer subsided. Ivan Felix Kschessinsky would have to continue to lie alone in the family vault in the Powalsky Cemetery, waiting for his wife and his son.

The court sent a wreath and the emperor sent a note of condolence to the family.

It was not until early autumn, after Niki finished his hunt and noted in his ledger the number of deer and pheasants bagged, that he seriously turned his attention to the great unrest. Have you ever seen those beautiful watercolored records of the imperial hunt? A sheet of card stock, forty-eight centimeters long, bore the illustration of a fall/winter scene—a muddy river flowing through a snow-covered field, a wood of fir trees and orange-leaved birch to one side, a sleigh, men in winter dress, dogs, and in brown ink the tally of pheasant, partridge, hare, and deer, the record signed by the head of the Imperial Hunt. The Old World. Niki kept these records in his Gothic Revival library at the Winter Palace. He liked order, hated disorder. The year 1905 was nothing if not disorderly, but you would never know it from the record of the hunt for that year. Yes, it was not until October, after the hunt, that Niki could bear to lift his head and look at the disturbances, at which time he reluctantly sued for peace with Japan in order to bring his army home to turn it on his people. Hadn't he given them enough time to settle down on their own? But because Russia was a country of many millions of souls and each soul had a voice, there was no end to the clatter. The army brought order to the cities, which the police and local regiments could not seem to establish, and then it restrained the peasants in the countryside. Niki called the army out three thousand times to help the Cossacks—who forced the peasants to remove their caps and scarves and bow down to them, after which they executed the men and raped the women—finally put down the peasant uprisings. What the army could not finish, Niki's new minister of the interior, Petr Arkadevich Stolypin, did. Stolypin, with his balding pate and ridiculous waxed moustache, might be one of Niki's aristocratic ministers, but he refused to be one of Niki's sycophantic courtiers—he wouldn't accompany the tsar on his annual hunt, for example, as did the rest of his suite, so Niki never really liked Stolypin, but Stolypin was effective. He had so many thousands of men hanged—fifteen thousand—to restore order that the people began to call a noose *Stolypin's necktie* and the train cars that hauled the forty-five thousand revolutionaries to Siberia *Stolypin carriages*. And though I more than anyone wanted to see order restored, I was uncertain about the means. Surely this brutality could only make Niki's people further hate him. On the other hand, look at his grandfather, who offered reforms and had been killed in the street for his trouble. That is what attention and forbearance brought. Regicide. So Niki cracked the whip and his people bowed their heads and this was the end of the first revolution, though most people know only of the second, in 1917. But really, I see now, there was just one.

Finally, thanks to Niki, was I able to move my father and his mother to the family vault by train from Petersburg to Warsaw, on the railway line Emperor Alexander III had once built so he could travel from Petersburg to his white-walled palace at Gatchina, south of the capital, and then the track was extended and extended until it reached the old capital of Poland, once a great nation with its own king, now its capital just an outpost of the Russian empire. My father arrived for the last time at the old railway station there with its circular archways, its latticework along the portico, its slanted slate roof off which the rain could sluice. And it was raining when we arrived, as it often does in early autumn, the pinks and greens, the peaches and yellows, of the buildings around us drenched by the weeping sky to the zenith of their coloration. We stood, my brother, his wife, Sima, my sister with her husband, Ali, my mother, and I, holding Vova's hand, in the vaulted main hall of the station. My father's body and that of his mother were loaded onto the cortege that would be drawn to the Powalsky Cemetery. There is no other way to approach a cemetery than by horse and carriage. The stately approach echoes the heartbeat and allows one to prepare. Why do you think the cars we use today for funeral processions slow to a crawl as they follow one another on the long trek from church to grave-yard? The cars move at a horse's pace. I have been now to many fu-nerals and I have had time to think about these things. All along the streets, from the station to the cemetery, my father's fans—he had never neglected them, making an annual pilgrimage to Warsaw to perform—stood weeping, hats removed, for as my brother later wrote to his son: *tears of gladness or of sorrow show the feeling and heart of a man, only in Poland are people accustomed to love those close to them, to become attached to them and esteem them.* They did not blame my father for devoting his life to the entertainment of the Rus-sian tsars. And now that that was done, they welcomed him home.

The Powalsky Cemetery is one of the most beautiful cemeteries in Europe, you know. It rivals the Père Lachaise here in Paris. In Père Lachaise, death feels orderly, but in Powalsky death is wild, rustic, the cemetery paths leaf-strewn, its trees massed closely to-gether, as are the graves and monuments, many of them slabs marked by a simple cross. Stone angels fly with wings outstretched; stone women draped in togas point to the sky; stone men stand in hooded robes or stretch out a hand to the passersby. *Join me.* At some crypts a statue weeps, at others the door bears a knocker—so you can knock for whom, the soul? Or perhaps the soul itself opens the door, knocker clapping, to make its way to heaven. The peasants buried their dead with a candle and a bread ladder, but we buried my father with a crucifix in his hands. My brother closed the bronze door to the chapel I had built over the crypt with my Romanov money, and he embraced his wife and my sister embraced her husband, and I took my mother's hand. However many imperial bodies I have lain beneath, I have observed the great moments, the ceremonial moments of my private life, alone. And when my Romanovs observed the great moments of their private lives, I was not with them either; I was, always, the shoe under the bed.

Before we left, I picked up pebbles from around the crypt and pulled thick green leaves from the trees there, and these I put in my reticule.

When we returned to Petersburg from Warsaw, my sister went with her husband to their house at No. 40, English Prospekt, just down the street from where I had once been kept by the tsarevich a thousand years ago, and my brother went with his wife to their twelve-room apartment at No. 18, Spasskaya Ulitsa, and I, who had no husband, who had never had a husband, went home alone with my grief and with my son to my dacha at Berezoviya Alleya in Strelna. I went out to the veranda, and I remember there I could smell the gulf and real autumn swiftly coming and behind her, the long, long winter. I rolled the pebbles I'd taken from my father's grave around and around in my hands. The peasants left breadcrumbs, not pebbles, on the graves of their relatives at Easter, and when the sparrows flew down to eat, the peasants knew the souls of their loved ones were well. A fairly certain way to comfort oneself about the dead, no? The peasants believed heaven existed in some faraway cleft of the Russian steppe, where long green grass swayed and rivers of milk bubbled and foamed unseen by the living. And what kind of heaven did dancers believe in? An abandoned theater where their souls amused themselves all day in face paint and magnificent costume, perpetually playing the parts they had played here on earth to a decaying house?

When I heard the sound of a horse's hooves on my front drive, I opened my hands in surprise—I was expecting no one—and my pebbles rolled across the wooden porch floor. I crouched, as desperate to find them as if they were my father's bones, when a man's boot appeared, first one, then the other on the whitewashed planks. The boot belonged to Sergei Mikhailovich, and when I looked up into his bearded face, he said kindly, *What are you looking for, Mala?*, as if he had never been gone or had been gone for just an afternoon, instead of three years, and had come upon me kneeling on the porch. I wanted, suddenly, to kiss him as answer, for how could I explain to him why I was trying to gather up these little stones? But I didn't have to explain. Because I wanted them, he knelt beside me and began to collect them, and all at once I found the tears that had eluded me in Warsaw. He let me cry as he squatted there on the porch. He had heard of the death of my father, he said, and he had come here to Strelna on the day I was to return from the funeral to offer his condolences. He knew what my father had meant to me.

And he came also, he said, to express his regret at having abandoned me the very hour I gave birth. He had ridden home to the New Mikhailovsky Palace that night without knowing how he got there and when Sergei did, his brothers poured vodka down his throat in an effort to calm him, the trollop's lapdog. But when the plans for my palace were published, the golden double-headed eagles tiny gray scratches on the page one needed a magnifying glass to discern, and when my new home appeared in all its magnificence on Petersburg Island, where one needed no optical device to read its message, he and all of Petersburg knew: Kschessinska has given birth to a Romanov—though perhaps only Sergei knew my son's father must be Niki himself.

But Niki was still an unfaithful lover, was he not? I nodded. And in that case, perhaps I still needed a protector, for Niki could not leave Alix's side, as she lived in a state of perpetual hysteria over the health of Alexei. As Niki struggled to control the country, Sergei told me, so he struggled also with Alix. She was desperate for a cure for some mysterious ailment from which the baby suffered, and because of this ailment, they had kept Alexei hidden since his christening even from the family. And Alix, frustrated by the court doctors, had begun to enlist the aid of healers and mystics, believing if St. Seraf had given her a son, perhaps a man of God could save him. Another man like Philippe Vachot had appeared in the capital, brought there as M. Philippe had been, by the Montenegrins, the Black Sisters, another of their mystics to parade about the Petersburg palaces like a monkey on a leash. This man had sent a telegram to the tsar as so many peasants did—*Father Tsar, I wish to bring you a tamed sable. Father Tsar, I wish to bring you a potato as big as a dog. Little Father Tsar! I would like to bring you an icon of the blessed St. Simon Verkhotursky the miracle worker.* And the tsar, on occasion, let the peasants come. The tamed sable was brought to the palace to play with the children. And Alix, who had seen the telegram about the icon, and who could not resist it or anything like it—had it brought to the palace by this man, Gregorii Rasputin. So once again, through Sergei, I was privy to the most secret life of the tsar. By then Sergei had gathered all the pebbles and put them in my hands, then held my hands in his own.

And that was how Sergei came back to me, out of pity and obligation, and perhaps love, though whether for me or for Niki, I could not fully tell. He would not marry Countess Vorontzov-Dashkov, currently pregnant with his child. Unlike Niki, he could not love two women at once. Or two sons. It was my son, not his own, to whom Sergei would give his attention. And I was not sorry for the countess, did you think I would be?, only grateful that my son, at age three, finally had a father.

And, of course, I had once again a man in my bed, smelling of leather and oranges and horses, and I had missed Sergei. The tsar had his Alix, so why should I be alone?

Yes, the fall of 1905 brought compromises for us all. Nicholas, who had wanted to appoint a military dictator and use martial law to crush the last of the disturbances, instead gave in and granted reforms. With the October Manifesto, written up by his ministers, the tsar managed to retain his throne by agreeing reluctantly to freedom of speech and assembly, to amnesty for all strikers, to a cabinet and a Duma—a parliament, in effect, of elected officials, which he resolved to dissolve as soon as he could.

So for now there was the Duma with its Social Democrats, a tiny number of them Bolsheviks and the majority Mensheviks, with its Constitutional Democrats, its Jewish Bundists, its Ukrainians, Poles, and Tartars—the Duma for which Alix would always blame Grand Duke Nicholas Nikolaevich, Niki's uncle, who commanded the St. Petersburg military district and had refused to be Russia's military dictator, the fist of the tsar, saying the time for repression had long passed. The Duma now sat in the Tauride Palace, a palace built by Catherine the Great in 1780 for her lover, Prince Grigory Potemkin, in gratitude for his having conquered the Crimea. What would she say to see the Duma in that palace now? The Tauride stood in Shpalernaya Street, out of sight of the Winter Palace, where the Neva wended its way in a great sandy shoehorn around the eastern part of the city. Out of sight, yes, but it was still there, desecrated by the men of the Duma, who stank of the animals they so recently tended, that smell so woven into the fibers of their clothes it could never be scoured out, by men who sucked in vodka and beer and spit out the husks of sunflower seeds sodden with it, until the corridors of the palace, eighteenth-century pictures hanging serenely from long wires, reeked of the peasantry.

Yes, there was a Duma, but Niki was still tsar, still commander of the army and the navy. He alone could declare war or make peace, and he alone could dissolve the Duma at will and make laws by emergency decree, and none of its laws could take effect until the tsar gave his approval, along with that of the State Council, the upper house of the Duma filled with nobles who ensured that no law counter to their interests ever passed. And so there was a Duma, but it had, as you can see, little power, which meant, as Sergei assured me, that little would change. But the Duma, by its very existence, meant, despite Sergei's assertions, that there *had* been change—there was now open and legitimized opposition to the regime, and I knew from what happened in my theater that the opposition could be reprimanded, threatened, strangled, but it would eventually have its way. Look at how I always got mine! And so though Niki could dissolve the Duma, as he did seventy-two days after the opening ceremony, hating even the appearance that it could inhibit him as autocrat, by law it had to be reconstituted. You see, the Tauride faced the St. Petersburg Main Waterworks, a big redbrick building where the city's water ebbed and flowed, forced through various pipes and valves and winches and pools and dams and into drains at will, and so Niki tried to control the will of the Duma—and of the country.

Sometimes, I imagined Niki, burdened with Alix, his fragile son, his roiling country, taking his solitary walks through the palace park from the yellow Alexander Palace to the blue, white, and gold Catherine Palace, its baroque grandeur evoking for him that time when a tsar ruled supreme, giving him strength to go on. Did he walk alone into the Great Hall, walk along its high windows and polished mirrors? I wished I could walk beside his reflection there and slip my little hand in his for comfort, whisper, *You will prevail*.

When the country quieted, so did the theater. Everyone who had opposed the regime and who had formed unions and committees and who had written up resolutions and had otherwise run about stirring up trouble was required to swear fealty once again to the tsar in writing before being granted amnesty as part of the larger general amnesty being offered to all in Russia who had taken part in strikes and protests. Dancers are not workers from the streets and they were easily intimidated. Most signed immediately. Fokine, Pavlova, Karsavina, and my brother, though, all refused to sign the loyalty oath, and when Josef slapped the face of a dancer who had signed and who Josef felt was a particular traitor, Josef was dismissed from the theater, and his wife, the princess, divorced him. Ironical, no, that it would be my imperial connections that saved his pension, my connections that would quietly find him a position with the court in charge of the tsar's hunting lodges—far from the stage, it's true, but the salary kept him alive. It was eight years, though, before I could arrange to have him reinstated at the theater, that's how deep the feelings ran over these matters. Sergei Legat, the brother of my beautiful partner Kolinka, signed the declaration and then, feeling himself a traitor who had betrayed his friends, sliced his throat open with a razor. There were other consequences—two of the dancers who led the strikes were dismissed along with my brother; another was sent to a psychiatric hospital; others were not promoted, were given poor roles, went abroad to dance, to Berlin, to London, to Paris. These disasters, like the hangings and rapes and deportations that subdued the peasants and intellectuals, subdued the dancers, though there was, for several months, resentment between the two factions, between the dancers who, like me, were regime loyalists and those who had acted against it. The simmering resentment would eventually lead to a bleeding of talent from the tsar's stages.

ballets russes

It was just a few years later, in 1909, that Fokine, along with Diaghilev and Benois and Bakst—the three free artists who had come to the theater—obtained the tsar's permission to prepare a season of Russian exports to take to Paris. They would present some of the tsar's greatest singers and dancers abroad, mounting a few operas mixed in with a few *scènes des ballets*.

Of these men, Diaghilev I loved the best. We called him *Chinchilla* because of the white streak that lay at the front of his hair on the right side and because his little white teeth looked exactly like those of a small animal. As a member of the theater staff—though briefly tenured, for he was dismissed within a few years after a dispute with Volkonsky—he came to all the performances at the Maryinsky, and though he prized music first and art second, he soon developed a great enthusiasm for the ballet. The dancers would sing under their breath whenever he arrived at the theater and took his seat in the administration's box:

> *Ya tolko shto uznal,*
> *Shto u nevo v korobkye shinshillah.*
> *Ya ochen boyus oshibitsya!*

I've just heard
That Chinchilla is in his box
And I'm terribly afraid to make a mistake!

Fokine I liked less. Why, he complained when I wore a tutu to rehearsal instead of the regulation practice clothes, as if I should be bound by some regulation. And when I had my maid bring Vova to a rehearsal, which I interrupted when Vova called for a kiss, Fokine erupted in rage. But what child does not deserve a kiss? We were only rehearsing Fokine's ballet *Le Pavilon d'Armide*, a pale copy of a ballet Petipa could have done three times better. As for Pavlova— why, she wasn't happy until she had the whole stage to herself, as she did in that mawkish solo *The Dying Swan* Fokine later made for her to that sugary music by Saint-Saëns, a solo she danced over and over again all around the world—even in Japan and India and South America to brown men with bones in their noses. Can you imagine? You've heard the legend of her death, the way she called for her swan costume to be brought to her and laid across her body, a pall of white feathers and gauze, a woman of the theater even to her last moment, mindful of the great story it would make from beyond the grave.

I've outlived her, you know.

Well, I was invited, *very* reluctantly, by Fokine to dance in Paris not in *Giselle* or *Les Sylphides* or *Prince Igor*, but in only one forgettable ballet, his *Le Pavilon d'Armide*, three acts set during the time of Louis XIV with a libretto of counts, roses, fiancées, slaves, dreams, gardens, weddings, and deaths, which Petipa himself would have loved and which I suppose Fokine thought I couldn't ruin with my old-fashioned talents. He had invited me only because, based on my participation, the tsar had committed one hundred thousand rubles to the project. But I was barely participating at all! It was clearly a Paris season of strikers and dissidents. Why, my brother Josef had been specifically invited by Fokine to join them—my brother, who had been dismissed from the Imperial Ballet!—to link arms with Pavlova and Karsavina, his fellow dissidents. *To raise our art to its highest level*, they had claimed was their cause. Yet even the mother of one of them, Karsavina, had said to her, *Be a great artist—that's how you raise your art to its highest level*. A great artist. Even the definition of that was changing.

For me, these young dancers were taller than I and my contemporaries, with long limbs and gorgeous feet. In the past, we didn't care so much about height or supple arched feet (Pavlova's were so high they spilled, absurdly, out of her shoes). We liked dancers who moved quickly and small dancers can move more quickly than tall ones—and faces didn't matter to us; one couldn't look like a monster, but it was the body that mattered, and that body was corseted, like the bodies of the women in the audience. Now these young dancers' bodies rippled like water. And their faces—Pavlova, well, she had the beak nose and the disconcerting habit of standing in the wings and gulping down meat sandwiches shortly before curtain, the smell of roast beef and ham all over her fingers and breath, but Karsavina was a real beauty, dark-eyed, with a pleasing nose and delicate lips. These girls wore their real hair in smooth chignons, none of these elaborate, curled wigs I preferred. Why, when I finally did dance for Diaghilev in 1911 as part of his season, the European critics' tastes had so changed, being fed this diet of new dancers, that they called me *fat, passé, stereotyped*, and worst of all, *competent,* and they speculated in print, *If one did not know she wore the tsar's jewels and was the wealthiest woman on the stage, would one notice her at all?*

But in 1909 I was otherwise insulted—if Diaghilev and Fokine did not really want me to dance for them, then this was not really a season of the tsar's dancers—for who was more of a tsar's dancer than I? And in that case, why should the tsar pay the bill? So I whispered this thought to Sergei, who whispered it to the tsar, who abruptly withdrew his palm full of rubles. Though the tsar had withdrawn his person from me, he would keep secure my place at the theater. One week the dancers were rehearsing in the Hermitage Theater, served tea and chocolates by the palace servants in full livery. The next week they had to find rehearsal space in a small rented theater on the Ekaterinsky Canal, leaning big flats of scenery for other productions up against the walls to give themselves room to move. Yes, I almost foiled that first season of Les Ballets Russes, but Diaghilev scraped together a few rubles anyway, running sweatily about with his top hat in his hand, begging, collecting enough money even to refurbish the Châtelet Theater in Paris, which he had cleaned and repainted and laid with new ruby-red carpets, the better to present his Russian jewels, his own unofficial season not sanctioned by the crown.

But to Diaghilev's surprise, his confections of *Pavillon*, *Giselle*, *Sylphides*, ballets that reflected the European court life the French themselves had perfected, were not the ones that seized the imagination of the Parisians. They stood on their seats to cheer the ancient Tartar Polovtsian dances from *Prince Igor*, its male warriors outfitted with bows, whirling savagely about the stage, arms raised, their bright costumes flowing, crisscrossing one another, mouths open, heads flung back. Diaghilev stood agog in the wings, and from then on he pursued a new tack. Why show the French the watercolored echoes of their own court? Show them instead a smattering of old Russian fairy tales about Ivan Tsarevich and Kashchei the Immortal and firebirds. Show them peasant life from the provinces. Yes, after his first cautious season in Paris, Diaghilev began to create ballets to showcase the Rus: *Petrouchka*, its puppets hanging in the peasants' stalls at a Shrovetide Fair by day, but at night, left to their own devices, they fought and loved; *Firebird*, a pastiche of Russian tales about a monster, a maiden princess, a tsarevich, and a golden bird, set in a sumptuously exotic garden; *Rite of Spring*, the depiction of an old peasant ritual sacrifice. Eventually the creators moved even farther afield to the vast curtained harem of Persia for *Schéhérazade*, to the Hindu rock temple of *Le Dieu bleu*, with the dancers' limbs and hands posed in imitation of Hindu sculpture, to the great columns and hieroglyphics of *Cléopâtre*, all the dancers bewigged and turned sideways as if they were painted on the walls of an Egyptian pyramid. Diaghilev and Benois and Fokine created ballet after ballet with folk tales for the libretto, with folk music mixed into the score, with peasant motifs of stars and animals painted on the canvas of the sets, with costumes dyed the bright reds and blues and yellows of peasant clothing.

Ballets Russes? Not really. Petersburg and Moscow had never seen ballets like these before—no one had. And Russia's *prima ballerina assoluta* was nowhere to be seen in them, either.

I ask you, Who does *Cléopâtre* or *Firebird* now? Who does *Rite of Spring*? *Petrouchka*? They are the oddities of the ballet, polished up for an occasion amid great efforts at reconstruction. No, it is the Romanov ballets that survive, Petipa's ballets—*Swan Lake*, *Sleeping Beauty*, *Raymonda*, *Le Corsaire*, *Coppélia*, *Nutcracker*, *La Bayadère*. Those are the true *ballets russes*. Those ballets outlived the regime, will outlive me, will outlive the Soviets.

Enough.

the twentieth court

I SHALL TELL YOU now of my life with Sergei and my son during the great lull after 1905, when the country returned to its senses and the aristocracy to its customary habits. If the tsar, the dowager empress, the grand dukes had their nineteen courts, I decided I would create the twentieth, my own court, equally fabulous, where I stirred together the men from the imperial family with the artists from the imperial theaters. With both the tsar's money and Sergei's and with my stupendous new palace, the double-headed eagles glinting on the gates, I could stage entertainments to rival those of Duchess Vladimir, the dowager empress, Princess Radziwill, Countess Schouvaloff, if not in ostentation, for, after all, I didn't *quite* have their coffers, then in merriment. I didn't have to compete with Empress Alexandra because the Winter Palace sat dark ever since the birth of the tsarevich, though the country and the court did not know exactly why. It was the Vladimir Palace that hosted Peter's most extraordinary receptions now, tables laid for a thousand in her *enfilades*. When offered congratulations after an especially brilliant ball, Duchess Vladimir responded pridefully, *One ought to know one's job. You may pass that on to the Great Court.* Whose court she had, of course, eclipsed. Like all Russians, she spared no expense when it came to playing the host—why, a Russian will knock down a wall of his house to better entertain a large gaggle of guests, will go into a debt he could never in this lifetime climb out of to feed them. But I did not need to go into debt. Invitations to my parties were quite sought after, for, like my father, I made each event into theater.

At Christmas, a tall tree towered at the entrance to my winter garden, the pine boughs heavy with gold tinsel and crystal pears, and tied to the lowest branches swung the toys I had bought from the peasants' stalls set up on the Champ de Mars and on the quays. For Vova's fourth birthday I brought in an elephant to distribute the presents with his long curved trunk, and the children climbed his leathery gray skin to sit upon his back and be led about by the clown Dourov, who'd fetched the beast to my house. At my dacha the next summer I transformed my veranda into a stage by hanging a length of velvet cloth at the edge of it and converting my big bedroom into a backstage wing. I cajoled Baron Golsch into my Russian costume, and the dancer Misha Alexandrov—the illegitimate nephew of Alexander II's widow, Ekaterina Dolgorukaya—into a long tutu, and, all moustaches and hairy legs, they played caricatures of myself and Pavlova. On another occasion I sent out invitations summoning my guests to dinner at Félicien, a famous Petersburg restaurant that stood in summer on a raft out on the Neva, only to escort my guests through my lantern-lit alley to the gulf, where I had dinner served out on the jetty in the open air. The lights of Petersburg, of Kronstadt, of Vachta across the green water were mere peeps of light compared to the brilliance of the Milky Way, with its silver stream of flooded light. At dessert the fireworks I ordered spanked their brilliant colors onto that white sky, and after this I hired a special train to ferry my guests back to Peter. And in all this, Sergei indulged me.

Almost every man in the imperial family save for the tsar found his way to my palace, though I suppose I hoped one day one of his uncles or cousins might bring him along—one of Sergei's brothers Nicholas or George or Mikhail, or perhaps their father or Grand

Duke Paul or his son Dimitri, the poet Konstantin and his sons Oleg and Igor, who acted in my theatricals, even perhaps Alexander Mossolov, the head of the Court Chancellery, or Grand Duke Vladimir, who brought with him his sons Kyril, Boris, and Andrei, though his daughter stayed at home—yes, they all came, but not the tsar, who never saw how well I entertained the Romanovs. They mixed at my parties with the greatest artists on the imperial stages: Bakst, Benois, and Fokine, Petipa, when he visited from the Crimea, the younger dancers Pavlova, Karsavina, and Nijinsky, who made my Kolinka jealous because he was Polish, too, you see, and with him I could speak the Polish I learned as a child but never used except *en famille*. Kolinka used to say, *One Pole can spot another Pole from far, far away*—and then he would put his hands over my eyes so that I would not make Nijinsky my partner, which I did anyway. Who else came? The composers Glazunov and Shenk, the balalaika player Victor Abaza, Fabergé, to whom someone would always show her jewels for appraisal or praise, the great basses Chaliapin and Sobinov, the latter of whom one night sang Vova to sleep in his bed with a lullaby, actors from the English Theater who tended to shout, and dancers from the Imperial Ballet you've never heard of. Even visiting artists like Isadora Duncan, her Greek tunic clipped closed with a brooch, and Sarah Bernhardt stopped by. (For the great Bernhardt I went to enormous effort to acquire the borzoi dog she wanted so, an act of kindness she did not bother to thank me for!) And with such a mix of talent, theatricals were the order of the day, either that or baccarat and poker. And yes, at my palace many mistresses were taken and many marriages made, like that of Nina Nesterovska to Grand Duke Konstantin's son, Prince Gabriel, and one could find there the odd son or daughter, the flower of a liaison between a theater artist and a prince, like Misha Alexandrov, who now served either as a dancer or as a member of the Guards, for there was a social fluidity at my house that existed almost nowhere else in Peter and all could swim there.

Because of my many and myriad relationships with the imperial men, the grand dukes began to call me not *Ma*-thilde, but *Notre*-tilde—*Our*-tilde—so intimate did I become with them all, though their wives had another name for me, of course, *that awful woman*, which I'm sure they would call me still today, had I not outlived them. Grand Duke Vladimir sent me each Easter an arrangement of lilies of the valley and my own jeweled Fabergé egg, and he sent me also a pair of porcelain vases that once belonged to Prince Vorontzov, a sapphire bracelet he bought for me in Paris at Cartier, even sheet music. The last piece, *La Valse triste* by Sibelius, was sent just a few weeks before Vladimir's death in 1909 and had been written for the play *Death*, penned by a relative of the composer. The music describes a dance between a dying woman and death itself. On the first page of it Vladimir scribbled a note by the title, *This is your ballet*. So he knew, Vladimir, of my private dance with the destroyer, the tsar. For Vladimir had ample opportunity to observe me. He not only came to my palace for my parties but also took me to dinners at Cubat's, and in the summers, he spent afternoons at my dacha, sometimes alone with me and sometimes he brought along his sons, for long sunlit hours of card games. Our favorite was *tëtke*, or aunt. One day it seemed Vladimir was dealt the queen of every suite and at the last abruptly folded his cards to ask me, *Does anyone like me for myself or is this respect and affection awarded to me solely because of my rank?* And I told him, swiftly, *Here you are loved for yourself*, though of course, there is no way to sever one's position from oneself, nor would he have wanted to try, I am sure. I loved him for his rank and his person but also for his friendship to me and for the friendship to me he prodded from his sons. I knew the elder two, already, Kyril and Boris. They came to the ballet on their father's *abonnement*, Kyril, with the long, handsome face and English-looking features, and Boris with a face bloated by his love of baccarat and liquor and women and a good joke—at my theatricals, he was always the first to stamp his feet and call *Curtain! Curtain!* as the French do.

Vladimir's youngest son, Andrei, though, had been studying at
the Mikhailovsky Artillery School all these years, one of those elite
military schools so strict they did not allow their pupils any holidays
with their families—to snap, I suppose, the boys' ties to home and
to have them forge instead new ones with their fellow officer candi-
dates and their country, and so him I had not met before 1905, when
Vladimir brought him one afternoon to luncheon. If I was his father's
dushka, Andrei became mine, stirring a finger into my heart. His
face was the face of the young sovereign I saw up close for the first
time at my school graduation dinner; and like Niki then, Andrei
was terribly shy, a baby, still, at twenty-seven, though I was no longer a girl but a woman of thirty-two. Each time I spoke to him, he
ducked his head with a charming terror. At luncheon, when I placed
my left hand on his wrist to ask him which dessert he preferred, I
startled him, and he knocked over his wineglass, spraying my white
dress with purple darts. His brothers laughed.

That day for luncheon he came with his father and his brothers,
but soon enough we made a date for him to come again alone, late
one evening, on his mother's name day, July 22, when the rest of the
family would be occupied. He rode over from Ropsha, the Vladimir country estate, leaving behind his mother's annual party in her
own honor, chairs filled with Romanovs, leaving behind the Gypsy
musicians fiddling in the garden, the food spoiling on tables set
among the flower beds. Petersburg was hot that month, the walls of
the buildings glowing red with the sun, the Neva thick and still.
But Strelna was part of a constellation of islands at the mouth of the
Gulf of Finland, and here the heat mellowed into a dreamy warmth
as the Neva surged toward the Baltic Sea. I waited outside on my
terrace for Andrei, pacing just as I had once paced at Krasnoye Selo
while waiting for the young tsarevich to take me for a ride in his
troika, reluctant to sit down, for I didn't want to crease my starched
summer dress. When Andrei finally arrived in the late evening's
dusk, he brought on his boots the yellow sand of the roads and on

his clothes the scent of the flowering jasmine and the lilies of the valley that grew at the sides of them. We lingered on the terrace listening to the nightingales, which are silenced only by the light, and it seemed when eventually he went to my bed we took the birds and the lilies of the valley there with us where Andrei, almost a virgin, made love to me as the tsar had once made love to me, with soft surprise. And it was as if the tsar, a fairer, blonder version of him, had been returned to me, and I could continue, through this proxy, to live the life I should have had with him.

Soon after that, Andrei bought his own palace on the English Embankment, No. 28, so that we would have a place to meet privately, out of the sight of Sergei and out of the sight of Andrei's mother—who had been horrified enough by my friendship with her husband and was enraged now by his forbearance at my friendship with their youngest son. Andrei's palace had belonged to Baron von Dervis, who had made his fortune in railroads, and his widow, in the few years left to her, had remade all the rooms in high style alternately rococo and Gothic, reminiscent of the Winter Palace. Andrei changed nothing about the mansion, did not even remove the von Dervis monograms and coats of arms, did not, in fact, even live there, but used the place as a stage set for our parties and our trysts. Yet Sergei, of course, knew about this purchase and knew also that I visited Andrei secretly there, and he endured this as penance. He had abandoned me when my son was one hour old, still coated with yellow wax, and he had heard me cry after him as he galloped through my garden and jumped my hedge. It had taken three years and my father's death for Sergei to offer me a word. Did I think of the deceit I offered him the day I told him I carried his son and all those days after when still I kept silent? Conveniently, I did not.

Andrei and I were nevertheless discreet. We conducted our affair in a different neighborhood or we went abroad, to the French Riviera, where Andrei, in a gesture to rival Sergei's, bought me a villa in Cap D'Ail. In Russia, too, we stayed out of sight, as the von

Dervis mansion stood where the English Embankment faced the Neva as it curved south, away from the Winter Palace and the New Mikhailovsky Palace, and from it one had a different view, that of Vasilievsky Island. The Rumyantsev Mansion stood at No. 44. The Vorontzov-Dashkovs at No. 10. Countess Laval at No. 4, where Pushkin himself read aloud his *Boris Godunov* in 1828. Diaghilev lived at No. 22. All of these mansions serve some other purpose now. The great noble families are long gone—some of their houses are museums. The Laval mansion is a historical archive. Andrei's home became first a Ministry of Agriculture under the Provisional Government. I hear in 1961 it became the USSR's first Palace of Weddings. I like to think of the young couples arriving there, perhaps the girl with orange blossoms tucked behind one ear, a little unsteady on her heels. Perhaps out of some prescience of what this palace would one day become, Andrei was driven one late afternoon to announce he wished to marry me, and he threw off our sable coverlet to dress and, leaving me there in the bed, rode immediately home to announce his intentions to his parents. And I thought, *How delightful, how perfect. Let me make trouble in the palace of every Romanov!*

Miechen, of course, railed at him that he had been bewitched into destroying his future. She was already maneuvering for her daughter, Elena, to marry a king and for her son Boris to marry Niki's eldest daughter, and she did not want Andrei to throw away his chances of a great match, as had his brother Kyril, who just that past year eloped with the divorcée Victoria Melita and as a consequence had been stripped of his titles, income, and country. Perhaps Kyril's recklessness had inspired Andrei? Grand Duke Vladimir admonished him that I was a pleasant enough diversion but nothing more. He should know. No, he could not marry me, Andrei said, returning to me, sheepishly. I laughed and snapped my fingers at him. How very like the young tsarevich! I knew I was unmarriageable. It was not only Andrei who could not marry me. No man of any real rank could, nor would one of lesser rank want to, I had been so well used. No, the tsar could not marry me, Sergei could not marry me, even Andrei could not marry me. When Princess Radziwill congratulated me later that year on having two grand dukes at my feet, I forced myself to laugh and reply, *And why not? I have two feet.*

What I did not have was the tsar, who had turned his face from me and my son no matter what trouble I stirred up in the beds of his capital.

When Vova saw me going off those afternoons to Andrei's, he was jealous and, as he assumed I was going off to rehearse at the theater, he said he was old enough now to come with me. He wanted to see the stage, he cried, he wanted to see me dance, he wanted to take lessons at the theater school, and as I had once done to my father—until, exasperated, he took me to Lev Ivanov, who watched me pose and dance and said, *All right. Let her come to the school straightaway!*— I was seven!—so Vova also launched an elaborate campaign. He would live at the school, he said, and I could be his teacher. *They will not take you until you are ten*, I told him. *Until then you will study with your tutors*. By the time he was ten, I figured, he would forget all this, and so I hoped, for at ten or twelve, boys could enroll not only at the Theater School, where I had no intention of enrolling him—where my brother Josef's children Slava and later Celina attended—but also at the prestigious Corps des Pages, where, just before Vova's birth, Sergei had, at my urging, placed his name on a list. For after all, the young tsarevich still lived—Alix's uncle, Leopold, had lived to thirty-one before a hemorrhage from a minor car accident claimed him—and Vova must have a life. The Corps des Pages admitted only the sons of grand dukes, lieutenant-generals, vice admirals, and privy councilors, and my son, as far as they knew,

was the son of Grand Duke Sergei Mikhailovich. The old Vorontzov palace, designed in the 1790s by the same Rastrelli who had
created the Catherine Palace and Peterhof for Empress Elizabeth,
had housed the school for over a hundred years, and on its grounds
were both an Orthodox and a Catholic church. Within the palace
were rooms for dormitories and classrooms and a ballroom with a
great gallery where the school hosted its seasonal balls.

The young cadets who decorated those rooms were given day
uniforms, full-dress uniforms for court appearances, evening clothes
of black broadcloth with gold lapels, and standard ball uniforms,
with weaponry to be removed while dancing, though the disasters
that occurred when spurs and swords met taffeta and satin were
legion. In their final years, the top students in the class were appointed pages to the court. The emperor was assigned a page, as
were the grand dukes and duchesses. The dowager empress and
Alix had four apiece. If Vova—when Vova—was appointed a court
page and assigned to one of the imperial family, he would be given
a court uniform of white doeskin breeches, a red-and-gold tunic,
and black Wellington boots and driven in a court carriage to the
Winter Palace, the pages all covered with sheets to keep their uniforms spotless en route. And when Vova completed his service he
would be awarded a gold watch engraved with the monogram of
the imperial personage he had served and commissioned as an officer, assigned as an adjutant to one of the men of the imperial family to begin what would be, I was certain, a brilliant career at court.
I could see already his initial appearance there, where he would be
formally presented to the imperial family, including Alix, whose
hand he would kiss and with whom he would exchange pleasant-
ries in French to the extent of her ability to deliver them. My son
had a French tutor already, so by eighteen, he would speak the language fluently. What would she think of him? Would she note
some imperial resemblance? See in him Niki's eyes, perhaps, Niki's
likeness in the face, his gait, his bearing? Or would Vova be to her

merely another of the many, many beautiful young men in uniform? Family, wealth, beauty, loyalty—those were the requirements for the Guards.

Yes, my son would get to his father in the Winter Palace one way or another, but for now my boy would remain at home with me, doted on by my family and cosseted by Sergei, who placated him for not attending the theater school by having a playhouse built for him at our dacha. And later when Vova complained, indignantly, that he had to stand in the garden to relieve himself into the rosebushes, Sergei added a working bathroom to the playhouse. He bought him a miniature motorcar that really drove, a fireman's hose that shot real water, a stuffed llama that towered above his bed. At night, beneath the llama, Sergei and Vova knelt to whisper their prayers together. When Vova was sick, Sergei brushed his thin hair up into a ribbon to cool his fever and telephoned his brother the hypochondriac to send his personal doctor to come and treat Vova; Sergei even had a camp bed set up in Vova's room so he could sleep by him until he was well. Though Sergei never rebuked me for my dalliance with Andrei, it seemed because of it Vova had supplanted me in Sergei's affections and the two of us were turned by it from each other to Vova, who became quite spoiled from all the attention. And so, this is how it all was until 1912.

see how we suffer

I N LATE SEPTEMBER OF THAT YEAR, the tsar and his suite traveled, as usual, to Poland for the hunt, to his estates at Skernevetski, Bielovezh, and Spala, and my brother Josef, now chairman of the Northerner, a hunting society, and who had been, through my influence, you remember, put in charge of the tsar's hunting lodges after his dismissal from the ballet, traveled with him. It wasn't long before rumors about matters in Poland began to make their way to Peter. People were saying the tsarevich had taken ill with typhus or cholera. The London *Times* had written the heir had been wounded by a terrorist's bomb. Of the truth, Sergei knew nothing. If the rumors were true, Niki was not speaking of them yet. And then, on the ninth of October, Josef sent me a terse telegram instructing me to come to Spala at once at the tsar's request and to bring Vova with me. I carried the telegram around in my hand so long that afternoon the paper began to disintegrate. What did the tsar want of me and my son after so long? What he wanted back in 1904? But when I answered my brother's message, Josef would give me no details other than *Don't use Sergei's railroad car*. I was to call him at the lodge when I arrived at the station in Warsaw. Josef the revolutionary as the tsar's servant? See how poverty and need can change a man!

I told Vova only that we would go to Poland to visit my brother who was serving the tsar at his hunting lodge. Yet at the train station I saw the *gazeta* with the black-bordered bulletin that announced the tsarevich was gravely ill, and though the bulletin did not specify the affliction, I knew the family would not allow such an announcement unless the tsarevich was near death. All the way south and west from Petersburg Vova chattered, could he go hunting and would we hunt elk and stag and would there be European bison there, too? Would he have his own gun or would Josef have to hold his for him? Could he take the antlers home and mount them on the wall of his bedroom, or, better yet, over the mantel in my White Hall so our guests could see them and demand to be told the tale? He wanted to practice with me the few Polish words I had taught him, but I was distracted and kept pulling out Josef's telegrams to read and reread as if some new information might appear there to explain away my dread. Eventually, in disgust with me, Vova wandered the aisle of the compartment. At each station he asked me to buy him strawberry-flavored *kvass* or tea or roasted nuts. He kept the vendors busy all along the route. At the Warsaw Station while we waited for the car Josef sent for me, I fussed over Vova, smoothing his hair, straightening and buttoning his coat, at one point drawing him close, but he was old enough now to be embarrassed by all this and so he squirmed away from me to kick at the leaves that blew about the station, and I pulled up the collar of my chinchilla coat.

Spala, once the hunting seat of the kings of Poland, was now the hunting seat of the tsar of Russia, who entertained the remaining subjugated Polish nobility there during his autumn visits. It was already dark by the time a car took us to the gates of the estate. Here in the forested countryside we were accompanied by a great, deep hush. A carriage brought us along a sandy road through the spruce and pine and fir trees to the lodge park. Josef, holding a torch, met me and Vova at the edge of the circular drive before the lodge, but Josef would not look at me directly; it was only after the carriage let us out and disappeared that Niki himself stepped from the shadows, holding his own torch like a weapon. The breath he blew toward me in the cold mingled with my own and his aging face confronted mine. His hairline had greatly receded, and beneath his beautiful eyes another color washed there, a purplish blue. The skin of his face was the texture of paper that had been folded again and again at every possible angle and then smoothed out. His moustache seemed to thrust from his sober mouth, or perhaps it was just the light or the grimace he made that had his moustache bristling so, and his eyes glittered far too brilliantly. Behind him on the grass lay a row of dead stags in two lines on their sides, back and front legs bound, branches thick with fall leaves pressed to their bellies like a garnish to hide where they had been gutted, their beautiful antlers lifted to the sky. At the sight of all those beasts, Vova cried out in delight, *Look, Uncle Iouzia*, and pulled at my brother's hand, but Josef shushed him and Vova fell silent. Niki's great sheepskin coat fell in folds to the grass and his tall black *papakha* made him a dark crown. He looked like the king of the underworld in full costume amid this carnage. Niki raised his free hand and gestured that Vova should approach, and beside me in his own little coat Vova began to shake. He was small for ten, with a delicate face, and people when they saw him on the street often called out to him, *Look here, pretty boy!* With a backward glance at me, my son took small steps toward Niki in the cold, stiff grass. *Do you know who I am?* Niki asked. Josef answered for Vova, *This is the tsar*, and Vova bowed and said, *Highly pleased, Your Majesty*. At this, Niki put his hand on Vova's shoulder and peered into his face. Did he see himself? No, he saw my son's brother. *He looks so much like Alexei*, Niki said to me, and then he held out his hand for my own. *Forgive me, Mala. You've had a long journey*. His palm was warm and rough, and it had been a long time since I had felt his skin against my own. *Come*. He walked not beside me, but slightly in front as we headed toward the lodge, leading me like a horse, Vova, the hound, trotting slightly behind, and my brother, whom I had forgotten, trailing us at the discreet distance of a servant.

The lodge at Spala did not look like much of a palace, being long and aging and ugly, the bottom story measured off by evergreens clipped into pyramids, the top by tall windows, side by side by side. The forest appeared to be penned back from it by a scalloped hem of clipped brush. As we drew closer, Niki, with a wave of his hand, sent Vova back to walk with Josef. When they were out of earshot, Niki gestured upward to a curtained balcony at one end of the lodge above a veranda. *Alexei is dying up there*. I believe I began to bite at my nails while he went on, those eyes scintillant, that face such a fine mesh of lines. It was the second week of Alexei's suffering, he said. Blood had begun to fill the cavity between his groin and his left leg to the point where the child had no choice but to draw his knee to his chest, but still the bleeding did not cease. The doctors alternately raised and lowered the springed frame of his bed to help him sit up or lie down, but in neither position, in no position, Niki said, could the tsarevich find comfort, and the blood began to press on the nerves, causing Alexei spasms of pain so great that he had begun, between shrieks, to beg to be allowed to die, crying, *Bury me in the woods and make me a monument of stones*. But the worst was the hemorrhage in the stomach, which the doctors could not stop either and from which he would soon expire. He was feverish and delusional, his heart was feeble, and he was so white-faced it seemed there was no blood left to circulate about the rest of him, but as he was a child and they did not want to give him morphine, his only relief was to faint. All this was the result of an unfortunate poke by the oarlocks when Alexei had jumped into a boat at Bielovezh, causing a small swelling that they thought had healed until he took a carriage ride here at Spala on one of the bumpy, sandy roads like the one we had walked together.

Niki said he could not bear to enter his son's bedroom, where Alix sat in an armchair day and night, without weeping. Though each day there was a hunt and each evening there were many guests to dinner, where on a makeshift stage his daughters performed for their entertainment, behind the painted canvas of that show hung a very different scene. Just the day before, Baron Freedericks, the minister of the imperial court, who oversaw all court protocol and carried out all Niki's instructions, had persuaded the family the tsarevich was so sick it was time to publish a bulletin announcing this to prepare the country for his death, and this bulletin had appeared in all the newspapers this morning. That was what I had seen in the *gazeta* at the train station. Another bulletin had also been prepared to announce his death. As Niki talked, we approached the house, and Niki paused to point out the green canvas tent in the garden, the fabric rippling in the dark wind. Up until today the weather had been warm, the tsar said. But now, as if in preparation for the tsarevich's death, the season had turned. The simple tent had been made into a chapel and now with the official announcement of Alexei's illness, all churches and chapels in Russia would hold prayer services twice a day. As Josef led Vova into the tent to see the altar, Niki said to me simply, *Come with me.*

Niki took me a half verst into the deep forest of tall, thin trees, birch trees with their white peeling trunks so tall and close together one could disappear within them, Niki holding up his torch to light the way. Everywhere I stepped, a root or a vine twisted under my shoe. On Niki walked, now and then offering me his hand or his elbow, and just as I was about to ask how much farther, he abruptly stopped counting off his paces and looked down. Before us lay a small grave, freshly dug, and by it a loose pile of stones. Niki knelt, picked up a pebble from the ground, and put it in my hand. The stone was cool and moist, and my fingers closed around it. The forest around us listened, waiting, and I heard myself exhale, slowly. Niki said not one word; his torch crackled and snapped. We stood there a minute, an hour, a year until I understood: this grave was for Alexei and it was meant to disappear, to be swallowed by the forest. We turned away from it, finally, and Niki led me back to the green tent, where Vova and Josef lingered. I tried to catch Josef's eye. What did he know? Everything, probably, and he considered it a curse I'd brought on myself. Niki took us to the white-paned doors of the lodge, where Niki and Josef thrust their torches into the ground at either side. We went into a hallway that smelled of damp and offered little light. We passed a small room that held two chairs with backs like the antlers of giant stags, a dining room with leather chairs pulled up to a long table, a dark covered porch spotted with wicker furniture. Everywhere we walked, we left a trail of gritty sand. Josef followed as Niki, Vova, and I went up a narrow wooden staircase. At the top of it Niki touched my elbow. We walked along a hall, and when we came down the corridor two young girls in costumes ran by us—one in full pirate regalia, the other in a white dress and white cap—and opened a door and then we could hear it, a long, low moaning sound. The tsarevich. The door closed. Niki's face pleated itself into a thousand furrows, and by the time we reached the curtained outdoor balcony at one end of the long hall by that door, he was a thousand years old.

A woman sat in a wicker chair on that balcony in the almost dark amid a miasma of stripes—striped fabric on the low walls, striped curtains floor to ceiling, striped cushions of the chairs. Alix. She rose. She wore a sable coat against the cold, its thick cuffs bracelets at her wrists. Her hair, which I had remembered only as red-blonde, had many gray strands now mixed with the gold at the temples, her hair parted in the center and crimped and arranged into large poufs at the sides of her head. We were the same age, but I was a girl and this was a grandmother, a German grandmother, whose skin had loosened and thickened at the jowl, whose nose had begun to hook, and whose eyelids now formed hoods. I gripped at the stone I still held in my hand. Why, Alix looked more like a man than a woman, as some women do when they age. At the theater, men always played the hags, the Baba Yaga, the Carabosse. This was Alix, the princess from Hesse-Darmstadt? She did not contrive to make her anguished face say anything but what she felt. She looked down at my son, the little boy with the big eyes I held in front of me, my arms across his chest, and smiled sadly at him.

And Niki said to me, *See how we suffer*.

When Josef himself brought our luggage up the back passage to the bedroom adjoining Alexei's, where we were to sleep, I understood we were unofficially here.

When are we going to hunt? Vova asked.

And my brother answered, *Later. The tsar's son is very sick.*

When will he be well?

I don't know, Josef told him, and he looked at me and shook his head, as if to say, *Look where your idyll has brought you now*, and then he looked at that adjoining door, and I understood that our immediate proximity to the tsarevich was purposeful, that at the exact moment of Alexei's death, he would be carried into this dark room and from there to the forest while Vova was pulled from this bed and ferreted into the sickroom, with Niki and Alix beside him, and he would be proclaimed miraculously healed. I supposed Niki believed he could appropriate my child as he appropriated the best furs, timber, vodka, and caviar for the profit of the crown. After all, I had long ago and foolishly offered my son to him. But my ambitions for Vova then had always involved me, as well—my marriage to Niki, my son and I together brought to the palace. Now I could see that Niki and Alix had been stitched together so tightly by the tragedy of their son's illness that there would be no sending of Alix to a convent and no divorce, no matter what happened to their boy. So all that remained of my long-ago fantasy was this tale by Dumas, in which my boy was required to assume the identity of another.

It was not that a quiet reassignment such as this did not have precedent. It had long been suspected by the wider court that Emperor Alexander I had one night walked by his sentries in his cap and greatcoat—the sentries swore it was he, they knew the sight of him well—disappeared into the streets of the capital, and a short time later his family announced his death in the south, in Taganrog. He had defeated Napoleon, and then despite, as he said, *the French air of liberty that had delighted me in my youth*, he had continued to oppress his own people, upholding the principles of aristocracy, until, exhausted, he told his brothers, *I can no longer bear the weight of being ruler*. His coffin was sent from Taganrog back to St. Petersburg. The casket, always open by custom during a state funeral, had for the funeral of Alexander I remained sealed. One of the grand dukes commented that the blackened face of the corpse, its features indiscernible, could be the face of anyone, as Alexander's family, determined to secure a serene transition and to hold on to its wealth, very well knew. And after his brother, Nicholas I, ascended the throne, defying the guards who wanted to establish a republic, there appeared in the wilderness of Siberia a holy man, a hermit, who gave his name as Fedor Kozmich and who bore a striking resemblance to the old emperor. An emperor in rags in Siberia is a hermit. The brother of the living emperor, dressed in ermine and standing in the Winter Palace, is the tsar. But Nicholas I was thirty years old when he assumed the throne and he had been raised at court. My son was ten years old and he had been raised by me. Unprepared, he would be forced into the tsarevich's bedclothes, while I would be driven from Spala, alone, escorted to the station by my brother, the two Kschessinskys in service to the court. Three Kschessinskys.

All that night on the other side of the door that connected us to Alexei's room we heard the many comings and goings of Doctors Raukhfus and Derevenko and Botkin and Federov and Ostrogorsky—all sent for from Petersburg—and through the door I could hear their voices and then Niki's voice and Alix's. Beneath the door on occasion the shadow of a shoe would appear and then be withdrawn. There would be light and then shadow. And, of course, we could hear the suffering of the child and his mother's croon as she attempted, helplessly, to soothe him. Although I put Vova into his dressing gown, I never undressed but sat in a chair drawn up to his bed, much as Niki had said Alix sat fully clothed by her son this night and every night for two weeks past, rarely sleeping. Vova lay in bed with his eyes open. We could see very clearly from our window the moon and stars made crisp by the frost; the earth seemed very large and heaven very far away. I stroked my son's brow and his silky brown hair and his slender beautiful fingers and I tried to answer his questions.

Why is the boy crying?

Something hurts him.

When will he stop crying?

I don't know.

But with the continuing moans and shrieks from next door, Vova's questions stumbled to a halt. He was listening, his eyes wide, to the boy's cries from the next room. *Lord, have mercy* or *Mama, help me* or, the worst, *Let me die*, and soon Vova began to whimper himself in sympathy. *Mama, is that boy dying?* But he put his hands over his ears for my answer. And then I heard the unmistakable sounds of prayer, one voice, not conversing, but intoning. *Through this holy anointing and His most loving mercy, may the Lord help you by the grace of the Holy Spirit*, and then several voices, *Amen*. This was the first part of the rite of extreme unction, the anointing of the sick, followed by the last confession, and finally, the administration of the viaticum, the Eucharist, food for the journey. The journey where? The journey to heaven. Alexei was dying, right now, in the next room, and at any moment Niki would open that adjoining door and take possession of his other son, without telling me, without asking me. And right there I decided I would tell Niki it was both too late and too soon. He could have Vova later, as a man, as a page, as an officer in the Guards, as a diplomat or a minister. He could make him a prince. But he could not take my baby from me now even if God took Alexei from him. And in the silence coming from the next room, I stroked my son's sleeping head, and I rehearsed my lines, *Batiushka, hear my plea.*

But Niki did not appear to us in this little room until the morning, and then he said only, *Alexei is better. Come and see him.*

So what or who had effected this sudden miracle? The *staretz* Rasputin. Alix had telephoned him in the night sometime between my arrival and the delivery of last rites. In her grief and despair she had reached out wildly for his help, just as Niki had reached out for mine. And just as I rushed to obey, so did Rasputin, far away in Pokrovskoe, Siberia. He did not have to travel, though; he simply prayed, interceded with God and then sent to the tsaritsa a telegram: *God has seen your tears and heard your prayers. Do not grieve. The Little One will not die.*

Perhaps a word here about Rasputin. He had begun to perform healings for Alexei and because of this he had become indispensable to Alix, which would not have been a problem had Rasputin been a quiet man, but, alas and alack, he was a man of the theater from start to finish, so perhaps I understood him better than most. Let's begin with the costume—the shabby black coat, the peasant's blouse, and the peasant's boots (all of which Alix soon replaced with silk shirts embroidered with cornflowers, with velveteen pants, with boots soft as butter, with a beaver cap and a beaver coat), the long, un-combed hair that fell past his shoulders like the hair worn by no man, peasant or prince, only by holy fools, the long, unkempt beard, the beard of all Old Believers, and then the eyes, a light blue like the pale gemstone tourmaline, just as sharp and piercing and as shot through with light as a crystal. I heard he could barely read a tract of Scripture, had trouble remembering any of its passages, and that his handwriting was a scrawl of big black letters, misshapen, of uneven size, the words misspelled, toppling onto each other. But when he spoke, it was an incantation, an almost incoherent ramble—*the world is like the day, look it's already evening; love the clouds, for that is where we live*. Most theatrical of all were his healings, where he took the hand of the patient, and then, using the greatest powers of concentration, made his face lose all color, turn yellow. Sweat dripped down his cheeks, and with his eyes closed he began to tremble—it was as if life left him and entered the body of the sick. Yet a storm of criticism always surrounded Rasputin because of his behavior at the margins of the stage—at the height of his popularity a stream of women came to his apartment in Petersburg to listen to his lectures, to give him money, even to be defiled by him, after which, in the night, he went to bathhouses, consorted with prostitutes, drank himself to public drunkenness beyond even that of an ordinary Russian, and once at the Moscow restaurant Yar, Rasputin, leering, exposed himself to a group of women and created a fracas that ended only when the management called high enough up the ladder of command until someone, the assistant minister of the interior, was well enough positioned to give permission for the arrest of the palace favorite. Alix believed the police reports were false, the ministers who spoke against her association with him his enemies—and hers. But when her letters to Rasputin began circulating in Petersburg in 1911, letters written in an effusive style so at odds with her chilly public demeanor, letters in which everyone was her *darling* and in which she longed to kiss them all, copies Rasputin himself released at first to the capital and then to cities all over Russia to silence his tormentors (*I only wish one thing, to fall asleep forever on your shoulders and in your arms. Where are you? Where have you gone? Will you soon be again close to me?*), it seemed all of Russia was in an uproar. What was the empress doing in the arms of this unwashed *staretz*?

The cartoons that resulted from these letters—caricatures of Rasputin, Alix, and the girls that appeared in the papers and could not be suppressed, now that the 1905 reforms had lifted censorship of the press and guaranteed freedom of speech—showed the women of the imperial family frolicking naked, the empress and Rasputin embracing. In another, a demonic, black-haired, oversized Rasputin held two small stupid-faced puppets in his hands: Niki and Alix. Behind Rasputin, the empress knelt naked, a yellow crown in her long flowing brown hair; Niki potbellied and castrated, sat in a palanquin, wearing only boots and a fur hat; clustered about the three of them chattered a legion of grand dukes and ministers, all now exiled or murdered. At this, the family, Niki's ministers, even the prime minister of the Duma, Petr Stolypin, insisted Rasputin had to be sent away. And so, bowing to pressure, which he never liked to do, Niki sent Grigory Rasputin back home to Siberia for a while, to his village of Pokrovskoe, which was why, in 1912, from Spala, Alix had to telegraph him there.

I saw Rasputin in St. Petersburg later that fall—for after his great success at Spala he had been allowed out of exile to return to the capital—on an evening after the theater while I was driving over the Troitsky Bridge. At first he was just a shape, a long black coat, a hood, hands gesticulating, two animals battling, and then as we drew closer, the lanterns on the outside of my carriage swung into his face. The man beneath the hood was suddenly illuminated, as if the figure had stepped up to the footlights of a stage. He had been turned toward the Neva, staring into the water, possibly importuning his own fate, but he turned his head toward me as I passed in my perfumed and heated carriage, and I saw the face of the creature that Petersburgers had begun to call *The Nameless One* or *The*

Unmentionable—a nose broad at the nostrils, like the gnarled root of a tree, a heavy brow like a ledge over two blue eyes, pale as electrified water. I knew immediately and unmistakably it was he, so much had his description circulated. When his eyes connected momentarily with mine I felt the shock of it as if I turned inside out and my mind was wiped clean. And then we passed and I looked back at him, but he had not turned to look back at me. He didn't know who I was or how my son could have seized from him his power.

So, where was I? Yes, how we saw Alexei for the first time, Vova and I. Although it was brilliant daylight outside, the electric lights were burning in the narrow, dark hallways. While my brother supervised the loading of our trunk into the carriage, our utility here over, the tsar escorted us down the hall. The door to Alexei's room had been flung open, and standing by the bed against a table of medicines and towels, useless palliatives, were Alexei's sisters, all four dressed alike as if they were a small *corps de ballet*—in high-necked, white lace blouses and pale, pleated linen skirts. Even their hair was similarly styled—half of it pulled back at the crown with a bow, the rest loose behind the ears and falling over their shoulders. Only the littlest one's, Anastasia's, hair was straight. The hair of the other three hung in soft waves. They were kissing at their brother's fingers and telling him about the bit of theater they had performed last night at dinner for the guests, the members of the imperial suite and the Polish noblemen who had been invited to join them—two scenes from *Le Bourgeois Gentilhomme* that must have called for two of them to be the lady and the pirate I had seen in the corridor last night—and their laughter stopped as they saw at the threshold Vova and me, a little boy and a little woman. They themselves were big, pink swans surrounding the small, white-faced form, who smiled at Vova from his bed. For a moment, with that smile, one could see the lively boy Sergei once described to me who at dinner even with company there licked his plate, squirmed through the meal, teased his sisters, stole the slipper from a lady-in-waiting and returned it to her with a strawberry stuffed into the toe of it, wrote little notes to Niki telling him of his day—*When I see you I am going to bathe in your bath—I kiss your hand.* The children had few friends, as Alix kept them away from what she considered the salacious influence of the court, which was everyone they knew. So the girls entertained each other, and Alexei was allowed the company of the son of his sailor nanny or when the family was in the Crimea the son of a peasant or on occasion a boy from the Corps des Pages, a well-behaved cadet who was summoned to the palace when they were in Petersburg. And now here was my son, his half brother, the latest to be summoned, standing in his bedroom doorway.

Perhaps Alexei thought Vova was one of those boys come to play with him during his convalescence, for he raised his hand and beckoned Vova to come, telling him not to bow. When Vova approached, toy in hand he had clutched for courage, Alexei said, *Is that for me?* and without protest Vova handed over to him the stuffed elephant I had given him at Christmas as a remembrance of the real elephant the clown Dourov had brought to the house. The cotton animal wore a red-and-gold cloth saddle and matching hat with a bell that jangled. The children fell upon it instantly—*Oh, how darling, look at its little trunk*—as Alix and I looked at each other. All night we had each contemplated losing a son, and this morning we shared the same relief. My son bent over the bed to show the heir the intricacies by which the elephant's legs could be made to move and their two heads touched. Alexei's hair had more chestnut to it, but Niki was right, the two boys looked remarkably alike, of similar age and build and similar features; it took my breath away to see how similar they were, but one had color and health and the other yellow skin stretched tight across his face. But Alexei was alive. He would not be buried in the cold woods by the

Pilitsa River. Soon enough Alexei asked one of his sisters—I don't know which one—to fetch his box of lead soldiers so they could play elephant hunt, and when she reappeared with the chest of beautifully painted toy men, each molded into a different posture, Niki followed behind her and stood in the doorway to watch the boys stand the soldiers one by one until they filled the hills and dales of the bedsheets around Alexei's legs—one leg up, the other leg down. It would be a year before the tsarevich could walk normally or fully straighten his left leg, for the stagnant blood that had filled his joint was like acid and it ate away at bone and cartilage and this deformation locked the leg into a bent position. For a year he would wear iron braces designed to slowly once again straighten out the limb, and during this year he would be photographed officially only when seated—on chairs, on sleighs, on steps. The boys aimed their soldiers at the elephant and made shooting sounds, and after a few rounds of this, the tsar said we would have a real hunt another time, when Alexei was all better, and Alix told Alexei to make a gift of those soldiers to Vova and the tsar helped the boys gather all the men and lay them back into the wood box.

My brother drove us to the station himself, fur hat pulled low on his forehead, his nose a mountain slope of rebuke, and we did not speak then of the tsarevich or anything we had seen. Instead, Josef amused Vova along the way with the numbers of beasts and birds the tsar's hunting party had bagged each day, and I was grateful to him, for on the long train ride back to Peter, Vova drew pictures of animals and forests, of guns and bows and arrows, and then he drew up lists of imaginary hunting records with numbers carefully chosen for rabbit, pheasant, partridge, elk, stag, and bison. In a few weeks, when Alexei was well enough, he also would travel to Petersburg, first by carriage on the sandy road I had walked that night, a road raked smooth by the servants there, and then by railroad car that crept along at fifteen miles an hour to spare him any further injury. By then the dark forest and the dark house would be bleached white with snow, but that wouldn't matter, for Alix had snatched her son back from the underworld. The imperial family would never return to Spala, never return to any of their Polish estates again.

For my part, for years I wondered what my son remembered of that night, of that small, plain room with the whitewashed walls, the single picture hanging of men at hunt, the iron bed, the window that held the vista of a cold night in Poland. But I never asked him, for once it was over, I never wanted to speak of it again. I understood now why Niki had withdrawn from me so totally—his son's illness was a tornado and it sucked everything around the boy into its powerful and lonely vortex.

B Y THE WINTER OF 1913 the tsarevich could walk but only short distances and then only with a limp, but the Great Ter-centenary, the celebration of three hundred years of Romanov rule, could not wait for his fuller recovery. For ceremonial events he would have to either remain at home or be carried by one of the Cossacks from the family's personal retinue, the tsarevich's eyes too large, his features wooden with fatigue, and Niki knew the country would stink with even further rumors: the tsarevich was an imbecile, the tsarevich had an incurable disease. And so, for the de rigueur gala performance of *A Life for the Tsar* at the Maryinsky, when the theater would be filled only with court officials and dip-lomats, an Old World audience of the wellborn who once ruled Russia very well, thank you, without any help from peasants, clerks, workers, Jews, and revolutionaries, Niki did not want to push through the curtain of the imperial box with his crippled son cradled in the arms of a Cossack from the Konvoi regiment. It was not my brother this time, but Sergei who brought me Niki's latest proposition.

Niki wanted Vova to wear Alexei's red dress tunic of the Preo-brazhensky Guards that night and join them in the imperial box. I could see in Sergei's face that this excited him—a great prank like the ones the Potato Club used to play, but he had not been to Spala to see how this prank was prelude to an abduction. Sergei thought we had gone to Poland so Vova could hunt with Josef, not so my son could be hunted. And so Sergei endeavored to persuade me. I would already be at the theater, Sergei said, and so it would be easy enough to bring Vova with me. Sergei would come visit in my dressing room as he often did and he would bring me Alexei's uniform. The imperial carriage would roll to a stop at my dressing room window to fetch Vova. *Let him be tsarevich for a night*, Sergei said, and I think he was bewitched by the picture of the young, illegitimate boy he adored being adored by the court that had so far shunned him. But Sergei could see my reluctance, and so he endeavored to trump it by reproaching me. *Mala, Niki needs our help.*

And so I asked Vova, *How would you like to play a part at the theater tonight?*, knowing, of course, that he would be mad to do it—he had not yet given up his dream of becoming a future Honored Artist of the Imperial Theaters. He had announced recently that he would rather be an actor than a dancer, after all, and he had taken to dressing up to perform skits in what he could find of Sergei's things—gloves, a cap, and once his boots, or in costumes we bought him, such as a Cossack's tunic and cuirassier or his fireman's uniform with its Teutonic helmet, which he wore otherwise while manning his miniature water truck, driving it about the grounds of the dacha. When I said, *Would you like this?*, Vova began to jump up and down at the prospect of performing.

What will I play? he asked me. *A peasant boy, a fairy page, a puppet?* He had seen my ballets. He knew all the children's roles.

No, I said. *A very special part. The tsarevich. The tsar's son is sick again and can't be with his father and mother in their box tonight. You will go there with them. Can you pretend to be very noble, the heir to the throne?*

And my son said, *Yes, yes*, too quickly, and he raised his chin and looked about the room in a very good approximation of a nobleman surveying his estate.

Very good, I said. *Very good, my little tsarevich.*

That night I arrived at the theater my usual two hours before curtain and had my dresser sew me into my costume a bit earlier so she would be gone long before Sergei's arrival with my son's costume. Only when Vova asked, *Why are you so nervous, Mama?* did I realize I was compulsively tracing the patterns of the white flowers against the blue of my dressing room's cretonne-covered walls.

When Sergei arrived, I hissed, *This is ridiculous. Everyone will know he's not the tsarevich.*

And Vova interrupted me, *Mama, I want my costume.*

Sergei said, *Mala, stop worrying*, and to Vova, *I've never known your mother to have such stage fright!* and with a big wolf's grin he opened up his greatcoat to reveal the little uniform hidden inside, the heir's uniform of the Life Guards, a miniature of Niki's uniform, the red breeches and the red tunic with its golden epaulettes, each button embossed with the imperial eagle, and the collar embroidered with the monogram H II, a monogram only the heir to the throne was permitted to wear. At the sight of all this, Vova let out a whoop and began to dance, he was ten and still childish from all my cosseting of him, and Sergei and I, playing his dressers, had to practically stuff him into the trousers, Sergei lifting him up off the ground and I holding open the breeches for him to be lowered into. *Hold still*, I told him, as I buttoned him into his shirt and tunic, Sergei laughing at Vova's glee, my movements awkward from nerves. My son was small for his age and Alexei tall for eight and this meant that the uniform fit almost perfectly, and with his two hands Sergei smoothed Vova's hair. *Look*, he said to me. *Is this not the picture of the little tsarevich?* More than a picture, I thought, and then we heard a carriage approaching, the bells on the horses' bridles jingling, and the carriage paused on the private driveway right outside the low windows of my dressing room, and that was the only sound, the police at the tsar's behest having stopped the theatergoing court traffic at both ends. Sergei looked out the glass and said,

It's Niki, and to Vova, *Are you ready?*, and when my son nodded vigorously, *Da, da*, Sergei opened the window, gave Vova a quick boost, and my son was a shadow slipped over the freezing window-sill and into the envelope of that carriage to ride the rest of the way up the drive to the private imperial entrance. There he would dis-embark with Nicholas and Alexandra and walk through the marble foyer and up the steps, along the carpeted corridor lined with gilded chairs and into the imperial anteroom, the walls of it a light blue, and from there through a velvet curtain, as if they themselves were entering a stage, and into the imperial box itself.

The entire audience stood at the family's entrance and the na-tional anthem was played, and by that time, of course, I had run out onto the stage to look through the peephole in the curtain. I believe I had to elbow someone out of the way. The three tiers of the boxes and all of the stalls seemed reddened by the color of all the scarlet tunics of all the uniforms worn by all the officers in attendance, that red punctuated in two spots by the greens, blues, and golds of the national costumes of the emir of Bokhara and the khan of Khiva and their retinues. My son stood proudly between Niki and Alix in his scarlet-and-gold uniform, looking down at the crowd from the imperial box with the exact aplomb he had shown when practicing his role at home. I had always thought Vova showed little talent for the theater, but it looked as if I had been his Teliakovsky, thwarting him, holding him back, for clearly Vova was enjoying this moment, even, at one point, raising one hand to execute a very good sem-blance of a noble wave. So, he was a Kschessinsky as much as he was a Romanov.

That night we performed *A Life for the Tsar*, which tells the story of the boy Mikhail Romanov, the first tsar of the dynasty, pro-tected from assassination by the peasant hero Ivan Susanin. Mikhail was sixteen years old and the grand nephew of Ivan the Terrible's wife, close enough, when the council of *boyare* decided in 1612 to offer him the throne. Ivan had died in 1584, the first to call himself *tsar*, from the Latin word *caesar*, and the last ruler of the Rurik dynasty that had controlled Russia for six hundred years. After his death, Russia stumbled this way and that until the council reached out for someone related, however tenuously, to Ivan. In the winter of 1612, the Poles had invaded Russia, intent on taking advantage of her during its time of troubles—ah, we have a long, tangled history, the Poles and the Rus—and intent on murdering Mikhail on the eve of his coronation, which managed to take place, thanks to the peasant Susanin, in the Ipatiev monastery where Mikhail had been hidden. No wonder his mother trembled as her son was crowned, listening for the men coming to murder him, her boy who had just last month lived quietly with her in a Volga River village. Susanin only pretended to lead the Polish regiment to the boy, and instead took them into a snowy mountainous impasse. For his trouble, Susanin paid with his life and Poland with partition, but Russia was given a new, stable dynasty, the Romanov dynasty of three hundred years.

I trembled in the wings, like Mikhail's mother, at this turn in *my* child's life, but luckily I did not have to enter the stage until Act II, at the ball at the palace of a Polish nobleman where the ensemble performs several Polish dances—a polonaise, the krakowiak, a waltz, a mazurka—and while dancing this last, the gentry's mazurka my father had taught me, it seemed over the shoulder of one capped dancer and then another I saw my father's face. *Mathilde-Maria, what are you doing?* Over the shoulders of another, I noted how often the court looked up at the imperial box. Vova was now seated slightly behind Niki and Alix, the dowager empress, and Niki's sisters and their husbands, but Niki's brother Mikhail was notably absent. He had eloped with a divorcée and been exiled just like Andrei's brother Kyril. In the grand ducal loges, Sergei sat beaming with his brothers and Andrei, bland-faced, completely ignorant of what was at hand, sat in his box with his brother Boris and with Miechen, now widowed, but no less rapacious, perhaps more so! The formidable Miechen had taken over her husband's position as minister of the arts, most unusual for a woman, but other ambitions, more traditional ones, had been thwarted—she had not managed entirely to unhook Andrei from me, she had not married her daughter off to a king but to Prince Nicholas of Greece, her suit to have Boris betrothed to Niki's daughter Olga had been rebuffed, Alix sniffing that she would not think to match a fresh young girl with Boris, so much older and in and out of so many beds, and Boris settled instead for a mistress. And though Miechen had quickly and expediently converted to Orthodoxy after the tsarevich's near-fatal illness and Mikhail's exile, her own son Kyril's unfortunate marriage might prevent him as well from ever being tsar. And Miechen did not even know the other obstacle that stood in his way to the throne—the one sitting in a velvet-cushioned chair behind Niki in the imperial box. Just let her try to tip my son from that chair! But it wasn't until I finished the mazurka and took my bow first to the imperial box, then to the grand ducal boxes, and finally to the house at large, that I even noted the grim face of the empress, another of the ambitious mothers here and one miserable despite her finery— the white velvet gown, the blue diagonal ribbon of the Order of St. Andrei, the diamond tiara, the white fan made of eagle feathers. She stood up at my bow, face covered in blotches, and removed herself to the back of the imperial box, where no one could see her and where she remained for the rest of the performance of the opera. One could hear the audience practically hiss its disapproval as the empress withdrew—and these mouths and tongues belonged not to the peasants, not to the students, not to the revolutionaries, not to the members of the Duma, but to the court. Niki kept his face impassive, but he heard the sound.

I am certain this is why he then gestured for my son to move to the front of the box to take the seat left vacant by the empress, and the audience made another noise then, one that sounded like a caress, that wrapped itself around the pretty boy who looked so happy, whose father smiled at him so fondly. From the modest distance of the stage, I could see Niki's pleasure at the murmur of approval emitted by the audience. And when, at the end of Act IV, after the coda that marks the opera's finale, the great bass Sobinov who had played the role of the hero, Ivan Susanin, walked to the proscenium in his long robe and his horsehair beard, dropped to his knees, raised his arms to Niki and Vova, and began to sing an impromptu "God Save the Tsar." He had once sung a lullaby to my son in his cradle—did Sobinov recognize him now? His voice filled the theater, at first a capella until the orchestra, stumbling a bit in its surprise, followed his lead and picked up their instruments. One by one we artists of the Imperial Theaters knelt alongside Sobinov and the audience, in a great wave, stood. At this Niki stood, as well, and at his signal my son rose beside him. Niki looked down at us all, silent, head bowed. My son, in imitation, did the same, and there was no doubt it had been *this*, the sight of the emperor with his young heir, that had prompted Sobinov's homage.

God save the tsar,
Mighty and powerful,
May he reign for our glory,
Reign that our foes may quake.

The son of a tsar belongs to his country, not to his mother. And Russia, or at least the Russia inside this theater, still loved its tsar, *this* tsar, and it also loved and needed his son, perhaps *this* son, should it come to that. And if and when the time came, Alix would agree to it, had, even tonight, reluctantly, unhappily agreed to it. For the alternative to my son as imposter was for the line to pass crookedly to Niki's brother, whom Alix hated, or to Kyril, whom she hated even more, or, if the imperial council negated those successions, to the tall, tsar-sized commander of the army, Nikolasha, whom she had hated since 1905, ever since he had told Niki if he did not install the Duma he would shoot himself on the spot rather than be charged with imposing martial law. Yes, she hated and feared them all, all the men of the imperial family—and, yes, she would take my son because he was Niki's and because a tsar without an heir is a weakened tsar. But what kind of mother was I, to send my child away, a sack of clothes in his hands, a note pinned to his shirt, *Take my son*. What kind of mother? The mother of a tsar. This opera was my object lesson, after all, with Mikhail Romanov's mother reluctantly submitting her son to his fate. Whenever I met Niki he wanted to take something from me, though when I was younger I thought I was taking something from him. But one never takes from the tsar, one always gives, and that my father saw—I was giving the tsar my life. After all, the opera is *A Life for the Tsar*, not *The Tsar's Life for His Subject*.

And if that time came the next week, next month, next season, I would have to say to everyone I knew, *My son has gone off to school in Paris*, and I would have to remain on the stage just to see him, as I had remained on the stage to see Niki. Perhaps I would have my father's sixty years in the theater, and each of those years, the imperial family would come to watch me from their box, and I would dance for them first as a princess and then as the Queen Mother, and finally at last, as a hag, an old woman noticed only when she had the capacity to frighten or harm or amuse. The family would arrive, as always, by means of the long private drive, where they would be greeted by the director of the Imperial Theaters and escorted through the private passageway to their chairs at the gilded proscenium of the box, which in both design and ornamentation echoes the proscenium of the stage, and eventually, Tsar Nicholas II would stand there with his hair all white, beside him Alix in a tiara with white hair also, and his daughters in the brimming beauty of their adulthood, and with them the tsarevich, the tsar's son, my son, also an adult, in his own red-and-gold dress uniform of the Preobrazhensky Guards, the oldest regiment in Petersburg, created by

Peter the Great himself, and at their appearance an excitement would course through the audience and around the dancers on the stage as we waited for the curtain. *The imperial family, the imperial family is here*. And then at a signal from the director, the orchestra would begin the overture and the curtain with a heavy lurch would sweep sideways and upward toward the catwalk and I would run forward on the sloping boards of the stage toward the audience, toward the imperial family I had aged alongside, and one day, when I looked to the imperial box for permission to perform an encore, my son would be the one to grant it.

But all this would not happen yet. By the next summer, 1914, my son was still with me and Russia was at war with Austria and Germany.

toy soldiers

I N CITIES ACROSS RUSSIA, from the east to the west, from Odessa to Irkutsk, the red flags of the revolution were suddenly and all at once replaced with portraits of the tsar and holy icons, the country spontaneously united against a new enemy, the Austrians who threatened the Slavic people and the Germans who were Austria's allies. The German embassy in Petersburg was vandalized by a mob, the equestrian statues on its roof toppled to the street, where enormous chunks of horses' heads, horses' legs, and thick horses' bodies lay as if dynamited in the roadway. In Moscow, Bechstein and Bluthner pianos were thrown from the top stories of the leading piano store, something satisfying, I suppose, in dropping large objects from a great height. The name of the capital was changed from the Germanic Petersburg to the Slavic Petrograd. But I will always call it Petersburg—not Petrograd, Leningrad, Stalingrad—and I know one day it will again be St. Petersburg. Bach, Brahms, and Beethoven were no longer played in concert. Christmas trees were banned by the Holy Synod for the 1914 holiday: the candlelit Christmas tree was a German custom. Anyone in the streets who spoke English, French, Italian—the common Russian was too ignorant to know French from German, *Bonjour* from *Guten Tag*—was hissed at: *Nemtsy! Germans!*

Sergei rolled out a great map of Europe and Russia onto the desk in Vova's room and Vova excitedly went through his toy soldiers to bring them to the table and place them where Sergei pointed as he explained the battles. Here in Sarajevo was where the heir to the throne of Austria-Hungary, Franz Ferdinand, had been killed by a Serbian assassin, and there Vova lay one of his men on his side. Here in Vienna was where the emperor Franz Joseph had drafted an ultimatum demanding that Austrian officers be permitted to enter Serbia to suppress all anti-Austrian sentiment and arrest all anti-Austrian officers. Vova stood a man at Vienna and made him a tiny paper crown. And here in Belgrade was where the Serbian crown prince telegraphed to the tsar in St. Petersburg for help, as by tradition the tsar was protector of all Slavic peoples. Our city Vova knew and he spent some time searching for the proper figure to represent the tsar, finally settling on the tallest soldier in the box, though Niki, of course, was not tall. But despite the tsar's mediations, the Austro-Hungarians attacked Belgrade—Vova placed cannons here and there, and Sergei pointed to where the Russians mobilized along the Austrian border. Then the kaiser declared Germany would enter the war to help its ally, Austria-Hungary, and he began to send his troops through Belgium to northern France to prevent the tsar's armies from being transported by railroad through France to Germany. So France entered the war. The tsar's armies began to fight both north and south, north against the Germans where they met many casualties and south against the Austrians where they had greater success. The Russian army in the south moved all the way to Gorlice, Cracow, Lodz, and the Carpathian Mountains. Through all the battles of 1914, Vova moved his lead soldiers steadily southwest and at the north he laid them down on their backs, dead. Sergei told Vova that the tsar had a map just like this one in his study at Alexander Palace which no one was allowed to enter and that he kept the key to that room in his pocket. The tsar wanted to use this war to enlarge the country, Sergei said, to make it an even greater Russia, to stretch it over East Prussia to the mouths of the Vistula and over Bukovina to the Carpathians. Armenia would be annexed, the Muslim Turks pushed out of Europe and back into Asia Minor. The Straits and Holy Constantinople would belong to Orthodox Russia, as they should. The Germanic empire, which Sergei told me Alix found so changed from the Germany of her childhood, the people transformed by the perfidy and ambition of the kaiser—who had once loved her own sister!—that she urged Niki to crush it. Sergei told Vova that Germany, once crushed, would be divided among France, England, and Denmark, and the kaiser's House of Hohenzollern would soon be no more and wasn't that a great thing, and Vova nodded. And I nodded too. A greater Russia meant a greater tsar, a greater future tsar, and Alix and I were united in our desire for that.

Each day Vova pestered Sergei for news of the war and Vova had me wash his first-year cadet uniform daily, for that was all he would wear. But I gladly had it washed, glad he was at home with me and not at the military school where we had planned to send him this fall had the war not interrupted our plans. I was sorry about the war, but not sorry to have Vova home. Perhaps, like my father, who wanted to keep his children close, I, too, wanted my child at my side, where I could pet and cosset him and where I could perpetuate his undiluted love for me, having so little of it, even diluted, from the tsar. But there were other reasons to keep Vova near. Because of the loss of so many officers at the northern front, graduates of the military schools were being commissioned early and sent to replace them. Though our officers allowed their men in the infantry to crawl along the ground as they moved forward under machine gun fire, their Russian pride would not allow them to do the same, and so in their colorful uniforms the officers strode into battle and were easily gunned down, still gripping the lances and sabers and bayonets they never lived to use. So new officers, teenagers fresh from school, replaced them, and the infantry of the Second and Third armies replaced the soldiers of the First, and these men were barely trained—some did not even know how to hold their rifles—and the worst of them were garrisoned in our cities to protect us from the Germans. And when the war dragged on and revolutionary sentiment was reawakened, these barracked soldiers turned on us—as the men in the field turned on their young, inexperienced officers. But not yet—this was still to come.

What was it like to live in Peter during the war? At first it was not so different. The cannons at the Peter and Paul Fortress still marked the noon hour; the swans still skimmed the waters of the canals along the Champ de Mars. Tea parties marked name days and at christenings babies were baptized, the leaves turned first yellow and then gold, and after they fell, children fought with snowballs before the backdrop of a pink winter sky. Long carriages still ferried the little theater students to the Maryinsky in the evenings, and the tsar's theaters still presented their seasons, for theater to us was like opium, though we at the Maryinsky returned now to the comfort of the old classics, pulling from the storage vaults our costumes, reminding ourselves of the choreography created by Didelot, Johansson, and early Petipa and Ivanov, divertissements we had almost forgotten how to dance, steps that dated back to tsars Alexander II and III, when the world we knew was comfortably secure, where one could find, in the words of an elderly court official, *order, punctiliousness, symmetry*. The opera company sang *Boris Godunov* and *Don Quixote*, and the Imperial Ballet danced *Sylvia* and *La Fille du Pharaon*, ballets about long-ago and faraway civilizations—ancient Greece and Rome and Egypt, once great civilizations now vanished. It's ridiculous to point out the irony, yes? So I won't.

But by the late fall of 1914, only a few of the young Guards who had walked our prospekts and danced at our balls still sat in the stalls of our theaters. There were no more rows of military tunics in the parterres and boxes, no medals gleaming in the footlights, and there were fewer shimmering jewels and evening dresses as their wearers also occupied themselves otherwise, running hospitals and forming charities. At the intervals when the houselights came on the audience demanded national anthems—at first just our own, but then also the French and the British as each country became a Russian ally, and our intervals soon became interminable, even by Russian standards. When the little students of Theater Street now looked out their windows onto the Maryinsky Theater Square, they saw recruits with bayonets at practice stabbing at dummies—uniforms stuffed with hay. The infantry marched in columns down Nevsky Prospekt to depart from Warsaw Station, and the men leaving were not only young men, but also men of thirty years or more, their wives trailing them until fatigue or grief made them give up and stop and simply stare after their husbands. The imperial family went to serve, as well, not because they were particularly gifted leaders, but because that was what their positions in the family demanded of them. The tsar's brother Mikhail was called back to Russia only to be sent to the southwestern front to fight in Galicia, in a battle productive but horrible, a hundred versts piled high with the Russian dead and not enough living to clear the ground of their bodies. Niki's older cousin Nikolasha continued to serve as commander in chief of the army. Vladimir's three sons also served. Andrei went to the northwest front to headquarters, or Stavka, an old Russian name for the camp of a military chief, at Baranovichi, but I didn't have long to miss him for the stress of the war made him ill with bronchitis and he soon came home. One would think living with Miechen would have prepared him better for battle, but since he was never able to stand up to her, this was just one more instance of overwhelming force inspiring Andrei to retreat. His brother Boris served as commander of the Ataman Cossacks. Kyril commanded the naval Garde Equipage. Sergei's brother George went to Kiev to supervise evacuation of the wounded. Sergei, suffering from arthritis, remained in Petersburg to run the Artillery Department as inspector general, and the tsar himself moved between Tsarskoye Selo and Stavka, sometimes taking Alexei with him to see the spots Vova only looked at on his map—Galicia, Reval, Odessa—until a nosebleed in December 1915 nearly killed the tsarevich. I will tell you more about that later. And then, of course, inevitably, the dead and the wounded began to be returned to Peter, the dead put into rough, wooden coffins and the wounded into makeshift hospitals. Alix transformed the golden Armorial Hall at the Winter Palace into a huge ward, removing the glass cases of silver trophies and placing in their stead hundreds of hospital cots. And she turned a hall in Catherine Palace at Tsarskoye Selo into yet another hospital, as well as two palaces in Moscow, and even a portion of the Feodorovsky Gorodsk at Tsarskoye Selo was made over into a lazaret. But for every man who called for the empress to hold his hand, there were a dozen others embarrassed to have her see them so vulnerable and ruined and a dozen more than that who were openly rude as the war went on. Not only she, but every woman of means opened a hospital, served as a nurse, or packed boxes to send to the front. Why, even I funded a hospital, though I did not nurse there, being no good with blood and amputations, but I visited the convalescing, helped them write letters home and performed for them my Russian dance, my *ruskaya*, and the men called me *radouchka*, bringer of joy, which I was! What could my enemies criticize about that?

By the beginning of 1915 the army began to run short not only of munitions, of bullets and rifles, but also of overcoats and uniforms and boots, and men could not shoot until the men in front of them were shot and they could snatch up their rifles. Eventually whole regiments of gunners could not even return fire, and they were stuck in the Carpathians without the means to fight their way down

the other side into Hungary. By the summer, the Germans had quietly assembled in southern Poland and in May they began to bom-
bard our men, who fought back with no cartridges or shells, but
with their bare hands and bayonets, the Germans pushing us east,
from Galicia and back out of Poland, our men running away in their
fur caps and greatcoats and empty hands in a bloodbath that massacred 180,000 men, and Sergei feared the Germans might make
it all the way to Moscow. At this Vova put his soldiers back in his
box—there weren't many left standing, anyway—rolled up his map
and stashed it away, and the country exploded, looking to place the
blame, not yet at the tsar—though the proverb says, *A fish begins to
stink from the head*—but at everyone around him. Petersburg blamed
for these disasters the inspector general of the Artillery, Grand Duke
Sergei Mikhailovich; the war minister, Vladimir Sukhomlinov; and
even, in its desperation, the imperial concubine, Mathilde Kschessinska. Yes, there were rumors that I took bribes of money and jewels
to convince Sergei to throw business to friends, the Petersburg arms
contractors and munitions factory owners and providers of matériel
who came to my parties and who could not possibly fill all the orders they took, while the munitions factories in the provinces sat
idle and eventually went bankrupt from lack of business. Articles
appeared in the press saying I used artillery documents and privileged information from Sergei to better negotiate a price for my
bribes—how else did I pay for my house?—and the president of
the infernal Duma spoke out against me, against *the thieving gang
operating under cover of the grand duke's name*. Sergei's brother Nicholas demanded Sergei break off all relations with me, accusing me
of exploiting him for profit. I was greatly affronted! And all these
rumors tingled the ears of the empress, who scribbled a note to Niki
about them—*There are very unclear, unclean stories about her and
bribes which all speak about*—a note I'm sure she purred while writing. Lewd poems about me and unflattering caricatures made the
rounds of the capital—I, planted naked in bed with a bevy of grand

dukes; I, surrounded by mounds of diamonds and rubies, fat munitions manufacturers laughing behind my sable-coated back while an
army private shook his empty rifle in despair. As if I could be happy
about this, about Warsaw, where my father and grandparents were
buried, rotten with Germans! The uproar around me grew so great
I had to leave for Strelna in May and could not return to the capital
until late fall.

But to be honest, what did I know of factories—of their capacity
for production? I had thought it made no difference if this factory
or that one made the bullets and so I had asked Sergei to offer the
arms contracts to our friends, men we knew, the ones who came to
Kronversky Prospekt with their gifts and their old-world manners.
Better than strangers to have them, right? Who was better to trust?
While I hid at Strelna, Sergei was forced to resign from the Artillery
Department and was sent to Baranovichi, where stripped of his
official duties he had nothing to do but grow a vegetable garden,
smoke cigars with Niki, and putter about like an old man, taking
long walks in the forest as if there were not a war on and this were not
headquarters but some kind of sanatorium. Now Vova and I could
not see him and my son wept himself to sleep. The unfortunate Sukhomlinov, who did not have the luck to be a cousin of the tsar or his
former mistress, was arrested and imprisoned in the Peter and Paul
Fortress. I sent him a note, which I'm sure he appreciated.

The country became obsessed with the idea of traitors and spies.
German bakeries and schools were attacked. Those with German-
sounding names came home to find their houses burned, the roofless
walls blackened behind their iron railings. And who in Russia did
not have a German-sounding name? Half the court was of German
ancestry; why, their very positions at court derived their titles from
their German counterparts—the *Ober-Tseremoniimeister*, the *Ober-
Gofmeister*, the *Kamer-Freilini*, the *Flag-Kapitan*. And of course the
country remembered that Empress Alexandra was German. Alix of
Hesse-Darmstadt. The people began to call her *Niemka, that German*

woman, and they were suspicious of her and her *staretz*, Rasputin, who they feared was a German spy. In Moscow, in Red Square, the crowd shouted that Rasputin should be hanged, the empress shut up in a convent, and Niki deposed.

To stem this great uproar over the despair about the Great Retreat, for that was what the ignominious backward march of men from the Carpathians toward Lublin and Lvov began to be called, the furor over the supply shortages, and the hysteria of the spy paranoia, the tsar shut down the Duma, replaced Nikolasha as commander in chief, and moved permanently to Stavka, which had to be moved, after the Great Retreat, two hundred miles east from Baranovichi to Mogilev, on the Dnieper River in the Ukraine to avoid being overrun by the advancing Germans. At Baranovichi, the generals and grand dukes had bunked in their own private luxury train cars at the railway junction, the cars pulled off the track and fanned out in the birch-and-pine forest, wood planks making walkways between them. But at Mogilev, the officers simply commandeered the house of the local governor and each took a room. Niki took two rooms for himself, one as a study, one as a bedroom— and prepared to be the country's figurehead as the tsar-warrior. With that decision, and with his mother sitting out the war in Kiev, Petersburg was left to the empress. And Rasputin.

Let me explain how Rasputin crawled into Alexander Palace and into Alix's lap. As always, it had to do with the health of the tsarevich. When Alexei had come in the autumn of 1915 to spend some months at Mogilev with his father, to sleep on a cot in his father's bedroom in the governor's mansion, Sergei told me, Alexei caught a winter cold and one sharp sneeze induced a nosebleed which could not be stopped. The doctors tried every bandage and nose plug in their flimsy black bags, while the boy's body continued to pump scarlet blood out his nostrils. Eventually Alexei lost consciousness. In this condition he was brought by his father by train back to Tsarskoye Selo, and Alix met him there at the little station, expecting Niki to carry off the corpse of her son, and when she saw his white face and his limp body, she begged Niki to allow her to call Rasputin. And Rasputin, as you can imagine, making the most of this opportunity, swept into the boy's room, made the sign of the cross over the boy's body, and said, *Don't be alarmed. Nothing will happen.* And the next day, Alexei was sitting up, bright-eyed, asking for his spaniel puppy, Joy, and for the cat he had left behind at headquarters.

Niki returned to Mogilev the next day, but it would take murder to dislodge Rasputin from Tsarskoye Selo. With Rasputin's guidance, Alix argued for the country's ministerial appointments to be given only to courtiers of the old school, men who worshipped the autocracy of the tsar, who believed the Duma a mistake, as she did, but most of all to men who were well-disposed to Rasputin. She was as charged with energy as she had been when Niki was sick with typhoid in Livadia and both times for the same reason—if the tsar was threatened, her son's future was also threatened—and she wanted to secure the country for both of them. Almost every week, it seemed, I would open the *gazeta* to read the name of a new minister Alix had persuaded Niki to appoint. Over the next six months, Russia had four prime ministers, five ministers of the interior, three war ministers, three foreign ministers, four ministers of agriculture, and three of transport, and the country was thrown into such disorder by the incessant replacement of competence with incompetence and then incompetence with ineptitude that the government could barely function. Rasputin, of course, had had a hand in all those appointments, and sometimes for ludicrous reasons—when the court chamberlain, A. N. Khostov, pleased Rasputin with his loud bass singing at the Gypsy restaurant the Villa Rode one night, Khostov found himself appointed minister of the interior the next month. So many people came to seek Rasputin's patronage, they had to line up

on the stairway to the door of his third-floor apartment on Goro-
khovaya Street, and the country seethed that among all those sup-
plicants sat a German agent who listened to Rasputin bluster and
blab about the confidential strategies and tactics the Russian army
planned, tactics Niki confided to Alix and she then to Rasputin, for
she craved his blessing on military maneuvers he understood nothing of. The crazed monk and the German woman were destroying
Russia from the inside and out the people said, and as the war continued to go badly, the officers in their hopelessness began to take
long, unauthorized leaves from the front; they appeared once again
at the palaces and at the embassies and even at the bars of the Astoria and the Europa hotels, and once more uniforms and medals began to stud the stalls and boxes of the Maryinsky.

Why, Petersburg had a new song:

We only want to know, next day,
What ministers will be on view,
Or who takes who to see the play,
Or who at Cubat's sat next to who

And does Rasputin still prevail
Or do we need another saint,
And is Kschessinska quite well
And how the feast at Shubin's went:

If the grand duke took Dina home,
What kind of luck MacDiddie had—
Oh, if a zeppelin would come
And smash the whole of Petrograd.

murders will follow

AND SO THE PLOTS BEGAN, and it was not only the Vladimirichi who schemed, but also the Mikhailovichi, the old Potato Club, who schemed with them—minus Sergei. In one plan, four Guards regiments would be sent to Tsarskoye Selo to capture the imperial family, dispatch Alix to a convent or a mental institution, arrest Rasputin, and force Niki's abdication. It was not an original idea. In most coups, mutinous guards were used to overthrow the tsar—Catherine the Great had used them. Another plan would have the guards seize the imperial train as it traveled between Stavka and Tsarskoye Selo, the tsar forced to abdicate and Alix arrested or, in Miechen's words, *annihilated*, and Rasputin hanged. Then, variously, depending on the conspirator, it would be Kyril installed on the throne or the tsarevich Alexei, with Nikolasha or the tsar's brother Mikhail entreated to serve as regent. Grand Duchess Vladimir, her three sons, Niki's ward Dimitri Pavlovich, the young Prince Yusupov who had married Xenia's daughter, even Sergei's brother, the now famous historian Grand Duke Nicholas Mikhailovich, met evenings at Vladimir Palace. Other plots fermented among officials of the Duma, and the plots eventually grew so multitudinous and were spoken of so openly that Sergei's brother

Nicholas finally felt compelled to write to Niki that if Alix didn't stop her interference in matters of government *murders will follow*.

Rasputin's assassins were those men who met at the Vladimir Palace: Grand Duke Nicholas Mikhailovich, Prince Yusupov, and Grand Duke Dimitri Pavlovich. The Vladimirichi—Kyril, Boris, and Andrei—the residents of that palace, why, they stayed safely at home, hands unbloodied, but no less guilty for that. Sergei's brother gave Sergei the details. They had lured Rasputin to the basement salon of the Yusupov Palace with the promise of meeting Yusupov's wife—Xenia and Sandro's daughter, Irina—famously the most beautiful woman in Peter. I've told you Rasputin had an eye for women. And while Rasputin waited for this beauty to appear, as the men assured him she shortly would, they served him cakes sprinkled with cyanide and wine into which the crystals of that same poison had been dissolved, hoping for an easy night. But the poison, apparently, amazingly, unnervingly, had no effect, and Yusupov, impatient and frantic, pulled out his revolver and shot Rasputin in the back. The *staretz*, eyes wide, crumpled, seemingly dead, and while the men conferred about the disposal of the body, inexplicably, the body rose from the floor of the salon and bolted across the courtyard to its iron gates, making for the street, and the men fumbled for their pistols and sent after him a spasm of bullets that once again brought him down. There on the cobblestones his panicked assassins kicked Rasputin's body and clubbed his face, then bound him with rope, and for good measure rolled him up in a blue curtain they yanked, improvising, from a basement window rod. But, apparently, Rasputin survived even all of that, as well as his rough journey to the rustic Petrovsky Bridge, to the hole beneath it in the ice through which he was shoved, drowning, finally, in the freezing water of the Little Neva. When he was found, one hand was freed of the ropes.

That was December 16, 1916, and all of Peter said, *sabakye, sabatchya smerte*—a dog's death for a dog. It was even rumored that the tsar's daughter Tatiana dressed as a guard and had Rasputin castrated before her eyes as vengeance for his alleged attempt to violate her, that she helped push him into the river. What must he have thought about under the black ice? Battered, chained, his clothes saturated with blood and river water, one leather boot on his foot, the other on the surface of the frozen Neva, a murky shape above him on the white ice, the outlines of it made visible by the moon's face, Rasputin reached out an arm. Was he reaching out his arm to his shoe, to the moon, to the ice shelf above him, the white marble slab of his sarcophagus? Was he lifting his arm to give a final benediction, a final prophecy? Or was he simply trying to untether himself, to crawl upside down along the ice in this black inverted world, to find the hole through which he had been pushed, to run, dripping water and ice, to the Alexander Palace, where, as he had screamed at his assassins on his dash through the Yusupov Palace courtyard, *Felix, I will tell the tsaritsa everything!*

She knew it soon enough.

When Dimitri Pavlovich entered his box at the Mikhailovsky Theater the night after the murder, the audience stood and applauded him. Penitents in Our Lady of Kazan Cathedral lit thick swatches of candles before the icons of his name saint. And the day after that, Andrei rode with his brother Kyril to Dimitri's palace on Nevsky Prospekt to assure Dimitri that the Vladimirichi were behind him, to urge him to turn his regiments against the tsar. But luckily, unexpectedly, Dimitri demurred. He might have hated Rasputin, but he loved his tsar. Soon enough everyone knew the triple-tongued Andrei and Kyril had tried to pry open the gates of hell. Ah, the baby of the family, Andrei, turned out to be quite a Vladimirichi, after all.

emperor vladimir

I F THE ROMANOVS COULD KILL RASPUTIN, it was possible that, encouraged, they might try to carry out the rest of their plots. And that is when I received a summons from Niki to come to Stavka with Vova.

The name of the provincial town Mogilev comes from the Russian word for a grave, you know, and the landscape we viewed from the train car all the way from Minsk looked foreboding enough. It was so cold that when I disembarked at one stop, within a few seconds I could not even wiggle my fingers. Vova was in high spirits at the thought of seeing Sergei again and he had insisted on carrying his present for him—a puppy—in his coat's big pocket. He was so busy with the animal, making up names for it and asking me what I thought of each one—*Nika*, born on Sunday, *Gasha*, good, *Kiska*, pure—that he did not look out the compartment window as he would normally. I was glad of this, for what would he have seen but trees standing dark against the sky, their limbs split or sometimes pocked by artillery fire. We passed abandoned trenches, the mud walls fortified with wooden boards, barbed wire hanging in scrolls and loops along the surface. The roads were wet and muddy and bore the thick treads of tank and truck tires, water pooled and froze in any depression in the ground, and in the fields white crosses cut their way out of the graves they marked.

A rough wooden fence surrounded the governor's house, and above the gate on a wooden arch cut in the shape of an Ionian dome was carved the word STAVKA. Sergei met us there. He had put on weight and he had gone almost completely bald, and, as if to compensate for this, he had allowed his beard to grow fuller and wilder than he normally wore it. And yet despite the extra weight and the denser beard there seemed something deflated about him—the disgrace, however unfair, and his resignation had made him uncertain. I could see it even in the way he moved, as if he might take a false step or lose his balance. He had defended me against all critics, including ones from his own family, writing his brother Nicholas, *I swear on the icon that she does not have any crime behind her. If they accuse her of bribery, that is all lies. I was dealing with all her business, I can show whoever needs it accurate details about how much money she has and where it came from.* He took the punishment for me, and now, because of it, he wore a plain brown tunic—for, having been forced to resign from the army, he could no longer wear his uniform.

Vova jogged ahead of me to greet him, oblivious to the great changes in Sergei, holding the puppy out to him happily in his two hands. The ribbon Vova had put around the puppy's neck at the start of our journey was long unraveled and gone. *It's for you. To keep you company! You can call it Kiska.* Vova grinned, offering up his most recent inspiration. Sergei embraced him and then inspected the black-haired puppy, a spaniel just like Alexei's. When I reached him, Sergei kissed me, and I felt absurdly comforted by the heft of him, by his familiar scent of tobacco, oranges, and whiskey, and I put my arm through his while Vova took Kiska on a wild run around the frozen, muddy courtyard, which had in the center of it a round fountain. The spouts of the fountain were the open eyes of porpoises, and in the summer those spouts must shoot streams of water, but now Vova picked up a stick to thrust into the empty eye holes.

On the opposite side of the wooden fence, a few boys called to him, peasant boys on a trek back from the river. Vova ducked through a broken and leaning section of the fence to join them, the puppy yapping hysterically as he followed Vova's stick. Sergei and I watched through the splintered planks as the four of them hurled Vova's stick like a baton for the puppy to retrieve but Kiska hadn't learned yet to return it, so inevitably the boys would give chase, laughing as the puppy avoided them with quick zigzags across the field. *I've missed him*, Sergei said. The whiskers under Sergei's nose looked frozen. *I've told my brothers everything I have should go to Vova when I die*, and I said, *Why are you talking about death? You're not going to die.* But Sergei didn't answer me, calling out to Vova, *It's too cold, let's go inside*, and to me he said only, *Niki wants to see you before dinner*.

One of the commanders had given us use of his quarters, a two-room hut, and from there Sergei led us to the governor's house, to the two rooms Niki had taken for himself. As we passed through the big dining room, I saw the long table was already being set for dinner, the round carved legs poking out from beneath a short white tablecloth, the rough planked floor and clapboard walls illuminated to the last splinter by the wall of windows at the far end of the room. Niki sat waiting for us in his study at an enormous mahogany desk, every inch of it etched and carved and ornamented. This room, after the brilliance of the dining hall, seemed blindingly dark—the stripes of the damask paper on the walls made a dull mirror; a lone dark chair crouched like a dwarf against the back wall. Niki rose to greet us, his face at first sepia, but then as he neared me, rosy, as if he were a photograph being painted over with color while I watched. Or perhaps I was that painter, and I felt myself color, too. He kissed my peach hand, shook Vova's, now almost the size of his own, and asked him about his studies, Was he learning French and geography? And did he like his subjects? He put a hand on my boy's shoulder as he listened, and now and then Niki looked over at me and smiled, and I thought, *Do I look as old to him as he does to me?* Because I was now forty-four, the age when a woman is well into her long, reluctant goodbye to the beauty she has worn as a right since she was sixteen.

Sergei stayed behind in the study when Niki showed us the other room in the house he had taken for himself, as if this next room, the carpeted bedroom, were too personal, too private for Sergei to enter, though we could, and he took from Vova the puppy. A camp bed had been placed by the great porcelain stove at the side of Niki's own bed, and through the window opposite, half-open, we could see the windows of the city hall and hear the noise in the street below, voices, the occasional car or cart. This was a town, after all, not a battle-ground. The cot was made up with a striped cover, the pillows plumped at the head as if expecting a visitor, and beneath the cot lay a leather box which Niki gestured Vova should open. Within the box Vova found some colored marbles and lead soldiers—toys that must have belonged to Alexei and which he had left behind. Vova looked at the tsar and Niki nodded that he should play with them, and Vova glanced at me, uncomfortable. He was fourteen now, and except for planting soldiers on his battle map, he did not play with toys anymore. It was clear, though, from his nod, that Niki saw Vova as the twelve-year-old Alexei, still child enough to be engaged by the lead men. Vova looked down and then with a small smile, he took the box to the chair by the window and began to line the sol-diers along the window ledge. Vova understood. If the tsar wanted him to be twelve, he would be twelve. Niki smiled as Vova made the marbles into cannonballs to fell the soldiers. Ah, if only our regi-ments could fight the Germans with that ease. Why, we had hoped to be in Berlin by Christmas 1914! *All over by Christmas*, everyone had said. Two years had passed since then.

Niki watched Vova pensively, shifting, his uniform wrinkling across the front. His boots bore dried mud. Every afternoon, Niki said, he would drive to the woods or walk by the Dnieper River, sometimes alone, sometimes with Sergei. He had begun, while here alone at Mogilev, to contemplate the colorlessness of life without Alexei. Rasputin had promised that Alexei would at thirteen outgrow his illness, but the doctors he spoke to last month had contradicted this, and the disease had certainly showed no sign yet of abating. Each month brought Alexei some new pain to his joints or brought him a headache or a fever. Each movement brought with it the potential for hemorrhage. And now with Rasputin's death, Niki said, what was to prevent the next hemorrhage from being a fatal one? Alix had wept for days after Rasputin's murder, now that catastrophe was certain for her son. She had read the congratulatory letters and telegrams between all their imperial relations, notes confiscated by the secret police, and she knew they stood alone. He and Alix had come to accept that Alexei would not live long now and certainly would not be able to serve as tsar. And, Niki said, it was not only Alexei's life that was in danger; Alix's was also, for different reasons. She had written him, *Don't let them send me to a convent. Don't separate Baby from me.* Had I heard the rumors? I nodded. Did he not know I had heard them all practically firsthand on the sable-covered bed at the von Dervis palace?

He had, Niki told me, decided to return to Peter at the end of December, to take charge of the roiling matters in the capital, and then to send Alix and the children to Livadia Palace in the Crimea, after Russian Christmas, where they would stay for a few years, until the war was safely over, until order had been brought both to the State Council and to the State Duma or else that two-chambered parliamentary body would be permanently dissolved. Eventually, according to his plan, Alix would return to Petersburg, but Alexei, if he still lived, would remain behind, tucked away, just as his English cousin George V and his wife, Mary, had concealed their sickly epileptic son John, just as Alix's sister, Irene, had hidden her hemophiliac son Henry. And there, just as John and Henry had, Alexei would eventually die.

We heard the cannonballs exploding, marbles clinking against one another as Vova played, and Niki turned his head toward him but spoke still to me. He wanted to take Vova home with him to Tsarskoye for Christmas, alone. He could help decorate the three trees at the Alexander Palace, the one in the Big Living Room, another in the passage for the servants, and the last in the playroom, the fir tree there, strung with crystal baubles and tinsel, so tall it almost reached the ceiling, and I thought, *Does the decree against Christmas trees not apply to the sovereigns, or is Niki recalling the hazy comfort of some Christmas past?* Though I knew Niki delivered these details to soothe me, he was the one who smiled as he recalled them. The candles on the playroom tree would be lit first, he said, and beneath it Vova and the other children would unwrap their gifts. After the New Year Vova could travel with them to the Crimea for Easter. And so on and so on, each holiday leading to another, one month to the next. Vova could call me once a week. I could see him in March before the family left for the Crimea. We would have to explain to him, slowly, the manner of his birth, the function of his new place, and eventually, his assumption of his new name, and this transfer must be cultivated as unhurriedly and as carefully as Petersburgers cultivated their vines and flowers in their greenhouses all winter, forcing their bulbs to flower, their vines to bear fruit, forcing nature to do the impossible, to make summer from ice. And when Alix returned to Peter with the girls, Vova would come with her. Did I understand?

I was not an idiot—how did he think I had memorized all those divertissements and adagios, one step leading to hundreds of others? I understood—without a clear line of succession, the various Romanov men from all branches of the family would furiously contend for the crown. And with this weakness and divisiveness from above and the ruinous fog of war all around us, the red flags of the revolution would once again be draped from the roofs and windows of Peter and the old revolutionaries would slink back into the capital to take full advantage of the instability of the three-hundred-year-old throne. No—there could be no rupture in the route to the throne. Yes, I understood. Niki's son—one of them—must be the tsarevich. We were quiet enough now to notice Vova had also grown silent. Niki might consider him a child, but I knew better. Vova had been listening intently. If he did not want to do this, if he did not want to go with the tsar, I knew he would let me know. He sat on the cot, motionless. Of course he wanted to go. This was the big adventure he yearned for, the path that led, finally, away from me. And then he let a marble roll slowly along the windowsill to topple the last soldier standing upright, which fell, with a clatter, to the floor.

At that moment, a real soldier came to the study door to tell Niki it was time for dinner. Sergei's face next appeared in the doorway and I could tell from it the tsar had already discussed with him his plans and that Sergei was distressed by them; it had distressed him even to overhear Niki repeating them to me, though Sergei did not know none of this was a surprise, that I had been preparing myself for this and dreading this since Spala. But I understood this was why Sergei had been talking of death, of leaving his estate to Vova: he wanted to lay some claim to Vova before Niki gobbled him all up. But what could Sergei do? Vova was not his son, no matter how much he doted on him, though Vova did not know this. Nor did Vova belong fully to me. This fate or something like it had been Vova's since his conception. And he did not know that either.

I touched Sergei's hand as I passed him and then Niki gestured to Vova to walk on ahead with Sergei and the soldier while we held back. Niki turned to me in the dim winter light of that bedroom. *I promise I will leave him the greatest empire Russia ever commanded.* Nicholas II's Christmas manifesto to his army would speak of his vision, as yet unfulfilled, of this Great Russia, and the peace that would follow from it that, its reach blanketing all the Slavic peoples and resolving all long-simmering conflicts, *a peace such that generations to come will bless your sacred memory*. Did I believe him? Like his most loyal subjects, I still believed him capable of anything. Then he kissed me, the triple kiss to the cheeks the divine tsar bestows upon his subjects at Easter, and then one last kiss, the one a man gives to a woman, his chapped lips to mine. I opened my mouth to his rough tongue, which I had not tasted in fourteen years and which he let me have now. Had he loved me all these years? If only, if only, he had ennobled *me* and made *me* his wife in 1894 instead of Alix. Our kiss was long, and though the twilight made around us a cloak of black fur, we were not invisible beneath it. When we broke apart, finally, I saw that Sergei had forged on ahead, the puppy at his heels, but my son had turned back to wait for us, and he stood there in the passageway, his face utterly astonished.

That night I dreamed I was following the tsar through the south gates at Tsarskoye, those grand gates, their Gothic façades like the doorways to a great church. The tsar was wearing his thick great-coat and his fur *papakha*, and I saw only the broad back of him as his big dogs, his fifteen Scottish sheepdogs, the large breed favored by Queen Victoria who first brought them to Balmoral, came to stick their long noses into the folds of his coat, and then they ran ahead of him in the grass toward the grove of birch trees and oak and then back, weaving his steps like shuttles through a loom. His favorite sheepdog, Iman, had been the only palace dog, but Iman had disappeared, had perhaps taken a nail in the paw or swum too far in one of the lakes, and now Niki did not want that attachment to a single dog again, so he enjoyed them as a pack, loving no particular one over the other. Spaced thirty feet apart at the tall iron fence stood the Cossack guards, and along the horizon one of them rode by on a huge horse, beast and man fused into a force of speed and strength, headed to the barracks of his regiment, built in the Muscovite style Niki so loved, an imitation medieval village christened the Feodorovsky Gorodk, or Townstead. Niki walked alone, ahead of me, unaware of me, but I followed him as he walked along the grass, along the glades of trees, along small bodies of water turned green and black by the reflection of these trees and their shadows and the grasses, the yellow walls and white columns of Alexander Palace rising like an ancient Greek temple at the other end of the long drive and the wide lawn. His children ran there, built snow towers, and sledded on the hills in the winter, canoed in the lakes and swam in the canals in the summer, served tea on Children's Island in the little playhouse, buried their pets in the small cemetery by the bridge, and marked their graves with headstones in the shapes of miniature pyramids. I followed him across the bridge to Children's Island where he climbed the few steps to the porch of the playhouse, the playhouse like the ones built for all privileged Russian children since Peter the Great, and where with his gloved hand he brushed the leaves from the seats of the two wicker chairs, and the wind came over the still water and rattled the little canoe at its small stone pier and the pine needles shifted in the tall trees that reached twice as high as the roof. Some of the needles, unhinged from their branches, fell like the lightest rain, and he brushed clean the table on which sat some crockery playthings—teapot, cups, and plates—and then he turned and faced me and raised one arm and held it out with the palm up and then I saw it was not Niki at all, but Vova, grown to manhood, and I woke just as I was racing across the grass to kiss his hand.

In Petersburg I told everyone only that I had left my son at Stavka with Sergei.

On January 1, Niki returned to the capital and, as he promised me, he began to rid the capital of his enemies to make it and the throne safe for our sons. He had consulted the ghost of his father and the ghost had given his blessing. Prince Dimitri Pavlovich was exiled to Persia. Grand Duke Nikolasha, who was already in Tiflis, having been sent there after his demotion from commander in chief of the army to commander of the regiments in the Caucasus, was ordered to remain there indefinitely. Prince Felix Yusupov, in his gray soldier's coat and under guard, was sent to his estate in the Kurskaya province in central Russia. Sergei's brother Nicholas was dispatched to Grushevka, his country estate in the Ukraine. The Vladimirichi were ordered to depart Peter, and Miechen, Andrei—with the swiftest of goodbyes to me—and eventually Boris went to the Caucasus, to Kislovodsk, with the face-saving excuse that they were taking the cure at a spa, and the Vladimir Palace and the von Dervis mansion stood abruptly empty. Andrei came to say goodbye to me on Kronversky Prospekt, and I blessed him with my father's icon of Our Lady of Czestokowa while he knelt, though he was not going off to war but to a place untouched by it where his safety could be assured and, frankly, I was happy to see him go. He was no longer an amusement and his treachery endangered my son—my ambitions for my son. Kyril, as a Navy commander, was ordered to Port Romanov on the Arctic Circle far, far from the capital and perhaps there, with any luck, he would freeze to death. After the war, Niki planned to turn his attention to his ministers of the State Council and to the members of the lower house of the Duma—to rid both of the incompetence that was crippling the country, but to reorganize the government now, he felt, in the middle of a war, could be disastrous. First, Russia must prevail over Germany.

The Christmas and New Year's holidays had fattened the country's spirits, and the weather had taken care of the rest, turning so cold, at fifteen degrees below zero, that the streets had emptied of troublemakers. It was so cold, in fact, that no supplies could make it either into the capital or out of it, for blizzards kept the trains frozen on their tracks and there was no one to sweep the snow as so many men had been conscripted. The bakeries were forced to stop making bread because the flour and sugar could not be moved from their warehouses and silos, and the big, fine pastries disappeared from the shops, followed by biscuits, buns, cakes, and finally humble loaves of bread. Women began queuing up in long lines for anything available. And there was trouble transporting coal, as well, and what there was of Peter's wooden fences began to vanish as people tore them down to burn them in their stoves. But on the tsar's orders, four trucks managed to unload coal at my Petersburg mansion, and the sight proved so novel that a crowd gathered, despite the temperature, just to stare at it. As I've said, my neighborhood stood far from the factories that harbored the strikers, and my house stood far from the tenements in which they lived, and so this crowd was a titled one, but no less hostile for that, the men slapping their gloved hands together, fur hats pulled down low on their heads, making remarks. I opened the door to Vova's balcony just a crack; it overlooked Kronversky Prospekt, and I heard the French ambassador, Maurice Paléologue—a busybody who kept a diary of events large and ridiculously small (the tsar's ministerial appointments noted alongside the chinchilla coat and gray taffeta dress worn by Niki's brother's beautiful new wife, Paléologue noted even her *superb pearls!*)—yes, Paléologue was declaiming loudly, *It seems we haven't the same claim as Madame Kschessinska to the attentions of the imperial authorities*. To which I thought, *Of course you haven't, you fumisterie. You are not the mother of the tsarevich!* But I said nothing and shut the door, for the phone was ringing with my weekly call from Vova.

The calls always began the same way, with a palace servant announcing, *You are receiving a telephone call from the imperial apartments of His Majesty the Tsarevich Alexei Nikolaevich*, and then my son would be on the line to chatter about the events of the past week—he was learning English with Alexei's tutor Mr. Gibbes, he had sledded down a big ice hill and beat the girls, both the Big Pair and the Little Pair, for supper they had had suckling pig with horse-radish, and when would I be coming to visit, as the emperor had said it would be soon, and I agreed that, yes, it would be soon, at the beginning of March. After those calls, I would dress and go to the theater.

Even at forty-four I was still dancing, though not as often, and I remember exactly my last performance, though, of course, I did not know it was to be my last. With Mikhail Fokine, I performed an excerpt from *Carnaval*. Poor Fokine. The war had tied him to the Imperial Theaters, where Diaghilev had no sway, and so Fokine had had to shuffle his way reluctantly back to partner me if he wanted to appear on the Maryinsky stage. When this ballet had its premiere in 1910 at the Pavlov Hall, Nicholas and Alexandra both were there to witness it, but now we performed it as part of a benefit for a war charity. The sets for this ballet were arranged in such a way and with such perspective as to make it seem the dancers were miniature beings and the audience were peering into a velvet maquette to watch us cavort. Usually, in this little hatbox of a ballroom, the characters slipped magically in and out of the folds in the blue curtains, but that night, it being a benefit for one of Alix's charities for wounded soldiers, Fokine and I performed only the duets and solos from the ballet, Fokine in his harlequinade costume and mask, I, his love, Columbine, in my many-layered ruffled dress with the puffed sleeves. We danced that bit of *commedia dell'arte* set to Schumann, and in it we exemplified the silliness and light of the form, the light in here against the dark of the war outside and the dark frozen mood of the people. Fokine moved to the flute and clarinet, and I to the strings, and yet beneath the frolic the music etched a dark line. I found myself unexpectedly weeping by the end of the ballet, when Harlequin brings his pirouettes to a finish by abruptly sitting on his bottom. Fokine's face, behind his mask, looked up at me quizzically. He was younger than I and he belonged to a different age. When the war was over, he would go abroad. But there was only one stage for me, one world for me—this one. And it was just twenty days before the revolution that would destroy it.

For a short time, though, it had seemed this world would last. The British ambassador, George Buchanan, took his usual vacation to Finland. Princess Radziwill hosted a great soiree at her palace on the Fontanka Canal, the light from her windows flickering across the water in all directions and illuminating Boris Vladimirich's car among the cars and carriages lined up outside. At M. Paléologue's dinner party at the French embassy, the guests discussed whether the palm for excellence should go to Pavlova, Karsavina, or me. And Niki decided to return for three weeks to Stavka, and Alix and his ministers could not dissuade him. The night he left, I received an unscheduled call from the imperial apartments of the tsarevich Alexei Nikolaevich. On the phone, Vova told me he was feeling ill, that Olga and then Alexei had come down with a headache and a high fever and the doctor had diagnosed measles and had put even Vova now to bed. *Mama, I want you*, Vova cried, his voice as thin as a five-year-old's, and when I hung up the phone, I pictured him hot with fever in some closet, abandoned while Alix rushed to and fro tending to her own children with the same fervor she had shown when nursing Niki through typhus. If only Niki had not gone back to Stavka so soon! When he was at Tsarskoye I knew he would look after Vova, but how could I trust that Alix would even take notice of him? And so I began to pack a small valise and telegraphed Sergei at Stavka that I would take the train the nine versts to Tsarskoye Selo to nurse Vova myself. When Sergei reported to Niki my intentions, Niki said no, that I must trust the imperial doctors and their ministrations, for who practiced better medicine than these men? Vova was in good hands. But when I insisted, reminding

Niki that my promised visit had been postponed by his departure to
Stavka, he relented, so long as my visit was made by night and of a
few hours' duration. He would tell Alix to expect me. And I must
use the servants' entrance, soberly dressed, so that my visit would
not be an official one, and would not be noted by the adjutant in the
leather-bound appointment book, though, of course, I would still
be observed by the secret police.

For my son I would endure these humiliations. For after all, what
more was I now, having given up my rights as parent, but a servant of
the tsar?

The sentry at the back gate took my name and my driver took me
to the side of the colonnade, to the servants' wing, where I was received by a policeman of the imperial court and a maid in a black
dress with a white ribbon in her hair. Alix, I had heard, liked her
palace servants to dress much like the English ones she grew up
with at Granny's, at Windsor Castle, but her Russian girls complained mightily about the corsets and the starched aprons and caps,
so they had been allowed dispensation, special Russian dispensation,
to wear just the dresses and the ribbons. I was taken by stairs, as the
elevator was broken, to the second floor of the east wing, to what
Alix called *the green room*, a large corner playroom. The maid waited
behind me in the doorway. I suppose Alix had instructed also that
I not be left unattended. What did she think I would do, strangle
her son and pin a note to my own with the word *tsarevich* scrawled
upon the paper?

My son lay with three other children, all in camp beds, all of them
asleep. Along two walls a cluster of peacocks strutted in a painted frieze
against a background of green, as green as the carpet on the floor.
The moonlight and starlight from the seven windows of the outer
two walls made clear the figures of the children, who looked as if
they had dropped, by virtue of some enchantment, into positions of

abandon on the grass of a magical park. And indeed they had been enchanted, I found out, all of them drugged by the imperial doctor, Eugene Botkin, with various potions against pain and for sleep. I stepped cautiously into the big room. The carpet had been cleared of toys, the paraphernalia pushed to the walls or heaped onto the great green and yellow sofas and chairs—railways and model towns and model ships, big dolls in carriages, smaller mechanical figures in factories and in miniature mines, tea sets, dollhouses, white-faced china dolls dressed in lace, teepees, wooden canoes with matching oars, open boxes of lead soldiers, their tunics painted green, blue, and red—the riot of it muted by the dim light. Dr. Botkin was just finishing his latest rounds, his wire-rimmed glasses glinting as he moved among the shadows, and with a nod at me he left, and another servant girl in a black dress, but this one with the white apron and cap so loved by *dear Alix*, brought me a chair. I pointed to a spot by my son's camp bed and she brought it there.

I sat and scrutinized my son's face; his skin had not yet erupted in the spots that measles inevitably brings. I laid my hand on his forehead. His skin was hot, very hot, and he was so drugged that he did not respond to my touch but slept on in this strange, deep sleep. On the row of beds beside him lay the imperial children whom I had seen only from the stages of the Maryinsky or the Hermitage. The girls would all be bald in a few weeks when their hair began to fall out from the fever and Alexandra would have their heads shaved, but for now they lay with their hair damp along their flushed faces—the broad cheekbones of Olga, the eldest; Tatiana with her delicate upturned nose and her wide-set eyes shaped like almonds, like a cat's, like her father's. And Alexei, a long, thin shape beneath his quilt, his face, like my son's, losing the round childishness of babyhood and drawing itself down into a long triangle. In August he would be thirteen; in June, my son would be fifteen. Niki was right to want to make the switch now, before the boys' faces became any more distinct from each other as they grew older.

Here, they and their lives were the same. They slept beside each other in Alexander Palace, they were tended to by the imperial physician, watched over by Alexei's two *dyadi*, his bodyguards. They took lessons from the imperial tutors, English from Charles Gibbes, French from Pierre Gilliard, history from Vladimir Voyekov, seven tutors in all, one for each subject. And Alexei at his birth had been enrolled as a member of the Imperial Guard Corps, made an honorary member of the 89th White Sea Infantry regiment and ataman of all Cossacks. His godparents were the dowager empress, King Christian IX of Denmark, King Edward VII of England, and Kaiser Wilhelm II. All these honors my son would one day assume.

Was this not his *sud'ba*, his fate? And so was his illness a warning to me or a test of my resolve? I pinched at my arms and in midpinch the door to the playroom suddenly opened and Alix appeared, a tall, white ghost dressed in the wimple and tunic she wore when nursing the war wounded, and she moved along the beds without looking my way or speaking to me, her hands adjusting a pillow, smoothing the lock of one's hair, the sheet beneath another, and when she reached my son, she laid her palm to his forehead as I had and then turned back his coverlet and gently moved his arms until they lay, palms up and free of the bedsheets to cool his temperature, and none of these actions had I thought to do. Vova stirred. His hand reached for and clasped hers, and comforted, he slept again. I knew then she would protect him as fiercely as she protected Alexei and I felt myself turn to vapor, as useless and as invisible. Alix loved my son—who would not?—and it appeared he loved her, too. And if he had here a mother's and a father's love in addition to all else, then did he not have everything he deserved? I was not needed here. I stood and started for the door when the maid caught my sleeve. I turned back. Alix beckoned to me.

I followed her unsteadily from the playroom and along the dark corridor to a wooden staircase that took us down past the mezzanine to the first floor. She smelled of lavender, which I breathed in each time I stepped onto the stair she had just left behind. There in the vestibule with its marble floors, its walls covered in cloth that gave off a low sheen, yet another footman in white gaiters waited with the empress's sable cloak. Through the archway and an open door I could see into a drawing room full of boxes and crates, some filled with sawdust and paper. The walls of that room had been stripped of some of their treasures, for exposed wires and nails made studs and loops along the cream-colored plaster. The court was packing to go, I thought wildly. To go where? Why, to the Crimea. To Livadia Palace. Of course. That was the plan. Niki had told me that. Vova had said in his call before last he was looking forward to Easter holiday there and to the parade on the Day of White Flowers, where the girls had told him he would carry a staff decorated with white marguerites and go into the shops with them to beg donations for the sanatoriums. Livadia was three thousand miles south, far from the war, from the troubles of the capital, and from me. I saw now that that, too, was part of the plan.

We stepped out then into the snow-filled courtyard. The only light came from the vestibule behind us and the tall lampposts ahead—the steps had snow shoveled to the sides of them and snow rested on the pointed tips and ornamental filigrees of the wrought-iron gates and fences that enclosed the palace, and as we walked snow once again began to fall from the sky. I followed Alix in her dark cloak as she led me across the courtyard and I could not feel my feet, whether from the cold or from fear I do not know, and the air buzzed and rustled about my ears, alive with the colliding snowflakes. She walked me all the way to the gate where my driver waited, and when she saw me settled into the car, she leaned forward and whispered to me the words executioners traditionally ask of their victims before they raise the ax: *Will you forgive me?* So. She understood, even if Niki did not, that she was taking from me my life. And I said, *Yes, I forgive you*, and she shut the door to my car then and straightened up. I watched her figure standing in the courtyard as my car turned the drive, her shape half-white and half-black, one part sable, one part linen: nurse, empress, mother.

I dreamed of my mother that night, for the first time. She died of a stroke in 1912, after having suffered an earlier one. She was eighty-two years old. For some weeks after the first stroke, she was confined to the bedroom she had once shared with my father in our old apartment on Liteiny Prospekt, and I would visit her there. In my dream I found the room unchanged, the same dark furniture, the same oil paintings of Polish landscapes in heavy gilded frames hanging on the wall from long loops of wire, the same patterned wall fabric, the same photographs of all of us, but my mother was not lying in the big bed. I found her in the big, dark ballroom where my father used to give his dancing lessons, her long yellow hair unbound, her eyes closed. When I approached her, she opened her eyes and her fingers reached for my wrist. *Mala*, she whispered, *how you've neglected me*.

masquerade

So SLEEP BROUGHT NO COMFORT, but the theater would. The next night I went to the Alexandrovsky, to see my old friend the actor Yuri Yuriev in his twenty-fifth-anniversary performance in Lermontov's *Masquerade*. Ah, how we clung to our old rituals in the very face of their dissolution—the anniversary tributes with the requisite gifts from the tsar and the court. Inside the theater's mustard yellow building, aristocrats were chockablock in the seats, having come to honor an imperial artist, to applaud a play set during the reign of Nicholas I, the Iron Tsar, a tsar Niki was now emulating with his own resolute behavior. Had he not cleared the capital of imperial malcontents? Was he not about to wash down the barnyard of the Duma? Would the Romanovs not reign another hundred years? On the stage the huge mirrors and gilded doors suggested the great ballroom of a great palace. It was the most elaborate set ever assembled on the tsar's stages, yet it was assembled even as the real sets of that real world were dismantled forever on the streets outside.

For the next day the newspapers printed that bread would be rationed starting March 1, setting off a panic and protests. Two hundred thousand people coursed down the Neva over the ice after the police raised the bridges to block their way to Admiralty Island and the palace square, where it was traditional to march, to claim the streets from and the attention of the imperial authorities. By night the streets still weren't completely safe. Many restaurants stayed dark, the rail lines were empty of trams and the streets of cabs, streetlights did not burn, and the beacon from the Admiralty lay like a white sword over the city. The next day, when the temperature, which had been as cold as in Lapland, suddenly rose to five degrees Celsius, it seemed the entire populace emerged from its dark hiding places into the sun to voice its misery, and by the afternoon, the crowd that had been shouting, *Bread, bread*, began shouting, *Down with the tsar!* And each day that week the police and brigades of Cossacks—reserve Cossacks new to Peter, not Niki's Cossacks—their horses skittish on cobblestone and their hands empty of the whips with which the regiment was normally equipped, half heartedly tried to control the crowds. And then Niki, from faraway Stavka, ordered the Pavlovsky, Volynsky, and Semenovsky regiments, which had put down the uprisings of 1905, into the streets, where they shot dead fifty people in Znamenskaya Square, and it seemed after that the remorse of the regiments spawned a mutiny. These junior officers of humble backgrounds, unlike all the aristocratic senior officers who had been killed at the front, joined the crowds as they took over the Arsenal, the Peter and Paul Fortress, the telephone exchange, and the railway stations, and together with the crowds and the Cossacks, the mutineers fought the tsar's police.

At midday, the mob breached the island and made its way across the Troitsky Bridge, and the chief of the 4th Petrograd Police District telephoned to tell me a large crowd was heading down the Bolshoi Dvorianskaya toward me. As I spoke to him, I saw a truck filled with elated soldiers, red flags flying, cross Kronversky Prospekt. By the time I hung up the phone, another truck. It seemed that all the city's soldiers, the whole 170,000 peasant infantry billeted in the Petersburg garrison for training before being shipped to the front, had absconded with their guns and their trucks. But they were not at the front, they were here, and their enemies were not the Germans but their own officers, along with the regiments, the police, and the Cossacks who remained loyal to the tsar, the court, and the *burzhui*.

And the imperial family? Were they safe in Tsarskoye Selo? When I called my brother—who was back in Petersburg, having been by this time reinstated at the Imperial Ballet at my request—he relayed to me what he had heard all day from the *isvozchiki*, the cab men, as they drove back and forth on the riotous city streets. All day, he had heard, drunken soldiers had been looting the Pavlosk shops of wine, bread, and boots, and a mob had headed to Tsarskoye Selo. A department store in Tsarskoye Selo was attacked, in the mistaken belief that it was the palace, by peasants so ignorant they couldn't tell one grand edifice from another. There were soldiers in the courtyard of Alexander Palace, regiments loyal to the tsar from the Garde Equipage who were used to protect the family at sea and on their yachts, standing in battle formation. So the rumors of the mob, if not the mob itself, had reached the palace.

The sound of a crowd is the sound of braying, unpredictable energy, and at the theater that sound coming from the audience is a sound of ecstatic adulation, a swell that rushes to one on the stage and seems to lift the dancers off their feet as it rises. The sound I heard from the street was not a sound to lift one up. Even if the mob didn't know that my house was the house of Kschessinska, the double-headed eagles glittered on my gates and those eagles alone would provoke attack. What delusion drove me to put the imperial eagles there? I remember I sat down. I remember thinking in no place in the city was there someone to call. Sergei and Niki were at Stavka, the tsar hiding, the people said, in the bosom of his army. Even the disgraced Andrei had found himself, by accident rather than by design, safely in Kislovodsk—in fact, the most powerful factions of the Romanov family, because of Niki's orders, were not even here. Grand Duke Vladimir and Stolypin were dead. And my family?

My sister lived on the other side of Petersburg, on English Prospekt, my brother Josef on Spasskaya Ulitsa, also over the bridge. At least my son was safe. No one would be more protected than he. But I could not remain here. Yet my car, my Rolls-Royce, was too well known, for in choice of cars, as in all things, I copied the Romanovs, and I had heard from my brother that Grand Duke Gavril Konstantinovich's Rolls had been commandeered by the crowd at will. To make my departure now I would need a different car. But when I called up the New Mikhailovsky Palace to beg for a car while the mob and the troops rioted their way down Bolshoi Dvorianskaya toward my house, I discovered Sergei's brother Nicholas had left written instructions to the servants to refuse any calls from me, to stop all communication *with the house on the Petrograd side of the city*. The great historian wanted me to run through the streets, carrying my reticule with my jewels, through the streets! where anyone with so much as a fancy hat was being murdered as a *borzhui*. And this was not all that was happening in the streets, but the rest I will tell you later. Sergei's family had always referred to him as my *lap dog* and thought I used him mercilessly, blamed me for his current disgrace and his virtual exile at Stavka, and now, even in Grand Duke Nicholas's absence, as he had been sent to Grushevka, his orders were being followed and the family were having their revenge. I sat there, nonplussed, the phone in my hand. And then I thought of Yuriev. The party after his tribute had been held at his apartment on Kamennostrovsky Prospekt just a few blocks away. The Romanovs might not help me, but surely my fellow theater artists would harbor me, and at this distance I could escape on foot.

And as the only thing safe to be at this time was a worker, this is what I did: I disguised myself as one, scissoring an ermine collar off an otherwise plain cloth coat, tying my maid's kerchief about my head like a peasant woman. I took with me my jewels that were not in storage at Fabergé, Niki's letters, the photograph he inscribed to me all those years ago, my father's icon and the ring of Count

Krassinsky, a photograph of Vova at age five—an odd ménage, I know, but when one runs from a burning house, only the most valuable items run with you, and you learn quickly what you value most. Believing my servants to be safe, I left alone. But the next morning, when my housekeeper opened the gate to the mob and called out to them, *Come in, come in, the bird has flown*—have I told you I had been described in Peter as a jeweled bird?—the mob came in bellowing for me, *Kschessinska! Where is Kschessinska?* and not finding me, seized my porter instead and stood him up against a courtyard wall as if to execute him, whereupon his wife died from shock before the crowd spied the Cross of St. George my porter had earned for valor in the war and released him. Over the next weeks my furniture disappeared from my home, as did my silver, my crystal, my Fabergé *objets*, my clothing, my furs, even my car, the car I had been so afraid to drive! My house had become a free market—all goods for the taking. No other house in the city was so looted as the mansion of the tsarist concubine Kschessinska, unless it was the mansion of the minister of the court, Baron Freedericks, dispenser of the tsar's punishments and favors. Yes, the minister and the trollop were famous in Peter, and I'm aware it is for my scandalous private life that I am still best known. Why, just this year, 1971, when Kenneth MacMillan created the ballet *Anastasia* for London's Royal Ballet, I was made a character in it, appearing in Act II to perform at a Winter Palace ball given in honor of the tsar's daughter Anastasia in a costume that befitted my reputation, my neck belted with diamonds, the décolletage of my black tutu split practically to the waist. As that, I live on.

If only I had thought to do what Countess Kleinmichel had done to save *her* mansion on Sergievskaya Street—put up a sign in my yard that shouted the lie: *This property already requisitioned by the citizens!*

For within weeks, the Bolshevik division of the Social Democrats took over my house and desecrated it by hanging a red flag from my roof, and soon enough it became the headquarters of the Bolshevik Central Committee. That night, though, I locked up my house with my key, under the illusion that would be all it took to keep it secure—and I rushed the few blocks to Kamennostrovsky Prospekt to pound on the door of the great actor Yuriev.

I stayed with him three days, hiding with his family in the hallways of his apartment from the stray bullets that ricocheted through the streets and sometimes punched their way through the windows. Outside, the crowds of workers, peasants, criminals sprung from prison, and soldiers who had mutinied fought the tsar's police, who had mounted machine guns on the roofs of many of the district's apartment houses. As Yuriev's apartment was on the top floor of his building, desperate soldiers, their greatcoats unbuttoned and their caps turned backward to signal their allegiance to the revolution, periodically broke into his apartment in order to climb to the roof to search it. Yuriev was a big man, with a strong nose and thick jowls, and the soldiers did not bother him, and as they had no idea who I was, a little middle-aged woman in a ripped coat, they did not question me. And the phone—mounted to the wall and operated by a crank—rang and rang as people hiding in their apartments called one another just to hear a sane voice, to tell the tale of what was happening on their particular street. After the third batch of soldiers came through, Yuriev moved his chairs away from the windows, and his vases and statuettes also, lest any of it be mistaken by the hysterical mob below for guns and we for police snipers and therefore fired upon. And when I went to help Yuriev and his wife move these things we saw a group of soldiers who had reached the rooftop of the building opposite ours throw someone off it—a policeman—

we watched the sail of his greatcoat spread wide as the wings of a great bird whose flight was short. When he fell to the pavement, a crowd gathered about him to beat at him with sticks.

Mala, Yuriev said, *this is madness. Where is the tsar? All they want is bread. There are no revolutionary leaders here*—and it was true! All of them would slip back into the capital only later and we would learn their names later still—Lenin and Martov from Zurich; Trotsky from New York; Chernov from Paris; Tsereteli, Dan, Gots, and Stalin from Siberia—Stalin was nobody then—a pockfaced bank robber for the revolution who worshipped Lenin and sent him his stolen rubles hidden in bottles emptied of Georgian wine, sent them all the way to Europe! Yes, these men still sat in armchairs and cafés in their places of exile since 1906 and we would learn their names only later; the leaders of these mobs were therefore impromptu and improvised—students, workers, and low-ranking officers who had once had revolutionary sympathies and now found those sympathies reawakened. Their photographs were placed in store-window shrines over the next weeks with the phrase *Heroes of the Revolution* printed on them. The names of these men—Linde, Kirpichnikov— would soon be forgotten, but they were the ones in the streets, organizing the crowd busy commandeering cars and trucks. One of those trucks sped by while we watched, a banner hung on it: *The First Revolutionary Flying Squad*, and Yuriev said, *What does that mean?* For there was no real revolution here, as yet, only what Gorky later described as a peasant riot. *Why does not the tsar bring in troops from the front to restore order?* Yuriev asked, and I found out only later, from Sergei, that General Alexeev, who served as Niki's chief of staff, feared that if he sent in his troops they would only lose all discipline and join in the mutiny and then all would be lost.

All through the streets walked men with swords, bayonets, butcher knives, revolvers, sticks—and we, five stories above the mass of people, heard the thin ends of screams, gunshots, glass shattering. The chief of the Petrograd Military District had tried to send a regiment loyal to the regime to the Winter Palace, but after fighting their way through the streets they found themselves turned away by the liveried palace servants on the orders of Niki's brother, Mikhail, who worried that the men in their dirty boots might muddy the palace floor and break the china; and so the troops, demoralized, simply joined the crowd. It was a comedy of errors, like an ill-rehearsed ballet, in which the dancers, unaccustomed to the sight of each other in their new costumes and unsure of their steps, bumped and waddled into one another and fell down.

The three days I hid at Yuriev's I never undressed but remained in the same clothes from the day I fled, and how quickly they grew soiled with sweat, dusty from the floors I squatted on, stained by bits of food, for we ate our meals sitting on the ground, hunched over our plates like animals. In our overcoats, our backs against the wall in the interior corridors of his grand rooms, we waited for news that the tsar was returning to the capital, that order was being restored, and at night we slept on mattresses we pulled to the floor. Yuriev's wife said to me one night, *How lucky for you your son is at Stavka with Grand Duke Sergei*, and I said, *Yes, how lucky*. And secretly I comforted myself with the fantasy of my son at Tsarskoye Selo, sitting up now, I was sure, eating from a silver tray brought to his bed, making slow rounds in his robe and slippers about the green-carpeted playroom, perhaps splashing in the tsar's big tub and talking to the parrot, Popov, which the tsar had inherited from his father and kept in his bathroom, the palace and park guarded by loyal Cossacks and the soldiers of the elite Garde Equipage. The rumors were that half the Pavlovsky regiment in Petersburg had mutinied, followed by some of the Litovsky and the Preobrazhensky—the Preobrazhensky!, the tsar's most prestigious regiment—and that in the Astoria Hotel the rank-and-file soldiers had hunted down their senior officers with rifles and bayonets until the lobby floor was turned into a junkyard of mirrored glass and crystal beads, its revolving door spinning in circles through the blood. If I had known

Kyril Vladimirich had the gall to return to Peter from the Arctic and call the men he commanded of the Garde Equipage away from the Alexander Palace, pin a red cockade to his cap and a red ribbon to his uniform, hoist a red flag on his roof, and march to the Duma to pledge his support for the revolution, to offer his services as tsar, I would have lost my mind. But I didn't know it. And so, somehow, I kept my sanity.

After three days at Yuriev's, the streets grew calm enough for my brother Josef to come and retrieve me. As I had saved him once, he now saved me. It was good, I suppose, at this moment, to have Kschessinkys on both sides of the revolution. I gave Yuriev a pair of Sergei's Fabergé cufflinks and we kissed each other's cheeks and then I kissed his hands. He wore on one finger the ring the tsar had given him as his gift at Yuriev's benefit. I heard that Yuriev wore that ring the rest of his life, even during the Great Terror, when he knew he could have been killed for it.

Josef and I had to walk all the way from Petersburg Island across the Troitsky Bridge to his apartment on Spasskaya Ulitsa. The wind blew from the north down the Great Neva and pushed at us as we crossed the bridge. The coat I had snatched up three days before, when the weather had briefly warmed, was too light for the weather which had turned cold once again, and the wind threatened to knock us against the triple lampposts that dotted the bridge or send us flying over the balustrades. Against this wind I held down the fabric of my coat and I tugged my kerchief low over my brow. Siberia, I thought, could not be colder than this. When we reached the palace embankment, I lifted my head. This was why Josef said we had to walk. Hundreds of smashed cars bottled up the streets, stolen by young girls who had no idea how to drive and yet inspired by revolutionary fever had jumped behind the wheel and pressed the gas. Their cars shot forward only to smash into one another and into all those taxis whose drivers refused to keep to the left now that *we are free!*, and from there into the lampposts and

walls and storefronts until finally the girls abandoned the cars altogether. Some of them were left with their tops down, frozen metal
sculptures, creased and gouged and functionless, and among them,
as if they didn't exist at all, roamed the crowds. Small groups of
people stood in circles around impromptu bonfires, and when we
drew close enough I could see they were burning the wooden emblems they had stripped from the shops about us, emblems the
shops used to advertise their imperial patronage, and on Nevsky
Prospekt a great crowd busied itself with the same, the gray smoke
like a puff from a giant hookah reaching two stories above a crowd
wearing kerchiefs, fur hats, and, worst of all, caps with army insignia. The charred pile of trash looked like an animal and the people
posed for a camera held by a comrade to record their great deed.
The soldiers wore their coats and tunics unbuttoned, their caps
backward, all deliberately against regulation in a city where a year
earlier a soldier could be reprimanded for the incorrect salutation
to his superior—why, a duel could be fought if an officer's inferior
did not walk on the left side of the street! Two women in men's
clothing walked by us. I suppose they, too, now were *free*—their
arms locked about each other's waists, while other women wandered, hatless, their hair frizzled and loosened. Everywhere I
stepped there were bits of glass and I put my hand to my brother's
back and held on to him as I followed his shape through the streets.
To the right of us a group of little boys threw loose cartridges into a
fire and scattered at the intermittent explosions. In the window of
one café stood a sign: *Fellow citizens! In honor of the great days of
freedom I bid you all welcome. Come inside, and eat and drink to your
heart's content.* Three steps from that café, against the side of a building, a woman stood with her skirt raised while a man, his dirty
fingers gripping the line of brick above her, took his pleasure, his
breath coming in a series of short, barking grunts. *Don't look,* my
brother said, but how could I not look? Never was I so relieved that
Vova was not with me. A man brushed by me dressed in women's

clothes, a skirt hanging beneath his greatcoat, big boots on his feet as he stomped past. *A policeman*, my brother said, *trying to get away disguised*. On his way to Finland Station, no doubt, to make his escape from a fate like the one who fell past the window of Yuriev's apartment. *Pharaohs*, the crowd was calling the policemen now. *Pigs*. I stepped on a pair of smashed eyeglasses and I began to see the detritus of this uprising everywhere—a watch chain, a bit of patterned silk, a woman's shoe with the heel snapped off, metal insignia, a fork, various signage reading *By Appointment to His Majesty Tsar Nicholas*, all bearing the double-headed eagles, waiting, next, to be burned, and in one gutter, a lace dress laid out as neatly as on a woman's bed. But when we turned the corner I looked up and saw what I would never forget: the stone head of Alexander II held up like the severed head of Medusa by a peasant with the broad nose and lips of some Eastern province. Josef said, *You should see what they've carved on the plinth of the statue of Alexander II in Znamenskaya Square: hippopotamus*—and at that I began to laugh, crazily. Into the gutter a man vomited, cap in hand, and the liquid splattered his boots. Everywhere I smelled fire, and when ashes blew toward us, my brother said, *That's the Palace of Justice burning to the ground*.

My brother lived at No. 18, in a twelve-room apartment. The Bolsheviks remembered him and his revolutionary activity of 1905, and when they made all the *formers* share their houses and apartments, when servants took the rooms of their masters or stole their furniture and whatever else they could carry, my brother Josef was allowed to keep his twelve rooms all for himself. He would enjoy them until Stalin came to power, after which he was allowed the use of only two. Josef didn't want to leave Russia even then. In 1924, after Lenin's death, I arranged from Paris visas and tickets for Josef and his family so he could come dance once again for Diaghilev. But Josef wrote me, *We artists have privileged positions here. I can't leave a country to which I am bound by so many memories.* We weren't the only ones with memories. When Stalin launched the Great Terror in the thirties, Josef was dismissed from his teaching position at the old Imperial Ballet School simply for writing to me.

He died, you know, of starvation, in 1942, during the siege of Leningrad, in the war after this one, and he was buried in a mass grave in the Piskarevskoe Memorial Cemetery.

On my second day at my brother's apartment, as Josef and I sat in his dining room and drank glasses of tea, some sweetened with sugar, some sweetened with jam, we heard the sound of singing in the street below. Josef stood and opened a window and I went and stood behind him. The crowd was singing their version of the "Marseillaise," which the workers had appropriated from the French revolutionaries and then, pronouncing it the *Marsiliuza*, stuffed with their own lyrics,

> *We renounce the old, old world*
> *We shake its dust from off our feet.*
> *We don't need a golden idol*
> *And we despise the tsarist devil.*

Something has happened, my brother said, and he put on his coat and went down to the street. I paced the floor, going to the window every few seconds, and it seemed each time I looked out one more red flag appeared on one more roof and yet another banner was unfurled from the windows of a building; and then church bells began to ring, and not just from one church but, it seemed, from everywhere, from every church. Was the war over? Then Niki could bring all his troops home as he had in 1905 and then these animals would be put into cages or hung from the scaffolds. At last I heard my brother's foot on the stairs and he rushed in clutching a handful of leaflets, the fronts of them printed with symbols we would soon see again and again—a chain broken into two bits, a sun emerging from the clouds, its rays spreading out from behind the mist, a throne and crown on their sides. The emblems of the revolution, though I didn't know that then.

What is this? I said to Josef. *What does it mean?*

It means, he said, *the tsar has been overthrown.*

I grabbed at his sleeve. *What? What?*

We sat at my brother's dining room table, reading the printed news, unable to speak, our fingertips blackening with ink as we turned the pages. The tsar had abdicated on March 2 on the train while it stood on the rails at Pskov, where he had been forced to stop on the way home to Peter, having gone east on a detour to give the direct route to troops being moved along that line. Once in Pskov, halfway between Stavka and Tsarskoye, he could not move, as the tracks ahead had been seized by revolutionaries. And Niki's efforts to halt the revolution were as choked as his train. General Ivanov, whom Niki had charged with bringing troops to the capital and establishing a dictatorship, had arrived with his men too late. General Khabalov, already there in the capital, was too much a fool to think to bring in loyalist troops, and instead hid in the Admiralty and drank cognac. And General Alexeev, an even bigger fool, thought the liberals in the Duma would settle the city by political means and keep the monarchy intact, and so he held his troops at bay—and when he saw none of this settled the roiling capital, Alexeev gathered all of Niki's leading generals to ask for the tsar's abdication for the good of the country, the war, and the dynasty. This was what made Niki write in his diary that he saw all around him only cowardice and deceit.

And so, ill-advised, Niki had handed the throne to his brother, Mikhail—Mikhail! whom Niki had allowed back into Russia only in 1914 at the start of the war! And I thought, *Why? Why have you done this? What did they say to you on that train?*, for I did not know any of this then. Oh, if only Niki had made it all the way home to Tsarskoye. Alix would never have let him abdicate on the advice of his beloved generals—he had always been too besotted by the military—and she certainly would not have let him shove the throne away from her son or mine! What had happened to the glorious greater Russia Niki had promised me for my son? Was he so tired that he allowed himself to be persuaded? At Mogilev, Sergei had told me the tsar's doctors had begun to prescribe cocaine for Niki to stem his exhaustion and that they were worried he was headed for a nervous breakdown. Perhaps it was a relief for him to give Russia away to his fool of a brother who hadn't even the courage to take the crown but instead had himself abdicated! When the mob had bellowed at this news of yet another tsar, Mikhail had hidden himself in the mansion of the Princess Putiatina at No. 12, Millionaia and allowed the prime minister of the Duma, Prince Lvov, and one of the republican ministers, an Alexander Kerensky, to persuade him to refuse the crown, telling him they could not guarantee his safety. Frightened, Mikhail quickly scribbled his abdication manifesto in a school notebook in the study of the princess's daughter, hunched over a child's desk. Another of the documents of the revolution scribbled in a child's practice book. Yes, Mikhail had broken the crown into little bits and distributed the fragments among the incompetent ministers and the disreputable men of the Duma Niki hadn't had time yet to fix! For the country, the leaflet said, would now be run by a Provisional Government. Niki had given up not only being emperor but the whole regime—the grand dukes, the princes, the barons and counts. I felt like one of the peasants in the provinces, the old *muzhiki*, who when hearing the news cried, *They have taken the tsar away from us. What will become of us now?* I looked at my brother's face to see if he was happy, for wasn't this what he and his comrades had wanted all those years ago, and still wanted?

But he didn't look happy. Perhaps this was more than he wanted, too radical even for him?

What is the tsar doing? my brother said, shaking his head. *It's not legal for him to hand over the crown to his brother!* No. Josef was right. It was not legal. The throne should pass to the heir and Alexei was the heir. Niki knew this. I sucked at a strand of my hair. Perhaps this act of abdication was just a tactic of delay—Niki knew his brother would not have the character to succeed him—and by signing an illegal manifesto he was preserving the throne for his sons. It was a trick, a prevarication to give him time! As my thoughts stampeded from one end of my brain to the other, Josef read to me from the paper, which reported that Colonel Nicholas Romanov, as the tsar would now be known, had returned by train from Stavka to Tsarskoye Selo, where he, his family, and some of his retinue were now prisoners of the Provisional Government. I made him repeat that last part. *He's a prisoner in Alexander Palace?* My brother nodded. *Along with his court.* At this, I took the leaflet from my brother to read it over myself. How could this be? How could this possibly be? The tsar under guard?

How *long* would the imperial family be at the mercy of the revolutionary soldiers who guarded them—the brothers of these men pillaging and vomiting in the streets below—as the Provisional Government struggled, despaired at the task, and then finally turned the country back over to Niki. Weeks? Months? For I was sure that was what would happen. The insolent soldiers who now stood guard in the park would be hanged along with all the mutinous troops. That couldn't happen quickly enough for me. Surely they could not hold Niki prisoner that whole time in Tsarskoye. Could Niki have foreseen any of this out there on those tracks, without view of the mob gutting his city, when he wrote, *Not wishing to part with our dear son, we hand over our inheritance to our brother, Grand Duke Mikhail Alexandrovich, and give him our blessing to mount the throne of the Russian state*. And then I remembered how he had looked at Mogilev, at dinner, smoking between courses, his eyes turned inward, fatigued and stressed, his inattention to the conversation of the men around him politely disguised—did that mood fore-shadow this act of which I could not then conceive? Was he debat-ing, *Should I strive for action or remain inert?* Perhaps he had returned to Peter to do the former and then halfway through had conceded to the latter.

I put down the paper and rapped on the table to get Josef's at-tention and he turned from the window. *What?* It was then I told Josef what I had done, that Vova was not tucked away safely at Stavka with Sergei as I had said, but was being held with the impe-rial family at Tsarskoye Selo, and in my brother's face I saw this was terrible for Vova, worse than I had thought. When I opened my arms along the table and put my head to its cloth, stained with droplets of jam, even I was surprised by the violence of my weep-ing. My brother paced the floor while I wailed. My crying grew so loud, eventually Josef's wife and daughter, Celina, five years old, clutching a doll in a purple dress—a little girl who would never be embroiled in an imperial misadventure but was to be safely en-sconced at the Imperial Ballet School (and now in this new world what would *that* be called?)—came to the tall doors of the dining room and peered in at us. At the sight of them, my big brother grew calmer and with this calm, arm in arm, came reason. No one would touch the tsar at Tsarskoye, Josef said. He was safer there than in the capital while this new Russia was configured, and so were his family and Vova. If the tsar was not reinstated, the imperial family would surely be sent away to live out the rest of their years in com-fortable exile. According to the report, Nicholas expected as much, commenting after he signed his document of abdication that he would retire to the country, adding, *I like flowers*. A lie, I am sure. But this must have been what the poet Mayakovsky was thinking of when he wrote in 1920 the verse primers by which the illiterate peasant soldiers on the southwest front learned to read.

> B—*The Bolsheviks hunt the borzhui.*
>   *The borzhui run a mile.*
> Ts—*Flowers smell sweet in the evening.*
>   *Tsar Nicholas loved them very much.*

So, Josef said. *We will have to wait and see.*

But of course I couldn't wait. When have I ever been able to wait?

The trains began running again by the end of the month, and so disguised as the new me, not Magnificent Mathilde, but Peasant Mathilde, I was able to travel in a second-class compartment the nine versts southwest to Tsarskoye Selo. I knew immediately the imperial family must be outside when I walked up from the village and saw the common people pressed to the park fence. I had heard when the family made a promenade of the palace park or, later, when the weather changed, broke ice in the canals or, desperate for some industry, worked on their kitchen vegetable garden, small groups of the curious would gather outside the black iron railings to gaze at the former tsar and the former tsaritsa in their former park, now their prison. In the past such access would have been unthinkable—the Cossack sentries would never have permitted anyone to gather and gawk, but the revolutionary guards had no such compunction. They let all who wished to come and stare. That day, the people were silent, though sometimes it was reported they jeered at the former tsar or balled up the greasy brown paper in which they had wrapped their lunch and hurled it into the park through the fence, a gift for the despot. When I arrived and stood a little apart from the crowd,

I could see Niki alone of the family was in view, a soldier with a bayonet fixed to a rifle a few paces behind him, and at that sight I felt my bones turn to powder. The tsar stood on the summer landing pier, a long, wooden pole in his hand, jabbing at the ice to crack the frozen surface, so one could see the liquidity beneath it, the color, the movement, the variety of it, the very elements denied the tsar by his guards. When not harassing the family, the guards shot at the deer and the swans in the estate's park because they were bored and because no one any longer had the power to forbid them to do so and because they believed, when the counterrevolution came from the old regime, they themselves would be hanged from gallows and the people pressed to these fences would jeer at their dangling bodies, and so why should they let anything, animal or man, live? I heard the guard call, *What will you do come spring, Nicholas Romanov?*, a remark that enflamed me but which Niki ignored. As the guard cackled at his own joke, a boy came into view, a boy too tall to be Vova and reed thin—Alexei, recovered now from the measles, but wasted by it. And so I continued to wait, for where there was Alexei, I figured, there would also be Vova, and so I stood, without moving, while onlookers came and went, and eventually, because I am so small and because I remained there so long and so motionless, I became a magnet. Nicholas was compelled to take note of me. He looked my way without giving any sign, but he stood still staring for long enough to attract the attention of the tsarevich, who stared where his father did and then said, *Papa?* I heard clearly the uncertainty and apprehension in that one question, and I knew from it that the guards must frighten and intimidate the children so used to the respect and servility which they were normally accorded. And sure enough, just as Alexei had feared, Niki's stone-still posture drew the attention of the guard, who took a single menacing step, looked piercingly at the rabble at the fence and held up his rifle in warning, addressing Niki not as *Gosoudar*, Sire, but as *Colonel Romanov!* Niki turned away, casually, as if to show he had been looking at nothing in particular at all, but the guard, suspicious, advanced to-ward the crowd to see who among us had caught the tsar's attention, who was a scout come to spring the family from their prison, for the only thing that frightened the guards more than the thought of a counterrevolution was letting their imperial prisoners escape, for which transgression they would be immediately shot by their own. As I found out later, they worried constantly about signals sent to the outside through parcels, through the turning on and off of lamps, through the single telephone line which the prisoners could use only in the presence of a guard, through the unsealed letters sent in and out and read by the commander at their ingress and egress.

I moved closer to the others at the fence and lowered my eyes, bent my knees, and shrank down beneath my hat—I was so tiny I could impersonate a child!—and as the guard, practically a child himself, paced left and right, behind him I saw Niki put a hand out to Alexei to reassure him, and then wave to someone behind the bridge, someone indistinguishable from the dark trunks of the leaf-less birch trees. Another boy appeared soon after, a boy who took up his own wooden pole, and together with Alexei and Niki began to pound at the ice. The shadows of the birch trees swept across the white snow, but Niki, acting with the self-discipline he had prac-ticed for the twenty-two years of his reign, never looked in my di-rection again. And so in this way Niki showed me my son.

After that, Vova wrote short weekly letters to Sergei at Stavka—most likely, Sergei told me, to conceal his association with me and to prevent me from coming to Tsarskoye again and endangering them all. Vova's letters always said the same thing, *I am well. I embrace you warmly. Always yours, Vladimir*—but Sergei said though the mis-sives were short—for after all, they must pass through the censors—they were in Vova's handwriting and so he and I must be reassured by this, for what other reassurance did we have, and at least some communication with the outside world was allowed.

Over the next months the streets of the capital grew shabby and unkempt—weeds found every crack in the pavement, no matter how slight, as if Nature had waited quietly all along to take back the versts Peter the Great had snatched from her. The snow turned yellow and then black and the windows of the buildings remained unpolished, a graffiti of streaks and smudges. The imperial statues and monuments the revolutionary crowds had deemed too large to topple had been covered in red cloth, bloodied spears stuck in the dirty snow, and along the iron railings of the Winter Palace wads of red cloth bound up the imperial emblems too difficult to remove. But for now, though this off-kilter world wobbled, it continued to turn, and so did the routines of the theater. The Imperial Theater Schools reopened and the governesses led their charges once again out to the parks. The ballet school had no hot water and the rooms of the school were cold, but soldiers were no longer shooting at the windows of Theater Street—why, little Alexandra Danilova had had to duck a bullet when she peeked over her dormitory windowsill— and classes could resume. There was no fuel to burn, so the governesses put the children into smaller dorm rooms and laid their cots close to one another, so that like animals in a barn, the heat of their bodies could warm them, and in the dressing room basins floated chips of ice. The Maryinsky Theater itself reopened March 15, and the children were now driven to the theater in long sleighs, for the school's carriages had been confiscated during Glorious February, and the students now danced before the common soldier, who smoked his cigarettes and spit his seeds right there in the parterres and used his boots to stomp in time to the music. I heard from my old partner Vladimirov that the great oil portrait of Nicholas was taken down from the lobby wall and the double-headed eagles and crowns that ornamented the boxes and the thresholds were also pried from the plaster and discarded. The ushers no longer wore their uniforms with the epaulets that bore the crown monogram. The Provisional Government gave them gray jackets, and because in this new life of deprivation there was no way to clean them, the fabric grew greasy with use. The evenings' programs were no longer embossed with the double-headed eagle but with Apollo's lyre, the same as the pin the boys at the ballet school had for a century worn on the collar of their school uniforms. So the lyre of a Greek god was still acceptable to the new regime. But I was forty-five years old and I was a *former*, with a son whose father was a Romanov, so I myself was not acceptable. I could not appear on the stage. Nor did I want to.

In May, the last class graduated from the great Corps des Pages, which my son had so wanted to attend but had never had the chance, and the school was closed—there was no need for pages if there no longer existed a court. And there was no longer any need either for the thousands of servants who had attended the imperial family or for the giant Abyssinians who in their white turbans and curved shoes had stood in majestic pairs outside the doors to any room that contained the emperor. They had all abandoned Tsarskoye Selo along with the courtiers who did not wish to remain with the Romanovs under house arrest. One day, on Nevsky Prospekt, I found myself facing one of those six-foot-tall Africans, now dressed in trousers and a tunic, a black-faced ghost, a relic, with no door to open for the tsar, no door to guard while the tsar busied himself behind it. *Where are you going?* I wanted to ask him. *What tales of the Russian court will you take with you?* I could have asked the same of almost everyone.

Yet, the Petersburg palaces were not entirely emptied at this time. The streets were full of rough-looking soldiers, yes, for the revolution favored black leather jackets, backward-turned caps, and a swagger, and the old revolutionary leaders of 1905, Lenin, Trotsky, Chernov, yes, found their ways back to Peter and took up residence in or made offices of requisitioned homes—including mine, which had a view of the Troitsky Bridge and the embankment, a strategic view for anyone planning an uprising—and so I remained at my brother's, in his daughter's bedroom. But the nobility was still here. It was as if all the aristocracy were under house arrest along with the tsar, waiting to see how the Provisional Government of the old Duma and the new Soviet would rein in unruly Russia and deal with the *formers*. Would they be allowed to keep their palaces, their treasures amassed over generations? The former imperial family, it appeared, would receive reduced *appanages*. The grand dukes, Sergei's brother Nicholas had heard, might receive 30,000 of their accustomed 280,000 rubles a year. Was that conspirator happy now that the tsar had been deposed, as he had wished? It appeared perhaps one of the Romanovs—Nikolasha, Kyril, or Niki's brother Mikhail—would assume a figurehead position as tsar, as head of Duma, as president, as no, no, as nothing. Russia's fate was evolving every day. In the spring of 1917 some former tsarist officials still served in the Duma and still led the army, but others of them, like the former minister of war, Sukhomlinov, were arrested—or in Sukhomlinov's case, rearrested—and taken to the Peter and Paul Fortress for questioning, and still others slipped away, to the Caucasus or the Crimea or Kiev, where they gambled, drank Abram champagne, ate caviar and sturgeon, set the clock back one hour to Petersburg time, and waited there, as we did here, to see which Russia would prevail.

Through all this, Sergei remained at Stavka on the advice of his brother Nicholas, who feared for his safety. There were no revolutionaries there at headquarters among the generals of the old regime— any unrest in the military was taking place among the infantry barracked in the cities and at the fronts. In his letters to me Sergei gave me news of the war. At the fronts, the soldiers were tired and refusing to fight, and though the new supreme commander, Brusilov, made a tour urging them to pull together for a fresh offensive, he met with men who didn't care about Galicia or France and just wanted to go home. The men wanted peace so badly they would put the tsar back on the throne if he promised it to them. At the eastern front men had even begun to fraternize with the Germans, who lured the Russians over the Dniester with vodka and prostitutes. Only in the southwest, far from the big cities, were the soldiers still disciplined. But when the offensive ordered by the commanders began in June, the men advanced only two miles toward Galicia to retake all the ground they had lost in the Great Retreat before they refused to go any further and began to desert, looting and raping along the way in Volschinsk, Konivkhy, and Lvov. Sergei feared these disgruntled soldiers and their like would eventually find their way to Peter and meet up with the several thousand troops garrisoned on the Vyborg side of the city, troops who had helped bring about the revolution in the first place and who could overthrow the shaky Provisional Government, as well. The members of the Duma were at odds with the Kadets from the Constitutional Democratic Party, the Socialist Revolutionaries, the Anarchists, and the Social Democrats, the Bolshevik splinter of which had begun to agitate and arm the Red Guards, the workers' brigades that had sprung up not only to protect the Vyborg factories that sat so close to the Vyborg regiments but the revolution itself against an imagined counterrevolution. And while the Provisional Government labored over the details of the perfect parliament to be elected in the fall, the Bolsheviks began to whisper in the streets, *The Provisional Government itself has become a puppet of the counterrevolutionaries who plan to reinstate the tsar. The tsar and tsaritsa are plotting to reinstate the monarchy.*

Exhausted and overwhelmed, the prime minister of the Duma, Prince Lvov, resigned and was replaced by a new man, that Alexander Kerensky who had helped secure Grand Duke Mikhail's abdication. Kerensky had served in the Duma as minister of justice and minister of war and now it seemed, in a ministerial leapfrog to rival Alix's appointments, he would be installed as prime minister in charge of the country. Rumor had it Kerensky had moved himself into the Winter Palace, into the suite of Alexander III, into his very bed, and when he couldn't sleep, he would pace the breadth of that grand room singing operatic arias, so giddy was he with his new power. He had once wanted to be an actor—his speeches were so impassioned that sometimes he would faint after delivering them—and as a boy, he had signed notes to his parents, *From the Future Artist of the Imperial Theaters, A. Kerensky*. If his guards had been less ignorant, all Peter would know which arias Kerensky sang and from which operas. This Kerensky, Sergei said, had been talking of moving the imperial family to England or Finland for their safety, where they would live—perhaps permanently—and if that happened, we, too, would apply for permission from Kerensky to go abroad. The Romanovs in the English countryside, hunting pheasant and drinking tea in some grace and favor house when they had once ruled one-sixth of the world? In that case, Vova would no longer be of use to them, nor would I.

So Sergei's letters weren't much comfort to me, nor were Andrei's. He sent me letters care of the theater, which Vladimirov ferried to me like some postrevolutionary mailman. Andrei described the large whitewashed villa his mother had rented for them, guarded by a dozen Cossacks for hire, the dinners, teas, and card games they enjoyed with the Sheremetievs and the Vrontzovs, who had also left Peter for the Caucasus, and when I read his merry letters I thought, *What is this strange mirror-world these people have found on the Black Sea, where the revolution cannot penetrate the quicksilver of that plane?*

There were no teas or dinners for me. Wherever I lived I was an embarrassment, and whomever I lived with I endangered. A pornographic movie was made about me that depicted me servicing one grand duke after another or two at a time in some revolutionary filmmaker's fantasy of a mistress's boudoir: *The Secret Story of the Ballerina Kschessinska*. I became the subject of many news articles—about the jewels and silver fleeced from my house: "16 Poods of Silver from the Palace of Kschessinska"; about the war bribes: "Espionage and the Ballerina"; about my long-ago affair with Nicholas: "Secrets of M. F. Kschessinska." But the most frightening of all was the novel, *The Tsarevich's Romance*, by Maria Evgenieva, which told the story that my early liaison with Nicholas had resulted in the birth of two sons, now grown, both of them spirited off to Paris after Glorious February. If only that were true, but my one son was not in Paris, he was here, just outside the city, right under their noses, sending off his letters to Sergei, a Romanov grand duke of the old regime—and therefore at peril. *I am well. We are planting a kitchen garden. Alexei and I showed movies in his room. I kiss your hands, Vladimir*.

My connections to the court, which once made me quite a prize to know, now made me a peril. At Vladimirov's I hid my reticule of jewels at the bottom of a potted plant. The tsar's signed photograph I had slipped between the pages of a magazine at Yuriev's, afraid to tell Yuriev what I had done for fear of compromising him, and later I discovered he had, all unknowing, thrown away the magazine! I hid the bundle of the tsar's letters with another friend for safekeeping, but she was arrested, her home searched and searched again, until finally, in terror, she burned all his letters to ash. *Forgive me, divine creature, for having disturbed your rest*, along with all the other lovely lines Niki stole from the greats or created for me of his own inspiration were gone. Even the lowest housemaid to Niki's daughters, Elizaveta Nikolaevna Evsberg, felt compelled to burn the little notes the girls had left for her and that she had saved as keepsakes—*Elizaveta, can you sew this button on for me, thank you, Tatiana*—because it was too dangerous to have been even the *exploited servant* in the Winter Palace, too dangerous to know anyone who knew *any* Romanov at all. And I, of course, knew many Romanovs, and I had flaunted those connections.

M. Fabergé finally asked me to come and remove my valuables from his vaults, as with all the upheaval he could no longer guarantee their safety.

The Fabergé Building boasted red-brown granite pillars at its entrance. Into one of them was chiseled his name, the *F*, the *A*, the *B* of the Fabergé so straight and so tall, their edges so precisely beveled, they seemed the only bit of order left in the capital. But inside the building all was chaos. The showroom's glass cases had been emptied, and through a door to the back I could see open crates and men bent over them stuffing valuables into sawdust to be shipped off— shipped off to where? Fabergé himself led me to my vault, the wisps of his white hair standing almost on end, as if alarmed, and his beard, when he turned to address me, shimmered as white and fine as spun sugar. *Look, look at this*, he told me, his voice cracking, and he halted at a wooden crate about to be hammered shut, thrust open the lid, and excavated from its shavings a luminous blue stone egg floating on a bank of clouds, the imperial Easter egg Niki had intended to give Alexandra that coming Easter of 1917.

Why he showed this to me I do not know, nor do I know what stone gave those clouds their milky opalescence, nor do I know what gleaming blue gem made up the egg itself, but Fabergé told me he had been working on this gift for a year and that it had been designed to honor the birthday of the tsarevich. Fabergé's face flushed pink and he looked down through his delicate nostrils at me and at the egg as he extolled its virtues. The lines etched into the surface of the luminous blue, he said, sketched out the lines of the earth's longitude and latitude, and the tiny diamonds embedded along those spokes winked like the constellations that shone in the northern hemisphere on the early August day the tsarevich was born. This egg marked the fortune of his birth, Fabergé said, and those stars spoke his fate—to rule one-sixth of the world. Fabergé suggested with his fingers the golden disk that like a ring of Saturn would have girdled this small planet, its thin surface also paved with diamonds. It would have been his most magnificent, his most poignant, his most meaningful egg yet presented to the tsar, and Fabergé's eyes brimmed with tears at how the revolution had foiled the presentation of his masterpiece. Now his egg would be buried in this crate filled with sawdust, the lid hammered closed, the box shipped into oblivion, into the chaos of this godforsaken country, to end up on a train commandeered in the upheaval of some province, in the wet basement of some requisitioned municipal building, in the rough hut of some peasant, where it would wait to be rediscovered.

I did not say to him, *My son was born in June. If the world rights itself, you will have designed the wrong constellations for the tsarevich.*

Then in July, a crowd of fifty thousand Bolshevik sympathizers—Kronstadt sailors, Putilov workers in their blue factory tunics, and soldiers—surrounded the Tauride Palace where the Soviet met and tried to force it to seize power from the weak Provisional Government, crying, *Seize power, you bastards! All Power to the Soviet!* Then in frustration, when Trotsky and Chernov refused to do so, saying the time for a Soviet revolution had not yet come and certainly would not be decided by bayonets in the street, the mob ran through the city attacking the *burzhui* until a sudden rainstorm cleared the streets. The mob caused such a disturbance that Kerensky feared the monarchist right, indignant at this mayhem and the Provisional Government's inability to control it, might bring in the armies from the front, after all, and move to reinstate the tsar and the civil order of that regime. And so Kerensky laid down a series of decrees—no public gatherings, death penalty to deserters and insubordinates at the front, no more soldiers' committees. But it was his release of

leaflets accusing the Bolsheviks of being traitors, their movement
financed by German money with the purpose of overturning the
revolution and all the new freedoms and forcing Russia into a hu-
miliating peace treaty that finally turned the workers and the troops
against them. Arrest warrants for the Bolshevik leaders were issued, and those who didn't flee were jailed in the Peter and Paul
Fortress alongside the corrupt loyalist officials from the old regime
already there. This sudden wave of sentiment against the Bolsheviks, which meant perhaps the imperial family would also be released, worked unexpectedly in my favor. In this new atmosphere,
the public began to agitate against the traitors who with their dirty
boots and tobacco juice tromped their way through the house of a
prima ballerina, even if that ballerina *was* the imperialist trollop
Kschessinska. And so the Provisional Government sent eight ar-
mored cars and several batteries of artillery over the bridges to my
house and turned the remaining Bolsheviks out.

Sergei's brother now judged it safe enough for Sergei to return
to Peter, and Sergei came at once to see me at my brother's apartment, driving there in the lone car the Provisional Government had
permitted him to keep—he who had once had half a dozen motorcars! The arthritis that sometimes troubled him had now flared like
a pulsing star, scorching his every joint, and that was why Sergei
limped into the foyer, where I stopped him to kiss his beard, untamed as a peasant's and tangled with silver just as the tinsel we
threw each year on our Christmas trees tangled with the pine needles. When I kissed at his fingers, I saw the knuckles of them had
become so misshapen that his insignia ring sat on a little finger as
curled and reddened as a boiled shrimp. I took his hat from him and
suddenly I found myself on the floor with it in my two hands like a
giant saucer. Sergei stooped awkwardly and tried to pat my shoulder. He missed. His hand batted the air, the tip of my ear. I peered
up at him—had he lost his sight, along with everything else? No.
He was simply, suddenly, at forty-eight, an old man. And I knew—I

would not be permitted to sit down on the floor, cry into this saucer of a hat, and hand him my tears.

While Sergei had moved back into his apartments at the New Mikhailovsky Palace, where he and his brother Nicholas dined together every night, the Napoleonic memorabilia Nicholas collected scattered about, I had not yet been able to return to my home, which the Bolsheviks made famous and which would be forever referred to in the history books as *the Kschessinska Palace*. But when the Provisional Government finally put the keys back in my hand, I, along with Josef and Sergei and two of Sergei's loyal dragoons—for not every soldier, you must remember, was sympathetic to the revolution—drove to Petersburg Island in Sergei's one car to take stock of the ruin.

Shall I tell you a bit of the ruin, for I remember it exactly? My intimate Louis XVI drawing room had been looted of all its period furniture and its silk walls shone a dull gray now rather than soft yellow from smoke and filth. Apparently, the Bolsheviks did not employ housekeepers. My piano had been, inexplicably, pitched by a crazy man almost into my winter garden, where, caught between two white pillars like an officer pinched between two of his infantry, it could go no farther. My winter garden itself had become a thicket of dead plants, the marble basin in its center a toilet circled by brown palms. My dining room floor had clearly functioned as a spittoon for the husks of those ubiquitous sunflower seeds. The bottles in my wine cellar, all carefully selected by the dilettante Andrei at his long-ago ease, had vanished, drunk to the bottom, I am sure, the moment they were discovered. But there were some provisions in the pantry cupboards; the Bolsheviks had been booted out too quickly to pack everything, though they had tried. The staircase to my bedrooms was covered with the books and leaflets someone had tried to carry out before the men gave up hope of removing their literature and decided to burn it instead; in almost every fireplace and stove in the house I found a big pile of ash. Ink stained my bedroom carpet, and I found cigarette butts and wads of tobacco spittle lying like cockroaches in the bottom of the sunken bath I had with such imperial delusions built for the tsar. The cedar wardrobes in which I had stored my furs had their doors ripped off. Need I say there were no furs remaining within? The numbered plaques above my dressing room cubbies had been pried off, as well. The Bolsheviks did not like numbers? They liked well enough the clothing that had been assigned those numbers, I saw, because not a stitch of it remained, either. The next weeks, it seemed to me I saw bits and pieces of my wardrobe on the backs of young women everywhere on the streets—my black velvet skirt on one, my ermine coat on another, my lace shawl around the shoulders of a bucktoothed girl. I went then into Vova's suite, threw open the doors to his balcony, and sat at his desk, a student desk but large enough for me, the drawers still stuffed with notebooks and papers from Vova's lessons with his tutors, a map with the major cities of Europe, even those hated German ones, marked in red ink, a line of script on the frontispiece of his French notebook, *Je m'appelle Vladimir Sergeivich Kschessinsky, quatorze ans*. I fingered the spine of one of Vova's notebooks and then held it to my nose to breathe in the scent of my boy. How long had it been since he had fidgeted here at this desk? Half a year. But instead of breathing in my son, I inhaled something else, a foreign smell. I lowered the notebook to the desk and opened the cover.

> The country is passing from the first stage of the revolution—which, owing to the insufficient class consciousness and organization of the proletariat, placed power in the hands of the bourgeoisie—to its second stage, which must place power in the hands of the proletariat and the poorest sections of the peasantry . . .

All power to the brutish peasantry, the social equivalent of the theater's Near the Water girls? They were to run the country? Those

rank-and-file workers who threw a man off a roof while their brethren on the street below beat at his body with sticks?

> The masses must be made to see that the Soviets of Workers' Dep-
> uties are the only possible form of revolutionary government . . .
> no support of the Provisional Government.

So the Provisional Government was not revolutionary enough for
this writer?

> Abolition of the police, the army, and the bureaucracy . . . nation-
> alization of all land . . . the union of all banks in the country into a
> single national bank.

And what was this? No police? No landowners? One bank?
There were cross-outs as the writer revised and blotches and
pools of ink where he had paused to think, nib of the pen against
the paper. I flipped the page to see a list of names I did not recognize
and had never heard of, perhaps the names of his own comrades,
and next to each name an epithet—*pig, cunt, whore, bastard*.
I shut the notebook. It was certainly one of my son's school com-
position books. I opened the cover again. On the inside cover the
writer had signed his name, one word, *Lenin*. The handwriting was
large, graceful, almost the handwriting of an older woman lying at
her case on her chaise, but these words, this *Theses*, as the document
was titled, had not been written by some bourgeois but by some
maniacal anarchist who sat hunched here at my son's desk composing these stark sentences. Actually, I was correct in my assessment
of the two sides of the man, though I couldn't know it then. Lenin
was Vladimir Ilyich Ul'ianov, a hereditary nobleman whose father
had slowly earned enough *chin* as inspector of schools to be addressed as *Your Excellency* and whose mother had inherited her fa-

ther's country estate at Kokushkino, where Lenin strutted about like any good squire, sniffing the fragrance of its lime trees, strawberries, raspberries, and hay, and where, in 1891, during the great famine, he had the gall to sue a starving peasant neighbor for damaging a fence. That was one side of Lenin, but the other side had seen his older brother, Alexander, hanged for plotting to kill Alexander III. And when Lenin later arrived to study law at Kazan University as had his brother, he joined the same neo–People's Will groups that his brother had joined, and Lenin was expelled for taking part in a student demonstration—if only they had hanged him like his brother! But, no, Lenin survived a prison sentence, a three-year Siberian exile imposed by the tsar, and then a further exile of his own in Europe, before the war had done to this country what all his treatises could not. Lenin had been a revolutionary for twenty years now, and a man like that was not going to give up just because Kerensky had put out a paper warrant for his arrest. Not that I knew this then—but this ugly writing foretold that if it were up to this Lenin, the Provisional Government would have it no easier governing than had the tsar. And would meet, perhaps, the same fate.

I was still sitting there with that notebook when I heard Josef call out my name, *Mala, Mala*, and I went to the top of the staircase. Josef and Sergei stood at the bottom and Josef said tightly, *Sergei's just heard from his brother*, and I thought, why is he speaking for Sergei? When I looked to Sergei he said, *Niki and the family are being moved at midnight tonight*, and then I understood. Josef had meant to prepare me for bad news.

They were being moved? Moved where? My fingers curled themselves around the notebook and I started down the stairs. Did Kerensky fear the loyalists would put Nicholas back on the throne? Or did he worry the Bolsheviks would try to stage another putsch and that this time there would be none of the meteorological luck which in July had brought the heavy rain to put out the chaos? Nothing this time to keep back the crowd that had shattered the windows and splintered the doors of the Tauride Palace and had almost lynched the Social Revolutionary leader Chernov in his black frock coat right in the street before his comrade, the Menshevik Trotsky, intervened, giving one of his impromptu speeches to the crowd from the bonnet of a car? *Pride and Glory of the Revolution, you've come to declare your will and show the Soviet that the working class no longer wants to see the bourgeoisie in power. But why hurt your own cause by petty acts of violence against casual individuals?* And thus having hypnotized the crowd, Trotsky announced, *Citizen Chernov, you are free!* Was Kerensky afraid that this month or next month at the Tauride or Tsarskoye or the Winter Palace, the crowd would drag out the tsar, the ministers of the Provisional Government, possibly even Kerensky himself and beat them all to death or string them up in the trees? I looked into Sergei's face, trying to guess what *he* thought of this news. I could already tell what Josef thought, what Josef always thought: anything to do with the Romanovs was a bad idea.

Where are they moving them? I asked Sergei. Sergei shook his head. *They were told only to pack warm clothes.*

Warm clothes? Niki's mother, sisters, cousins were now all in the south, in the Caucasus and the Crimea. Niki would not need warm clothes there.

But they were going south, to Livadia Palace, I said.

There's too much unrest along that route, Sergei told me. *The steppe is empty. They are probably taking them east*. And at the look on my face, he said, *Kerensky promises the family can come back by the fall, once the Constituent Assembly has met, and Niki will be free to go where he wishes.*

I looked at Josef, who was shaking his head, and then at Sergei. I took the notebook I was carrying and put it into his hand. *Look, look at this*. And I opened it to the page that said,

We fully regard civil wars, wars waged by the oppressed class against the oppressing class, slaves against slave owners, serfs against landowners, and wage workers against the bourgeoisie, as legitimate, progressive, and necessary.

Sergei read the lines and then tore the page out of the notebook, crumpled the paper in his fist, and threw it down. I pointed to the paper ball. *They want a civil war.*

Sergei smiled. *Where is this writer now? Chased out of your house so quickly he didn't even have time to take his big speech with him.*

But the writer had gotten into my house. In 1905 he had not gotten this far. By 1918 he might be writing on manuscript paper instead of schoolbooks, issuing his own *ukazy* from the tsar's desk in the Winter Palace where Kerensky now sat. I thought, *Only you Romanovs cannot imagine a Russia without you.* While the Romanovs left in Peter were dreaming, in Siberia, with the droves of mosquitoes in summer and the cold so extreme in winter only reindeer skins could help a man withstand it, Niki and his family would be shrunk into such tiny figures on the horizon eventually they would be not even seen, this *former tsar*, with his *former* sons. In the outlier of Siberia their guards, drunk on vodka and far from the moderating reason of Kerensky, could turn surly from the boredom of their inglorious posts, and no one from the capital or the old court, no Vladimirichi, no Mikhailovichi, no Alexandrovichi, would hear the imperial family cry out if they were suffering. And how would I hear my son's cry as it flew over the Urals, across thousands of miles of empty steppe, from whatever small town Kerensky saw fit to stash the family? I could see already the Tura and Tobol rivers, the endless versts, a meadowland in this season but an ice sheet soon enough. And so I said to Sergei, *Take me to Tsarskoye. Vova cannot go with them to Siberia.*

———

Halfway to the Alexandrovsky Station near Tsarskoye Selo, our train, which had left the Warsaw Station in Petersburg at 8:00, with plenty of time to reach Tsarskoye before midnight, inexplicably slowed to a stop in the middle of nowhere. All trains to Tsarskoye had been temporarily halted, our conductor said. We would wait. One hour slipped into two, before Sergei and I realized that our train was being held back purposely: the secret of the tsar's departure, Kerensky's great secret, was no longer a secret, and the radicalized railroad workers all along the Warsaw line, hearing the rumors, suspicious, must have decided to refuse to allow any trains into Tsarskoye, no doubt to keep any friends of the Romanovs away until the train chosen to carry the family away had set out. And at this, I began to paw at the sleeve of Sergei's tunic.

We climbed down from the back of the last car onto the great plain upon which Petersburg also sat, these versts between the capital and Tsarskoye being a small collection of villages and country estates before one reached Krasnoye Selo and Tsarskoye itself. It was late enough now even in a Russian summer to be dusk, and Sergei took the lead as we trudged back toward the village we had just passed. The peasant clothes my brother gave us—my light cloth coat and kerchief, Sergei's soft cap, loose tunic, and baggy pants— would, I hoped, make us look as if we belonged on foot. Sergei limped ahead of me; his arthritis, which had swollen the knuckles of his fingers, had also torched his joints so that he moved tenderly, back bent. As we followed the track through a thick wood of fir trees, I found myself falling, my grace and balance useless on this ground churned by roots and gullies. Eventually we found a rutted dirt road and Sergei said the village was down below, let's hurry. Every few minutes I called to Sergei for the time and he checked his watch in its leather pouch: 10:30, 10:42, 10:56, and finally he said, *Mala, don't ask*. It was 11:04 when a peasant driving a horse and wooden cart appeared. Sergei limped forward to hail him and I watched their pantomime. Sergei's arms moved, the peasant, capless but wearing the classic bowl haircut, shook his head, bangs flapping, and gestured to the open back of his cart. Was he offering us a ride? Sergei then brought out his purse. I'd heard that when Niki went out riding these country roads each afternoon at two o'clock, he would stop and speak to the villagers he passed, and that, knowing this to be his habit, peasants from this district and beyond would line the road to beg a favor from the tsar or to hand him a petition, knowing Nicholas liked to honor all these requests. Their Father Tsar loved a supplicant, loved to grant permission. I edged closer. Sergei placed a thick pad of rubles into the callused hands of the peasant. The man wore a short navy blue coat and beneath it a tunic and trousers almost exactly like the ones my brother had given Sergei, but too filthy to be worn by someone merely playing a part. We should have dirtied Sergei's face and hands with a pot of black makeup from the Maryinsky storage room. Even Father Gapon, in hiding in Petersburg after the debacle of Bloody Sunday, had known to cut his hair, to shave his beard, and to paint his face with theatrical makeup in order to avoid discovery and arrest. We had not had the time to create verisimilitude, though that would matter more later; for now Sergei's rubles had been real enough. The old peasant lowered himself to the ground and Sergei gestured to me, *Come*. As he helped me up onto the driver's bench, the man stood unmoving, staring blankly at the small fortune in his big hands. Surely the world had gone mad, when one was tossed great mounds of money for a rotting cart and a broken-down horse. Was this the new order of things?

Sergei bellowed and snapped the reins to turn the swaybacked horse, and after a hesitation, it lurched forward, straining to get the oversized wheels of the wooden cart in motion once more. Sergei cursed and leaned forward to slap the horse's rump, hard. The horse snorted, its scrotum swaying gently as it took each heavy step. From the animal's bowed legs and protruding ribs, I could see we would plod all the way to the Alexandrovsky Station. I turned back to ask the peasant if he had another horse, a faster one—but the man was gone, having vanished into the surrounding forest with his newfound wealth before we could change our minds and turn his pockets inside out. I took a deep breath. We wouldn't make it by midnight. We'd be lucky to make it before the sun rose. But Sergei and I said nothing to each other, nothing aloud. We would go on because there was nowhere else to go.

By the time Sergei and I arrived at the Alexandrovsky, the sky had changed from ebony to magenta to the marble green that preceded dawn. The family had boarded a train for the abyss of Siberia more than five hours ago. The station house glimmered in this almost light, the building a yellow-and-white slice cut from the yellow-and-white cake of the Alexander Palace, now empty. I used my hands, elbows, and knees to ratchet myself down from the cart, Sergei laboring to keep up with me as I made for the big station doors, twice the height of a man, and from there to the tracks on the other side. Behind me, Sergei called that Vova would be fine, that he could learn where the family was taken, we could still get him back, but my terror made me deaf. I stepped out onto the small platform by the two tracks to sniff the scent of my boy, ready to lie down on the empty tracks that had guided him away from me. But, to my astonishment, the platform was a crush of people.

On the tracks waited a long gray train that flew the Japanese flag—it was not, in fact, Japanese but an ordinary passenger train that bore a placard, *Red Cross Mission*, though the train was not on a mission of mercy. It was more poorly disguised than we were. Milling about the platform was half a regiment of Russian soldiers in their brass-buttoned tunics, rifles slung over their shoulders, taking long pulls on their cigarettes. The uniforms looked new, as if issued for this particular assignment. Sergei put a hand on my shoulder and pulled me back against one of the tall, many-paned station windows; while we watched from this recess, an officer with a high forehead and a small moustache emerged from the train and descended to the platform to speak to the soldiers. *That's Colonel Koby-linsky*, Sergei said to me quietly. *He's a war hero, detailed to Tsarskoye to oversee the family.*

Although I could not hear Kobylinsky as he spoke to the men, it was clear from his posture and from the relaxed stances of the soldiers that the train's departure was not imminent. In fact, there was not the slightest hint of tension. The imperial family must not yet be on board. Perhaps the family had not even left the palace. I turned to Sergei, my face a question, and he said, *If Kobylinsky's still here, they haven't left yet.*

By some holy miracle, the family must still be at Tsarskoye. I would later learn it was no holy miracle. The same revolutionary railway workers who had stopped all the trains had refused to shunt and couple these, suspecting the tsar was being spirited out of the country, an action they were determined to prevent: the tsar was a prisoner of the revolutionaries, he was to stand trial, he was not to live out his life in some comfortable exile. It had taken Kerensky multiple calls to the rail yards, shouting into the receiver in his loud, excitable voice, to prod the men—who now by new habit questioned all authority and respected none.

We need to go, Sergei said to me softly.

The streets of the town of Tsarskoye were quiet. In our cart, we passed the racetrack, the storage houses and slaughter yards, the cathedral, the police station, the post office, all the municipal buildings that made the little town hum so efficiently when the tsar was still tsar. Sergei knew the streets well—Malaya, Kolpinskaya, Stredniaya, Sadovaya, Dvortsovaya—having traveled them all in his Rolls-Royce in happier days, following the tsar with the rest of the court—and all the streets we rode lay like a well-pressed apron, its strings tied up neatly in front of the massive compound of Tsarskoye Selo, the Tsar's Village itself. The imposing mansions of the former court made a silent honor regiment for our approach. I prayed that we would not see the family and its entourage barreling toward us in their motorcars in a race to the train station. Before I could lift my hand or shout a name, they would be gone, and Vova would be whisked away from me again, like a cruel joke.

Sergei began to rehearse aloud a plan to rescue Vova, choreographing bold dashes, feints, flanking maneuvers, but just like all of Russia's battle plans, his relied more on fantasy than on reality—an overestimation of our strengths, a fatal underestimation of the enemy. Finally I cut him off.

We are two. Do you hear yourself?

Sergei started to protest, then fell silent.

The wheels of the wagon groaned and sounded as if they would splinter.

Listen to me, I began. *If there were fifty soldiers at the station, there will be a hundred more at Tsarskoye. If they see you, they will recognize you and believe you part of a plot to save the tsar. You could be arrested. Or shot.*

Or, and this I did not say, they might—enraged still by the ammunition shortages of the war in which they had served—lynch him on the spot; lynching had become a far too common practice in Peter. There would be ten thousand by the end of the year alone. A mob would capture a thief and cut off his hands, snatch up a murderer and throw him into the Neva to shoot him when he tried to climb out, tie up a *borzhui* and string him by the foot from a tree the better to torture him.

I watched Sergei stare ahead, jaw set.

These men have never attended a ballet in their lives. I will be just another old woman to them.

The black wrought-iron fence that enclosed the Tsar's Village abruptly rose before us and Sergei pulled the cart over on Dvortsovaya, not far from the mouth of the short drive that led up to the palace gates. I could hear the trees high above me shuffling their leaves like hands to cards and that wind also dispatched the sweet scent of lilacs planted by a half-dozen empresses over the span of the last two centuries. The last time I was here, it had been winter, snow-flakes spiraling like ice insects around the lamps mounted high on either side of the palace doors. I had left my son behind at Tsar-skoye in March, but I could not leave him behind now in August.

Until this moment, my mind had been playing out my worst imag-inings for Vova again and again, like a scratched gramophone record, but the needle had been lifted and uncertainty filled the emptiness. There would be guards at the gate. What would I say to persuade the guards to let a member of the tsar's suite go free? And what if Niki had no intention of letting him go? An idea began to form, in its own way as foolishly simple as Sergei's battle plans were elaborate—I would simply ask for a chance to say goodbye to my son. Surely they would give an old woman that, and from there, what? No matter. I needed to get only there. The end would take care of itself. I only had to invent the beginning. And the beginning lay ahead of me. Against the pink sky behind the birch trees that lined the road, I could see the top of the yellow-and-white palace.

As I got down from the cart, Sergei said, *Mala, vot zapomni— now remember*—and I nodded, yes, yes, I would call to him if I faced any danger.

I walked along the black fence, and as the Russian saying goes, I felt as lonesome as a blade of grass in a field. Two trucks carrying a contingent of soldiers drove noisily past me and turned in, stop-ping at the two sets of locked gates. I knew they must have come to escort the family back to the train, and my tongue went numb. The bed of the truck was open; within it were the soldiers from the sta-tion, and this close I could see their uniforms were ill-fitting, their buttons at the neck undone and their shirts untucked. Some of them looked only a few years older than Vova, but the combination of their rifles and their youth made me uneasy. The young have little attachment to the past, to the history of their fathers. The gates, each one embellished with a great wrought-iron wreath, swung open, and a sentry stepped forward to wave the trucks in, then pulled the gates shut with a solid, unyielding clank.

Here, the trees had thinned and I had a clear view through the iron bars of the drive that rose slightly as it made its short journey from the gate to the palace courtyard. The trucks rumbled up to the courtyard and slowed to a stop. I could see only the heads of the soldiers now, bouncing, disembodied, as they clambered out of the trucks to the ground, their rifles floating beside them. Unholy dread had blown me to these gates, and if opportunity presented itself, I hoped God would signal me. But whose side was God now on? Not Niki's, by all appearances. And I had spent many years tying my fate to his.

The wind made the trees hiss and that sound brought with it a chill and I was chilled also by the sight of a mass of dark figures shuffling across the courtyard. What was this? The dead fleeing a dying empire? Yes. As the mass started down the drive, toward the gates, I could see from their long dark coats and dark hats that they were the underservants, the ones who earned little notice but who were necessary to the smooth running of the palace. They had been dismissed. They were not making this trip with the tsar and his family, these *kamer-diners* and *kamer-jungferi* and *komnatnlye dev-yushki*, who after years of service ferrying plates or boiling linen were now free to find glorious employment with the new regime. Their faces were strangely emotionless, showing neither relief nor sorrow. For most of them, the palace was their home. They were being exiled just as surely as Niki and Alix were, though their journey would not be as far.

A horn bleated behind me, and I started. I turned to see a grinning soldier swerve another truck into the drive. He braked, then nudged his vehicle forward, alternately leaning on the horn and waving his arm out the window, shouting as he motioned the knot of servants out of the way. The sentries fell in to help, clearing the drive with a push here or a shove there, and I saw my chance. With a quick glance back to Sergei, watching intently beside the cart, I followed the truck through the gates. And that easily, I was one of them. A servant of the court. Wasn't that what I had been all my life?

I was moving against the flow of the crowd, though, and so I decided I was looking for something I had dropped, and in my mind I made this a silver buckle. Ahead I could now see much more of the courtyard—the wide palace steps of gray stone, three waiting cars, long touring motorcars made especially for the emperor by Delauney-Belleville, a model the French firm dubbed Son Impérial Majesté, and it appeared that in these the emperor and his family would be escorted from the Alexander Palace. To my left glittered the gold emblems on the cornices of the Catherine Palace, and between here and there lay the green water of the pond that during the day captured the reflection of this palace, a pale yellow crescent against the blue cornflower of the sky. In the imperial menagerie, in better days, the animals given the tsar by the foreign ambassadors, Siamese elephants and South American llamas and Tyrolese bulls, had chewed at their breakfasts at this hour.

Keeping my head down, I crossed the drive to the shade of a lone, full tree, and the soldiers' eyes flitted quickly past me, a nobody in a kerchief. Next to the first truck idled another, already heaped high with bags and boxes, and beyond it, another one still, this one stacked with rolled rugs and pieces of furniture. It seemed as if every stitch and crumb of the palace were being removed. It was not a simple matter to send a former tsar into exile. A convoy of trucks wound around the side of the palace. Soldiers stirred and coughed everywhere, squatting on the stone steps, leaning against the palace columns, strolling the sandy ground, at least sixty, seventy men in uniforms less presentable than the ones I had seen earlier, uniforms without the tsar's insignias, without decoration, no braid, no medals. A large group of sweating soldiers heaved dozens of trunks and cases and crates into the back of the empty truck as if trying to break them wide open, while an older man, familiar to me—yes, it was Count Beckendorff, a member of the imperial suite, tall polished boots, trim white beard—supervised from the steps. Sergei had told me that although Kerensky had kept the tsar's exact destination, departure date, and members of his retinue a secret from his ministers, the tsar's old court knew exactly which of his suite would make this voyage east with the tsar. Word had traveled softly from one prince to another the past few days—the Countess Hendrikov, Prince Dolgoruky, and General Tatishelev would go now, the Baroness Buxhoeveden and Count Beckendorff to follow later. So thrilled was I to see a familiar face that, like a fool, I almost called out and ran to his side to enlist his help. But I knew the count, as a member of the tsar's suite, was now as much a prisoner as the imperial family, and there would be no advantage in revealing myself to him. The soldiers hoisted the last crate into the truck and surrounded the count, who pulled some paper money from his pocket and held it out. One of the soldiers snatched it from the count's hand and as the men circled to divvy up their pay, *three rubles apiece*, I heard one of them say, *for three hours' sweat*, I understood the count had not been supervising the soldiers, but had bribed them to follow their orders.

The count retreated to the central hall, which, luckily for me, had been designed with floor-to-ceiling French windows, and I could watch him as he moved behind those windows among several figures, some of whom now began to file out the main entrance. These were the higher-ranking servants, the ones who would accompany the family on its flight—the valets, the chambermaids, the footmen, the cooks and assistant cooks, the wine steward. At a soldier's shouted direction, they climbed up into the bed of one of the empty trucks, the men helping the women, and sat down on its wooden benches.

Then came the sound of muffled hooves on grass, and one black shape, then five, then another five charged over a small rise. Niki's Cossacks were riding their mounts toward the courtyard from their barracks in the Feodorovsky Gorodok. I counted twenty-five Cossacks in all. Were they coming to save the tsar? They made a fierce sight, waxed moustaches slashing their cheekbones, long red tunics topped with silver, the tall black *papakhi* giving the Cossacks, already tall enough on their horses, an even greater height. In a moment, they would pull their curved sabers—the body of each blade inscribed with the gold monogram H II, the top of each blade with the double-headed eagle—out from their leather scabbards and, whooping, raise them above their heads and bring them down on the heads of these impudent soldiers.

But that did not happen. Nothing remotely like it happened. The soldiers, instead of readying themselves against the approaching horde, barely looked up. And the Cossacks slowed their horses to a walk, sabers still sheathed, to take up positions along the curving drive. They were in the employ of the Duma. For three hundred years, the ferocious Cossacks had pledged their complete devotion to the tsar, each promising to protect the tsar and his family *until the last minute of my life*. Every man gave twenty years to the military, and no matter how embattled, how desperate a tsar became, he could always count on his Cossacks. Expert horsemen, master swordsmen, unparalleled marksmen, they were the mighty fist of the emperor. They were the enemy Napoleon most dreaded to face. They were the men who tied the Stolypin neckties around the necks of the revolutionaries and who with the army put down the peasant revolts of 1905. These Cossacks had loved this tsar, and this tsar had loved these Cossacks, wore their tunic, practiced the overhand sweep and deadly thrust of the *klych*. Even Alexei owned a miniature Cossack uniform. But Niki's Cossacks, no longer his, were here to help escort their master into oblivion.

Two Rolls-Royces raced down the mounted line, and I recognized the first as one of the tsar's own; as it passed I saw Kerensky sitting within. I knew his face, with the bulbous nose and hair like a thicket, though I had not seen him in person, but only on the postcards he had distributed everywhere, as if to say to the people, as the tsars once had, *Know me, love me*. He stepped out of the Rolls—the new leader arriving to bid his predecessor a polite farewell?—and then another man emerged. I recognized him, as well: the tsar's brother Mikhail. The grand duke must be here to say goodbye, with Kerensky acting as monitor, that is, unless Mikhail was going with the family—but why would he go with them? He had been tsar for only three days and Kerensky, reportedly, had been so pleased by the grand duke's aborted term that he had called Mikhail a *patriot*. The presumption! Another man followed them up the palace steps. It was the officer from the train station, Colonel Kobylinsky.

Mikhail entered the palace but Kobylinsky paused on the steps to survey his soldiers, who watched him but didn't rise to attention or salute. He made a curt gesture. Eight soldiers eventually stirred themselves and climbed into the trucks to start the engines. Gears protested as the drivers battled the transmissions, then, after a few false starts, they lurched toward the gates, the servants holding on to one another on their benches, the crates rattling. The evacuation had begun.

Mikhail reemerged with Kerensky, head bent, hand over his eyes, to hide what, his tears? Relief at the fate he had averted for himself with his act of *patriotism*, the fate his brother the tsar now faced? Kobylinsky shook both Kerensky's and Mikhail's hands and closed the car door after them; the car made a slow circle, went down the drive, and was gone.

Kobylinsky waited until the gates were closed again and then motioned the soldiers to form a cordon around the few motorcars that remained. The soldiers reluctantly made an asymmetrical half-circle around the perimeter and two uneven rows from the bottom step to the cars. Several of the Cossacks exchanged glances at this slovenly formation, and I understood that, slovenly or not, this was the gauntlet through which the imperial family must pass, and that I must get inside the palace, quickly, *now*, and request my private farewell with Vova before these cars were loaded. I stepped away from the tree and started toward the palace. But I had waited too long.

Out from the circular hall of the Alexander Palace and down the stone steps came Niki's daughters, flanked by Colonel Kobylinsky. The girls all wore wide-brimmed, black straw hats and what must have been wigs, for the hair that had been shaved from their scalps in March surely could not yet have grown back to these lengths, and in their white shirts and long, tweed skirts, they seemed quite adult, which, of course, they must now be! The oldest, Olga, had to be almost twenty-two, my age when Niki trimmed my heart down to nothing to marry Alix. Was it possible I had lived so many years? One of the girls carried a little lap dog and when it struggled out of her sleeve and made to run away, a soldier gave it a kick, the *muzhik*, and it ran, yapping, back to her. Colonel Kobylinsky stared at the offending soldier but said nothing.

The colonel settled Olga Nikolaevna in the first open car and the three other girls were joined by a woman who must have been Countess Hendrikov, the only female courtier making the journey at this time, in the second. Then came the boys, both of them, tall and thin in their just-adolescent bodies, their hair cut in identical unflattering styles, a short fringe of bangs drawn across their foreheads. The man who led them from the house did not seem to be a revolutionary soldier but some sort of valet in sailor garb, one of the sailor nannies, the *dyadi* Nagorny or Derevenko, though the boys would soon be too old for nannies and would need batmen or valets. Vova looked so much older, so much taller! They had each celebrated a birthday in captivity. Vova's fifteenth was marked, he wrote Sergei, with a cake sprinkled with lilac petals, and Alexei's thirteenth by a special procession of clergy from Our Lady of the Sign, who had carried with them a holy icon, which even the revolutionary soldiers had felt compelled to kiss. So there was some element of the old world they still respected. Vova walked close beside Alexei, the two probably inseparable now, as they moved quickly down the line of soldiers who stared openly at them. If I pushed through that line, I could hold my son in my arms, but I knew our embrace would be violently broken, so I remained silent. Not yet, but when?

The two boys were followed by the doctor, Botkin, in his blue coat, and a thin man in a hat with a cheap black band which I recognized from Vova's gleeful description. This must be the children's French tutor, M. Gilliard. Two other men I recognized, as well, Prince Dolgoruky and General Tatishelev—both of them frequented the ballet. At a sudden shout, we all turned back to the palace. One remaining servant had called to another for help lifting the empress in her wheelchair through one of the French windows onto the terrace.

The wheelchair astonished me. What had happened to all the energy with which she had nursed the children just a few months earlier? Alix now looked drugged, and perhaps she was, by those same helpful, soothing drops Dr. Botkin had squeezed into the children's mouths when they were all so sick with the measles in February. She wept as the two men struggled with the chair, her body swaying this way and that, until one of them lifted the empress out of the chair and carried her, the long, wide sleeves of her blouse flapping, down the sloping ramp to the courtyard. The other trailed behind, pushing the empty rattan wheelchair with sharp, hard jerks, letting its wide, thin wheels make a rattle over the flat, gray stones. Niki was the last to step through that window. He paused on the terrace, his bearing slightly stooped, until, with conscious effort, he squared his shoulders, the better to balance on them the weight of his family in their solitary exile. Even the horses seemed to still as Niki scanned the scene before him. He gazed at me but his eyes didn't linger. I was just another subject, come to watch the tsar's departure. I saw him study the sunrise over the park the Russians had once called *Sarskaya Myza*—or high farm—and this farmstead had become, for a time, the tsar's private paradise. And now his expulsion east. Oh, why had not Niki insisted on going to the White Palace in Livadia or to his brother's estate in Orel, both estates Kerensky perhaps could have been persuaded to reconsider?

I watched Niki walk down the long ramp and take Alix's arm at the bottom of it, for without her chair she had stood, hesitantly, seemingly afraid to walk, and together, they followed the boys into the first car. Niki helped each of them into the open carriage and onto the three rows of high-backed leather seats. Colonel Kobylinsky climbed onto the box at the head of the running board and turned toward the Cossacks. To them, he need not say a thing. They knew their roles; a few of them guided their horses in front of and alongside the tsar's car and along the two others as escort. And now, as the soldiers swarmed aboard the remaining trucks in that long convoy, I realized that I would be left behind if I did not act. There would be no later moment. A Cossack gestured with his big arm that I should move out of the way, down the drive, stop gawking. *Babushka!* Me—a babushka! So I wasn't invisible. He urged his horse toward me. *Everyone is leaving.* I nodded and began walking backward, then sideways, trying to keep my eyes on the family seated in the first of the Son Impérial Majestés, the Cossack and his black horse shadowing me, the trucks and cars and horses circling the courtyard, clop, clop, clop, making their way around the light sand to the drive proper, the Cossacks' horses keeping pace with the slow turning of the wheels. I supposed they would ride with them all the way to the station, the last assignment of the tsar's retinue.

The sun gave a luster now to everything, the buttercream palace, the blue cornflower sky, the black doors of the automobiles, the chocolate eyes of the horses upon which the Cossacks sat. The park birds had begun to herald this exodus which was to have been made in the desolation of night, but which was now taking place, thanks to Russia's short summer nights, less safely, in plain view. And in this sunlight I was plainly walking backward toward a life I couldn't conceive continuing without my son. What would I tell Sergei when

I reached the bottom of the drive, Sergei who hoped his Magnificent Mathilde would bring back our beautiful boy? How could I tell him the truth of my failure? But now, with the column starting down the drive, the truth was all I had left.

And so I stepped in front of the first vehicle and the Cossack beside it, waved my short arms, and began to yell in my vulgar-sounding Russian—yes, I admit it, I speak more like a peasant than like a *boyar*, even in the French I acquired in exile this is the case, so perhaps my costume was not so much an impersonation as a revelation of my truest self—*Stop! Wait!* And at the unexpected sight of me the lead Cossack halted his horse and the drivers braked their vehicles to stare at this demented woman, and to them all I cried, *I want my boy!*

Would he bring his whip down on me as I had seen his comrade do to that poor man on the Troitsky Bridge in 1905? Like a mechanical toy, wound almost to breaking, I began to repeat over and over—*I want my boy. I want my boy*—until the Cossack looked back in bewilderment at one of the trucks that held the soldiers. From within the cab, someone shouted at him to move the old woman, and the Cossack spurred his horse forward. But when I stood my ground, instead of trampling me, he simply reined in his horse. I could hear both of them breathing and I raised my hands to him.

He called over his shoulder to Kobylinsky, standing on the running board of that first car, *She wants her boy*. The Cossacks let their horses stamp their huge feet and shake their long manes impatiently to signal me there was only so much of this foolishness they would allow. *What is the delay? Move the woman*, called a voice from the back of the line. I saw Niki lean forward in his seat, squint in my direction to take in my small shape, and abruptly straighten up. He had recognized me. But I could tell that Vova had not, as he peered around at the soldiers surrounding the motorcar. And then Niki pushed open the door and stepped out, walking forward past the lanterns fixed to the front of the hood, with Alix protesting from her seat; and at the tsar's movements, the soldiers, all brass buttons and alarmed caps, began jumping down from their trucks, racing forward with raised rifles and fixed bayonets. Kobylinsky held his hand up to Niki, *Her son must have left earlier with the underservants.*

Her son is not an underservant, Niki said. *He is part of my suite*, and he gestured to the interior of the carriage to Vova, who sat next to Alexei on the middle seat. Kobylinsky looked clearly perplexed— Why would the tsar have a peasant boy as a member of his suite? Why would the tsarevich have the son of a peasant as a playmate?— but he said nothing, looking at Vova and then over at me. Niki studied my face as the soldiers converged about him, and I thought, *Niki is not going to give Vova back to me, he still thinks as Sergei does that he will return to Peter in the fall, he thinks I'm acting precipitously, he doesn't understand that Kerensky, with one shift of the winds, will soon be running for his own train to save his own skin*. But then Niki reached into the car and took Vova's hand and Vova climbed out onto the running board and jumped down.

He stood very close to Niki, pressed tightly against him in a posture of filial intimacy that set the soldiers to shouting, *Look, that is the heir. This is a trick*—their worst nightmare come true, someone in the imperial family was about to slip from their grasp. One regiment was posted at the station, but two remained here, and so there were many men to make a commotion and over it Niki held Vova to him with one arm around his shoulder, and Kobylinsky stepped back on the running board and called, futilely, to the excited soldiers, *Move back*, but his soldiers had no intention of moving back now, and they surrounded the cars, calling, *Who is this boy?* and, *Where is the heir?*, as if wondering for the first time why the tsar's entourage counted in its number two boys instead of one. And I thought, *What game is this?* Surely they know who is who— they had been guarding the family for months. It was only later that I would learn that these men had been newly assigned to accom-

pany the family, and what help were imperial portraits and genea-
logical charts (if these men had ever laid eyes on such things) in
sorting out the bedraggled human reality of their prisoners? In
Siberia the guards would take photographs of the family and servants and assign each one an identity card which, ridiculously, had
to be produced on demand.

The soldiers encircled the carriage and one of them pushed by
the tsar to reach into its interior. I could see Vova still had no idea
who I was. Why had Niki drawn Vova from the motorcar and yet
not sent him toward me? Perhaps he had in mind we were only
to say goodbye, and the farewell I had been prepared to pretend I
wanted might be all that I would, finally, be allowed—but with the
soldiers all around, we were not even to have that chance. With a
few shouts, one of the men pulled Alexei from his seat in the black
automobile and stood him side by side with Vova as if to inspect
them both, and the men began to shout, *Which one is the heir? Which
one is Alexei Nikolaevich?* For how could they tell which was which?
If Niki were so inclined, if he feared what lay ahead, he could push
Alexei my way and take Vova with him to Siberia. And from the
car I saw Alix reach for Vova's tunic as if to pull him back within
and I thought, *Does she, too, know what is at stake? Or can she simply
not bear to let him go?* And from the girls in their car behind came
a wailing which seemed only to further excite the soldiers, who
pointed their rifles first at Niki and then at the boys, and when they
remembered, at me. The soldiers closest to the car began to shout at
the boys, *What is your name?*, but both remained silent with terror,
looking mutely at those wide peasant faces, and through all this
Niki remained with his arm around Vova, his eyes on the boys to
keep them calm. What was he thinking now? And Kobylinsky from
the running board called, *Back to your trucks!* The soldiers ignored
him, but his words had some effect—they had been up all night and
the train was ready at the station and on the train they could sleep—
and so they called out to one another, *Let's take them both with us,*

and they gestured with their rifles to herd the boys back into the first car. After a quick look at me, Niki gave a nod to the boys. Alexei clambered back in immediately, but as Vova ducked his head to follow, I cried out and took a step forward. My son looked back at me, but the Cossack was closer and he leaned over on his horse and put out his hand, big as a wall, to stop me—but my son had paused and I took advantage of that moment to drop to my knees like a serf on the roadway with a petition in my hand. Yes, I played the beggar, but really, in my defiance of the tsar's clear wish to keep our son for himself I was more the revolutionary, was I not? On my knees I called out to Niki as he turned from me toward the car, *Tsar-Batiushka, remember Taras Bulba!*, an incantation so bizarre the entire party halted, the soldiers, the Cossacks, even Kobylinsky, atop the car, and Niki, one hand on the car's open door. Would Niki remember the opera whose hero gave up his country for the love of a young Polish girl? Would he remember how he had once toyed with me in his letter, playing at giving up the crown for me? Now his crown was gone. I needed him only to give up our son.

Unexpectedly, Niki laughed. Yes. He remembered *Taras Bulba*, and he laughed. And when he turned from me, decisively, still smiling, it was to grasp Vova by the shoulders as he stood on the running board of *le grand* Son Impérial Majesté, to guide him away from the car. And then, after a triple kiss to my son's cheeks and an embrace, he whispered something into his ear and pushed him along in my direction, saying aloud, *Go*. But to my frustration Vova did not run toward me, but moved vaguely, like a somnambulist, so that I began to wonder if he, too, had not been drugged by the dispensary of Dr. Botkin, and I clapped my hands at him as if he were a dog—*hurry, hurry*—even as the weeping girls, their faces contorted, had the girls become so attached to my son in this short time?, began now to climb from their seats, while Niki tried to hold them back. I had disrupted the entire convoy! Vova looked over his shoulder at Niki as if hoping to be called back. What madness was this?

Through the tall thin trees I could see the tiny figure of Sergei watching helplessly from the road. I turned back. Vova had neared the last Cossack, the one with the big fist, a hulking man with a beard that spread across his chest like a shield, and just as he was almost within reach of me, the soldiers, infuriated that their fellows had not impeded this decision of the tsar, recovered themselves and shouted out orders of their own. Prisoners were not to give orders. Nicholas Romanov was no longer tsar. The boy would come with them. The Cossack reached down and gripped Vova, mid-step, by the neck, and I could see Vova's features twist in pain; with this, he seemed, finally, to wake. He took in my small shape, my dark hair beneath my babushka, my brown eyes, and when I smiled at him, encouragingly, the distinct outward tilt of my dog teeth: the peasant woman in front of him was his mother, and his mouth opened. I thought he might speak, but whatever word he thought to say became a wince as the Cossack, still holding Vova, began to turn his horse around to lead him back. Seeing this, Niki barked, *Ostanovites!*—Stop!—with such authority that all these men, the Cossacks still enough the tsar's servants, the soldiers still so much the peasant with their hundreds of years of subjugation at the hands of the squire, paused. Even the Cossack's horse paused, one hoof in the air to await the pleasure of the master.

And Niki marched uncontested down the line of them toward my son, the revolutionary soldiers stepping back involuntarily in deference, cowed, their insolence abruptly evaporating, as well it should in the presence of the tsar. Still, a few followed after him, calling ineffectually, *Gospodin Polkovnik*—Mister Colonel—*Colonel Romanov!* until Niki whipped around abruptly and thrust his face to these soldiers' faces, one breath apart, and, uncertain, off-balance, the men backed away. *I have only one son*, Niki said, his voice a scythe. *And I know who he is.* And with a flat gesture of his hand, without taking his eyes off the men, Niki signaled the Cossack to release Vova, which he did at once. Vova stepped away quickly, rubbing his neck as the Cossack looked back and forth from the commander to the tsar, his big hand still open as if surprised by itself. The tsar at that moment could have done anything, could have called the Cossacks to charge, could have ordered the Cossacks to hang these soldiers from the trees, could have sent them to the Winter Palace to drag Kerensky and his ministers off to the Peter and Paul Fortress. But he did none of that, as he had done nothing on the train in March of last year in Pskov. Perhaps he was now afraid of further endangering us all, as he had been afraid of endangering his country and his subjects.

And so, he made Vova the only subject of his orders, telling him, *Go to your mother*, and then Niki strode back to *his* family, and the group of soldiers behind him rallied, shrugged, and waved their rifles to corral everyone back to their various places, Niki having snatched from them, temporarily, their precious authority, a humiliation for which the soldiers would later make the family pay. Vova and I stumbled back as the cavalcade of horses and trucks passed in a cyclone of wind and sand; as the first black car flew by I saw Niki staring straight ahead, Alix, beside him, head down. But in the middle seat, there was a face turned toward Vova, the small white sad face of the tsarevich Alexei, who raised one hand to his friend in farewell.

In Siberia, they killed everyone with the imperial family, you know—Dr. Botkin, the valet Trupp, the cook Kharitonov, the maid Demidova.

We're not going back to the Alexandrovsky Station, Sergei said when we reached him, and so after he embraced Vova and kissed his cheeks, he hurried us onto the cart and we drove it and the horse all the way back to Petersburg. At first, Vova wanted to marvel at how the tsar had stood up to the soldiers, *Did you see his face when he looked at that Cossack?* And then he told us how the tsar had once used his walking stick to whip at the ankles of a soldier who had followed him too closely around the palace park and who had stepped on the heel of the tsar's boot. But other times the tsar had done nothing when the soldiers behaved with insolence, signaling the empress to do nothing also, and Vova's face grew dark to recall this. In a voice that rattled, careening between the high thin treble of childhood and the lower register of young manhood, he told us how they had stayed awake that last night at Tsarskoye, sitting on their suitcases for hours in the semicircular hall, then going up to the playroom to nap until the guards called out again, *The cars are coming*, and then, when it appeared the train cars had still not been coupled because the surly railway men had refused to couple cars for the tsar and the motorcars were not coming either, the children wandered back up to the green room. The last few months the soldiers had followed them everywhere, Vova said, and they listened at doors, refused to let them speak any language but Russian, which was the only language the ill-educated soldiers could understand, and this made it difficult as the empress always spoke to her daughters and her husband in English; Alexei was terrified of them, Vova said. They once took a toy gun away from him and some afternoons came to the doorway of his room just to look at him and to whisper about him and about his many-paneled, elaborate iconostasis, an oddity in a child's room, which usually hosted only a single candle and icon. *And you?* Sergei asked. *Did the men want to look at you?* Not so much, Vova said, though he wished they had and ignored the sensitive Alexei. But everybody knew Vova was not the heir but the ward of Sergei Mikhailovich and that as the grand duke was at Stavka, the tsar had temporarily made Vova *his* ward. So that was the story Niki had cut and pressed for the family, and I exchanged glances with Sergei. All spring, Vova said, when they were better from the measles, they had amused themselves by watching one of the movies given Alexei by the Pathé film company at Christmastime—*Atlantis*, *Luke's Double*, *Fantômas*—which the boys would set up on the projector in Alexei's room. He and Alexei lined up chairs and then invited the family in, guiding them as if they were theater attendants to their seats and then introducing the films, which Alexei would rate Excellent, Very Good, or Satisfactory. Or they played outside with Vanka, an old donkey who had once performed at Cinizelli's Circus, who pulled them on a sled when there was snow and would chew the rubber balls they fed him, one big eye closed with pleasure. The girls showed him how to embroider a row of swastikas, the empress's favorite symbol of good luck, across a handkerchief, and at embroidery Tatiana was the best. *And we had lessons*, he said. *The tsar taught us history and geography and from the newspapers he read to us about the war, about the street violence, about Kerensky and the Provisional Government.* The tsar did not like the way the soldiers who guarded them didn't polish their boots. The tsar knew all his family had left Petersburg except for his brother. Vova would read Sergei's letters to him before putting them in his valise, and at night Vova would take one out, read the line that said, *Your mother is well and sends you her love*, and put it under his pillow. In Siberia, the tsar had said, they would hunt and fish, and I thought, *In the Siberian exile of the past the tsars used to order, perhaps, but not in this one*, and then Vova wanted to know when he could rejoin the family, because he and Alexei had planned to erect a tent in their bedroom and to build a trap for wolves. So Vova had relished his captivity, where he had been a part of a family I could not give him, with a mother and father, with sisters and a brother, and the family had all been together every hour—held there by force, yes, but still.

The sun was high by the time we reached the capital and Vova said, *Why aren't we going home?* when Sergei turned the cart up Spasskaya Ulitsa toward Josef's apartment, our home for now. When I told him our own home had been taken from us and that I had just now gotten it back and that it was empty of furniture. Vova could not quite grasp this. All I had gone through these past months was a novelty to him.

What about our dacha? he asked.

The soldiers are using it as a club, but we *will have it back, too*, I told him.

And Vova said, *And the tsar will have his house back from the soldiers as well?*

And Sergei spoke, *Yes, of course. Yes.*

When? Vova asked. *How long will it be before the tsar comes back? A few months. When things are settled here.*

I think it will be longer than that, Vova said, after a pause, *because they packed so many things.* Another pause. *I'm not going to join them, am I?*

Kerensky later said he had picked Tobolsk because he believed there the tsar would be safe, and because the choice of Siberia as a place of exile would most likely satisfy the agitators—had their comrades not been sent there for the last hundred years? They may have been, but the revolution itself had not yet traveled those three thousand versts east to the backwater town of Tobolsk. The imperial family was given the old governor's mansion there, a dirty, boarded-up house, only thirteen rooms, hardly a mansion. The walls were painted and papered for them, their carpets unrolled and beaten and laid, their furniture dusted and polished and arranged in the various rooms, but still the girls were four to a room and the toilets overflowed, and I thought of Alix, who, out of modesty, used to cover her toilet at Tsarskoye with a cretonne cloth to mask its form and function. The townspeople, as Kerensky had expected, were respectful of the former tsar and sent over in welcome butter, eggs, and sugar, tipped their hats when they passed the front door. And when the family walked from the mansion to church, their route from the former to the latter flanked by two lines of revolutionary guards, the townspeople gathered to see the processional and fell to their knees at the appearance of the emperor. The stupidity of the people for loving their tsar infuriated the guards, whose commander finally decreed that the family could no longer walk to church. Mass would be said for them privately in the house.

That evening I put my son to sleep in Josef's daughter's bed, which was the bed of a child and my son's feet hung over the end of it—Celina would sleep with her parents—and Vova asked me then, finally, about the puppy he had given Sergei in December. So his stay at Tsarskoye Selo had not wiped his mind completely clean of our life together—how easily we could all be washed away from him, slipping from his fingertips down some dark drain, how easily Niki's plan could have worked. *The puppy is now almost a dog*, I told him, *and he is at Stavka, a mascot there, Sergei tells me*. My son smiled and I covered him halfway with a blanket. *When will we go home?* he asked me, and I said, *Soon. Sergei is here now and he will fix everything*.

I studied the sleeping son I had not seen for six months. The small pink lamp on Celina's dresser revealed the light black hairs scattered above his upper lip and between his thickening brows; his nose stood large in his face. He wore a thin, sleeveless undershirt, unfamiliar to me, and around his neck a thin velvet cord; a small bump at the neckline of his shirt hid something. I teased out the lump and found a homemade paper pendant: an oval shape with a photograph of Rasputin on the front and a hand-printed prayer on the back. I stared down at the face of the *staretz* Rasputin in the palm of my hand. This picture had been touching my child's skin. The electric eyes, pale gray in the black-and-white photograph, stared out from that face framed by the wild hair. I turned the photograph over and read, *Dear Martyr, give me thy blessing and remember us from on high in your holy prayers*. The family's executioners would find an amulet like this on each one of the children's bodies when they stripped them in the forest twelve miles from Ekaterinburg in order to burn their clothes and conceal their identities. I understood that this amulet was meant to protect Vova, and that Alix, Rasputin's most fervent disciple, had probably given it to him. It meant that she feared for Vova as she feared for her own children and that she loved him as she loved them. When did she hang this around my son's neck? When he was sick with measles? The day Niki abdicated? Or was it on the very night Niki returned to his family from Stavka as *Colonel Romanov*, when a band of revolutionary soldiers broke into the little chapel Alix had had built at Tsarskoye as Rasputin's tomb, dug up Rasputin's corpse, stuffed it in a piano case, and drove it to the Pargolovo Forest, where they soaked the body and the case in kerosene and set it on fire? Vova told me that in the night the wind had howled and he and Alexei had thought it sounded like a man's voice wailing, but they didn't find out until the next day from his big sister Olga what had happened.

No, a photograph of Rasputin was not enough to save the Romanovs. The humble name Kschessinsky was much better protection. With a pair of my brother's small manicure scissors I cut the necklace from my son's neck.

When I went out into the sitting room where Sergei waited for me, I said to him, *We need to leave Peter.*

But it was early September before Vova and I could get permission from Kerensky to leave the capital, and while Sergei agreed I should go to Kislovodsk, sixteen hundred versts south of the capital, where we would have at least the Vladimirichi to help us, he would not go with us and I could not persuade him otherwise. *Some adults must remain in the capital*, he said, *while the children try to rule Russia.* Should there be a reversal of fortune, a few Romanovs should be there to receive it. And if that happened, Vova and I could return.

And if that did not happen, Sergei would join us in the south and we could go to his estate in the Crimea or over the Caucasus in Georgia, to Borjomi.

We said goodbye to Sergei on the last day of September 1917 at the Nikolaevsky Station, the station named for Nicholas I, the Iron Tsar, who had faced down his mutinous guards in the Senate Square, who had created the secret police, who had ruled Russia with an iron fist for thirty years. Would he not laugh in disbelief to see us now in flight from a legion of peasants and workers? At the station the attendants stood at the train doors and porters in big fur caps and tall boots collected bags and workmen in sheepskin jackets and felt boots moved about the tracks, loading the luggage or coupling the cars. It was raining and it was dark, and Sergei sat with us on a sofa in the first-class waiting room, wearing his thick military greatcoat without his epaulettes. I supposed Kerensky now used the imperial waiting room, with its suite—sitting room, dining room, and bedroom—where the imperial family could rest or eat or sleep, and where Emperor Kerensky could now do the same. When he had returned to Peter from a trip to the front, I heard he had insisted on being met at the station by an honor guard, as were the tsars. A train whistled from somewhere down the line and soon we could feel the trembling beneath our feet that meant the train would soon arrive. The stationmaster stood on the platform along with a few peasants in their peaked caps and their long greasy beards. A boy sold *kvass*, a woman pushed a samovar on a cart. All as it had been two years earlier, three years earlier, before the war, when we still had a tsar. A bell rang and Sergei escorted us from the waiting room and helped us up the high step onto the train and down the narrow passage to our compartment, where I took a seat against the glass and Vova the one next to me. Sergei compulsively smoked one cigarette after another, taking a new cigarette from his case before he had fully exhaled the smoke from the last. It was warm in the compartment, a steamy heat, and then when the blast of heat dissipated, the compartment grew slowly cold until the next blast once again warmed the car. When the second bell rang, Sergei put out his last cigarette and bent to embrace Vova, who pressed his lips to Sergei's, and then Sergei and I kissed cheek to cheek. I am embarrassed to recall I was trembling. We still had to travel six days through Tver, Moscow, Bobriki, built on the manor of Count Bobrinsky, and through territory Kerensky had deemed too dangerous for the tsar to travel. We would, in fact, be stopped just past Moscow by a mob of deserters who declared we were all *free!* and we would barricade ourselves in our compartment against the exercise of their freedom. Then through Voronezh, Rostov-on-Don, and finally to Kislovodsk, in the foothills of the Caucasus Mountains.

When we see each other again, Mala, Sergei said, into my ear, *we will marry*. And that's how I knew this new world, whatever happened to it, had irrevocably changed the old one. Six months of revolution had granted me what my twenty-five years of wrangling could not. A whistle sounded. I gripped the sleeve of Sergei's wool coat. The train on the track alongside ours began to pull away, its iron wheels and pistons and joints going round, and our train would depart next. With the third bell, Sergei was gone, a blast of cold air stamping his departure, and then Vova pointed his finger at the figure of Sergei standing on the platform once again to watch us go. His face looked so unhappy, I thought to myself, we should get off this train and wait with him in Peter until the reign is restored or until we are certain there is nothing left of the Romanovs' three-hundred-year stranglehold on the land and wealth of All the Russias. But we did not get off. I stayed in my springed seat, my son's hand on my shoulder as he looked past me out the window. Our train began to pull away with many knocks and lurches and squeaks. I crossed myself, then touched my gloved fingers to the glass to encircle Sergei's sad face until the face grew too small to hold, and it was only then as his face vanished from my grasp that I understood I loved him.

sour waters

INTO SOUTHERN RUSSIA along with us poured Romanovs, *boyars*, banking families, oil magnates, theater artists—all of Peter it seemed had emptied itself into Kiev in the Ukraine or into the Crimea or here into the Caucasus. Kislovodsk, or Sour Waters, was a spa town, one of three famous spa towns, Kislovodsk, Yessentuki, and Pyatigorsk, strung along the Olkhovka and Beresvka rivers, all known for their healing mineral springs and fashionable baths. Kislovodsk sat in a valley north of the great Caucasus Mountains, and Georgia, where Sergei had lived as a boy, lay on the other side of those mountains to the south, closer to Turkey and Persia, in the Asiatic region of Russia, and it was here I came to breathe in the cherry blossoms, almond blossoms, and oleander that perfumed Sergei's childhood, to see the gold-domed churches elbowed by minarets and the mosaics of Arabia. Though the Mikhailovichi might not have been Armenian or Persian or Chechen or Abkhaz, and though they might not have worn *chokha*, those long, skirted coats of the Georgians with the pouches for bullets, for twenty years they had inhaled the woolly fragrance of that place and so they were, as the Romanovs had always sniffed, not quite Petersburgers. So much the better for them.

Andrei met our train in Kislovodsk, wearing a *papakha*, which, when removed, exposed the dome of his half-bald head; we kissed cheek to cheek. He was clean-shaven, so when I stepped back I had a good view of the weak chin I had not seen for half a year, longer. I had not missed it, or him. At the open-air restaurant he took us for dinner, I remember we sat at a table beneath a grape arbor, the big, flat grape leaves making a patchwork over us, Andrei talking, my son and I silent. I watched Vova slowly, uncertainly, unfold his linen napkin in his lap—did he not remember how to perform this nicety? Andrei placed his jeweled cigarette lighter on the table and ordered us a few local dishes, *khachapuri*—cheese pies—and *shashlik*—lamb kebobs. While we ate, Andrei smoking between courses, a small band played, and then, unexpectedly, a boy a few years younger than Vova rose from his table and began to dance and I recognized his dance—the *lezginka*, a Caucasian dance my brother Josef had taught me years ago for a performance at Krasnoye Selo. Who would have thought I would see an example of it here, performed on its native ground, by a boy who was not one of the tsar's dancers? The boy imitated an eagle, making big flapping motions with his arms while taking small, quick, light steps, birdlike steps, and then he dropped to his knees and lifted himself quickly up again, like a bird taking flight. At the end of his performance, we and all the other diners toasted him with our vodka and cognac, *To your health*. But I toasted also the spirit of this place, where people were not too broken to dance.

We spent that first night in rooms Andrei had found for us, and when Vova had gone to sleep, Andrei reached for my hand. I withdrew it, and Andrei lowered his eyes. He understood. I am certain, though, he believed it was because he had no funds to keep us, being entirely dependent upon his mother, but that was not why I withdrew my hand. Since when had he not been dependent upon his mother? That I could abide, for wasn't I myself dependent on the fortunes of the Romanovs? No, perhaps it was just that the opportunist in me no longer enjoyed her own reflection. Or perhaps it was that I no longer wished to kiss at this pale copy of the tsar. Or perhaps it was simply that Mathilde Felixovna Kschessinska had at long last fallen in love. So the next day I dug into the big reticule of jewels I had brought with me, among them the diadem of cabochon sapphires Andrei had Fabergé make for me long ago for the ballet *La Fille du Pharoan*, the emerald and diamond bracelet the tsar had given me while first courting me in 1891, the various-sized yellow diamonds from the number Sergei put in a little casket for my twentieth tribute in 1911, the walnut-sized diamonds from the tsar's necklace, the one with which Nicholas had marked our consummation in 1892. I used first the jewel I liked the least—the great cabochon sapphire from the serpent brooch given me by the tsar and the empress for my tenth-anniversary tribute, and with it I rented the Beliaievsky villa—two and a half stories tall, white, with a green tile roof, the property rested on a tuft of a hill. From my windows I could hear all day long the muezzin chanting from a nearby minaret, calling the faithful to prayer. It was not my mansion on Kronversky Prospekt, but it had a pale charm, and there Vova and I lived together, for Andrei, of course, lived with his mother, who remained obstinately oblivious to the great social changes the revolution had wrought. I was to comport myself, as usual, out of her sight. Even in her reduced circumstances here, Miechen wielded her power. Her son Boris and his British diplomat friend had disguised themselves as workers and made two trips to Peter to smuggle out the jewels and rubles she had stashed in her secret bedroom safe at the Vladimir Palace. The men walked the treasure here in their boots, and some of it Miechen, big-bosomed and stout, squatted over here in Kislovodsk. The rest of it Miechen had couriered to the safe-deposit box of a British bank. One of Miechen's tiaras is worn today by the English queen, Elizabeth II, did you know, bought on the cheap by George V's consort, Queen Mary, at the great fire sale of Romanov jewels in the 1920s. But when Sergei asked the British ambassador, George Buchanan, for help in doing the same with the jewels I had left behind, the ambassador flat out refused—perhaps he was among the diplomats who watched in disbelief as the coal trucks unloaded their cache at my house, not theirs, on that cold day ten months before in Peter. If only Sergei had not mentioned my name!

Sergei sent me daily letters, though they appeared irregularly, sometimes in batches of threes, with tales of his adventures in Petersburg—he had stashed my remaining furniture at Meltzer's (as if that shop were some impregnable fortress). Kerensky had recently arrested his new commander in chief of the army, General Kornilov, suspecting him of being a counterrevolutionary. The infantry had begun killing their officers of whom they suspected the same. Many soldiers had deserted to help for the harvest and with the guns they took with them they were now helping the peasants not only harvest the crops but seize the land and kill the squires. The Bolsheviks had somehow managed to increase their share of representation in the city Duma elections. The dapper Trotsky had been released from jail. And out of the continuing governmental chaos the joke on the streets was, *What is the difference between Russia today and at the end of last year?*, and the answer was, *Then we had Alexandra Fedorovna and now we have Alexander Fedorovich*—Kerensky. I've told you Russians love wordplay. Sergei did not think Kerensky would last much longer: people were saying he was a Jew or that he dressed in women's clothing or that he was addicted to morphine and cocaine. Though nobody liked Kerensky, nobody was prepared to get rid of him either—the feeling was that if the Bolsheviks did seize power they would soon enough ruin the country and the people would call for the return of the tsar, or if not that, perhaps the Germans would invade Peter and bring order with their tanks and machine guns, and I thought how long have the *borzhui* been pining for that? They'd been hoping a zeppelin might smash Petersburg to bits since that song of 1916!

After reading those letters, I dislodged the diamonds from a brooch given me in 1896 by Sergei's father and the grand dukes Vladimir, Alexei, and Pavel Alexandrovich and used them for tuition for Vova at the local school, for what likelihood was there that we would return to Peter anytime soon? But Vova did not work hard at his studies, made certain by all the dreaming he overheard at our teas and card parties and dinners—*Do you remember?* and *When will things be again as before?*—that we would be back to Peter and to his real studies with his former tutors by Easter, and though he didn't say this, perhaps he hoped also to be back in the bosom of the imperial family, as well. He spoke of them sometimes, wistfully, of how while working in the kitchen garden they had gleefully pelted one another with clods of dirt and Anastasia had drawn the word *darling* on his forehead with one muddy finger or of the riddles they had one evening made up, written down on slips of paper, and passed to one another to solve. Yes, Vova skipped his classes, spent his afternoons running wild through the hilly streets with some companions from the school as undisciplined as he, and when Vova did finally come in for dinner, he refused to do any schoolwork—not that he had brought home his books. He resented Andrei's regular appearance each afternoon at our tea table, Andrei having been released by his mother for a few hours' furlough. *Who is he?* Vova would say. *He's not my father*, and so he would not listen to Andrei's admonitions, nor would he sit with us, but, instead, stood hunched over his plate to eat his biscuit. Or worse, he took his plate to the kitchen, preferring the company of my plump, red-haired cook, sitting at *her* table, his long legs shoved beneath it, his coat torn, and his hair standing on end from his adventures up and down Vokzalnaya Avenue. At night he would come into my room to read over Sergei's letters and only then would he ask for whatever news of the tsar and Alexei I had gleaned at tea from Andrei—who had heard it thirdhand from the tsar's letters to his sisters or his mother, who then told friends who told friends who told the news to Miechen.

Andrei knew only, I told Vova, that the family were in Tobolsk, several hundred miles east of the Urals, that the children had built a snow mountain in the yard, that the family chopped firewood for exercise by day and at night they embroidered or read aloud or played bezique—that it was as it had been before at Tsarskoye, except much farther east. Vova took all this in soberly and said, *If I were there I would have a purpose, here there is nothing for me*—and then he would stand, his long shape a rebuke. I know this day comes to all mothers, when one's son steps away from the circle of her arms, but that knowledge made his actions no less painful. I consoled myself with the notion that when we returned to Peter or Sergei joined us here, then all would really be *as before*. In each letter to Sergei I begged him to join us, but he seemed determined to wait until the Provisional Government's assembly in late October, which would decide how Russia would be governed, in which he and his brother Nicholas hoped to have a hand.

Then we heard that even before the All-Russian Soviet Congress could meet at long last after all their deliberations to propose a government in which all political parties had representation, the Bolsheviks decided to act. Lenin, who had sat at my son's desk and whom Sergei had so easily dismissed with a crumpling of paper, had slipped back into Russia to stage another *putsch*, though a disorganized and scattered one, true, nothing like the great spontaneous eruption in July. But it didn't have to be. For Kerensky, believing the Bolshevik party so small their party name nothing but an empty boast, the *Majority-ites*, had not bothered to rout out or arrest what remained of their number. In fact, he crowed that he wanted them to show themselves so he could *crush* them. Meanwhile he planned to force the unruly peasant infantry the Bolsheviks had radicalized from their Petersburg barracks and off to the northern front to fight the Germans. But the regiments balked when the Bolsheviks assured them Kerensky was ridding the capital of them in order to shut down the revolution. Yes, Lenin was wily and Kerensky, without the army, was impotent—despite the absurdity of Lenin's *putsch*. The rusted old cannons the Bolsheviks tried to fire from the Peter and Paul failed to go off, as they had not been properly maintained by the inept regime, and from the cruiser *Aurora*, shells fell far short, plopping, ridiculously, into the Neva. It was an uprising so pitifully small that the performance of *Boris Godunov* ground through its scenes at the Maryinsky and Chaliapin continued singing every bar of his arias in *Don Carlo* at the Narodny Dom, the people's theater Niki built, where one could hear Chaliapin sing for twenty kopeks, the audiences of both theaters blissfully unaware of a counterrevolution. The streets were so quiet, even in the usually riotous Vyborg district, that only two drunks were reported arrested there. Sergei said he did not even know the Provisional Government had been overthrown until the next day when the newspapers told of it, declaring of the Bolsheviks, *Caliphs for an Hour*. The Bolshevik soldiers and armed workers had found entry to the Winter Palace from the cellar of the east wing and stumbled through the labyrinth of gates and doorways and passages into the palace proper. Despite the three thousand soldiers Kerensky had detailed there, sleeping at night on mattresses in the great halls to prevent this, the Bolsheviks marched the ministers of the Provisional Government from the palace right to the fortress of Peter and Paul. Kerensky did run, as I had predicted; he fled by car to summon his loyalist troops at the northern front and never returned. He ended up, I believe, in Finland, and from there he went, like so many of us, to Paris and then on to America. There he wrote and rewrote his story. His ministers had been arrested so abruptly they left with their pens still warm resting on the papers on which they had been scribbling plans and proclamations against the Bolsheviks and the upheaval they were newly creating—*The Provisional Government appeals to all classes to support the Provisional Government!* And the Bolsheviks, in a frenzy of occupation, ran about stuffing their pockets and hiding within their coats bottles of ink and clocks and swords and bedspreads with the imperial mono-gram and statuettes and leather cut from chairs, even cakes of soap, others shouting, *No, comrades, this is for the people!* When the sol-diers discovered the cavernous palace wine cellar, a three-week orgy of drinking ensued, wine and vodka streaming through the gutters where people stooped to guzzle it, and women brought sacks and cases to catch it and haul it home and all night the drunkards sang Russian folk songs, *Under the pine, Under the green pine, Lay me down to sleep*, and no matter how many guards the Bolsheviks sent over to stop the drinking, they themselves joined in the orgy, which did not end until the supply finally ran out and men lay un-conscious in the streets and broken bottles glittered on the pave-ment and the white snow had been tinted purple. And I wrote to Sergei, *Get out. Get out of Peter*.

We heard the Bolsheviks opened up all the bank vaults and at gunpoint forced the reluctant employees to hand over every kopek, every bar of silver, every piece of jewelry to finance their new gov-ernment. So much for my boxes of silver at the Bank of Azov and Don and for all the receipts to them I had stitched into my under-skirts. The Bolsheviks' new motto was *Looting the looters*, and they encouraged the people to go from house to house and store to store, to grab everything the wealthy *parasites* had once hoarded, and the workers took rugs, furniture, china, paintings, and from churches their silver and wine, and building committees composed of former servants forced the wealthy from their rooms in their own homes and consigned them to their servants' old quarters, and I thought, *How quickly and with what pleasure my old housekeeper would have relieved me of my bedroom and my drawing room and my great hall, relegating me to her narrow bed off by the cloakroom*. More ominously, we heard all the Romanovs had been ordered to register with the Bolshevik secret police, the Cheka, a new security force, the name of which stood for the All Russian Extraordinary Commission for Struggle Against Counterrevolution and Sabotage, and this Cheka then began to persecute and imprison even their old revolutionary comrades from the other political parties—the *pigs* and *whores*, I suppose, against whom Lenin had ranted in my son's school notebooks. The registered Romanovs were forbidden to leave Peter, which meant Sergei was now trapped there with his brother, who wrote, *We are marked for the gallows.* The empty Romanov palaces had been requisitioned and turned into orphanages, hospitals, and schools. My house, no longer the headquarters of the Bolshevik Central Committee, became a clinic and then a home for retarded children and after that the clubhouse for the Society of Old Bolsheviks—if they lived that long.

Worse, Russia no longer had much of an army to fight the kaiser's army, for all this while the Great War still went on—so many men had deserted and so many officers had been killed by their men that when the Germans advanced toward Peter they swiftly took city after city with laughable ease, sending a few troops with machine guns by train or motorcar to sweep up our soldiers along the way, and when they reached Peter they planned to do the same thing there. So in a panic Lenin moved the capital to Moscow and to stop the advance he signed a peace treaty that surrendered to the Germans the Ukraine, Finland, Estonia, Lithuania, and Poland— where my parents lay buried, now on German soil! Prince Lvov, the nobleman who had first headed the old Provisional Government right after the February revolution, became so distraught when he heard of this Treaty of Brest-Litovsk that he took to his bed and threatened to slit his own throat. We read that a general shot himself. But the treaty did not hold, for America entered the war and with her help the Allies defeated Germany within six months. Our poor Allies—trying to fight alongside a country that was fighting against itself! Democratic America was happy to see an emperor deposed. Did I mention I had been invited to dance in America in 1903, offered 40,000 dollars for just five performances in New York—and that was 40,000 dollars back then!—but I turned the offer down, for who in America knew anything about the ballet? Or about kings, emperors, or tsars, for that matter? Britain did, and as such, she, unlike America, halfheartedly supported the old regime, fearful that the disease of revolution was contagious. Let's see. I've lost my place. Brest-Litovsk. Yes. This treaty, briefly as it lasted, doomed the imperial family, for as soon as Russia signed it, Lenin turned his attention that summer to the problem of what to do with all those dozens of Romanovs.

We heard that four of them—Sergei's brothers the grand dukes Nicholas and George among them—were taken to Shpaterraia Prison in Peter, but that Niki's brother Mikhail was sent instead a thousand miles east to Perm. At this time Niki and his family were moved too, southwest from slow-paced Tobolsk to the grittier industrial city of Ekaterinburg, closer to the Urals, and there they were stuffed into the house of a merchant named Ipatiev, who was given twenty-four hours to pack up and get out, after which his home was rechristened, ominously, the House of Special Purpose. Half of Niki's suite who had been able to visit him daily in Tobolsk was now put in prison in Ekaterinburg and the other half of his suite was expelled from the city entirely, and we heard through the children's French tutor, Pierre Gilliard, before he left, that the family was confined to two bedrooms and that Alexei had had another hemorrhage from sledding in a tea tray down a staircase, that the guards from Tobolsk had been replaced and the new guards were hostile and deliberately, provocatively cruel, and that Niki's beard was now gray and the family was entirely alone. And at this I despaired. Finally, word came of Sergei. He, too, had been sent east, first to Viatka and then over the Ural Mountains to Ekaterinburg near Niki, though neither of them knew the other was so close, and then Sergei was shuttled a little farther north to Alapayevsk, a few hundred miles from Mikhail in Perm. Sergei was imprisoned in an old schoolhouse along with Alix's sister and three sons of Grand Duke Konstantin. And I thought, *Why have they concentrated all the Romanov men there in the*

Urals? But I knew the answer—that area was militantly Bolshevik, radically anti-tsarist, the miners and workers having slaved underground so long that they erupted like their red-hot furnaces. We received one letter from Sergei in which he tried to reassure me—he and the others were allowed to plant a vegetable garden and they could take their exercise in town, he and the Konstantin princes were teaching the schoolchildren to play soccer, a sport new to Russia, and he would surely teach it to Vova when he saw him again. On rainy days, he said, they read aloud to one another from *War and Peace*.

And so I wrote him, daily, but that first letter was the only one I had from him until, months later, a last, in June, a telegram, wishing Vova *Pazdravlyayu s dnem rozhdeniya*—a happy birthday. And then a great silence. I brooded over this, locked in my hot bedroom, for the temperature was warmer here than in Peter in July, sending my thoughts to Sergei—Get out of that schoolhouse. Climb over the desks and through a window and come to me. Vova harangued me, *See, they are all there together*. But I could not tell him, *It is not a good thing that they are all together in Siberia*. He wanted me to travel there. One of the princes' wives had followed this group of Romanovs to Alapayevsk of her own volition, the way wives and families of the revolutionaries exiled to Siberia for the last one hundred years had traditionally done, but this was a different Siberia, not the loosely monitored Siberia of the tsars, and within a few months, *she* was arrested and put in a Perm prison.

The capital we had already abandoned had now, with the exit of Lenin and the remains of the aristocracy, become a ghost town, with men and women ghosts floating slowly through the deserted streets looking for food or fuel. We heard the two hundred thousand beautiful horses of the city could no longer be fed and they died, often in the streets, where dogs ate at them if the people did not get there with their knives first. Trees disappeared. Then the houses, three thousand wooden houses—floorboards, wall panels, doors, window frames—anything that could be burned. We heard people burned their own furniture, their books, and they made light— there was electric current only a few hours each evening—with a bottle of fat and a wick, whose stinking smoke blackened the walls. We heard people piled their garbage on street corners and the rats ran to it. We heard the *formers* who weren't killed and who had anything at all to sell sold it on the streets or took the trains out to the countryside, where they bartered their shoes and clothes for bags of food—those *formers* had a new name, *bagmen*. And I thought, *Why could I not have been born in 1772 instead of 1872?* For then I could have lived out my life peacefully in the Peter of the tsars.

Through all this, Miechen bided her time in the Caucasus. And the dowager empress waited in the Crimea—the two women who had once lived in rival palaces and had run rival courts now squared off across the Black Sea. For here in the south, in the fall of 1917, around the time I arrived, an incipient resistance was taking root. Two former commanders of the Russian army, generals Alexeev and Kornilov, had made their headquarters in Novocherkassk, just north of us, in the territory of the Don Cossacks, only some of whom were tsarist loyalists but all of whom hated the Bolsheviks. These men were slowly joined by landowners' sons and students who had been made junior officers in the army and who hated this new regime and hated the common people who had expropriated their homes and burned their oriental carpets and the leatherbound books in their libraries and who with their axes had chopped up their chairs and consoles. These young officers wanted to rout the peasants out and send them back into their huts where they belonged. Why, they hated even the sight of the peasants' grotesque rough faces and greasy hair as they sat side by side with them in the fourth-class compartment on the train to Novocherkassk. And more of the old regime followed, including the old Duma politicians who hated Lenin. Even the poet Tsvetaeva and her husband went south, and he joined the Volunteers, as this new group was first called, and she wrote verse about them all, *White Guards: black nails / in the ribs of the Antichrist*. In Novocherkassk, the men donned their old tsarist uniforms or formal frock coats to distinguish themselves from the revolutionary rabble, and as this army of men grew in size and ambition, so did the hopes of Miechen and the dowager empress. After the Volunteers had a major victory at Rostov, just north of us, Andrei announced he would travel to Novocherkassk to join the ranks of what had now been renamed, rather grandly, the White Army, but Miechen forbade him to do so—and so Andrei deferred his plans, and Vova laughed at the news, saying, *Your suitor is a forty-year-old devushka!*—a girl!

This White Army might be made up of volunteers, but these volunteers, well-schooled and well-trained generals and Cossack atamans and officers, not only won their first battle at Rostov but a next at nearby Ekaterinodov and they were joined in Siberia in the spring of 1918 by the Czechs and the Allies. Emboldened, the Whites moved north from the Caucasus into the Ukraine, where they reclaimed Odessa and Kiev and Orel, and then they then began their march farther north to Tula, with its great arsenal, and from there it was not far to Moscow, where the Bolsheviks were in a panic, preparing to evacuate once again, this time to their stronghold in the Urals. I wish I could have seen Lenin scamper about as the workers and peasants tore up their party cards and tried to curry quick favor with the Moscow *borzhui* before the White deluge. We heard that the Whites were simultaneously preparing a charge on Peter and that they had encircled Ekaterinburg in the east, and after that we heard on the radio that the imperial family had been rescued by the White Army and I told Vova that Sergei would soon be saved as well. Then we heard rumors that the tsar's brother Mikhail had been shot, that Sergei had been freed by loyalist Cossacks, that he had been transported to another location, that two of his brothers had been executed in the courtyard of Shpaterraia prison, that the tsarevich Alexei had died, that the imperial family had been massacred, that the tsar had been hidden by the Pope in the Vatican, that the tsar had been seen on the streets of London, his hair snow white, that the imperial family were on a ship sailing ceaselessly on the White Sea, never touching the shore.

If Niki was alive, if Alexei or even Grand Duke Mikhail was alive, then the dowager empress had won. If not, then it would be Miechen's victory, for the crown would pass to Kyril—if his own marriage to a divorcée and his mother's over-late conversion to Orthodoxy did not disqualify him. In these special times, perhaps something as trifling as Miechen's Lutheran womb would no longer matter. And so these two willful women refused to leave Russia until what was unknown became known. Minnie's and Miechen's sons and daughters, however, had had enough of this waiting. The dowager empress's daughter Olga traveled by train, cart, and foot to the Black Sea port of Novorossiysk. Sergei's brother Sandro took his eldest son and left for England. Boris, for after all, *he* was never going to be tsar, left Russia for Paris. Kyril left Finland for his wife's home in Coburg, of all places! But Andrei, unable to leave his mother, out of either duty or attachment—and I suspected the latter—stayed, and I stayed, as well, because Kislovodsk was where Sergei knew to find me.

Then, in April 1919, at King George's urgent concern about the growing civil war, the dowager empress and the rest of the Niko-laevichi put down their dishes of rose-leaf jam, clotted cream, and hot honey cakes and left the Crimea on two British battleships, the *Marlborough* and the *Lord Nelson*—and then Miechen and Andrei and Vova and I were alone in the bottom of Russia in our two rented villas, Andrei running up and down the streets between them with news. If one flank of the White Army took Peter in the north and another pushed up from the Caucasus through the Ukraine and still a third came west from Siberia, Andrei said, then the Reds would be surrounded and crushed, and Peter would open itself to the Vladimirichi like the Fabergé coronation egg and Miechen would snatch up the egg's golden stagecoach and put Kyril within it. But that was not what happened. Instead, the Red Army deserters returned to their regiments when the Whites moved through the countryside, for the peasants suspected, correctly, that a White victory would mean the loss of their land and the return of it to their old squires. And in Tula, Lenin hastily conscripted the factory workers to dig trenches and erect barricades and arm themselves to protect the arsenal against the Whites, who would grab the munitions and guns and cannons and run with them to Moscow. And when Peter was threatened, the Red Army swelled yet again to defend *it*, for Peter was the seat of their revolution and a symbol of it. And through all this Miechen paced, her pet spaniels and bulldog dumped from her lap as she pondered her empire. But there was no empire. The Whites were eventually outnumbered and outfought in all three theaters, and by the end of 1919, the White Army and the Cossacks had begun their long, ugly retreat, fleeing from Moscow, through the Ukraine, and down to the Black Sea ports, drinking and pillaging and killing along the way anyone they blamed for the destruction of the empire in an orgy of furious defeat. And the people closed their shops and cafés and patients crawled from their hospital beds and they all followed the army, knowing that anyone who had been a White sympathizer would be executed by the Bolsheviks when they retook their cities.

We ourselves had to flee Kislovodsk for Novorossiysk in January by train, Miechen's personal car linked to the back of it, and Andrei rode with her there while Vova and I sat on our bags in a third-class car. I left a note with the postmaster for Sergei, telling him we were headed for the Black Sea port. The journey of three hundred miles, because of the stops and delays and searches, took an arduous two weeks, and at each small stop along the way, people's faces and hands would appear at the windows and the doors, the hands and faces wrapped in rags and clinging to any pipe or railing or to the sides of the carriages, even after the train had begun once again to move. And my son, seeing this, shrank against me, his sullen bravado of the past year gone after the first ten versts. When we arrived, finally, at the port, we found many people had already set up camp on the embankments or on the piers or in the warehouses, had pinched themselves between the great cranes and winches that bent themselves in metal angles to the sky. Former tsarist generals, former counts, former princes, former grand dukes had moved with the retreating Cossacks and Whites toward this port, where they piled now into consulates or hotel rooms. On the shaky dock a hundred thousand officers, army men, Cossacks, ministers of the government, members of the former court, and ordinary people converged. Niki's sister Olga, as irony would have it, also waited here with us for evacuation by whatever ship came into this popular harbor. But when Andrei called on her, she had no more news of Niki and Sergei than did I.

Everywhere I saw tents with bunches of garlic strung at the front flap, an old Rus amulet against epidemics, and this epidemic was typhus, the same illness that had nearly killed Niki so long ago right here in the Crimea. When the pharmacy ran out of medicine, it began to sell Orthodox medals to the most desperate, usually parents of young children. The rest of us hung garlic and held our breath when the ambulance trains brought the sick and the dead to the station, where we, for lack of anywhere else to go, remained in our railroad cars on the tracks. The general inspector, at Andrei's prodding, found me a saloon car, with two beds and a lavatory, to live in. Of the living, I asked for word of Sergei Mikhailovich. Of the dead, I could ask nothing, but I looked into their faces to see if he was among them. From my compartment window each day I saw the corpses of the typhus victims lifted from the arriving trains, put unceremoniously on carts, and dragged to the cemetery. I chased after them like a ghoul, arm over my nose, for a peek. We tied the cuffs of our sleeves tight against crawling lice, we put kerchiefs over our mouths, and we waited for a ship to take us across the Black Sea. But every boat had a problem. One was too small to take more passengers. Another was going only across the Black Sea to Turkey, which the Bolsheviks had already declared as the Turkestan Soviet Republic and which was embroiled in various tribal uprisings. On another ship the voyagers already had typhus, and yet another asked for more than we could pay. We were trapped in the rail yard, which slowly, with the rain, turned into an enormous mud hole. It seemed the wind was wet with ice and, like the figure painted on a Maryinsky backdrop, filled its cheeks with the cold air and blew it down through the tracks, and we resorted to sawing up telegraph poles to burn for fuel. Each cold evening Andrei came from his mother's first-class compartment to my tiny carriage to visit and sip tea or the occasional hot chocolate with me and Vova, who sat there silently, glowering, until, I swear, he seemed to wear the face of a *muzhik* grimacing at a *borzhui*. And we did look like peasants, for by now I had only two dresses left and my son one outfit and a coat. In the mornings, in the bleak light, I stepped out on the ice, my heels cracking the thin sheets that lay over the mud, and at the dark corners of the station the stray dogs emerged for the scraps from our dinner the night before. How they ran to me when I called them, thin, ribs visible beneath their fur, spots of mange covering their legs, their backs, even their faces. Yes, we were as ragged as those dogs, and I pitied them as I could not afford to pity us.

In February, through old friends from better days at the British consulate, Miechen found herself and Andrei a place out of this tumult on an Italian luxury liner, the *Semiramisa*, bound for Venice; Andrei trudged down to my car through the mud to tell me they would leave tonight, that he could not allow his mother to travel alone but that she had been unable to secure passage for me or Vova and what could he do about that? This was her lie, of course, but I'm certain Andrei believed it to be true. He handed us a small package of biscuits from the British canteen and then sat, awkwardly, on the springed seat opposite, one leg crossed over the other, showing us his empty hands. I pursed my lips at him. Of course, she did not want to secure passage for us—what better way to rid Andrei of me than to allow the nightmare that was Russia to swallow me whole. And my son. Vova opened the paper package and began to eat without offering Andrei a bite and I did not correct his manners. Once Miechen and Andrei left the Caucasus, Vova and I would sink into this crowd of refugees, our privileges lost. We had no connection to the British consulate and who among the sick and desperate aristocracy remembered or cared that I was once *prima ballerina assoluta* of the imperial stages? No, my power, what remained of it, extended only to the Romanovs I had bedded, two of them either imprisoned or dead and the third about to sail out of sight. And though I fantasized about Sergei's escape from Alapayevsk, what if he never arrived at this dock and Vova and I were here waiting for him still when the Bolshevik cavalry rode up over the hills, ringed this small city, and began to imprison, execute, or starve any *formers* they could scoop up in *their* red caps? They might put me in a cage on a cart and drag me from village to village to dance like a monkey on a chain, the tsar's former dancer, and my son they would take out into the woods and shoot straightaway. No, though I would like to say I waited faithfully for Sergei until certain death, until the Bolsheviks on horseback raced their way up those hills, I did not. No, I was more like the Messieurs Sabin and Grabbe and Leuchtenberg, members of the imperial entourage of Nicholas II who'd slunk away when the tsar's train from Pskov drew into the Tsarskoye station in 1917 after his abdication, much more like Dr. Ostrogorsky, who, after years of treating the imperial children, who had even gone all the way to Spala for the tsarevich's great hemorrhage!, told the empress that the roads to the palace were much too snowy and slushy for him to travel now that the family was under house arrest. No, I would not wait for Sergei in Novorossiysk. Vova and I must have passage out.

And so, while Andrei remained behind with my biscuit-eating son, I slogged up the muddy, icy path to Miechen's battered train car, mounted the steps, and rapped on the door. One of her staff admitted me to her sitting room, which was hung with blue drapes looking a bit soiled now, as were the narrow frosted glass windows that alternated with larger, smeared ones, the carpet, the embossed leather lining of the compartment walls, the blue upholstery of the chairs. How difficult it was even for Miechen to keep up appearances— difficult for her, impossible for me! But still she held court here, her brass samovar steaming amid the grime, her tulip-shaped reading lamps aglow. She sat in the largest chair in the small room, three dogs in her wide lap, wearing a heavy black shuba and a long gray scarf which she had wound several times around her neck. Her face was a mushroom, heavy and bloated, her jaw now thick as a man's, the nose broad, and clipped incongruously to her ears, as if to remind one of her original sex, were a pair of pearl drop earrings. At my entrance she lowered the fruit knife she had been using as she read to cut the pages of her book. She did not smile to greet me, not that I expected her to. She hated all her sons' women and we knew it; she called us, Andrei told me, *the harem*—me, Boris's mistress, Zinaida, even Kyril's wife, Victoria—all odalisques. Miechen blinked those eyes, hooded like a lizard's, at me. She showed no surprise at my appearance, although it was the first time we'd ever been alone together. Perhaps she knew I would come, knew that I would not accept my omission from the *Semiramisa* manifest without a fight— when had I ever allowed my name to be scratched off a list?—yet she gave not the slightest sign of pity or regret that my son and I would be left behind in this crumbling country to a fate that looked bleaker each day.

She said to me only, *I have no time to visit.*

If Miechen had spoken kindly, I might have lost my nerve, but the tiny tip of a smile she used to punctuate her remark acted like her fruit knife to cut the page from my imaginary script. And so I began, I began with my son, my son of suddenly, felicitously indefinite parentage.

Your husband was always a dear friend to me, I said, and her lips became paper thin. *A very dear friend.*

I stepped closer, taking care to use the small stage of this car. *He visited me often, as you know. We shared lunches, dinners. Breakfasts. He interceded on my behalf many times. Why, he even arranged my performance at the coronation gala, over the protests of the dowager empress herself. But of course you know that, too.*

Her face was flushing then and I moved to admire a portrait of the grand duke that sat, in its frame, on a console. There was no need to rush. Let the audience catch her breath. I straightened the portrait and let my fingers cling possessively to the frame for a moment before I turned back. Yes, I don't believe her eyes had left me for one second.

I said, *This is difficult for me*, but it wasn't, not at all!, not now that I had begun. *There was one summer, a particularly lonely summer for me. And for Vladimir.*

From what I hear, you had many lonely summers, Miechen said.

As did he. I paused. Her face reddened further. Perhaps she would have a stroke, in which case I would not need to go on. With the ridding of her, the ridding of my troubles. But no such luck. Though I waited a moment, she remained upright and sentient, so I was forced to continue.

Have you never wondered why my son's name is Vladimir? I lowered my voice. *My son wears a green stone cross around his neck on a*

platinum chain. Have you never noticed? It was your husband's chris-
tening gift to him, along with his name.

It's a common name.

Have you not seen the photographs of my son as a baby? He is the
image of Vladimir at the same age.

I've not had the pleasure.

Vladimir himself often commented that he and my son had the same
shape of the head.

You are saying my husband fathered your son. But if that were true,
he would have told me.

No. I smiled, giving her the smile of pity that she had refused
earlier to give me. *He wouldn't have. He loved you and he knew it*
would have pained you deeply, as did his earlier infidelities. I gave her
this, though it pained me to do it. But, after all, this wasn't a contest
of wills. It would do me no good to crush her completely. I needed her.
The grand duke is Vova's father. I've told this to no one. I would have
taken our secret to the grave, for his sake, if this unfortunate situation
hadn't arisen.

I took a deep breath. The final act. *Vladimir would never have*
wanted his son to be left behind here. His blood runs through Vova's
veins. What will you tell him on that day you meet again in heaven?
That you knew of his last son and abandoned him anyway?

Outside, a drunken chorus could be heard in the distance. A
baby cried. In here, the samovar steamed, but I would not be offered a glass of tea. Miechen pushed the dogs from her lap and, ig-
noring their yelps of protest, stood to face me, her fruit knife a small
dagger. *You are a whore*, she said.

A whore. She called me a whore. But not a liar.

Was I proud of my performance? When the world is ending, pride
is the first thing to go.

W E RAISED ANCHOR ON MARCH 3, at night, prepared to weave our way through the harbor waters laced with mines and crowded with every kind of vessel, their stark lights blanching our faces. I heard when the dowager empress departed Russia on the *Marlborough*, a Russian ship glided past her own in the Yalta Harbor, and the guardsmen on the ship opposite, spotting the distinctive black-swathed figure of their empress, began a booming rendition of the national anthem, "God Save the Tsar." There was no such serenade for us, though we, like Minnie, also stood on deck for a last look at the Russian coast. Three weeks later, the civil war would be over, and on that same dock, thousands of White Russians would cram themselves onto whatever could float. A British squadron would board several thousand White Army troops. Of those who were left behind, the Cossacks shot their horses rather than give them to the Bolsheviks, the White Army officers shot themselves in the heads with their military revolvers rather than allow the Bolsheviks that pleasure, their men shed their greatcoats and dove into the water in an attempt to swim to Turkey, drowning preferable to living. But tonight we looked out only at the encampment of the desperate rather than the hysterical. Andrei stood erect at attention at the brass rail by his mother, clothed in his uniform of the commander of the horse artillery of the guard, a uniform he would not don again until he lay in his coffin. Vova and I stood a short distance away, Miechen delivering to us the occasional sideways glance, reassessing my son. And then, along the dock, I saw a man in a greatcoat running running down the dock and out onto the jetty toward our ship, waving his arms and calling out a name that distance made into a thin thread, but I thought I pinched the end of it between two fingers—*M*—and I gripped the ship's railing and peered into the darkness. If Andrei had somehow managed to secure a tin or two of cocoa and biscuits from the British canteen for our teatimes, surely Sergei, so much more clever, could manage in all this upheaval to find a way to outwit his Bolshevik guards, to steal clothes from a peasant, to hop a train across the white steppe and then down a line south from Moscow, to make his way by cart and by foot to this dock just in time to run down its pier and leap over this rail to us. And just as I opened my mouth to make a spectacle of myself by calling out to him, Vova leaned toward me and said, *It's not him*.

No. It was not Sergei. He did not join us in Novorossiysk. Nor in Touapse, Pati, Batum, Constantinople, Piraeus, Venice, Milan, Cannes, or Cap d'Ail.

a frightening nothing

SLOWLY, SLOWLY, IN PARIS and on the Riviera that spring and summer appeared the faces of those who survived—various theater artists, among them Chaliapin, Karsavina, Fokine, Preobrajenska. Pavlova and Diaghilev were already in the West, and so Russian ballet was reborn in Paris, London, and New York, our dancers—or students touched by our dancers—founding some of the world's great ballet troupes. And there appeared, as well, many variations of grand dukes, princes, and counts. We found one another at our villas, at the Hôtel de Paris, at the Château de Madrid, at the Pavillon d'Armenonville, at the Théâtre de Sarah Bernhardt—but other faces did not appear, though they seemed to stand at our sides or just behind us, their forms washed in with a thin gray paint. We looked for the lost, asking ourselves, *Where are they? What has happened to them?* And then the terrible answers to these questions arrived in Paris, in the person of Nicholas Sokolov, a legal investigator who had been assigned to the mystery of the disappeared Romanovs. After the White Army took Ekaterinburg briefly back from the Bolsheviks, a few officers had hurried to the Ipatiev house where the tsar and his family had been held until just eight days earlier and found it scrubbed and emptied. Perhaps history would have been changed entirely if they had found Niki and his family there, for by 1920 Russia was in the depths of a famine so great the people of the eastern provinces had begun to eat their snow-frozen dead just to survive. Yes, the starving Russian people would have thrown flowers along the roads to Peter if the tsar were still alive and promised them bread. But the White officers did not find Niki or Alix or Alexei or the girls or any of the imperial suite; they found only Alexei's spaniel, Joy, wandering the house, hungry. They found hairpins, toothbrushes, books, a wheelchair, the board the frail Alexei had used as a desk while in bed. A frightening nothing. Sokolov knew how to conduct a proper search. He knew how to interrogate, how to enlist the help of interested parties, how to survey the pockmarked walls of the basement, the tire and rut marks and the imprint of horses' hooves leading from the house to the forest around the Four Brothers Mine, twelve miles outside Ekaterinburg. He knew how to sift the earth, to spot evidence. He was good at cataloging—charred bone fragments, belt buckles, a pearl earring, a few centimeters of a woman's finger, three icons, shoe buckles, shreds of a military cap, and the contents of the tsarevich's pockets—tinfoil, nails, copper coins, a lock. And from these he surmised that the imperial family had been shot, their bodies carried by truck and then by cart through the forest, where they were stripped, cut into bits, and burned, their ashes thrown into the mine. This would have been my son's fate, too, had he journeyed with them to Siberia that August night in 1917.

Sokolov had put what was left of the imperial family's belongings into a suitcase nobody wanted until finally the Orthodox Church in Brussels accepted it. All this Sokolov managed to collect before the Red Army retook Siberia in 1919, and in the same wave that sent us fleeing the country altogether, he, too, fled—with his suitcase and his notes and his theories and his photographs—to the French Riviera, where he visited Niki's uncle Nikolasha; to London, where he visited Niki's sister Xenia; to Denmark, where he attempted to visit Niki's mother the dowager empress, who refused to see him, who refused ever to believe that her son and his family had been murdered or to allow prayers for their souls; and finally to Paris, where Andrei and I met with him and saw his reports and photographs. We sat in the Hôtel Lotti, in an alcove of the dining room, our plates untouched, the steel gray sky pressed up against the window at my back. I peered at Sokolov's reports and documents, the photograph of the gouged wallpaper of the Ipatiev cellar, the gruesome list of hundreds of objects recovered, and then I could not read anymore, my arms shaking to the elbow, but looked into Sokolov's face—at his deep-set eyes, his long, waxed moustache as he spoke very properly of the family ground to ash. The Bolsheviks had sent a dozen men to the doorway to shoot and hack at Niki and at Alix and the children lined up with him in that cellar, on the excuse that they were to be photographed. From the Bolsheviks' own accounts of it later, every assassin had wanted to kill the tsar and tell the story of it. After they read him their orders, *In view of the fact that your relatives are continuing their attack on Soviet Russia, the Ural Executive Committee has decided to execute you*, Niki had cried out, *What? What?* He was the first to die in that little basement room in distant Ekaterinburg. Alix, sitting in her chair, second. Olga, third. But the other girls had begun to run, their corsets so sewn up with jewels the bullets could not pierce them. They ran in circles in that small space, tripping over the bodies of their parents blown from their chairs, crouching against the walls. Where do you find men to shoot at screaming girls, to club and bayonet them, to murder a fifteen-year-old boy crawling toward his father? The Bolsheviks found such men—and many more like them.

And then Sokolov told us this was not all. He had also learned that Sergei's brothers George and Nicholas had been shot in the courtyard of the Shpaterraia Prison and their corpses thrown into a mass grave. Niki's brother Mikhail had been shot in the woods outside Perm while smoking a cigarette. Sokolov had gone also to Alapayevsk, and there in his account he paused and cleared his throat.

In Alapayevsk he had discovered that Sergei, Alix's sister, and the three Konstantin princes had been taken from their schoolhouse prison on July 17, 1918, Sergei's name day—not long after Sergei had sent his birthday wishes to Vova—put into peasant carts, and driven to an abandoned mine shaft, and I knew then that his story would not end well. Sergei, Ella, and the three princes had been thrown into the shaft, Sergei with a bullet in his head. Sokolov had surmised that Sergei alone must have resisted his captors (and I thought, *Of course you would resist them, my fierce Georgian*), and therefore he had been shot before the long fall down, while the others had landed at the bottom still alive, to die a slow death of broken bones and starvation, and after them their murderers threw down pieces of timber to conceal their crime. And at this I put a napkin to my mouth. Sokolov had pictures of the bodies, which had been winched back up, laid out on sheets, and photographed, and Andrei, pulling out his reading glasses, inspected these, as I could not look at them. While Andrei did so, Sokolov passed to me across the table other evidence: a small envelope that contained two items, Sergei's gold potato charm and the kopek medallion I had given him thirty years before. Both pieces, he said, Grand Duchess Xenia had asked him to give to me. Eventually I would give them to Vova, for had Sergei not planned to leave all that was his to my son? In 1914 that was an annual *appanage* of 280,000 rubles along with the income from the vast family estates in northern, central, and southern Russia, and houses in every city and resort where the court traveled. By 1920, this was all that was left.

That night I dreamed I was returned to Petersburg, to the Imperial Ballet School, and as I headed down the long corridor to the little student theater where I had once danced at my graduation, someone behind me I could not see cried out, *The imperial family, the imperial family is coming!* And I asked, *But how can they come? They are all dead*, and the voice answered, *Their souls are coming*, and all around me voices began to sing,

> *Christ is risen from the dead*
> *Trampling down death by death*
> *And upon those in the tombs bestowing life—*

and I ran down the passage to fling open the door to the little theater, but there was no room beyond the door, no room with its small stage and its wooden chairs lined up in rows. The door opened instead into nothing at all, into a dark abyss where it was raining great sheets of rain and where a great wind moaned and sent the rain in all directions, and I stood there on the threshold, my skirts blowing, calling out into the wild dark, *Christ is risen from the dead*, and though I stood there a long time until I was quite wet, no one answered me at all.

What do the dead occupy themselves with, do you think, when they aren't haunting us? Do they find in the grave a pocket of the past? I know some souls rest in peace, but I don't think the souls of émigrés do, nor do the souls of the murdered. The souls of the Romanovs probably march west across the churning soil of Russia, through Omik, Ekaterinburg, Life, Kazan, Tambov, Tula, Moscow, all the way back to what is now called Leningrad, looking for what they have lost.

the princess romanovsky-krassinsky

WITH SOKOLOV'S REPORT DISSEMINATED, Kyril declared himself emperor in exile and thus forever alienated the dowager empress and the Nikolaevichi. What did he care? The
dowager empress was in Denmark, he was here in the
heart of Russian Paris, where one's worth among the émigrés was
still measured by one's old rank and where to be received by a grand
duke was still considered a social triumph. On Easter, Christmas,
and New Year's Day, the émigrés crowded the grand ducal houses
to sign the guest books, to sip a bit of vodka, to be in the company of
the men who once ruled Russia. And I? I did better than that. Why,
I married Andrei as soon as Miechen was snapped shut in her vault
in the chapel she built for herself at Contrexéville. Are you surprised? Then you have not been paying attention. I didn't have long
to wait—she was dead within six months of her arrival in France,
having decided to spare herself the diminution of stature served up
like a stale pastry to any refugee. Before Andrei and I took our vows
in the Church of St. George in Cannes, Andrei, ever obedient, wrote
to warn the dowager empress of what was to come and petitioned
his brother Kyril, as head of the family, for permission; and this
deference to the old protocol had its rewards. Grand Duchess Olga
sent us her mother's best wishes and Kyril issued a *ukase* whereby I,

Mathilde-Maria Felixovna Kschessinska, became Her Serene Highness the Princess Romanovsky-Krassinsky. My son was ennobled, too, after my marriage, when I pressured Andrei to adopt him, and he became Miechen's grandson rather than her husband's son, if this makes any difference to her. After our wedding, Andrei took me to be formally presented to Emperor Kyril and his wife, to Queen Alexandrine of Denmark, to Queen Marie of Romania, to Queen Olga of Greece. And in time I came to be received by King Gustav V of Sweden, King Alexander of Yugoslavia, the Shah of Persia, the old king Ferdinand of Bulgaria and the new king Boris, his son, not only by all the Russian grand dukes, but also by Grand Duchess Xenia, by Prince Dimitri Pavlovich and his sister Princess Marie Pavlovna, by the princesses Radziwill and Golitzin, by Prince Volkonsky, my old enemy, if you remember, as director of the Imperial Theaters, by the dukes of Coburg, Mecklenburg-Schwerin, and Leuchtenberg. Yes, by all these people my son and I were now received.

My name is in all the genealogy charts, you know, the ones that trace the lines of European and Russian royalty. I sit on the page below Queen Victoria of England, King Christian IX of Denmark, and Tsar Alexander II of Russia, though to be frank I am not positioned where I had hoped, next to Niki but beneath Alix of Hesse-Darmstadt, who as his first wife would be listed above, or even next to Sergei, off to the side with the Mikhailovichi branch of the family. No. I am a Vladimirichi, and perhaps, after all, that is where I belong, with the wily and the cunning, the schemers, the plotters, the intriguers, the Machiavellians. But my son, Prince Romanov, is not on the genealogy charts at all, for the line to the throne runs through Kyril, you see, so it is through Kyril's issue that the line is traced. You will see the name of *his* son Vladimir there, not mine. *Tant pis.*

We lived in style on the Riviera for nine years off the sale of the magnificent rubies Miechen bequeathed Andrei—she left her daughter, Elena, her diamonds, Boris her emeralds, and Kyril her pearls—but the huge price the rubies brought, twenty million francs, is not, after all, so much money for a Romanov; and when those francs were gone, I was forced to sell, stone by stone, my own gems, which did not bring me the price they should have, as the market was by then, of course, flooded with the imperial jewels of the impoverished Russian court-in-exile. At last, in 1929, we had to sell our villa at Cap d'Ail and purchase a home in Paris, where real estate was not so dear, a modest house with a long front garden at 10 Villa Molitor in the 16th Arrondissement and, additionally, a maisonette at 6 avenue Vion-Whitcomb to serve as my ballet school, the Studio of the Princess Krassinsky, for once again, it appeared, I would have to work for a living. Andrei was reluctant to lend his name to the sale of champagne, caviar, or cigars, feeling it beneath him, and, anyway, such an endorsement paid only a pittance, otherwise I would have insisted. Instead, I put out my placard and hired the wife of a former tsarist general as my pianist and employed Grand Duke Andrei Vladimirich to keep my books and sweep my studio floors, which he did daily, in his three-piece suits.

OR MY SON, however, I did not wish such a coda, such an *infernal gallop*. I did not want *him* sweeping my studio floors, and yet there is no proper occupation for a prince-in-exile, no institutions of government or military to run. Like the sons of other émigrés of his rank, Vova lived with his parents, attended royal family weddings and funerals, supported various charities, and waited in vain for the world he had been groomed to rule to be restored. In anticipation of this, Kyril established his Council for Building Imperial Russia; his grand ducal advisors included Boris and Andrei, as well as Sergei's two surviving brothers, Sandro and Mikhail, and lest you think the five of them alone were such dreamers, let me tell you that in 1930, in a forest outside Paris, Kyril conducted a review of two thousand former officers of the tsar's guard regiments, who cheered at the sight of him as they had once cheered for Niki, *The day of glory is near*. My son, along with Prince Dimitri Pavlovich and other frustrated young men, joined the Union of Young Russia, organized by Alexander Kazem-Bek, a great-nephew of Tolstoy, which envisioned a Russia that embraced both the reforms of the Bolsheviks and the throne of its tsar. Like those old officers in the Paris forest, they, too, had a uniform (a dark blue shirt), a symbol (the cross and the orb), and a motto (*Tsar and the Soviets!*). And they, too, held their rallies and yodeled paeans, theirs to the Red Army, of which most of them were too young to know almost anything, and when Andrei admonished him, Vova bristled— *Your council is a council of doddering old men.* It was not until Kazem-Bek was discovered in 1937 to be a Soviet agent that Vova finally left the movement, which itself collapsed after the Second World War.

And my son's tale worsens. With Andrei's death in 1956 and the closing of my school, I had to sell this house, too, though Vova and I have lived on here as tenants. Without Andrei, I'm afraid the other Romanovs forgot about us—just look how the émigrés ignore my son, the son of the last emperor of all the Russias—and Vova, my prince, had to take on work. He bore the indignity of this as Niki had borne the indignity of imprisonment—with humility and patience. Yes, it is in these last years that I have seen Vova become most like his father, who had been born on the Feast of Job and who perceived his life as a series of struggles and burdens to be endured, of which I am now one for my son. Each day, he delivers wine on his motorized bicycle, receives my visitors, types my correspondence in which I beg for money for us. The benevolent societies of the theater send us their francs only because I am alive, because of what I gave to my art. But when I am gone, they, like the others, will forget my son. I would be gone already but for him, for I see Sergei in his summer whites and his young body waiting for me by the door, and I need only to rise from this bed to join him. But without me, what will Vova do? He has never married. He has devoted himself entirely to me. Why, he sits in a chair beside me, now, wearing one of Andrei's remade three-piece suits and carrying in his pocket the gold cigarette case Andrei set out on the dinner table fifty years ago when we finally arrived so shabbily in Venice, to reassure the waiters we could pay the bill. Yes, he sits here alone with me, and, yes, he is sixty-nine years old, but this is still *young* for a Kschessinsky, if not for a Romanov—he may have thirty years more, and what will he do with them? Life must have a purpose.

The world has not forgotten Nicholas II, you know. Why, just last week I received in the mail tickets to the premiere of the film *Nicholas and Alexandra*. Their lives still have the power to excite the imagination. If Vova had lost his life with them at Ekaterinburg, the world would know his name, too, ponder his place in the tsar's suite—kitchen boy, playmate of Alexei's, ward of the tsar? They would search for *his* bones, weigh them, ponder the contents of *his* pockets, examine the bits and pieces *he* left behind in the House of Special Purpose—and perhaps by now the mystery of his birth would have been revealed and the world would know his great place in it.

But because of me he is alive here in Paris, not burned to ash in a forest near Ekaterinburg.

You understand that by keeping his paternity secret, I kept him alive? Lenin feared us so much he murdered as many Romanovs as he could grab in his fists. Stalin chased down anyone who had ever been touched by so much as the shadow of the tsars, and then he sent his agents abroad to ferret out the monarchists among us. Why, in the thirties his agents kidnapped two White Army generals right off the streets of Paris! Yes, as far away as Paris we still made Stalin shake. Khrushchev told the West, *My ves pokhoronim*—We will bury you. Ha. He died three months ago. *I* buried *him*. I have outlived all of them, even poor Kerensky. So whatever you think of me, don't pity me. I had a beautiful life. I was loved, admired, feted, copied, mocked, treasured, and feared. I am one hundred years old and I am no longer afraid of anything and I say to the Bolsheviks,

You will not last one hundred years, and when Soviet Russia falls, then the Russian people will come looking once again for their tsar, seeking the last link in the imperial line, and who stands closer to Nicholas II than his son, his one living son? Emperor Vladimir. Yes, it is time to say now what I could not say in 1954 when I wrote my first memoirs, full of fiction and lies. This time I will write for my son and these will be my *true* memoirs. I will dictate and he will put my words to the page. He thinks he has nothing, but in a moment, I will open my eyes and give him everything. I will tell him a story. I will start this way. *I was the lover of two grand dukes, the mistress of the tsar. The last tsar. He called me Little K.*

acknowledgments

In creating *my* concoction of fiction and lies, I have, of course, twisted the details of Kschessinska's life, conflating rumor into fact, excising inconvenient truths, and reconfiguring events and relationships to suit dramatic purpose; though conversations are imagined, I have used excerpts from the letters and journals of the principal characters when so indicated, with the exception of Little K herself, who, when it comes to her epistles, as with everything else, serves mostly at the pleasure of my imagination.

For details of Russian history, Russian culture, and the court of the Romanovs, I am indebted to works by Orlando Figes, *Natasha's Dance: A Cultural History of Russia* and *A People's Tragedy: The Russian Revolution, 1891–1924*; Richard Pipes's *Russia Under the Old Regime* and *The Russian Revolution*; Solomon Volkov's *The Magical Chorus: A History of Russian Culture from Tolstoy to Solzhenitsyn, St. Petersburg: A Cultural History*, and *Balanchine's Tchaikovsky: Interviews with George Balanchine*; Robert Massie's *Nicholas and Alexandra* and *The Romanovs: The Final Chapter*; Suzanne Massie's *Land of the Firebird: The Beauty of Old Russia* and *Pavlovsk: The Life of a Russian Palace*; Andrei Maylunas and Sergei Mironenko's *A Lifelong Passion: Nicholas and Alexandra, Their Own Story*; Maurice Paléologue's *An Ambassador's Memoirs*; John Curtis Perry and Constantine Pleshakov's

The Flight of the Romanovs: A Family Saga; Edvard Radzinsky's trio of books *The Rasputin File, Alexander II: The Last Great Tsar*, and *The Last Tsar: The Life and Death of Nicholas II*; Thomas Berry's *Memoirs of the Pages to the Tsars*; Simon Sebag Montefiore's *Young Stalin*; James P. Duffy and Vincent L. Ricci's *Czars: Russia's Rulers for Over One Thousand Years*; Peter Kurth's *Tsar: The Lost World of Nicholas and Alexandra*; Charlotte Zeepvat's *The Camera and the Tsars: A Romanov Family Album*; the exhibition catalog *Czars: 400 Years of Imperial Grandeur: The Splendor of Russia*, for a traveling exhibit from the State Historical and Cultural Museum and Preserve of the Moscow Kremlin; the State Hermitage Museum and the State Archive of the Russian Federation's *Nicholas and Alexandra: The Last Imperial Family of Tsarist Russia*; Greg King's *The Court of the Last Tsar: Pomp, Power, and Pageantry in the Reign of Nicholas II*; Edmund Wilson's *To the Finland Station: A Study in the Writing and Acting of History*; John Reed's *Ten Days That Shook the World*; Alexander Mikhailovich's *Once a Grand Duke*; Meriel Buchanan's *The Dissolution of an Empire* and *Recollections of Imperial Russia*; Pierre Gilliard's *Thirteen Years at the Russian Court*; Felix Youssupoff's *Lost Splendour: The Amazing Memoirs of the Man Who Killed Rasputin*; John van der Kiste and Coryne Hall's *Once a Grand Duchess: Xenia, Sister of Nicholas II*; Pauline Gray's *The Grand Duke's Woman: The Story of the Morganatic Marriage of Michael Romanoff, the Tsar Nicholas II's Brother, and Nathalia Cheremetevskaya*; Tatyana Tolstaya's *Pushkin's Children: Writings on Russia and Russians*; Francine du Plessix Gray's *Them: A Memoir of Parents*; Marina Tsvetaeva's *Selected Poems*; Anna Akhmatova's *The Complete Poems*; Ivan Bunin's *Collected Stories*; Tolstoy's novels, in particular *Anna Karenina*; Vladimir Nabokov's *Speak, Memory*; the photographs and historical documents on Bob Atchison's website, the Alexander Palace Time Machine; and Alexander Sokurov's film *Russian Ark*.

For information on the Russian ballet and its figures, I am indebted to Roland John Wiley's *A Century of Russian Ballet, Tchaikovsky's*

Ballets, and *The Life and Ballets of Lev Ivanov*; V. A. Teliakovsky's memoirs, part two, "St. Petersburg Ballet"; Alexandre Benois's *Reminiscences of the Russian Ballet*; Tim Scholl's *"Sleeping Beauty," A Legend in Progress*; Stanley Rabinowitz's translation of Akim Volynsky's *Ballet's Magic Kingdom*; Richard Buckle's *George Balanchine: Ballet Master* and *Diaghilev*; Bernard Taper's *Balanchine: A Biography*; Francis Mason and George Balanchine's *Balanchine's Complete Stories of the Great Ballets*; Alexandra Danilova's *Choura*; Tamara Geva's *Split Seconds*; Mikhail Fokine's *Fokine: Memoirs of a Ballet Master*; Lynn Garafola's *Diaghilev's Ballet Russes*; Tamara Karsavina's *Theatre Street*; Marius Petipa's *Russian Ballet Master*; Toni Bentley's *Costumes by Karinska*; Joshua Waletsky's film *Sacred Stage: The Mariinsky Theater*; and Bertrand Normand's film *Ballerina*.

For particular information on Kschessinska, I am indebted to her own memoirs, *Dancing in Petersburg: The Memoirs of Mathilde Kschessinska*, from which I drew many details and appropriated (with a few embellishments) the compelling dream that inspired her to write about her life—or so she claims; Coryne Hall's biography *Imperial Dancer: Mathilde Kschessinska and the Romanovs*, which tracks down the truths Kschessinska preferred to overlook; and three articles from *Dance Magazine*: Olga Maynard's "Kschessinska at Ninety-Nine," Helene Breazeale's "Mathilde Kschessinska," and Eileen O'Connor's "Portrait of an Era." Penelope Jowitt's entry "Matilda Kshessinskaya" in the *International Encyclopedia of Ballet* and the entry "Kshessinsky Family" from the same source were also helpful. Tim Scholl's conference paper "My Usual Triumph: Mathilde Kschessinska and the Artist's Memoir" was an invaluable resource.

My great appreciation to the dance historians Lynn Garafola, professor of dance at Barnard College, and Tim Scholl, chair of Russian Language, Literature, and Culture at Oberlin College, for their time in reviewing the novel and for offering their insights and expertise on both the period and the person of Mathilde Kschessinska.

I would also like to thank my editor, Courtney Hodell, for her brilliant work on this manuscript; her able and courteous assistant, Mark Krotov; my agent, Sandy Dijkstra, in all ways fabulous; and the Dijkstra Agency's most wonderful Elise Capron and Andrea Cavallaro.

And to my family, most especially my husband, my gratitude always.

DISCUSSION QUESTIONS FOR

The True Memoirs of Little K

ADRIENNE SHARP

1. The novel's title claims these are Mathilde's true memoirs. Is any memoir entirely true? What aspects of his or her life might a memoirist attempt to conceal—or rewrite? What is illuminating about reading a fictionalized account of someone's life as opposed to an autobiography or a biography?

2. In what ways did Mathilde's affair with Nicholas give her both more power and less? Consider her position both in the theater and in society. How did this affair empower her or limit her in these realms? How did other prominent women, such as the empress dowager, the empress, and the wife of Grand Duke Vladimir, exert power in a society that denied official status to women?

3. The love between Nicholas and Mathilde was affected from the start by the knowledge that they could never be husband and wife. How did this knowledge define their relationship early on, and how did their expectations of each other change over time as their relationship continued?

4. How does Alix's experience of mothering the frail Alexei mirror Mathilde's experience as a mother? In what ways does this suffocating mothering infantilize both boys? Was it this—or the disruption of the revolution—that tied Mathilde to her son, who remained her caregiver later in life instead of marrying and creating a life of his own? How might Alexei's relationship with his mother, had he lived, have mirrored that of Vova?

5. What do Vova's father figures teach him about being a man and being a leader? When both Sergei and Nicholas encourage him to impersonate the tsarevich, what does this promise him? How is Vova's attitude about himself irrevocably shaped by this impersonation and by his induction into the imperial family in the latter part of the novel?

6. Under the Romanovs, the art of ballet experienced its greatest flowering. What circumstances contributed to this? Consider the wealth of the Romanovs; the interconnection among the various theaters, schools, and conservatories in St. Petersburg, and therefore among composers, choreographers, set designers, and the theater, opera, and ballet; and the social relationships between the court and the theater. In what ways did being the daughter of an Honored Artist of the Imperial Theater's benefit Mathilde? What pressures did it exert on both her and her siblings? What were Mathilde's strengths and weaknesses on the stage?

7. Discuss Rasputin's role in the Romanov family. Why did Alix obstinately ignore the furor that surrounded Rasputin, a furor that became one of the incendiary factors in the people's anger against their sovereigns? In what ways did Rasputin's murder foreshadow the revolution and the strike at the crown two months later?

8. What advantage does Mathilde have over Nicholas, imprisoned at Tsarskoye Selo, when she makes her decision to retrieve her son before the family is moved to Siberia? What future does Nicholas envision for himself and his family at that point, the summer of 1917—and what future does Mathilde see ahead for them?

9. Which of Mathilde's history lessons surprised you the most? What aspects of the Russian revolution had you been unaware of? Was a violent revolution, resulting in a brutal police state, the only way the suffering of the lower classes could have been resolved in that society? What kept the Romanovs, and members of their circle such as Mathilde, from addressing the demands for change that came from all levels of society—from the workers, the peasants, the intelligentsia, even from members of the aristocracy itself?

10. Sergei was one of the dozens of Romanovs who did not survive the revolution, along with many other members of the aristocracy and the bourgeoisie. What does *The True Memoirs of Little K* reveal about the nature of survival?

11. Once Mathilde and the Romanovs find themselves in exile, they attempt to re-create their former lives—but the rules that formerly governed that society have loosened, enabling Mathilde's marriage to Andrei. What did each of them gain from this marriage—and in what ways did it help to legitimize Vova's place in Russian society in exile? How effectively were Vova and his parents able to establish a place for their son?

12. In 2008, DNA evidence confirmed that no members of Tsar Nicholas's immediate family escaped execution by the Bolsheviks. In fact, Sokolov's theories about how the imperial family's bodies were burned to ash were found not to be true. How might Mathilde's dreams of the imperial family be changed if she knew their bones lay in the mud beneath a wooden bridge in the forest near Ekaterinburg? If she knew their bones had been returned to St. Petersburg and interred in the tombs at Peter and Paul?

13. In the novel's closing pages, Mathilde is proud that her name appears in the genealogy charts of European and Russian royalty, though she expresses disappointment that her name is not included next to Nicholas's and that her son's name does not appear at all. Does she, after all, find the sacrifices she made and her exclusion from a place in normal society and normal family life worth this status?